Daily RVICE

'A very fine novel, which is more of a re-imagining of th[e]
story than a carbon copy – and with the bonus of a br[a...]
twist to the ending'   *Daily* [...]

'David Hewson's literary translation . . . allows the characters
more room to breathe . . . Hewson's greatest achievement is that
it's compelling reading'   *Observer*

'Not just a novelization. Hewson is a highly regarded crime writer
in his own right; he spent a lot of time with the creators of the
original to ensure that he did not offend its spirit and mood, and
he has provided his own, different solution to the central murder
mystery . . . for those who missed watching Sarah Lund and the
Danish police in action, I believe they will get a great deal of
pleasure from reading about them'   Marcel Berlins, *The Times*

'A fast-paced crime novel that's five-star from start to finish'
                                                     Irish Examiner

'The book is an excellent read in which the author manages to
dig deeper into the characters without having to rewrite their
original television characterization. For those who haven't seen
the series, this is a very cleverly constructed and beautifully
written crime drama; for those who already know the ending, a
new twist awaits'   *Irish Times*

LITTLE SISTER

Former *Sunday Times* journalist **David Hewson** is well known for his crime-thriller fiction set in European cities. He is the author of the highly acclaimed *The Killing* novels set in Denmark and the Detective Nic Costa series set in Italy. *The Killing* trilogy is based on the BAFTA-award-winning Danish TV series created by Søren Sveistrup and produced by DR, the Danish Broadcasting Corporation.

Hewson's ability to capture the sense of place and atmosphere in his fiction comes from spending considerable research time in the cities in which the books are set: Copenhagen, Rome, Venice and now Amsterdam. *Little Sister* is the third title to feature Detective Pieter Vos, following *The House of Dolls* and *The Wrong Girl*.

Also by David Hewson

The Killing trilogy

The Killing

The Killing II

The Killing III

Nic Costa series

A Season for the Dead

The Villa of Mysteries

The Sacred Cut

The Lizard's Bite

The Seventh Sacrament

The Garden of Evil

Dante's Numbers

The Blue Demon

The Fallen Angel

Carnival for the Dead

Pieter Vos series

The House of Dolls

The Wrong Girl

Other titles

The Promised Land

The Cemetery of Secrets

(previously published as *Lucifer's Shadow*)

Death in Seville

(previously published as *Semana Santa*)

DAVID HEWSON

LITTLE SISTER

PAN BOOKS

First published 2016 by Macmillan

This paperback edition published 2016 by Pan Books
an imprint of Pan Macmillan
20 New Wharf Road, London N1 9RR
Associated companies throughout the world
www.panmacmillan.com

ISBN 978-1-4472-9340-8

1 3 5 7 9 8 6 4 2

A CIP catalogue record for this book is available from the British Library.

Printed and bound by CPI Group (UK) Ltd, Croydon, CR0 4YY

Visit www.panmacmillan.com to read more about all our books
and to buy them. You will also find features, author interviews and
news of any author events, and you can sign up for e-newsletters
so that you're always first to hear about our new releases.

LITTLE SISTER

1

The prison, for such it seemed, was a dun-coloured two-storey block hidden away in a solitary wood on the edge of the island of Marken. Sixteen rooms for young patients with nothing to do but listen to their handlers, read books, watch TV, walk the small enclosed garden and stare out at the still, grey waters surrounding them.

On this hot summer Monday swarms of insects rose like mist from the scrubland, swallows swooping through the teeming haze, darting, hungry. They hovered above the high electrified fence that kept out any curious walkers who'd wandered away from the village's cobbled streets and pretty timber-gabled houses. Security ran twenty-four hours a day with cameras at regular intervals along the perimeter. At the end of the long drive stood a barred gate with an entry post, and beyond it a sign that indicated the presence of a justice ministry building.

People on the island village understood there was some kind of psychiatric institution on their doorstep. Only the few who worked there knew it housed a handful of the most disturbed female juvenile criminals in the Netherlands. The positioning was deliberate. On one side was the Gouwzee lake stretching west to Waterland and the main road to Amsterdam. On the other the larger Markermeer, part of a vast expanse of inland water that ran all the way out to the North Sea.

Nothing but a grassy dyke joined Marken to the outside world, a narrow lane above it. Any inmate who escaped would have to make their way along that. None had tried in the eighteen years of its existence. Nor did many visitors come the other way. Certainly not for Mia and Kim Timmers, two orphaned sisters

1

forgotten for the most part, out of convenience and an unspoken sense of communal guilt.

They'd been there since they were eleven years old and detained for killing a man. That was a decade before. Since being committed they'd never set foot out of the place. Lately though the atmosphere had changed. Irene Visser, the psychiatrist who'd been assigned to their care all the long decade they'd been incarcerated, had started putting them through a variety of intelligence tests. Some were boring. Some funny. The sisters approached each steadfastly, earnestly, answering all of Visser's questions in her office. It was a small, clinical room looking out along the flat green dyke of marshy land that stretched out like a stubby finger towards Volendam across the *meer*. Four weeks before she'd called them for what they assumed was another set of tests. Instead Visser told Kim and Mia they were getting too old for Marken and deserved better than to spend their days cooped up in a psychiatric institution for a crime committed when they were children. An offence, furthermore, for which most citizens might excuse, if not pardon, them.

Simon Klerk, their ever-smiling personal day nurse, was there when Visser went through the results. Both he and the psychiatrist agreed. The sisters were easily bright enough to get a scholarship to university if they wanted. Arts. Science. Whatever they felt like. The authorities could help with the exams. In the meantime they would provide books, computers, limited virtual access to the outside world. This was all the start of what the medical team called the 'process of rehabilitation'. A way of finding them a route back into a society they barely knew.

But Visser frowned and shook her head when they asked for a visit home to Volendam by way of reward.

That was a step too far. Because the modest fishing town across the water was where they murdered Rogier Glas. Two young girls of eleven found in a back street next to the musician's savaged body, a bloody kitchen knife on the ground beside them.

So instead, when they weren't at the computer burrowing, thinking, they'd sit in the garden beneath the trees, fingers wrapped in the iron mesh of the high fence, staring out towards home, watching the propellers of the white wind turbines in the water turn like second hands on a gigantic, invisible clock. Volendam's harbour, the boats, their tall masts taunted them. Sometimes they clung to that perimeter fence so desperately, fingers hard through the gaps, noses pressed to the wire, they came away with its marks upon their flesh. Like stigmata, a reminder of an earthly sin, impossible to dispel.

Marken smelled like home, salty from the brackish water around them, not fresh, not stale. Just how the placid, endless lake was meant to be. From March to November ferries ran from Volendam taking tourists to and from the tiny port half a kilometre from the institution.

A thirty-five-minute crossing. They could still picture the waterfront even though they'd not set foot there for almost half their short lives.

A landing stage.

Flocks of tourists taking pictures of the few locals wearing traditional dress.

And in summer, the week of the talent contest, a temporary rostrum next to the museum where, once upon a time, they'd sung together with Jo, the third triplet, youngest by thirty minutes, providing the high notes in their harmonies.

The Timmers Sisters. One day they'd be famous. Until death came visiting one night and stole Jo, their mother Freya and father Gus from them.

Two streets behind the picturesque harbour was their shabby black-timbered cottage, the place they died. Gus, a fisherman, worked all hours to pay the rent while Freya sang in local bars for pennies and performed backing vocals for the local bands when she could.

Volendam was where the Palingsound, the Netherlands

equivalent of Beatlemania, began. For decades a bohemian oasis for musicians, far enough from Amsterdam to escape the attention of the authorities. Freya had grown up surrounded by pop tunes and folk songs playing on the radio, in the cafes and bars. Her daughters had inherited their mother's calm, clear singing voice, matched to perfect pitch, and her beauty. The girls – they thought of themselves that way as did everyone in Marken – could still hear Jo in their heads ten years on from the black night that took their family from them. That gift was, perhaps, the only satisfactory legacy they had from their mother, or so some people said when the smoke, the blood and the fury cleared and the inevitable recriminations followed.

Now they sat in the office of the director Henk Veerman, a dour and bulky man in his late fifties forever playing with a pen over a notepad and glancing at his computer. Next to him was the psychiatrist Visser, a thin, intense woman with cropped blonde hair and a craggy face that smiled too easily. She seemed interested as always, smartly dressed in a blue jacket and skirt. By her side sat Simon Klerk, sweet, handsome, fair-haired Simon with his too-bright shirt and crumpled jeans, caring, curious, the closest thing either of them had to a friend. Or so he wished to believe.

Mia and Kim had explored their own biological history in depth, going through the books in the library, checking on the web when they were finally allowed access to a limited number of reference sites. Triplets were not unusual. One in five hundred births. They were rarely identical however and in this they were no exception.

Both tall with natural blonde hair long around their shoulders, cut themselves when necessary with a single pair of not very sharp scissors watched always by Simon. They wore similar cheap clothes for this hot summer day. Cotton shirts, red and blue, jeans and sandals bought by Simon and Visser from a discount store in the city. Their faces as usual were set to neutral, not smiling, not sad either. Mia's the narrower, with high angular cheekbones, while Kim, the eldest, slower and heavier, possessed the soft round features of their mother.

Twenty-one, they looked all of seventeen. And they were beautiful. Of that they were certain. Freya, the loveliest woman in town, had said so, promising all three of them, even little Jo, the loudest and most mischievous, that one day they'd be even more bewitching than her.

The Golden Angels she dubbed them that first – and last – day they appeared on stage alone.

Three tiny saints from Volendam. Children of the lake.

They had that magnetic quality. It had been there from the start. The sisters saw it in the way people turned and stared as they walked down the street. They noticed it every day in Marken, in the eyes of the nurses, of Irene Visser and Simon Klerk. There was something special about the two of them. A power in the way they looked, one handed down in their genes. It would have been foolish not to use it.

'Mia . . . Kim . . .' Visser said in her quiet, pleasant city voice. 'You know why you're here?'

'Because we killed Rogier Glas,' Kim said straight out.

'You're sure of that?' the director demanded. 'No more arguments?'

'There never were arguments. Only regrets,' Mia added carefully, wishing her sister would think before she spoke, not that she would ever tell her this.

Simon sighed and glanced at them. This was the wrong answer.

'That was a long time ago,' the psychiatrist told them. 'Almost a lifetime for you. And besides . . .'

'We need the details again,' Veerman intervened.

Things happened between them without a word exchanged. One would begin a sentence only for the other to finish it. When Mia got a headache Kim did too. Their clothes complemented one another and they never spoke of it. And once a month they bled in unison, sharing the same grim fevered mood in angry silence.

That was over the week before. Now they were calm. Normal. Ready.

'You're here because we think it's time you were given a chance,' Visser said in that careful, attentive way she had. 'We think you're well enough to see more of the outside world.'

'We're free?' Kim whispered.

Visser laughed. Mia sighed.

'Not free. Not yet. Just . . . more free than you have been. We've watched you. Both of you. The progress you've made this last year is—'

Veerman picked up a report on his desk, uttered an audible sigh and started to read.

'It's been wonderful,' the psychiatrist added.

'Where?' Mia asked. 'Where can we go? Home to Volendam?'

'Not yet,' Visser said. 'One day, I'm sure. When you're ready.'

'Not that you have a home there any more,' Veerman added, staring at his papers.

The sisters smiled at one another, then at the officials across the desk. Mia reached out and took Kim's hands, toying with her fingers.

'All we want is to be well, Mr Director. Just to be together. To sing. To be . . . like everyone else.'

'That's the idea,' Veerman muttered.

'We will do whatever you want. Where may we go?'

Simon leaned forward.

'To a place we have in Amsterdam. A sheltered house. Near the museums. You won't be on your own. I'll visit you every weekday. There'll be people there to help. You must do as we say otherwise you'll have to return to custody. Somewhere else probably. An adult institution.'

'And you have to keep taking your medication,' the director cut in. 'That's a condition. You understand what a condition is?'

Kim had to stop herself laughing. Even so she rolled her eyes.

'It means doing what we're told. We do that already, don't we?'

The water seemed to stretch forever beyond the office window. The modest fishing town with its boats and houses and memories beckoned from across the lake. It was summer. Perhaps they'd built a stage there, a platform made for singing.

'You can't go back to Volendam yet,' Visser repeated, watching them. 'There are too many bad memories there.'

Mia nodded. Then Kim.

Henk Veerman kept fiddling with his pen, turning it up and down, clicking the button nervously.

'I want this absolutely clear,' he said. 'If I'm to agree to this request from your psychiatrist you must undertake to do everything you're asked. No arguments. No excursions outside the sheltered house without supervision.'

'Sir,' Mia replied with the sweetest smile she could manage. 'We've tried to do our best here for years. Have we disappointed you lately?'

'No,' Visser answered. 'Not in a very long time. You've been perfect.' She glanced at Kim, the last to lose her stubbornness. 'Both of you.'

The girls nodded. Mia withdrew her hand from her sister's then ran her fingers through her long yellow hair. Sensing this, Kim did the same.

All eyes on them. As they usually were.

'When do we leave?' Mia asked.

'We need to talk about this among ourselves,' Veerman announced, glancing at the psychiatrist and the nurse. 'Ladies . . .'

They hated being called that. It made them sound old and ugly.

'Yes?' Mia asked.

'Wait outside, please,' the director said. 'We won't be long.'

The sisters stared across the desk. Two men, one woman. Everything in their lives came in threes. Three sisters. Three adults responsible for their fate.

Three.

It was important Visser believed this obsession of theirs was now lost.

So they got up and walked steadily out of the room, hoping that no one would notice that their steps drummed across the wooden floor in triplets . . . one, two, three . . . one, two, three.

There were three chairs in the corridor when they got there and no one else in sight. The closed door of Veerman's office was so far away they couldn't hear the voices behind.

Kim tapped her fingers on the thick plate glass of the window. Three times.

Mia watched and tried to smile.

2

August in Amsterdam and the city dozed in the grip of sultry summer. Of an evening people dined on their outside steps above the street, sipping wine, picking lethargically at takeaway pizza and plates of salad. During the day they went about their work with a genial listlessness. It was too hot, too sticky to get mad at anything. Even the bemused tourists who had the temerity to wander in front of cyclists rarely got a curse.

Nowhere was this sleepy, sweaty lassitude more obvious than the serious crimes office of the Marnixstraat police headquarters where, bang on cue as the heatwave hit, the air conditioning had groaned three times then failed completely.

Most of the windows were sealed shut so the place was stuffy, overheated and idle. Pieter Vos, the senior officer in charge, sat at his desk, long dark hair uncombed, a threadbare blue jacket over the back of his chair. In his late thirties he still retained a boyish face and a ready smile that fooled people from time to time, especially if he was out with his diminutive wire fox terrier Sam.

The two of them lived in a shambolic houseboat on the Prinsengracht canal just a short walk away. Sam usually stayed at the Drie Vaten bar opposite the boat when Vos was working. Today that was impossible. Sofia Albers, the owner, had gone to the Rijksmuseum with a friend and couldn't look after him. So now the green plastic dog basket from the main cabin sat next to the brigadier's desk. Not that there was much to do.

Laura Bakker was trying to catch up on paperwork while Dirk Van der Berg, twenty years her senior, the same rank, lobbed a rubber ball up and down the office for the dog.

Sam chased it into the area near the photocopier and sent the waste bin flying.

Bakker, a tall and striking woman in her mid-twenties, with long red hair, an awkward Friesland accent, and an occasional attitude looked up and complained, 'I'm trying to concentrate here.'

'Why bother?' Van der Berg replied. He was a hefty man with a pockmarked face and salt-and-pepper hair. Beer figured high on his list of personal priorities. He started picking up the mess while Sam ran round the office, head turning madly, trying to shake the ball to death.

'Because it has to be done?'

'You could always finish it tomorrow,' Vos suggested. He looked at his watch. The minutes were crawling by. Sofia wouldn't be back in the bar for an hour or more. When she was he'd walk Sam home and enjoy a beer. Van der Berg and Bakker would probably join him.

'I hate procrastination,' the young policewoman declared.

'I love it,' Van der Berg cried. 'Well . . . if it means you don't have to fill in a load of stupid forms.'

'Without forms . . . without organization we'd be lost,' she insisted.

The phone on Koeman's empty desk rang. Vos looked at it and didn't move. So did Van der Berg. Bakker sighed and marched over to take the call.

There was a bright and cheery woman on the other end.

'I want to talk to Ollie,' she said. 'Tell him Vicky's back in town. It's his lucky day.'

'Ollie who?'

'Ollie Haas,' the woman replied briskly. 'Don't you know your boss's name?'

'Yes. I do. Who's Ollie Haas?'

'Your brigadier!'

Van der Berg was at the desk already. His hand was the size of a goalkeeper's glove, fingers like sausages, out and beckoning.

'No,' Bakker said. 'I think you've got the wrong—'

She let Van der Berg retrieve the phone and listened. Vos was there now too. A brief conversation. Vicky was newly returned from a long stay in Turkey. Ollie Haas was an old friend. Lover maybe. She wanted to get in touch.

'He doesn't work here any more,' Van der Berg told her. 'Hasn't for . . . I don't know . . . years.'

'We had a falling-out. Lost touch. I went to live abroad. I really want to see him again.'

'I'm sorry . . .'

'Do you have his address? His phone number?'

Van der Berg put his hand over the speaker and relayed the questions to Vos. He shook his head and took the phone.

'I'm brigadier here now. Vos. Officer Haas is retired.'

'I'm an old friend! Surely you can tell me where he lives.'

'Write me a letter,' Vos suggested. 'I'll pass it on to human resources. They can try and—'

'This is all to do with that shit you lot got yourselves in, isn't it? Volendam? The Timmers kids? I thought you people had buried that once and for all.'

After that the line went dead.

'What the hell was going on there?' Van der Berg wondered. 'No one wants to get in touch with Ollie Haas.'

'Who?' Bakker asked.

'You won't remember,' Vos said. 'You were a kid. It was . . . years ago.'

'Ten years,' Van der Berg said. 'We watched that whole farce fall apart in front of our eyes. They wouldn't let me and Pieter anywhere near it. And then—'

'It was just an old girlfriend,' Vos suggested.

Van der Berg was staring at Bakker.

11

'You remember The Cupids, don't you? The pop group?'

She tugged at her long red hair and wrinkled her nose.

'Rings a bell. Didn't they break up? There was a scandal or something?'

He snorted.

'A scandal? One of them wound up dead. One went missing. As for Gert Brugman . . . well, you can still catch him singing for beer in the bars around here. Used to be a ladies' man. Looked a real mess the last time I saw him.'

'There was a murder,' Bakker remembered. 'A family. It was in all the papers for a while. I was in Friesland. At school. Volendam . . .'

Van der Berg grunted at the name of the fishing town half an hour away from the city.

'Have you ever been there?' Vos asked.

She stretched out her long legs, yawned and said, 'No. Everyone says it's full of tourists.'

Vos checked his watch.

'Not just tourists. Career development, Laura. You're supposed to read up on old cases from time to time. Cold ones too.'

'I am,' she agreed.

'Well there's your assignment. Go down to records and pull out what you can on the Timmers murders. Read through the files. Tell me where Ollie Haas went wrong.'

'Stop at twenty screw-ups,' Van der Berg added. 'After that you just might go crazy. At least it cost that idiot his job in the end. They should have snatched his pension too.'

She brightened at that. The day had been long and boring.

'So who's going to take me through it all? Or do I get the pleasure of both of you?'

'Sam's going to need his supper in a while,' Vos said. 'I've got some washing to pick up.'

'May I hold his lead, sir?' Van der Berg asked meekly. 'Along the way?'

'It's half past three!' Bakker cried. 'Even you two can't bunk off work this early.'

Vos checked his watch again and wondered if there was something wrong with the battery. The minute hand had scarcely moved. They had another hour to kill at least. Time seemed to have got stuck in this steamy, slow weather.

'Expense forms!' he said, raising a finger into the air. Van der Berg groaned then banged his head gently on the desk. 'After that I'm buying.'

Bakker closed her eyes and made weeping noises.

'This is all your fault,' Van der Berg told her.

She got to her feet.

'I'm going to look for those files. What was his name again?'

'Ollie Haas,' the two men replied in unison.

'The Timmers case,' Van der Berg added. 'Don't delve too deep, Laura. Not if you want to sleep tonight.'

3

Sisters, brought into the world thirty – ten times three – minutes apart, Kim and Mia stayed by the heavy window staring at Volendam across the placid water, understanding each other's thoughts the way they always did, knowing they both saw the same thing.

Three boats broke the bright horizon.

Three states of existence. Past. Present. Future.

Three parts to the world now visible. Earth. Water. Sky.

The seafront of Volendam seemed closer than usual. Without speaking a word each knew what the other was remembering. A warm summer evening ten years before. A backing band was starting up on a platform near the landing stage.

Three days and three nights Jonah lingered in the belly of the whale.

Three days and three nights Jesus spent in the heart of the earth before he rose to glory.

Three girls in blue hot pants, sparkly scarlet shirts, patent red leather shoes, yellow hair tied back in buns, faces heavy with mascara and lipstick, walking up the stairs onto the stage.

Three men before them. Famous once upon a time. Revered. Lucky escapees from the round of fishing and drink and hard leisure that was the lot of many in the town by the water.

Applause then. Shouts from the audience. A few yelled phrases that eleven-year-old girls didn't really understand.

They stood on the waterfront stage dancing slowly to the ballad their mother had taught them from the CD player in their living room.

Then the girls began to sing in perfect harmony with such delicacy, charm and precision they silenced the half-drunk audience and kept the rapt attention of the lone TV camera that had come out from Amsterdam seeking cheery sequences to fill the empty minutes of local summer news.

The camera loved them, Freya said.

The audience too.

Everyone.

And those three men who mattered most, grinning figures in denim seated at the front of the stage on chairs placed like thrones, judging everyone the moment they rose to take the steps.

This was a talent contest, Freya said. One of those win-or-lose moments in life when everything might change for the better. A chance to be spotted. To rise from obscure poverty in Volendam to something bigger, in the Netherlands, perhaps abroad one day.

The lovely singing sisters. The Golden Angels. Children now but teenagers soon. Freya had that transition mapped out all along. Cute then sultry. Adorable then desirable. An inch or two of that line had to be crossed at the start.

'You can save us,' she told them, putting on their make-up at the back of the grubby bar where she waited tables. The place both tantalized and scared them. It was called the Taveerne van de Zeven Duivels, the Inn of the Seven Devils. From the ceiling leering demons stared down at the customers, waving pitchforks. They met their mother there almost every day. 'You can take us out of this shitty backwater, darlings. You'd like that, wouldn't you?'

The men who judged them were called The Cupids. They had been famous throughout Holland once. Then the years and changing fashion had taken hold.

Freya Timmers knew them well. She'd sung on a few of their records. The old songs from the Eighties. The later stuff when they moved awkwardly into trance and rock and anything else their manager threw at them, trying to keep a grip on any audience they could find. Even now the girls could hear their mother's voice on the last song she made with them, a slow, sad ballad that was a return to form, going somewhere in the charts until that August night when three little sisters sang it and knew they would never forget the words again.

The lines remained burned in their memories, in English, the language The Cupids liked most of all.

In a soft, calm voice, almost a whisper, Kim stared out of the window and sang the first line.

Love is like a chain that binds me.

Mia followed with the second.

Love is like a last goodbye.

Together they sang the third.

Love is all I have to keep you.

Eyes closed, memories sweeping over them. Kim thinking the lower note, Mia the middle, they waited, listening, praying.

A high tone. Jo. A kid's name. A kid she'd always be. Jo took the last line in their head and the three of them sang it together, note perfect, all seven syllables in the key of F.

Love is gone. And so am I.

Kim's hand reached out and squeezed her sister's.

Four brief fragments. As much as they could manage.

Mia wiped away her tears.

No words. They weren't necessary.

Behind the closed door of the director's office their fate was being decided. For years they'd been praying for this moment. All they could do now was wait.

4

Henk Veerman pulled out some of the photos passed on by the police after Rogier Glas was found dead in his van not far from the Timmers' home.

'Do you want to take a look?' he asked, scattering a few pictures across the desk.

Simon Klerk frowned and asked, 'Why?'

'It was a long time ago,' Visser pointed out once more. 'They were children. They didn't understand the difference between right and wrong. And even if they did . . .'

She pulled up the nearest photograph and showed it to them. A burly middle-aged man stuck behind the wheel of a Ford Transit. Throat cut. Trousers down. Something bloody stuck in his mouth.

'Even if they were aware of what they were doing,' she went on, 'there are plenty of people out there who think they had good reason.'

Veerman groaned then tidied the papers back into the file.

'Except they got the wrong man. The police said there was no evidence to link Glas . . . or the other two in that group . . . The Cupids . . . to what happened.'

'By what happened . . . you mean the murder of their mother, father and sister?' she demanded.

'Precisely,' he agreed. 'No one's arguing it was a picnic—'

'A *picnic*?'

'I worded that badly. It was horrendous. God knows it would have screwed up any kid who witnessed it. But—'

'They didn't actually see him there, did they?' Klerk asked. 'I thought that was the whole point.'

17

'This was ten years ago,' Visser insisted. 'Mia and Kim wouldn't talk about it then. Any more than they'll talk about it now—'

'Haas investigated,' Veerman interrupted. 'He said Rogier Glas had nothing to do with the family's murder. Not that it mattered because, well . . .' He took out one of the photos again and pushed it round the desk. 'Those two little angels caught him in his van. Slashed him to ribbons. Then cut off his cock and rammed it down his throat. And now you want to let them loose in Amsterdam.'

Klerk shook his head.

'They wouldn't be loose. They'd be under constant supervision. When I'm not there we'll have someone else. If I see any sign they're likely to abscond. To misbehave—'

'Misbehave?' Veerman's index finger stabbed at the file. 'You call that misbehaving?'

Visser groaned.

'They were distraught children. They acted on the spur of the moment after witnessing the aftermath of a gruesome and dreadful crime. We've been observing them closely for eighteen months. They've been punished enough. It's our duty now to at least try to give them a chance of rehabilitation.'

'They're smart as hell,' the director interrupted. 'You said that yourself. This could all be an act.'

'For what purpose?' she wondered. 'They came in here as children. They've been good as gold lately. Marken's an institution for severely disturbed adolescents. Kim and Mia have turned twenty-one. Either we hand them over to an adult mental institution or we make other arrangements.' She hesitated to make sure he understood what came next. 'If we pass them on to someone else that will be marked down against us, you know. They'll say we had those girls for ten years and didn't do a damned thing for them. They'd be right too. There'll be questions asked. Do we want that?'

Veerman didn't answer.

'I think,' she added, 'your response is coloured by the nature of the crime. Men attack women in the vilest of ways all the time. We're used to it. We accept it.'

'Accept it?' Veerman glared at her. 'Are you serious?'

'I meant that we accept the fact it happens. But when a woman fights back . . . when two young girls do that especially.' She pulled out the photo again. 'Yes. They cut off his cock. And that's what you all found so shocking, isn't it? If it hadn't been for that they'd have been out of here years ago.'

He brushed the picture back into the file then said, 'Do you have any idea what will happen if you're wrong? If you let that pair out into the world and they go bad again?'

'It won't—'

'But if it does, Irene. We'd be dead here. You. Me. Everything.'

'It won't,' she insisted. 'I guarantee it. Simon will watch their every move. I won't allow them back to Volendam. That would be dangerous. We'll just keep them in the house in the Museum Quarter. Watch them. See how it goes.'

'For how long?' Veerman wondered.

'For as long as it takes,' Klerk said. 'I'm not saying they're cured. But they're close to it. They're nice kids.'

'They're twenty-one,' the director objected. 'Not kids any more.'

'I know.' The nurse laughed. 'I forget that sometimes. They come across as so young. Naive.' He thought for a moment then said it anyway. 'Innocent.'

'And they do sing beautifully,' Visser added. 'I think that could be good therapy for them. If we could put them in touch with an amateur choir or something.'

'I don't like it.'

'Obviously,' she said. 'But we can't keep them locked up here forever. The ministry's got civil rights people asking awkward questions about mental health committals already. All we need is for them to make the girls—'

'They're not girls!'

'All we need is for them to make the Timmers sisters a test case and then we'll have everyone on us. Lawyers. The media. You name it.' She leaned back and looked out of the window. 'That would be a shame, Henk. It's quiet here. Beautiful. We can work . . . undisturbed. I know you like that. We all do.'

The papers were in front of him on the desk. All he had to do was sign.

'I want to ask them a question,' Veerman said. 'Get them in here. If they answer right you can have what you want.'

'What question?' the nurse asked.

The director pushed his glasses up his nose and glared at him. 'That's for them. Not you.'

5

Simon Klerk stuck his head round the door. The girls stopped singing. They could still hear a third voice dying in their heads.

'Can we go?' Kim asked.

'Soon,' he said. 'The director wants to talk to you first. He wants . . .'

The nurse stepped out of the room and gently closed the door behind him.

'He wants to ask you a question.'

Mia said, 'What question?'

'I don't know. But it's important. You need to give the right answer.'

They walked up to him . . . *one, two, three, one, two, three.*

'What's the right answer, Simon?' Kim pleaded.

Mia laughed and said straight off, 'If he doesn't know the question . . .'

He struggled for a moment as he often did with them of late. They were so . . . confident.

'Just tell the truth,' he suggested. 'You can't go wrong with that.'

They giggled and looked at him.

'All the truth?' Kim asked.

He blushed.

'It'll just be a silly question.'

Klerk went back and opened the door then led them in.

Veerman sat at the desk. Freya, their mother, had a phrase for that expression. She said it looked as if someone had swallowed an angry wasp. Irene Visser stroked her short blonde hair and told them to sit.

21

It was like the hearing they'd had when they were eleven. They were about to be judged.

Across the water Volendam sat listening.

'What you did . . . the reason you're here,' Veerman began awkwardly. 'It was very bad. You know that?'

'Of course we do,' Kim said.

'Not a day goes by when we don't regret it,' Mia added, always the one to soften her sister's curt candour.

'You killed a man—'

'So they told us,' Kim cut in.

'You murdered him,' Veerman said. 'You do accept that, don't you?'

'They punished us,' Mia agreed with a nod. 'They said we deserved it.'

'Did he?' Veerman asked in a firm, loud voice now. 'Did Rogier Glas?'

The girls sat in silence.

Irene Visser moved forward and placed her elbows on the desk, the way she did when they were talking in her office.

'Did Rogier Glas murder your parents?' she asked. 'Your sister Jo? Do you still think that?'

The girls looked at each other. They seemed ready to cry.

'No,' Mia whimpered.

'No!' Kim was breaking too. 'You said he didn't, Irene. You wouldn't lie. Mr Glas . . .'

Tears did fill her eyes then. And her sister's.

'Give them a minute,' Visser pleaded. 'Henk. You can see for yourself. We're going somewhere that should be private. Between the two of them and me.'

'I'm the director,' Veerman insisted. 'I sign the release.'

'Mr Glas . . . we're sorry,' Mia said in a timid voice close to a hurt whisper. 'We were scared. We were young. We didn't know what we were doing—'

'Innocent,' her sister added. 'Mr Glas was innocent.'

'There!' Irene Visser declared. 'You wanted an admission, Henk. You've got it. No one knows who killed your family, girls. Do they now?'

They nodded.

'No one,' Kim agreed.

'And,' Mia added, 'they never will.'

Visser looked at Veerman. So did Simon Klerk.

'Very well,' the director said and got his pen. 'You can leave. Go with the nurse. He'll drive you into the city. Do as he says. We don't want you back here. Please . . .'

They blinked as if ready to cry. Then got to their feet and stuttered out their thanks.

'May we pack?' Mia asked. 'We have a few things. Just a few. No case though.'

'We'll find you something,' Visser said.

Mia added, 'You've been so kind. Director Veerman. Irene. Simon. So very kind. We didn't deserve such . . . such a *family*. Yes. That's the right word.'

'The proper word,' Kim agreed.

'Go and get ready,' Klerk said. 'I'll come for you. We'll take my car.'

They left, arm in arm, nodding, bowing, grateful.

Veerman sat in silence. Visser checked her messages. Klerk texted his wife to say he'd be late home.

Down the corridor Mia and Kim Timmers walked, happy, hand in hand.

Two voices in harmony singing an old and happy folk song. A third accompanying them in their head.

6

Bakker never came back from records. At ten to five Vos gave up on the paperwork and the minute hand on his watch and the two men walked Sam down Elandsgracht at a constant steady pace. They made the terrier's supper on Vos's houseboat, watched, laughing, as he wolfed it down then strolled over to his bed in the stern and fell fast asleep.

'Have we earned a beer now?' Van der Berg asked.

'Not really,' Vos said. 'But who cares?'

Two minutes later the pair of them were perched on rickety stools at the counter of the Drie Vaten staring warily at a new bottled beer Sofia Albers had bought in from a microbrewery start-up.

'I hate change,' Van der Berg declared.

'But do you like the beer?' she asked.

He sipped the pale ale again and said, 'It's different. Does that answer your question?'

The door opened and Laura Bakker came in and stood over them, arms folded.

'We're trying Sofia's new beer,' Vos told her.

'Was that your idea of a joke?'

'Ollie Haas?' Van der Berg said. 'The Timmers case? The Cupids?'

'The Cupids,' Sofia muttered and headed for the kitchen, shaking her head.

'No joke, Laura,' Vos added. 'You can't have read through all those files. Not so quickly. Not even you—'

'What files? I've spent an hour and a half chasing thin air.'

The two men sipped at their beer and waited, knowing no comment on their part was required.

'I went to the digital archive first,' Bakker declared. 'Nothing. Then the paper archive. All that's there are a few statements, a handful of photos and a set of psychiatric reports on the two sisters who survived.'

Vos nodded at the table by the toilet. It was empty as usual.

'Four people were murdered,' Van der Berg said. 'Father, mother, daughter. Then the guitarist in the band. There's a lot more to it than a few files.'

'I'm telling you, Dirk. I know how the system works. That's all there is.'

Sofia came and placed a fresh bottle of the new beer in front of her then retreated. Van der Berg poured the drink.

'I'll take a look in the morning,' he said, handing her the glass. 'Sometimes these things lurk in places a newcomer like you might not know.'

'How many decades do I need to spend here before I cease to be a newcomer? Look. I went through the archive records. I can see they were there. Lots of them. They got marked for deletion five years ago. By—'

'No,' Vos insisted. 'That's not possible. Technically it's still an open case. Not that anyone's—'

'They're gone! I'm telling you. It's there on the file. De Groot marked them down for deletion one week after he became commissaris. Every investigative report that Ollie Haas wrote has been erased by the system. Every paper copy shredded.'

Van der Berg raised his glass and peered at the clear chestnut liquid. Sofia arrived with four freshly boiled eggs and a saucer of salt. Then she returned with Vos's washing neatly folded and ironed in a wicker basket. He handed over a twenty-euro note and said thanks.

'I like this beer,' Van der Berg announced. 'I think it'll make the perfect marriage with an egg.'

Laura Bakker closed her eyes and whispered, 'Oh the life we lead.'

Beyond the window the Prinsengracht was busy with early-evening traffic. Tourist boats full of visitors gazing out at the city on the water. The world seemed quiet and at peace.

'Let's deal with this in the morning,' Vos said. 'I'm sure it's all just a . . . misunderstanding.'

7

Simon Klerk gave them a bag and left them to pack their things. Then the girls went to the accommodation block and said goodbye to the other nurses and the two men in the security office. After that they went to the kitchen and kissed the two big friendly women who worked there. The cooks wept and that brought tears all round.

'Time,' the nurse said after a while.

The kitchen women got a small audience together and pleaded for one last song. The girls looked at Klerk. He nodded. So there, watched in silence by the gardener, the security men, four nurses and the cooks, Kim and Mia sang the one they were always asked for.

Draai het wieletje nog eens om.

Turn the wheel around again.

A silly ditty for toddlers but they performed it beautifully, did the dance, clapped their hands when it was called for.

Everyone applauded and wept a little more.

'We haven't said goodbye to Dr Visser,' Mia pleaded. 'Or Director Veerman. Or—'

'They're busy,' Klerk told her.

'Or any of the patients,' Kim added. 'Kaatje. We've got to say goodbye to Kaatje—'

'We think it's best the patients stay inside. It might upset them, seeing you leave.'

Kim frowned and stamped her feet but, to her sister's relief, stayed quiet.

'They could be jealous,' Klerk added.

He picked up the bag. Now they saw it had Disney characters on the side.

'We need to go, girls.'

The sisters dried their eyes and went outside to stand in the car park next to the lime trees and the rubbish bins, taking one last look around.

'We won't come back, Simon,' Mia asked. 'Will we?'

'Not if you do as I say.'

The pair of them gazed at him.

'You will do as I say, won't you?'

'We promised, didn't we?' Kim replied.

'Promised,' her sister agreed.

The Marken sanatorium had been their home for so long. Its grey walls, the high wire fence, the wood by the water, branches swaying in the warm lake breeze . . . all these things had served as their world as they grew from children to teenagers to serious, introverted young adults.

Leaving the place meant entering a universe without boundaries, real form or substance, a mysterious destination they only knew from a distance. Through television, through the carefully monitored Internet connection the communications room provided. From the gossip and stories, some true, some fantastic, of the other inmates there. Not that Kim and Mia talked to them much. They were different. Even Kaatje Lammers, who could so easily get them into trouble. Unlike them the others were *sick*.

They waved back to the buildings as Klerk led them to his car, a shiny bright yellow SEAT parked behind the residential block.

'Sit in the back,' he ordered.

'How far?' Mia asked.

'How long?' Kim added.

'A while.'

'You said we could have watches,' Kim reminded him.

'I did.'

He reached into his jacket pocket and pulled out two cheap digital ones. Both pink. Kiddy things.

'Also,' Mia went on, 'you promised—'

'No more favours for the moment,' Klerk said curtly, opening the back door one side, then the other. 'Not until you've earned them.'

He held up the bag. Kim took it and they climbed in.

They didn't really know what the village was like. They'd been there a couple of times when their parents and Jo were alive. Fun visits wandering round the narrow streets. But the institution never let them out, not even when some of the other patients were allowed controlled, supervised walks. They weren't, Veerman always insisted, sufficiently 'normalized'.

Klerk got in the front and drove slowly down the long gravel drive to the gate. The man on the barrier knew they were coming. The nurse had to give him some paperwork all the same. He stared at the form and the signature of the director.

The blue-and-white pole went up. The car nosed out onto the single-track lane. They didn't say anything for a while. All this was so new.

In a minute they were crawling through the narrow streets of Marken, noses to the glass. Tourists wandered round taking photographs. A woman was posing for them in traditional dress. Black skirt. A striped red blouse. A white mob cap. Black clogs.

The girls giggled. Simon Klerk drove on.

Past the houses, leaving the centre behind, they remembered something and turned to look back at the eastern finger of land at the edge of the island, pointing out into the larger lake of the Markermeer.

'The horse!' Kim cried. 'I remember it now. The horse!'

A tall white building nicknamed the *Paard van Marken*. A monumental lighthouse that seemed to be sprouting from a grand white wooden mansion, a stallion stretching its neck for the sky.

'When we were tiny,' Mia said. 'We went there. Remember?'

Klerk switched on the radio. Pop music.

'No!' the girls shrieked in unison. 'Not that. *Not that!*'

He shrugged, turned it off then drove to the long dyke road crossing the water back to the mainland, past yet more wind turbines.

They stared at the green dam wall blocking the view and the cyclists on the bike path. The place seemed so flat, so devoid of any form, they had to imagine Volendam to the north, past the distant spike of another white lighthouse, much smaller than the *Paard*.

Then the sea dyke ended and they were on land proper. The 311 from Amsterdam meandered towards them.

'There's a bus!' Kim squealed and her sister shrieked too.

'Girls!' Klerk cried from behind the wheel. '*Girls!* It's just a bus.'

'I know,' Kim answered.

'But we haven't seen one,' her sister added. 'Not since . . .'

They went quiet and Simon Klerk didn't push it.

The yellow SEAT stuck to the main road for half a kilometre or more. A single-track lane came up on the left with a sign saying, 'Cars and bicycles, local access only'.

Klerk turned in. The way ahead was so narrow he could only drive at a snail's pace. There were drainage dykes on both sides, flat green fields of pasture beyond them, low, modest bridges that led to sprawling meadows where scattered herds of cattle munched idly on lush grass.

The sisters turned to the windows and stared up at the sky. It was a bright and beautiful day with puffy white clouds moving slowly east to west. Gulls hung in the air. As they passed a low hedge separating one bare field from the next a grey heron, all puffy feathers, descended towards the green channel next to them, stuck its long legs in the water and stabbed down, looking for prey.

'We'll never get there,' Mia said. 'Not at this rate.'

'What's the rush?' Simon Klerk asked.

About four hundred metres ahead lay a spinney of low trees, weeping willows by the narrow dyke next to a thicket of overgrown elder bushes. Behind stood what looked like a derelict farmhouse. They got to the drive. The rusty gate was half off its hinges. Klerk climbed out.

While he was messing around Kim tried the doors. They were locked. She patted her jacket. Mia did the same and smiled.

Ahead of them Klerk pushed down the gate then dragged it to one side. He came back to the car and drove over the wooden bridge. The tyres made a rhythmic sound across the planks.

One, two, three. One, two, three, the sisters counted.

He parked on the dried mud drive by the back door. Rotting furniture stood outside, fabric ripped, bare foam hanging out like torn flesh.

The sisters sat and waited.

Klerk leaned back in the driver's seat then turned, a stupid grin on his face.

'You remember what we agreed, girls? There's a price. There's a price for everything.'

'*Ja*,' they said together.

'So who's first?'

The wind picked up. The weeping willows shifted under its breath. They were nowhere and knew it. No passing traffic down this remote lane. No one to see. No one to hear.

'Me,' Mia said in a quiet, flat voice. 'But you have to open the doors.'

He laughed at his own stupidity then found the button beneath the window. Something clicked. She stepped outside.

This place didn't smell like Marken at all. It had a rotten stink about it. Stagnant water. A blocked dyke. All the things you got on land, away from the lake that swept everything clean.

'I'm waiting,' Klerk cried as she stood by the car door seeing how the abandoned farmhouse was hidden from everywhere by the spinney's green shade.

'Sorry,' she muttered and climbed in.

'You should be grateful.' He pointed at her in the passenger seat. 'You will be too. The pair of you. If it wasn't for me—'

'We know, Simon,' Kim insisted from the back. 'You don't need to tell us.'

'We're grateful,' Mia added.

His eyes were bright and anxious and greedy.

'One word from me and you're back in Marken. Or somewhere worse. Years before they let you out again. *Years.* They'll split you up. Probably never see each other again.'

'Very grateful,' Mia repeated.

'Get on with it then,' Klerk ordered. 'Had enough of your teasing.' He nodded at the back seat. 'And she's straight after.'

'Sure,' Mia said and didn't move.

A sound then. Klerk couldn't believe his ears. It was Kim behind him, singing in that pure clear voice of theirs. The kid's tune they'd performed back in Marken.

Draai het wieletje nog eens om.

Turn the wheel around again.

'For Christ's sake,' he grunted. 'Are you two little bitches listening to a word I—?'

Then he saw the thing Kim was dragging out of her waistband, knew what it was straight away too. One of the knives the staff used in their private canteen. Metal, unlike the plastic cutlery they allowed the patients.

This one looked brighter, sharper than any he'd ever seen, as if they'd been working on it for ages, planning for this moment.

'Girls—'

Kim sang something else.

Love is like a chain that binds me.

Mia tapped the windscreen – one two three – and came in note perfect.

Love is like a last goodbye.

8

As the summer sun faded over the water they waited by the main road for the bus from Marken to the city. There were two hundred euros in Simon Klerk's wallet. Maybe nurses didn't get paid much.

'The pills,' Kim said and both of them retrieved four weeks of medication carefully stashed inside old shampoo bottles, laughing as they emptied the multicoloured tablets on the grass.

Twenty minutes later the bus arrived. Just two people on it with the driver. Four euros each for two tickets to Amsterdam. They sat together at the back as they drove though the flat green fields criss-crossed by glimmering channels of water.

Waterland.

Earth that once was sea until men came along and tamed the vast, relentless expanse of ocean, reclaiming the land as polder, kept whole by dykes and dams. Not that the water, the sweet green water, ever went away. They'd grown up with that idea, seen their father and his brother fish for the diminishing supply of eels, in the lake and in the dykes. Theirs was a world where solitary herons stood like grey guardians, spear-like beaks at the ready, always watching from the margins. Where life teemed beneath the emerald surface and nothing was quite what it seemed.

Mia whispered in her sister's ear as they approached the town of Monnickendam, tantalizingly close to home. She'd retrieved a memory from when they were tiny, a precious one, full of meaning. It was a warm day that last summer when they were out in the old Renault with their mother. Somewhere close to where the bus now ambled they saw them: a fat and happy duck with her chicks standing by the side of the road, waiting for a safe moment to cross.

'You remember?' Mia asked.

'Of course I do!' Kim answered, not cross, just offended by the thought she might have forgotten.

The duck had a plump breast, puffed out proudly in front of her. The chicks looked like tiny black balls of furry feathers.

Their mother had slowed the car then stopped. All three girls in the back had put their hands over their mouths to stifle their giggles as Freya wound down the window, stuck her head outside and called, in a firm but friendly voice, 'After you, Mother Duck. Take care of your young ones.'

Then the bird had lifted her beak, quacked something, and the tiny band had waddled from the lake side of the road to the dyke opposite.

'That,' said their mother as they watched the procession reach the weed-strewn water and happily clamber in, 'is what mummies do. Look after their chicks. Always. And like good little chicks they do as they're told.'

In the back of the bus crossing Waterland Mia started to cry. Kim did too but not so much and then she wiped away her sister's tears.

Evening fell around them. The countryside slowly gave way to the city, to wide roads and highways, a new and alien environment of concrete and noise, heavy with the dusty dark smell of pollution. The bus slowed down with the traffic. Through the IJtunnel they went.

The sisters sat more closely to one another. This place was busy and so strange. They'd barely visited Amsterdam as children and that was half a lifetime away. Mia had the map they'd been left in their room at Marken. She took it out to show her sister. So many streets. So many canals bigger than any dyke they'd seen.

Finally they stopped at the terminus behind Centraal station, so shiny and clean it had to be new. Street lights were coming on everywhere, boats and ferries crossing the busy water.

The driver scratched his head as they wandered to the front and asked if they were all right.

'Of course,' Kim answered. 'We are sisters. Together we look after each other the way families do.'

The man had dark skin and shiny black hair. He smiled at them and said in a foreign accent, 'Enjoy your evening, ladies.'

They didn't smile back so he shrugged and opened the door.

They walked through the vast station to the city side and bought two hot dogs and cans of soft drink from a stall. The map they'd been left had a route to a place with a heavy felt-tip asterisk against it. There was a street name, a number and a short message scribbled at the top: *Go here girls. And be free.*

Ten minutes it took and with every passing second they felt the world was watching them, staring at them, judging them. Finally they wandered down the busy street of Haarlemmer-straat where gaggles of men and women, half-drunk, half-stoned, were going out for the night. The number was for a tiny narrow terraced house in Vinkenstraat behind.

A cheery English woman who called herself Vera answered the door. She was expecting them, made welcoming noises and showed them inside.

In the hallway Mia offered her money there and then. She'd no idea how these things worked.

'No need for that now, love,' the woman said. Her face was wrinkled and the colour of old wood. The sisters weren't good at guessing ages. Perhaps she was fifty. Perhaps more. In spite of the tan she didn't look well. Halfway up the steep and narrow stairs she had to stop to catch her breath, taking out an inhaler from her pocket, gasping at it before she could go on.

'Are you all right?' Mia asked.

The woman laughed and said, 'For now, kiddo. You Dutchies don't half like to make steps difficult for an old bird like me.'

Then she waited a while until she was steady and led them to a small room on the top floor. A couple of single beds sat either side of a narrow window that overlooked a dark courtyard where pigeons cooed.

'You can work out where the bathroom is,' she said. 'I'm off for a lie-down.'

They had scissors and hair dye, stolen from the staff quarters. Mia cut Kim's hair first. She began to cry as the golden locks fell on the grubby terracotta tiles. Kim started gently weeping too. They stopped, hugged each other in their girlish clothes and carried on.

After twenty minutes a yellow pile of locks sat in a heap on the dirty floor. They used their bottles of mineral water to dampen their hair then took it in turns to apply the dye. Black for Mia, a lurid shade of purple-red for Kim.

A set of stick-on tattoos came from the handbag of a temporary night nurse. Dragons mostly. They stripped down to their underwear. Kim put a green one on Mia's right shoulder. Mia did the same for her on her left, red this time.

Inside the bag they'd got some different clothes stolen gradually over the months. Kim was bigger, more muscular, but not so much that the sisters couldn't swap clothes. They spread out what they had on the table and decided who got what.

For Kim, with her purple-red hair, a black fake leather jacket, green T-shirt and old ripped jeans. Mia went more conservative. Brown cotton trousers, a white T-shirt. A cardigan of red and blue zigzags.

By the door was an ancient wardrobe with broken glass in the door. The sisters stood in front of it and stared at themselves transformed.

'That works,' Mia said.

'It does,' Kim agreed.

Mia stretched out on the single bed nearest the window, lay

back, hands behind her head. Kim did the same on the mattress opposite. They started to sing quietly then stopped.

One of the phones they'd brought was making a noise. Not ringing. A short buzz for a message.

Kim got it, stared at the screen and squealed with delight.

> Perfect, darling sisters. Now we begin.
>
> Love Jo

9

At nine the following morning Henk Veerman summoned Irene
Visser to his office. She looked as if she hadn't slept. Jeans, a
crumpled shirt, short fair hair uncombed, a mess. Veerman was
in his customary work suit, a heavy man, always dressed for the
office. He didn't like it when standards slipped.

'The last thing I need in the present circumstances is you
going to pieces,' he told her as she came in and took a chair at the
desk where, the day before, they'd interviewed the Timmers sisters, Simon Klerk nodding his assent to their partial release. 'I've
had his wife on the phone. She's threatening to go to the police.'

Visser rubbed her eyes. They were red. From crying. Tired-
ness. He'd no idea and didn't much care.

'She called me too. The woman's hysterical. I talked her out of
it. Don't worry. We've got time.'

'Jesus. This is a mess, Irene. I warned you about those girls—'

'They passed every test! Every single criterion we use to
measure their suitability for release. We couldn't have kept them
here anyway. Do you really not understand?'

Veerman was sick of that refrain. It was true. But they could
have handed the sisters over to an adult institution and kept them
incarcerated somewhere else.

'Do you have any idea where they are?' he asked, trying to
keep calm. 'What's happened to that idiot Klerk?'

Visser leaned back in the hard office chair and stared out of
the window. Another hot and airless day on the lake. Yachts in the
distance. Gulls in the air.

'They didn't turn up at the halfway house. Simon never
arrived home. He hasn't been in touch with his wife since he

texted her and said he'd be late.' She closed her eyes, trying to think. 'I don't know why he did that. All he had to do was drop the girls off in the city. I didn't get this wrong, Henk. Those girls are fine. Well, fine enough to release under supervision. If we could just get them acclimatized . . .'

'That's not really an issue right now, is it?'

She glared at him.

'Yes. It's the only issue. We're not here to incarcerate children. We're here to make them better. Get them back into the real world so they can make something of their lives.'

She gave him this lecture from time to time. Meant it too. He didn't disagree with her sentiments. They just seemed irrelevant at that moment.

'As I keep pointing out . . . they're not children. And now you're telling me one of our own nurses has run off with that pair?'

'I don't know what's happened! I've no idea. I just got a call from his wife at ten o'clock last night asking where he'd got to.'

Veerman was plotting an escape route from this mess already.

'You had a duty to inform me the moment you knew those women were missing. I'm supposed to inform the police. They're convicted murderers. It's not even parole.'

She gave him a black look.

'I've spent all night on this. I thought . . . I thought perhaps they'd just gone off to a hotel or something and they'd show up this morning. I'm sorry.'

'If they don't turn up soon—'

'Give me a couple more hours,' she pleaded. 'For the love of God . . . those girls haven't set foot outside this place in a decade. Whether Simon's with them or not they can't survive—'

'It's not their survival I'm worried about.'

She kicked the chair back from the desk and glared at him.

'They won't harm anyone. I guarantee—'

'There are no guarantees!' he screamed, losing it finally.

'Those kids could destroy us. Where's Klerk? Why hasn't he called home? Even if he had . . . ideas. He wouldn't just vanish like that. You should never have put them up for release.'

That hit home.

'If the police come hunting round here they'll start digging,' Visser warned. 'Don't think for one minute you're going to offer them my head on a plate.'

'Are you threatening me, Irene?' Veerman asked.

'No. I'm trying to cope. We need to be careful. Don't we?'

He turned to the window. The empty view out over the wood at the foot of the dyke, the grey expanse of the lake.

'I don't want the police crawling all over this place,' Visser added. 'Any more than you do.'

He got up and walked to the filing cabinets by the wall and began to sift through the folders.

'Best find them then. If you've nothing by eleven I'm calling the police. Amsterdam. Not the local clowns. I don't have a choice.'

10

Waterland was the place Simon Klerk had taken the sisters. A verdant panorama of meadow criss-crossed by narrow dykes. The place seemed perfectly flat; nothing defined it except the far-off horizon and a low grassy dam by the lake.

By rights this territory belonged to the ocean. The Zuiderzee, a vast shallow bay, once swamped the area, joining it to the wilful North Sea. Then, in the 1930s, the government acted against the recurrent threat of deadly floods, damming the mouth with the twenty-mile-long Afsluitdijk causeway from the tiny village of Zurich in Friesland to the north across the wild sea to Den Oever.

The Zuiderzee vanished to be replaced by a lake called the IJsselmeer. Forty years later a second barrier, the Houtribdijk, was built further inland, from the old harbour of Enkhuizen to Lelystad, a new town built entirely on polder, reclaimed land that was once the floor of the Zuiderzee. The IJsselmeer was then split itself, spawning a smaller cousin, the Markermeer that stretched all the way to Amsterdam.

The Dutch genius for engineering changed the land and saved countless lives. But it changed the people too. The remote island of Marken became a peninsula, joined to the mainland by a narrow causeway. The closest stretch of water to land was re-named the Gouwzee. Over the years the lake shifted from salt to brackish, turning the attention of Volendam's fishermen from herring and cod to eel and perch until most of them accepted defeat and started trawling for the most valuable catch of all: endless streams of foreign tourists looking to find the sights and flavours of old Holland.

Beyond the ancient towns polder silt and earth turned to rich grass pasture, feeding the cattle that provided the milk for the cheese that men still rolled to market in Edam, though principally for the visitors these days. It was, at first sight, a beautiful, natural landscape. Yet all of this was engineered. A complex network of locks and dykes and channels kept the floods at bay, from the towns and villages around the lake and, ultimately, from Amsterdam itself.

That it worked at all was in part down to men like Tonny and Willy Kok, two brothers who lived in a ramshackle farmhouse outside Volendam bequeathed to them by their mother. In between raising chickens for the market, carrying out odd jobs, shooting ducks and rabbits for the pot, catching and smoking the occasional eel, the Koks took a small salary from the government for keeping the narrow dykes of Waterland clear of weed and other obstructions.

They were strong men with ruddy, bucolic faces that spoke of long nights in the few taverns from which they weren't barred. Tonny, fifty-three, and Willy, two years his junior, now laboured under hangovers that hadn't improved even with their customary breakfast of eggs, cheese, ham and liver sausage.

Still the council schedule was rigid and they needed the money. So at seven thirty that morning they started up their bright blue Fordson Dexta tractor, the one their late father bought new in 1975, hooked up a trailer and loaded their one working mini-digger on the back. Then, Willy at the wheel, Tonny behind in the seat of the mini-digger, they set out on a long, slow circuit of the dykes and drains that lay behind the road from Marken back to the city.

After an hour they were in the single-track lane that ran beside a narrow channel of green water. Tonny had the worst of the headaches. So Willy was baiting him.

'You should try eating the weed, boy,' he called out from the cab as his brother dropped the digger scoop into the dense green mass blocking the waterway. 'I heard that was good for a thick head.'

The older man chuckled, let the scoop go deep, came up with a load of filthy slime that he dumped on the bank.

'If that were the case, Brother, I'd have been feeding it to you ever since you learned to walk.'

The bucket jammed on the bank, as it was wont to do at times. Maintenance was something the brothers performed themselves, not that they knew much about it. Willy got out and gave the thing a kick. Then he looked up the lane.

'Oh Lordy,' he whispered and forgot all about the digger and his brother.

Tonny cricked his neck and spotted what his brother saw. He climbed out of the cab and followed him. The pair had worked these lanes and channels for twenty years. In all that time they'd seen six cars find their way into the dykes. The Kok brothers weren't ones to wait around for the police to see what they contained.

The rear end of a small saloon was just poking out of the green algae and duckweed on the surface of the drain. It was shiny yellow with a SEAT badge on the tailgate. The back window had smashed in the impact. Water and surface vegetation had poured inside.

'I have taken three bodies from them things over the years,' Willy declared. 'Not this time, Brother. You always make me look first. Ain't fair.'

'You're younger than me. More nimble.'

'Yeah. And I get to see what the eels and the rats have done. Don't go down good for when you want to sleep that, does it?'

'Not for me neither,' Tonny replied. 'I see it too, you know.'

'In that case best we ring the police and leave them to deal with it.' The water covered everything apart from the back window and hatch. They'd no idea what was inside. 'Maybe it's empty.'

'Only one way to find out, ain't there? I'll get the digger back on the trailer. You drive us down here. I'll do some exploring.'

Willy stamped his big foot on the ground.

'I'm telling you, Brother. We should be calling the police.'

Tonny grinned and said, 'But we ain't got phones, have we? And I'll be damned if we're taking the tractor back home just so's we can call 'em and have 'em drag us back out here again. We have a look. If there's no one there we amble off home once we've done and report the car.'

A cocky duck swam through the green weed towards them, chest puffed out, quacking all the way. The bird looked at the crashed car blocking its path.

'Mr Mallard . . . he don't like having that thing there in his home,' Willy said. 'Don't blame the gent either.'

Then the duck eyed something and swam through the shattered back window. They watched its head go down, the white and brown tail go up. They'd seen this in Waterland a thousand times or more. But not what came next.

The bird retreated tail first through the shattered glass, shaking its head, back into the open green channel.

There was something in its beak. Both men stared, wanting to make sure of what they saw.

'Them's men's underpants,' Willy said. 'He's thinking it's for a nest.'

His brother nodded.

'I'll get the tractor.'

11

The three-storey terrace house in Vinkenstraat was quiet at the front. But their room was at the rear and overlooked a coffee shop and kebab bar in the neighbouring tourist thoroughfare of Haarlemmerstraat. From the grubby window, across a soot-stained courtyard, they could see drowsy people smoking in a tiny, shady room. Quiet, tired-looking foreigners laboured in a kitchen behind the restaurant. People came and went all the time.

In Marken they always felt close to home. There was the grey still water, the marine air, the squawks of gulls, ship's horns across the lake. Here their senses were assaulted by unwanted and unfamiliar sensations. Even with the window closed it was impossible to escape the stink of traffic fumes, cooking and an occasional exotic waft of what had to be dope smoke, not that they could be certain. The noise – voices, car horns, music, distant trains – was constant. Their new short hair, black for Mia, purple-red for Kim, so exciting the night before, now felt odd and wrong.

In the middle of the night Kim had got up and washed off the temporary tattoo. Then her sister did the same. After that the two of them sat on Kim's single bed, hugging each other for an hour. Not crying. Not afraid. Just drained of everything.

For years they'd dreamed of freedom and what it might bring. Now the moment was upon them it seemed a small and useless commodity. Marken possessed a kind of comfort in the daily routines, the sanitized, hands-off care the institution provided, the knowledge that their entire world was constrained by that high-security fence with its video cameras posted around, always watching, always recording.

Here they seemed unobserved. Anonymous. It was almost as if they didn't exist at all.

At a quarter past eight there'd been a knock on the door. Vera, the Englishwoman, stood there, gasping from the effort of climbing the steep staircase. Her lined face no longer seemed the colour of walnut, more that of a dull and fading parchment. Still she smiled the way the nurses did back in Marken. Genial but in control.

There was a tray in her trembling hands, two cups of coffee on it, two glasses of orange juice, two pieces of cake.

'Best you have breakfast in your room, girls,' she said in English. 'I've got to go and see some people. You don't want to be wandering outside without me.'

Mia took the tray and asked why.

'Because,' Vera said. 'I may be a while. I'd like you both to stay here until I get back. I'll bring us a nice lunch. We'll have a little chat. OK?'

It was almost nine when the woman left. Gone eleven when she returned. They used the time to explore. The house was narrow but so tall the wooden staircase sloped perilously from floor to floor. They had a cramped, scruffy bathroom next to them. The Englishwoman seemed to occupy all of the floor below. The ground was given over to a kitchen, a living room with a TV set, a music centre and computer, and a dining room with a table, four chairs around it, a single window looking out onto the courtyard where an old refrigerator was slowly rotting away.

Vera had locked the heavy front door behind her. They wandered around, tried the computer, couldn't guess the password, and hunted for a spare set of keys without success.

Then Kim remembered something and they clambered up the staircase, using their hands and feet like children, and went back to the bedroom to search for the phones they'd brought from Marken. Two. One for each of them. Both were missing.

'They've got to be here somewhere,' Kim insisted, going through the case Simon Klerk had given her.

'You put it in your pocket,' her sister said.

Kim found her jacket. There was nothing there. They talked about it and agreed. When they reached Vera's house they'd found just one phone, the handset with the message from Little Jo. The other must have fallen out somewhere along the way. Now the second one was gone and they knew: the Englishwoman must have taken it while they slept.

'I'm clumsy as hell,' Kim said, suddenly furious with herself.

There was no need for an argument, Mia told her. No point in trying to assess blame. Things happened to them, things that required no explanation. They knew life was like this and accepted it.

'At least in Marken we could go for a walk,' Kim grumbled.

'Marken's behind us,' Mia insisted.

'She shouldn't take things like that. Not when they're ours.'

When Vera came back she had fresh orange juice, eggs and ham and cheese. She cooked them pancakes too and then the three of them sat down for lunch.

Kim asked for her phone back. Vera grinned.

'What phone? I don't know anything about phones, sweetheart. Have you got one then?'

'I had one. We both did.'

Vera took out a plastic pill box, checked the time, fiddled with the lid, rolled a couple of white tablets onto the table and swallowed them with some juice.

'You must have lost them somewhere.'

Mia said, 'We'd like to go for a walk soon. We always have a walk.'

Vera laughed and shook her head.

'Not yet, luvvies. I mean . . . there are people out looking for you, aren't there? Give it a while. When I get the word . . . then it's OK.'

'Who from?'

The smile on the Englishwoman's face never cracked.

'So you don't know who sent you here?'

'They just . . . we just got the map. And a note.'

'One step at a time, eh? You just take it easy. Don't have to worry about a thing. This is a nice house. A safe house. Enjoy yourself. Until we hear.'

'Hear what?' Kim asked.

'What we have to do,' Vera told them. 'I mean . . . everyone's here for a reason, aren't they?' She reached over and touched the sleeve of Mia's T-shirt. Something about the way she did this seemed . . . wrong. 'You know that, don't you?'

The sisters kept quiet.

'Until we're sure where you're going . . . until someone's said,' Vera added, 'best you two keep your heads down. Watch the telly. Listen to some music—'

'Can we use the computer?' Mia asked.

'I'd let you if I could,' the woman said with a shake of her dyed hair. 'But it's been playing up lately and I don't know how to fix it. You finish your lunch. I've got to go out again. Won't be long. I'll have you out there soon enough. It'll be like a new world for you two, I bet. There'll be a treat too. More than one.'

She got up from the table and the smile fell from her face.

'You can manage the washing-up I'm sure. We're all in this together, aren't we? You and me.'

They gave her ten minutes after she left just in case this was a test. Then, very gingerly, they went to the front door and tried it. Locked again. After that the two of them tested all the windows on the ground floor. Every one was sealed shut and refused to move.

Kim wandered back into the living room and turned on the TV. Nervous, together on the sofa, holding hands, they watched the news. There was no mention of two sisters escaped from an institution on Marken. Or anything else about Waterland.

They switched off the programme and sorted through the CDs by the side of the music centre. Finally Kim found something they recognized. *The Love of a Stranger*. The penultimate album by The Cupids.

'I don't want this,' Mia said and threw the thing into the corner.

Her sister retrieved the disc, put the music on, and the two of them listened in a dull and angry silence.

All they'd done was exchange one prison for another. They didn't even need to say it.

12

First thing in Marnixstraat Pieter Vos dispatched Laura Bakker to look for the missing papers concerning the Timmers case. When she came back with nothing he told Van der Berg to join her. Normal service was resumed in the Drie Vaten so Sam had stayed with Sofia Albers. The office remained quiet. It was August. So many people on holiday. So little to do.

After three hours of tedious paperwork Vos went and joined them in the archives. The duty officer was getting sick of the sight of them.

Bakker said, 'I told you, there's hardly anything here.'

'You did,' Vos agreed and led them back to the office and the coffee machine.

Frank de Groot, the commissaris whose name was on the file deletion records, was off for the day. His daughter was getting married in Utrecht.

'We could always phone him,' Bakker suggested, more in hope than expectation.

'They're just missing files,' Vos said. 'There's probably a simple explanation. It can wait a day.'

He handed out the coffees and they went to sit around his desk. Vos listened to their ideas in his customary non-committal fashion.

'Besides,' Van der Berg added, 'if we didn't know those files were missing we wouldn't even be bothered. The case is as good as dead . . .'

'You said we never found who killed that family,' Bakker pointed out. 'This Ollie Haas screwed it up. How can it be closed?'

'It's not closed,' Vos said.

'If there are no files how can it be open?' she wondered.

Bakker smiled, preened her long red hair at that. A persistent young woman, she was never shy of an argument and both Vos and Van der Berg had learned to avoid these unless they were absolutely necessary.

'How about Haas?' she added.

Van der Berg sighed and said, 'We don't know where he lives. If that old girlfriend of his hadn't phoned yesterday we wouldn't even be—'

'Ollie Haas has a house on the outskirts of Volendam,' Vos cut in. 'Quite an expensive one. He retired there just under five years ago. I checked.' He pulled a sheet of paper out of his drawer. It was a page from an estate agency website. 'The place is valued at three-quarters of a million euros. He lives there alone. It's up for sale.'

He passed Van der Berg the printout.

'That's a lot of bricks for a police pension,' the detective noted. 'Ollie Haas is an Amsterdammer. He was brought up in Oud-Zuid. Why the hell would he move out to Volendam? The locals won't even talk to you until you've been in the place thirty years or more.' He slapped the page on the desk. 'Something's wrong. I'm with Laura. If we've nothing better to do – and I don't see we have – I think we should poke our noses round a bit. Talk to Haas again. Find out what happened to those files.'

Bakker retrieved one of the few folders still remaining from the Timmers case and opened it. There were photos of the parents, a gruff-looking man, angry, coarse face, faded blue fisherman's smock. A pretty fair-haired woman, too good-looking for him most would think. Then three little blonde girls in tight scarlet satin shorts and white shirts grinning for the camera.

'What a way to dress up kids of that age,' she grumbled.

Gus and Freya Timmers were thirty-nine when they were killed. The mother and daughter died of multiple stab wounds in their tiny fisherman's cottage behind the Volendam seafront. Her father suffered a single shotgun blast. Freya and Jo were found in the parents' bedroom. He was in the room the triplets shared. Ollie Haas believed Mia and Kim only survived because they were at the waterfront collecting a prize in the talent contest from Gert Brugman, the singer with The Cupids. He could find no motive for the crime and no likely culprit.

Brugman had stayed on the waterfront all night, drinking. Rogier Glas left the event for a meeting with the band's manager, Jaap Blom, in the cafe Blom ran in the town. Frans Lambert had taken a cab to Schiphol as soon as the contest was over and flown to Bangkok. He'd never been heard of since.

'That's odd,' Bakker said. 'Why didn't he come back?'

'It is funny,' Van der Berg agreed. 'But they have him on camera going through Schiphol at six in the evening. He couldn't have been anywhere near Volendam when it happened.'

Bakker wasn't giving up.

'Blom?' she said, pointing a finger at the report. 'That's not the same as . . .'

'The politician,' Vos cut in. 'Yes. That's how he made his money. Media. Pop music to begin with. Now . . .'

Bakker turned to the nearest PC and did a quick search. It was all there: Jaap Blom, fifty-six. Former pop group manager. Founder of an advertising and online media company sold to an American corporation six years before. Rich as Croesus, now a member of the *Tweede Kamer*, the second chamber. When he wasn't in The Hague on political business he lived in a mansion in Edam, Volendam's more affluent neighbour just two kilometres away.

'Irrelevant,' Vos said and went back to the papers.

Glas was found murdered in the front seat of the band's van three hundred metres from the Timmers' home. The two sisters were there with a bloodied knife. Haas believed they wrongly thought they saw the musician leaving their house just before they turned up and found their parents and sister Jo dead. So they followed Glas to his van and killed him there.

'Bit extreme,' Van der Berg commented. 'Two kids. Eleven years old. I mean . . . why?'

Bakker pointed to the concluding paragraph of the report. It said the Timmers children had been reported for disruptive behaviour by their school. Social services had been planning to talk to the parents to try to find the cause.

'Perhaps they were in shock,' she suggested. 'Rogier Glas just happened to be the first victim they saw. I found a newspaper cutting that said he was really popular with all the kids. Used to go to charity events. Hospitals.'

She put it in front of them. Glas surrounded by happy children. The headline read, 'The Candy Man'.

'It says he always carried sweets with him. Used to hand them out to the kids all the time.' She was thinking. 'I'm assuming this is all harmless? I mean . . . just because he handed out stuff to children. It doesn't mean . . .'

Bakker left it there. Vos said nothing. Nor did Van der Berg.

Haas could find no evidence to place the musician at the scene of the crime. Jaap Blom was adamant that he'd walked with Glas from the talent contest, talked to him about management matters in his cafe below the recording studio The Cupids used and seen him head off back towards the van afterwards.

Forensic believed the murder of the Timmers family and Glas's death happened around the same time. They were unable to trace the owner of the shotgun but there was no record of Glas ever owning a firearm. Whatever the sisters thought it seemed impossible he was responsible. Vos shuffled through the few documents they had.

'What are you looking for?' Bakker asked.

'The interview with the sisters. This is just a summary.'

'De Groot deleted all that stuff. Lots else besides.'

Vos stared at the red document folder. These murders had

taken place outside Amsterdam. It wasn't unusual for city police to get called into serious investigations in rural areas. But there had to be a reason.

'Why did we handle this?' he asked. 'Why didn't we leave it to the locals?'

'I asked at the time,' Van der Berg told him. 'There was all that terrible publicity. Two parents. A child. That pop singer dead, killed by kids. The locals were pleading with us to take it on. Ollie Haas had worked in Waterland before. He couldn't wait to get his paws on it. I was hoping I could steer it our way.'

He looked round the office. It was almost deserted.

'Frank de Groot was deputy commissaris back then. He gave it to Haas. He said Ollie knew the ropes out there and we didn't.'

'Can we pick it up now?' Bakker wondered. 'Do we have the right to barge in? I mean—'

Vos's desk phone rang. He took the call and listened.

The other two watched, sensing something from his manner.

The conversation lasted a minute, no more. Vos put down the phone, thought for a moment, then said, 'Mia and Kim Timmers were allowed out of a secure institution in Marken yesterday on some kind of . . . parole or something. They never turned up at the halfway house where they were supposed to stay. The male nurse who was driving them is missing. Perhaps with them. Perhaps not.'

'Yesterday?' Bakker cut in. 'What time yesterday?'

'About half past five. Not long after we got that phone call.'

'Those kids have to be high-security detainees,' Van der Berg said. 'They've been missing nearly eighteen hours and they tell us now?'

Vos got his jacket. He'd have to call the bar and ask Sofia Albers to look after Sam for longer than usual.

'The institution said they wanted to make sure. They have to inform us when prisoners abscond. This is our case now. Laura?'

She leapt to her feet, grabbed her phone, her bag.

'Get someone here to deal with chasing that phone call. I need a car.'

'You mean *we* need a car?'

'We need a car,' he agreed. 'Dirk can drive.'

Her big eyes widened.

'What's wrong with me?'

'Nothing. But Dirk knows the way.'

13

Twenty minutes later they were in an unmarked police saloon, Van der Berg at the wheel, Vos and Bakker in the rear, going through the suburbs on the way out to Waterland. She was a country girl, Vos said. She ought to feel at home with the people there.

'At home?' Bakker wondered.

'What he means,' Van der Berg suggested from the front, 'is they might open up to you in a way they won't with us. These places aren't like Amsterdam. They've got their own way of living. And talking, too.'

'And because I come from the country I'm supposed to . . . empathize with them?'

'That would be helpful,' Vos added. 'Dirk's right. It's never easy when you come out here. They keep everything to themselves. Perhaps . . .'

He stopped. A sudden idea had struck him. What if Marnixstraat had been called into the Timmers case in the first place precisely because someone knew they'd struggle in the foreign, hostile environment of Volendam?

'Perhaps what?' Bakker asked.

'Perhaps nothing.'

At Broek they left the main road and travelled east into Waterland, not more than a kilometre from the narrow channel where the Kok brothers laboured over a yellow SEAT nose down in thickly weeded water. Then they rejoined the main road to Marken along the margin of the dyke and finally drove onto the causeway that linked the island to the mainland.

A breeze kicked up sending a couple of gulls scuttling into the bright blue sky. There were yachts bent over in the wind on the lake. Across the water sat Volendam. To its right their destination, a ragged skyline of rooftops set on what was once so obviously an island.

'It's beautiful,' Laura Bakker said with a smile. 'I never knew there was anywhere like this so close to the city.' She clapped her hands then let down her long red hair. 'We could cycle here one day.'

Van der Berg's eyes widened. In the driver's mirror he looked terrified.

'One day,' Vos agreed.

They navigated the winding streets of Marken as Bakker laughed at the cute wooden houses. Then they found the single-track lane to the institution and came up to the security gate by the wooded entrance. Two minutes later they were in Henk Veerman's office watching the TV news. The disappearance of Mia and Kim Timmers was the lead item.

'Who released this?' Vos asked.

'Not us,' Veerman replied. 'Why would we?'

'You didn't tell us for eighteen hours that two dangerous prisoners were missing,' Bakker broke in. 'Now it's on the news—'

'They're not dangerous,' Visser insisted. 'We don't believe that for one moment. I'd never have allowed them out of here if they were.'

There was a knock on the door. The psychiatrist wandered over wearily to answer it. A sturdy young woman of about thirty stood there. Short black hair, eyes red from crying, plain blue dress, something almost military about her bearing. She marched straight in, introduced herself as Simon Klerk's wife, then asked Veerman what he was doing.

'We have the police here,' the director muttered, not meeting her gaze.

'Where's my husband?' she demanded. 'You let him out of here with those murdering bitches. *Where is he?*'

Vos waited for their answer. Finally Visser said, 'We don't know. I'm sorry. We don't understand what's gone wrong.'

Bakker's phone went. She walked outside to answer it. Vos kept quiet, thinking about the people in this room. Their attitude. What appeared to worry them. Klerk's wife, irate, confused, looking for someone to blame. Visser, a thin, nervous woman . . . Veerman, everyone's idea of a cold, practical manager . . .

Something remained unsaid between them and there could only be one reason: there were strangers, police officers, present.

Laura Bakker walked to the door and asked to speak to him. Vos and Van der Berg joined her in the corridor.

'Two things,' she said. 'After that TV news item a bus driver called in to say he picked up the sisters from the dyke road on the mainland just after eight last night. We must have come past the place. They stayed on the bus all the way to Centraal station. Got off around twenty to nine.'

'And?' Vos asked.

'We had a uniform patrol car near the dyke. They went to take a look.' She took a deep breath. 'They found a couple of yokels pulling a car out of a ditch. Yellow SEAT. Simon Klerk's car.'

A howl of grief broke behind them. The nurse's wife was there, eavesdropping.

'I'm coming,' the woman cried, jabbing at Van der Berg with fierce elbows when he tried to stop her. 'Wherever he is . . . you take me . . . I am coming.'

Vos grabbed her arm as she tried to push past.

'Mrs Klerk. I need to know your name. We have to talk.'

'Sara,' she said firmly.

'Sara. I'll let you know as soon as we find something. But you have to stay here. That will help us . . . help your husband more.'

'I can't!' she bellowed. 'Don't you understand—'

'Of course I do,' Vos cut in. 'Dirk?'

The detective was on it straight away, saying all the right

things, edging the protesting woman into the room with Visser and Veerman.

She reached out and pointed a finger in Vos's face.

'Don't you screw with me!' Then a jab back at the room. 'I'm not taking any shit from them either.'

Vos didn't budge.

'My officer will remain here and keep you up to date on anything that happens.' He glanced at Visser. 'I want your files on the Timmers sisters—'

'Can't do that,' the woman said immediately. 'They're confidential. Medical records.'

'She's right,' Veerman added. 'Only a court can give you those and we'll oppose it every inch of the way.'

'My husband . . .' Sara Klerk wailed.

'Do your best,' Vos told Van der Berg and left him there.

This time he drove. Bakker still wasn't so good behind the wheel. He didn't want more than one car in a ditch that day.

Back through the narrow houses they wound, past the sign to the little harbour, out onto the narrow causeway across the dyke to Waterland.

'You can see why Simon Klerk wasn't keen to go home,' Bakker observed as they hit the long straight road.

14

A solitary traffic car had come across the Kok brothers as they struggled with the yellow saloon almost submerged in the green waters of the channel. When Vos and Laura Bakker turned up Willy and Tonny were standing by the side of their tractor in their faded blue dungarees and waders, both smoking smelly pipes and taunting the young uniformed officer who was watching them.

Vos introduced himself. The uniform took him and Bakker to one side and told them what he'd found. The two men, both known to the local police, appeared to be trying to recover a crashed car from the dyke when he turned up.

'They never called us,' the young officer said. 'God knows what they might have done if I hadn't come along.'

'Got it out of the ditch?' Bakker suggested.

He gave her a caustic look and told them about the Kok brothers. They'd been spoken to regularly about minor offences: drunken arguments in Volendam, poaching, scavenging for scrap without permission.

'Big time hoods then,' Bakker added with a smile.

The uniform grunted something and then Willy Kok called over, 'Whatever that young man's telling you about us . . . it's all lies. All we do is have a few too many beers from time to time. You go arresting fellers in Volendam for that and you'll be building new jails all the way back to that city of yours.'

Vos and Bakker walked over to them. They were staring at her as if she were some kind of unexpected apparition in these parts.

'That's a policewoman?' Tonny asked.

'That is,' Bakker replied.

Willy nodded at the uniform officer.

'Don't suppose you'd fancy his job, would you? They sent that young chap here all the way from Eindhoven. No wonder he don't look happy. Don't belong . . .'

Vos asked about the car and what they'd found.

'We're paid to clean out the channels,' Tonny said firmly. 'That's what we do. Grass. Weed. Prams. Bikes. Them townies . . .' He cast a glance at the uniform. 'Specially ones from down south . . . I reckon they think the countryside's just one big dump for them to chuck whatever crap they feel like.'

Vos wandered over to the dyke. The back end of the SEAT was sticking out. The number plate was clearly visible. It was Simon Klerk's vehicle.

'Do you have a rope?' he asked the brothers.

'Got two,' Willy replied. 'Who'd go working out here without a couple of ropes to—'

'Get them,' Vos ordered. He looked at Bakker. 'There's a bunny suit in the back of the car. More your size than mine.'

She put her hands on her hips. All four men stared at her.

'Shouldn't we wait for forensic to bring a team out?'

'We don't know we need a team, Laura.'

'Laura,' Tonny Kok repeated. 'That's a good name. She seems a nice girl, that lass of yours, sir. Friesland from her voice I'd say. A northerner . . .' He scowled at the uniform. 'You can trust people from up there. Unlike . . .'

Bakker swore, went to the car, got out the bunny suit and was about to put it on. She looked at her neat red shoes. Willy climbed out of his waders and said, 'Never let it be said the blokes of Volendam aren't gentlemen.'

The uniform uttered a pained sigh and said, 'It's all right. I'll do it.'

She gave him the suit and the giant waders. Tonny Kok tied a thick rope to the frame of the digger, tugged on it and handed the thing over. Then the young officer clambered down the muddy green side of the ditch and half-walked, half-fell into the slimy water.

'If there is something there try not to disturb it too much,' Vos suggested.

He smiled up somewhat viciously and said, 'Of course.'

'Just a quick look.'

The man in the clean white plastic suit crooked one leg against the submerged saloon, pinched his nose with his left hand then used his right to steady himself as he sank down into the algae and weed.

'Who'd have thought it?' Willy wondered. 'The lad's got manners. When it comes to pretty ladies anyway.'

He broke the surface with a loud curse. They all went silent and watched. There was something in his hand.

'Rope,' he cried, tugging on the thing. Willy and Tonny got their leathery hands to it and heaved him to the surface. Green weed and algae covered the suit and his dark hair. He did his best to shake it free then dumped the things on the verge.

'Clothes,' he said, then kicked off the giant waders onto the grass. 'Men's clothes.'

'This boy here's nothing but a genius,' Willy declared, patting him heavily on the shoulder. 'I reckon you should snap him up swiftish before Interpol or someone nabs him.'

'That's all there is?' Vos asked. 'Just clothes.'

'One man's?' Bakker added. 'Nothing else?'

'Nothing,' Willy agreed.

The uniform shook his head again then pulled a long strand of weed from his hair.

'So you knew?'

'Course we knew,' Tonny said. 'We saw Mr Mallard swim in through that broken back window and come out with a pair of underpants. Got to take a look after that, haven't you?'

'And you didn't say?' Vos asked.

'You didn't ask,' Willy told him. 'Not you.' A nod at the uniform. 'Specially not him. He just came along here and started yelling at us. Couldn't get a word in edgeways.'

He went to the back of the tractor and came back with a pair of yellow underpants, wet and stained with weed, then threw them on the pile of clothes on the grass.

'There you are. Full set.'

The uniform climbed out of the ruined bunny suit. Tonny looked in a box on the back of the tractor and found a towel.

'The airbag didn't blow,' the officer said. 'The doors were closed. No sign someone was inside when it went in. I'd guess they got out and pushed the car into the ditch. Empty.'

'So where on earth is Simon Klerk?' Vos asked.

'Simon Klerk?' Willy asked. 'Who's he?'

'The man who owns the car,' Bakker replied.

The Kok brothers shrugged.

'Running stark naked across Waterland?' Tonny flicked a thumb at the young officer in uniform. 'Though if that were the case I suspect Boy Genius here might have spotted the chap. Him and his sort are dead good at picking up a spot of immorality here and there. A man with a bit of beer in him can't even take a leak down an alley late one night . . .'

Vos called Marnixstraat. No one had seen the Timmers sisters. CCTV had lost them after they left the station. There'd been no word of Simon Klerk but his wife had been screaming at headquarters demanding action.

'We can take the car out if you like,' Willy said when he came off the call. 'By rights we ought to. It's blocking the channel. That's our job. Clearing up crap after people.'

'Leave it there for the moment,' Vos ordered, scanning the low horizon. Blue sky, green fields. Nothing much else. 'We may need a forensic team out here. Laura?'

She was picking through the clothes with a pen.

'Yes?'

'Where do we start?' Vos wondered.

For once she looked lost too.

'Not here, I'd venture,' Willy Kok said. 'I don't understand a thing about policing and don't want to. But us two know these fields. These dykes. We grew up with them. Fished every last one of them.'

'Illegally,' the uniform moaned.

'Who owns the water?' Tonny asked. 'Who gave you the rights over what creatures live there?'

'Enough—' Vos began.

'We're telling you, mister,' Willy continued. 'There's nobody here. Not in that car. Not anywhere we've passed along the road. You're looking in the wrong place.'

'Wrong place,' his brother repeated.

Vos called Van der Berg.

'Dirk,' he said. 'You can tell Mrs Klerk we're still looking for her husband. We've got his car. He's not here.'

Van der Berg's breathing wasn't so great. Cigarettes. Beer. Lack of exercise. He sounded rougher than usual.

'OK,' the detective replied. 'She won't like it.'

Vos shut his eyes, recalling the desperate, angry shrieks of Sara Klerk as she followed them down the corridor in Marken.

'Be gentle with her.'

'I always am. Thing is, Pieter . . .'

'What?'

'There's something very odd about this place. I can't quite put my finger on it.'

'You will,' Vos told him and wondered where they might look next.

15

Three.

That was the number, the holy number. The only one that mattered.

Three little girls on the waterfront in Volendam.

Three, the magic symbol of family: mummy, daddy, children.

Three for The Cupids too. A drummer, a bass player who sang more than the others, a guitarist who wrote their tunes.

Listening to them now in the narrow house in Amsterdam the sisters agreed this was a cheat. There were only three of them but they played tricks when it came to music. They had their own studio not far from the museum by the lake. It was upstairs, above a cafe owned by their manager, the big man who smiled a lot and never really looked as if he meant it. Jaap. Jaap Blom.

He didn't push himself but The Cupids did. Their fame was on the wane nationally but in Volendam a touch of tacky stardust remained. For some reason they had still had glitzy friends too, celebrities who visited, foreign musicians looking for somewhere interesting to record. Show business people and other rich strangers, from the city and beyond. In the small, insular lakeside town that upstairs studio was a special place. When their mother finally took them there – she'd been hired to sing backing vocals for a demo – she'd dressed the three of them carefully in their school uniforms. It was important to make an impression.

Did they? This was a lifetime ago, part of a childhood they remembered only dimly and with difficulty. It was hard to divorce what was real from the dream. They were eleven when the bloody evening fell upon them. Its details remained elusive, as much the fiction of others as themselves.

Some things seemed certain. The Cupids were big men, forceful and full of themselves. They laughed too loudly. They sang off-key. And somehow, in the studio above the cafe that other, quiet, unsmiling man Jaap fixed all their errors with a subtle brand of magic. A wrong note was corrected. A thin vocal got duplicated until it sounded fuller than the three of them could ever achieve in real life. When the girls listened to the tune that came out of the session – technically perfect but lacking in emotion and spirit – it was hard to associate it with the shambling, middle-aged men who sat around the studio drinking beer and smoking dope.

Freya Timmers and her daughters could sing. Loud and clear and true. The men in The Cupids were charlatans. Not that it stopped them getting rich and famous for a while.

After a few minutes Kim announced she was bored with the music and made coffee. They didn't talk much. Since the phones were lost there was no way anyone could get a message to them.

Especially Jo.

Cute Jo.

Clever Jo.

Lost Jo.

Kim closed her eyes and sang the first line of an old hymn.

I will bless the Lord.

Mia waited for her moment and sang the middle harmony.

They waited.

Jo was the soprano.

Jo completed their harmony. Without her nothing worked.

Back in Marken they heard her. But that place was familiar. It was *theirs*.

Here in the strange cold city she was missing from their lives.

Kim sang the lower line again. Mia came in on cue.

Outside pigeons cooed as if they wanted to join in. Someone walked past laughing. A car horn tapped out an angry shriek. A dog barked. Then another.

They waited for the third voice, so reliable in Marken, but it never came. Instead there was the sound of a key in the front door. The Englishwoman bustled in carrying two blue-and-white Albert Heijn carrier bags, full to the brim judging by the way she struggled with them.

'All set up for the duration now,' she announced. Then she put them on the table and added, 'I'll let you two unpack. You want to earn your keep here, don't you?'

Cheese and eggs, bread and milk, ham and packs of ready-to-eat fruit. She watched them carry everything into the kitchen and put the food in the fridge, telling them what went where. They'd never done this in years, not since their mother asked for it.

When the shopping was put away she asked them what they wanted. Then she told the sisters to take the food out again, cook it and serve it out on plates.

An hour they spent preparing the meal, eating it, washing the dishes afterwards and cleaning up the kitchen.

'Your Auntie Vera wants to help you back into the world,' the Englishwoman said when they were done.

'You're not our auntie,' Kim pointed out. 'We don't have an auntie. Only an uncle.'

'Just a way of speaking. You remember your uncle's name?'

'Stefan,' Mia told her.

'Never came to see you in that place, did he?'

'No,' she agreed.

Lots of other people did though.

'Do you know why that was?'

Kim raised her hands, waved her fingers like claws, pulled a wicked face and hissed, 'Because we're *monsters*.'

Vera laughed.

'That's right, girls. Monsters.' She got up and patted them on the shoulder, one after the other, not noticing they didn't like this. 'My monsters now.'

'What do we do next?' Mia asked.

'You do as you're told. What your Auntie Vera asks.'

'We want to see things. On our own.'

The woman reached into the pocket of her denim jacket and pulled out two plastic cards then threw them on the table.

'Know what they are?'

The sisters didn't speak.

'They're your passports to freedom. Anonymous chip cards. Weren't even around when they locked you two up. I've put a bit of money on them. You can use them on buses. On trams. On trains if you know how.' The smile grew more cold. 'But you don't, do you? Two little songbirds stuck in a cage. Haven't got a clue what it's like . . .' She nodded at the front door. 'Out there.'

'We can't stay here all the time,' Mia complained, shocked when she heard the whining tone in her own voice. 'We'll go mad.'

Vera laughed and when she did her shoulders shook up and down.

'Go mad? Well we can't allow that to happen. All hell breaks loose, don't it? Go mad again and they'll only lock you up some-where worse than Marken. For good. Forever.' She leaned down and looked into their faces, serious now. 'Apart probably.'

'Apart?' Kim whispered.

'You heard me. They've spent ten years trying to fix the two of you. If they think it didn't work . . . you reckon they'll bother a second time?'

Mia's fingers clutched her sister's underneath the kitchen table.

'Don't need to happen,' the woman insisted. 'Won't either. Not so long as you do as your Auntie Vera says. Everything. Every last thing.'

She lit a cigarette, had the briefest of coughing fits, then blew the smoke out of her mouth in a curious way, turning her lips into an awkward O, closing her eyes as fumes rose to the ceiling.

'You will do that now, won't you?'

'Yes,' Mia replied.

Vera stared at Kim.

'Yes. We will.'

'Good. I'm having a lie-down. All this walking tires me out. After that I'll show you how to use them cards. I'll tell you where to go. What to do. We'll have a nice time. I've got a treat in store.'

Another drag on the cigarette.

'Don't ever think your Auntie Vera's not watching, will you? 'Cos I am.'

16

Dirk Van der Berg soon got bored with taking statements and listening to Simon Klerk's wife moaning about nothing getting done. He'd made notes, nodded, tried to seem sympathetic and interested. But largely failed. She wanted her husband back and he couldn't deliver that.

The Marken institution puzzled him too. The place had the antiseptic, dead feel of a half-deserted hospital. A few patients wandered around the garden close to the trees near the shore-line. They looked like ordinary kids. Cheap clothes. Glum faces. All female. When he returned to Veerman's office he asked if he could talk to them. The director asked why.

'No particular reason,' he answered.

'I don't think that would be appropriate.'

Van der Berg didn't push it. He just wanted to know what the answer would be.

He wandered back into the corridor overlooking the rear of the building. The administrative wing was attached to a two-storey residential annexe by the wood. Through the branches he could just make out the shoreline of the lake. There were a few boats on the water. A few faces at the window of the adjoining block. As he watched the male nurse out in the garden with four or five patients got called on his phone. The man looked up at Veerman's office and nodded. Then he walked the girls with him over the neatly tended lawns back into the building.

Van der Berg returned to Veerman's office. The director was bent over papers on his desk, the psychiatrist Visser by his side.

'How many inmates do you have here?' he asked.

'Patients,' Visser corrected him. 'They're not convicts. Not prisoners. They're patients. This isn't a jail. We're here to help people.'

'How many patients?' he asked.

'Twelve now the Timmers girls have gone.'

'Knock before you come in again,' Veerman added.

He got the impression Visser wanted to say something, but not while Veerman was around.

'How many do you cure?' he asked.

She winced and said, 'Not as many as I'd like. It's hard. Some of these kids have been screwed up almost since birth. Putting them in a place like this isn't always—'

'It's what the law demands,' Veerman broke in.

'I know that! All I'm saying is it doesn't make the task any easier, locking them up somewhere that cuts them off from the outside world.'

'Your job makes mine look easy,' Van der Berg told her.

'Very funny.'

'No. I mean it. Can we . . . can we talk in your office?'

Veerman was onto that straight away.

'There's nothing you can ask Irene that I can't deal with. Ask it here. We've got work to do.'

'True,' Van der Berg agreed.

Big place to keep a handful of young girls out of sight from the public, he thought. Remote too. He wondered who from outside kept an eye on the institution. Whether Veerman and the Visser woman answered much to anyone at all.

'I need to take a break,' he said and walked down the stairs, out into the car park then round the back of the residential block. There were cooking smells from what must have been a canteen. A dog was barking somewhere. Big dog from the sound of it.

A light breeze was blowing in from the lake, rustling the leaves of the trees in the spinney. The sound mingled with the squawks of gulls in the blue sky. He wandered towards the pebbly shoreline and lit a cigarette. If this were a hotel it would be a fine place, he thought. They could clear up the area around the wood and have weddings and parties there. The wild scrubland that ran from the car park all the way to the trees then onto the shoreline could easily be removed. The location was peaceful, a good half a kilometre from the pretty wooden houses of the island village. Someone could make a go of it. Instead it was a kind of jail. Quite unlike any he'd ever seen.

There was a sound behind him, so loud and sudden Van der Berg jumped. He turned and saw a stout woman in a white kitchen uniform, a blue plastic mob cap on her head. She looked fifty or so with a fierce, jowly face and was holding back a large German shepherd dog, struggling to keep a grip on the animal's chain lead.

'So you're the policeman? Took your time,' she said in an accent he recognized immediately: a Volendammer.

'That I am.' He showed her his ID. 'And you are . . . ?'

The woman swore at the dog and dragged it back on the chain. The animal whined then sat on its haunches. Tamed.

'Bea Arends,' she said and stuck out a giant hand covered in flour.

'You work in the kitchen.'

She laughed, a pleasant sound, unexpectedly warm.

'Oh my. We've got Sherlock Holmes on the premises.'

Van der Berg grinned and winked. Everyone else in Marken had been so reticent and nervous at his presence. This woman didn't seem nonplussed by him at all.

'And they let a cook bring their dog to work,' he added.

'Rex is my only companion these days. He don't like being left on his own. Besides some of the girls here adore him. What else they got? He only acts funny with strangers. Rex!'

The dog crouched down on its front paws and wagged its tail. Van der Berg did what Vos had taught him with Sam. He bent down, held out the back of his hand, let the dog sniff it then, slowly, very visibly, lifted his fingers and stroked his head.

'My Rex is the best judge of character I know,' Bea Arends said. 'If he likes you then I reckon you're OK.'

'Flattered. I don't suppose you've any idea what's been going on here? Where Simon Klerk might be?'

Her expression changed, becoming fierce once more.

'I'm just a cook. What would I know? Of that man or anything else . . .'

She stuck a floury fist on her right hip. A woman with something to say. That was obvious.

'I've no idea. That's why I asked.'

'Simon Klerk's wherever he wishes to be. That man's like the rest of them. Does as he likes. And no one in there . . .' She nodded at the admin block. '. . . thinks to stop him.'

The dog was getting restless for no obvious reason, tugging at his chain, whining in a soft high tone like a puppy.

Suddenly the whimpers turned frantic. Rex was up then, leaping for the woods. With both hands on the heavy lead she fought to jerk him back. Van der Berg went over to help but before he could get there the German shepherd was free, bounding towards the trees.

'Rex!' Bea Arends yelled. She stamped her right foot and Van der Berg saw, to his surprise, that she was wearing wooden clogs. 'He never behaves like this. Never. Good as gold usually.'

There was a face at the window in the admin block. Visser. Then Veerman and Simon Klerk's wife joined her. Interested in the commotion. Perhaps worried too.

'He must have seen something. Or smelled it,' the detective said. He threw his cigarette on the grass and set off for the woods.

The spinney was dank with the stink of mould and decay. Rex was easy to track. In its frenzy the animal had carved a clear path of flattened weeds and grass straight through.

Van der Berg followed, Bea Arends behind. The small dark wood enclosed them both. He felt nervous for some reason and found himself pulling his phone out of his pocket. A quick glance showed the signal had vanished entirely at this distant edge of Marken.

'Rex!' the woman called.

They emerged from the spinney onto a narrow line of shingle running to the water's edge.

The dog wasn't barking any more.

'Naughty boy!' she cried.

Van der Berg looked both ways. Back to the village, barely visible here. Then to the finger of land that ran into the lake towards the colourful outline of Volendam on the horizon.

The German shepherd had stopped at the edge of the wood close to the point at which the dyke rose from the pebble shore like a round green vein.

'Best leave this to me,' he said.

'That's my dog,' the woman objected.

'He's found something.'

Twenty steps or so it took and then they were there.

'Rex,' the woman said softly, close to tears.

Gingerly, aware of the animal's strength and mood, Van der Berg bent down and picked up the leather loop at the end of the lead.

'I can manage that,' Bea Arends insisted, snatching it from him.

She pulled. The dog turned and snarled madly at both of them, showing a set of sharp fangs.

They were white and bloodied.

'Oh my God,' the woman said and put a hand to her mouth.

Van der Berg looked. Rex had found a shallow grave. There was a body in it, one pale naked arm dragged out of the sandy earth by Rex's busy jaws. Much worse to see after that.

He took the lead from her, wrapped his arm around it and tugged the snarling animal away, back to the line of trees. She followed.

'Do what you can,' he ordered, handing over the dog. 'Just keep him away. I need to call.'

Hand out, phone in his fingers, he wandered back into the wood seeking a signal.

Just when he got one Sara Klerk ran out from the car park, shrieking again, arms flailing.

'What is it? *What did you find?*'

Van der Berg got in the way and held her back.

'Stay here,' he said.

'What—'

'Please. Mrs Klerk. Stay here.'

She was a strong woman and brushed past him easily. The dog was barking again. Bea Arends was shrieking at it.

The call got through. Then the screams got louder. Two women this time.

'Pieter,' he said when Vos answered. 'There's a body here. Down by the shoreline. Buried. I don't know how long.'

17

The sisters were back in their room, bored. Mia was reading a teenage magazine Vera had bought them. It was about boys and music and clothes. And sex, though that was handled in guarded terms as if the subject were too dirty and embarrassing to be approached directly. Kim pretended to sleep. Both of them were aware of the city noise from beyond the grimy windows. People and traffic. Planes overhead, music from open windows. The distant clatter of a tram across iron tracks.

A church bell somewhere sounded four. Not long after the door opened and Vera returned and called for them. She had a plastic shopping bag with her.

'Got presents for the pair of you,' she said and took out two blonde wigs.

The sisters stared at them wondering if this was a joke. They were blonde before. And then they changed hair colour. Now this odd, controlling woman seemed to wish to turn back the clock.

Mia took the first wig as the woman offered it. Kim the second.

'Is this real hair?' Mia asked.

'Maybe.'

'Whose?'

'How would I know?'

Mia ran her fingers through the things. The locks were long, quite like their own hair before the previous evening's scissors and colouring changed things. A reasonable impersonation. Inside the scalp was a kind of cotton mesh.

'It's not real at all,' she said. 'It's like . . . like . . . plastic.'

'Yeah,' the Englishwoman agreed. 'Still cost a pretty penny

77

though. It's not as if you have to wear them much. There are people out there looking for you two girls. They don't know how you look now. They just think you look like before. So we fool them a bit.'

She took out her phone and told them to put the wigs on and stand by the window.

'Why?' Kim wanted to know.

'Because I want you to. Come on.'

They did and she lifted the phone and snapped them, five times or more. Vera fiddled with the thing then showed them a series of snaps. Blonde hair. Puzzled expressions.

'That's what they think you look like, kiddos. That's how we want it to stay.'

'If they don't know what we look like,' Kim said, taking off her wig, 'we can go somewhere and they won't chase us. We can be free. Like—'

'Free?' Vera had a hard, cruel laugh sometimes. 'What do you mean . . . free? You two have been locked up for the best part of your lives. Without me you can't do nothing. Can't walk them streets. Can't buy a thing. Catch a bus. A train. Go anywhere.' She picked up the blonde wigs and stroked the odd, stiff hair. 'Haven't I got this across to you yet? Without your friends you're buggered. They'll just pick you up, chuck you back in a cell some-where and throw away the keys.'

'Is Little Jo a friend?' Kim asked and didn't notice the quick intake of breath from her sister with those words.

Vera looked downcast, guilty.

'Little Jo's . . .' She tapped her head. 'Your sister's up here now, isn't she? That's where she lives.'

The one phone they had left had gone missing. Only Vera could have taken it. The message there . . .

'She sent us a text,' Kim said firmly.

'Did she?'

'She sent us a text. It's on that phone you took from our room.

You can read it for yourself.' Always the more forceful one, she stared the Englishwoman down. 'I think you have. I think she's talked to you as well.'

It was the briefest moment of confrontation and the sisters wondered how she'd react. Fiercely or meekly. It turned out to be somewhere in between.

'I know you've got lots of questions,' Vera said quite calmly. 'It's only to be expected. But I can't answer them, not straight out. I'm like you. In the dark too. I am your friend, though. It's people like me . . . people with your best interests at heart . . . they're the ones who'll save you. So long as you do what you're told.'

Kim retrieved a wig from the bag and put it on again. She looked at herself in the mirror. It was like seeing a different her. Someone half-known, locked in a past she didn't want.

'That's enough,' Vera said. 'It's not a toy.' She snatched the wig off her head and stuffed it in the bag. 'When you leave here I want you looking like you do now. They've got cameras everywhere. Every policeman in Amsterdam's walking round with your photos. I bet there's a reward if someone spots you. How does that feel?'

Mia took a deep breath and whispered, 'Cameras?'

'Right. So you come and go when I tell you. Them clothes. That hair. When we're out, if we duck down an alley and I say so . . . then you put these on.'

'Why would we do that?' asked Mia.

Vera leaned forward and shook her head.

'How many times do I have to say this? Because I bloody well tell you.'

Kim was about to get cross so Mia said very quickly, 'OK. When can we go somewhere on our own? If we—'

'Got to prove yourself first, girls. Can't do anything until I know I can rely on you.'

Ten minutes later they went downstairs. Vera checked the two of them over before they left. Then they walked outside.

The day before – the interview in Marken, the car ride, dealing with Simon Klerk – was now a blur, almost as if it had happened to someone else. Especially that strange, intimidating walk from Centraal station to the address they'd been given. They'd been too nervous to look around much. Now they couldn't stop. It felt as if the city was watching them, following every step as they trudged down the street, close together.

Vera seemed to mellow, acting more kindly while they were out. Maybe she was nervous too. After a while she treated the two of them as if they were tourists. Together they walked through the red-light district, gawping at the half-naked women in the windows beneath the fluorescent tubes. They stopped for espressos in a coffee shop and the Englishwoman bought some dope from the counter, using words and terms the two of them didn't understand. They went to a back room and watched her light up, waving away the hand-rolled joints she offered them. Vera shrugged and smoked one all by herself, coughing badly the whole time.

Men came and went, checking out the two of them, knowing they didn't belong and wondering, consequently, why they were in this dingy dope joint close to the Oude Kerk, a part of Amsterdam where timid church and boisterous depravity lived side by side and scarcely seemed to notice let alone care.

'I suppose you'd rather have ice cream than a smoke?' Vera asked when she was done.

'Ice cream would be nice,' Mia agreed.

For the first time Vera laughed as if she meant it.

'You really are a pair of kids, aren't you? After all that's happened.'

'All?' Mia asked and felt nervous.

'It's like you're stuck in time. Never grew up at all in that place they kept you.' She hesitated. 'You'd think it'd be the very opposite.'

It was hard for them to judge the tone she used. Sympathy perhaps. Or despair.

'What do you know?' Mia asked. 'About us?'

'Enough,' Vera said with a hard look on her craggy face. 'You're not the only ones it's happened to, you know. Not by a long shot.'

That was all she said but it was enough. When she finished her smoke she walked them round the corner to an ice-cream stall by the canal. Her footsteps weren't quite as steady as they had been before. She sat on the wall over the water while the two of them licked their cornets, discussing whether they'd picked the right flavours.

'Done?' she asked, watching them demolish the last of the cones.

Then she pulled out a clean tissue and wiped the traces of liquid ice cream from their mouths. They didn't know whether to laugh or not.

'Bloody hellfire,' Vera moaned with a grim laugh, chucking the tissue into the grey canal. 'What have I taken on here?'

'Didn't ask for this,' Kim grumbled. 'None of it.'

'No.' The Englishwoman seemed upset for some reason. 'You didn't. Life's like that, girls. You don't get what you ask for. You get what you're given. Or what you take. If you've got the guts for it.'

They wanted to ask her a question. Several. This seemed the right moment but before they had the chance she shooed them on. Close to the Flower Market, smelling the tulips from the stalls by the water, they stopped and listened to a tuneless, automatic carillon from the belfry of Munt Tower.

The city was quite unlike the fairy-tale place they half-recalled from childhood. The noise was deafening, the crowds relentless. So many foreign voices and strange faces. Trams and cars and bikes coming from all directions.

They didn't know where they were going. What was expected

of them. Where any of this led. After a while Kim stopped walking and went and sat on a wall amid a sea of bikes outside an imposing hotel overlooking the Keizersgracht canal. She was close to tears. Her sister joined her, leaned close, black hair against purple-red.

The Englishwoman came and sat next to them. Mia and Kim were holding hands. She added hers. Old skin, leathery and wrinkled, against young, pale, unblemished. They could hear her asthmatic, wheezy breathing, the rattle of her lungs as if something was moving inside.

'Not very good at this, am I?' Vera said in a quiet, sad voice. 'Sorry, loves. I am so sorry. I mean that. Like I said. We don't get to choose what comes our way. Life's what you make it. And if you don't make it for yourself some other bugger comes along and makes it for you.'

Mia took a deep breath and said, 'Maybe we should go to the police. We don't belong out here. They can put us somewhere . . .'

Vera's bright eyes flared with fury.

'Don't you dare say that! No one's going to tell you where you do and don't belong. Not me. Not anyone. I'm just helping you two get back on your feet. You'll be there one day.'

'But—'

'You decide. When you're ready. I'll make sure of that.' Her hands gripped both of theirs tightly. 'I promise. I'm not a woman who breaks her word. God knows you can . . .' Her foreign, smoke-stained voice was wavering. 'You can say a lot about me but not that. Girls . . .'

Tears then and they were hers. The sisters stared in amazement.

'Just a couple of days. A couple of favours. That's all that's needed of you. Then we're done. You can set things right. About your mum and dad. That's what you want, isn't it? That's what Little Jo wants too.'

'Little Jo's dead,' Mia whispered. 'You said so.'

Vera reached over and tapped her head gently, then did the same with Kim.

'Not dead in there, is she? You hear her. As long you can do that a bit of her's still alive.'

They nodded then and didn't say another word.

A bus went past. A tram clanging its bell as if it were trying to warn the world about something coming round the corner. Finally a noisy dredger chugged up the canal then stopped to drop its claw-like bucket into the greasy water so unlike the fresh green channels back home. No one seemed to notice the three of them. That was one positive aspect of the city. They were invisible.

The dredger came up with a black mangled bicycle in its jaws.

'There,' Vera said, pointing at the odd sight. 'I'll buy you a couple of bikes too. From that bloke on the boat. About as much as the likes of us can afford, eh?'

Kim laughed out loud and so did Mia.

'Good.' Vera withdrew her hands and patted their knees. 'Have you ever been to the pictures?'

'The pictures?' Kim asked.

'The cinema. The movies.'

Not since they were tiny, Mia told her. But they'd watched videos in Marken. The ones they were allowed, all seated together with the other inmates in the communal room.

'That's not going to the pictures,' Vera said. 'Look.'

She pulled three tickets from her pocket. They were for a new animated movie about a family of meerkats. A kids' movie, she said, but one that adults liked too. And since they were a bit of both she reckoned they'd love it.

'The picture house is just down the road. We'll watch a film. We'll have a . . . a nice time together. After that . . .'

Vera didn't go on.

'After that?' Mia asked.

The Englishwoman pulled out her phone, checked the message then showed it to them.

A name: Gert Brugman. A mobile phone number. And an address.

They couldn't take their eyes off the text. The message said it was from Jo.

'Some things we never get to understand,' Vera said. 'It's best that way. You just do your duty and go about your business. OK?'

'OK,' they said in unison.

18

Three hours later, as the light began to fade over the Markermeer, Pieter Vos was watching the opening of a piece of theatre he knew only too well: the scene-shifting and preliminary stage directions of a murder investigation. Teams of white-suited technicians had assembled around Simon Klerk's naked corpse, half-buried in the shingle and sand. The bite marks of Rex, the German shepherd, were dismissed as irrelevant. Even the most cursory of examinations revealed that. The nurse's head was a bloody mess, so bad no one but the forensic people wanted to look at it. All the same there was a ritual dance to be had here, one he had to follow even though he hated every mesmerizing moment.

A dead man, shot somewhere else, then taken to the remote shore in Marken. That process in itself remained a tantalizing mystery. The drive to the institution was secure. CCTV cameras covered the entrance and the area around the building. They had seemingly detected nothing suspicious since the Timmers sisters had been driven out of the place by Klerk twenty-four hours before.

He watched the forensic team get ready to lift the bruised and blood-streaked corpse from the strand then walked off to the low green dyke that projected out into the lake towards Volendam. There'd be another two hours of work here before he could return to the city.

By a spiky tussock of marram grass he stopped and called the Drie Vaten. The place didn't sound busy. He heard a lively bark behind Sofia Albers' voice. Sam, making a new friend. Playing a game. The dog lived in a heavenly world of his own, innocently unaware that within the next day, beyond the next corner, might lie something black and evil and shocking. Vos sometimes felt guilty about keeping him after going back to work in Marnix-straat. He loved Sam's company. In a way it had helped him stay sane when he was alone, lost, out of the police, hiding from the world in his houseboat, amused by nothing but the terrier's wild antics and fiery appetite for life. That was then. Now he was a brigadier with the police again and all too often it was Sofia who looked after Sam while running the busy cafe.

'Work?' she asked without the slightest side to her voice.

'I'm sorry.'

'You don't need to apologize, Pieter. It's the job you do. And this is mine.'

The dog barked again. She called out to him to be quiet and got another bark in return.

Vos heard her laughing and didn't feel so guilty.

'I should be back in a few hours. Still time to pick up Sam.'

'Are you all right?'

'I think . . . I think I may be busy over the next few days. I may have to lean on you more than usual. Even more . . .'

'Oh for pity's sake, Pieter! I ought to pay you for having Sam here. The customers love him. Everyone does. He almost makes up for the lousy beer.'

'Your beer's not lousy,' he said, and meant it. 'Nothing is. That's why people come.'

'Later,' she said happily and then the line went dead.

Van der Berg emerged from the trees with Bakker at his side. More forensic people were bringing in floodlights to deal with the scene after nightfall. The investigation was going the way of the technicians. Vos would leave that side of things to them. It took time. There was no rushing the process. He'd briefed the night team, asking them to look for somewhere Klerk might have been shot and to try to work out how his body got to the shoreline behind a well-guarded penal institution. Vos had his own ideas on that already.

'Anything?' he asked.

'I've been talking to the wife,' Van der Berg said.

'How is she?'

'I've seen worse,' the detective said with a shrug. 'It's not as if it's just happened. She's been going frantic all day. There's nothing else I've got to ask there, Pieter. No point now.'

Bakker was marching up and down the shingle, impatient. Vos watched her, wondering what was on her mind.

'Let's pick this up with the forensic reports in the morning,' he said. 'Eight thirty. We'll see what the night team have come up with. There's an alert out for the Timmers sisters. In the city. In Volendam and Waterland too. Maybe they came back after the bus. Who knows?'

'I don't see it,' Bakker said in her flat northern tone.

'Don't see what?' Van der Berg asked, interested as always.

'Two kids who grew up in this place.'

She nodded at the flat grey buildings behind. Lights on now. Veerman and Visser had taken the news of Klerk's death badly. They knew the man and seemed to like him. The killing would throw a light on Marken too, one they wouldn't welcome, Vos thought. They liked to keep their work and their patients out of sight.

'I mean . . . it's like a prison. How on earth could they get out of here and kill a man like that? With a gun? How?'

Someone from the forensic team shouted. The body was coming out of the beach, lifted gently by six caring arms towards a black body bag next to a gurney. Vos closed his eyes. He could see this process in his head. The van. The morgue. The cabinet. The shining silver table for the pathologist. And somewhere down the line the paperwork for release to a grieving wife. Then a belated and unsatisfactory funeral.

'Pieter . . .' Laura Bakker said gently. 'How can—'

He was back with them in an instant.

'The only way Simon Klerk could have been dumped here is

by boat. I asked the uniform people to check the harbour here. It's just half a kilometre away. Nothing moved there last night. So . . .'

He pointed along the green dyke, across the lake.

'I'm guessing someone took a small boat from over there. Near Volendam.' There was a harbour in the town, a marina nearby. Any number of access points where someone could have launched a dinghy and taken it across the lake. 'The night team are checking.'

'Those girls couldn't handle a boat,' Bakker said.

'I doubt it,' he agreed. 'We'll pick this up in the morning.'

Van der Berg mumbled something inaudible.

'Speak up, Dirk,' Bakker encouraged him.

'I said . . . there's more than one story here.'

'That's deep,' she noted.

'No it isn't.' He gave Vos a familiar look. 'If we're knocking off maybe there's time for a glass or two?'

'You two go off on your own,' Vos said with a wan smile. 'I'll clear up here. See you in the morning.'

She tried to argue. Van der Berg stopped her. Then they left.

In the car Bakker said, 'We could always go for a quick one in the Drie Vaten anyway. He looks like he needs company.'

Van der Berg started the engine.

'No he doesn't.'

She folded her long arms and stared at him. They all knew that look by now.

'He worries me. When he's like this.'

Van der Berg turned and wagged a finger in her face.

'We've been here before, Laura. That's how he is. If you push him . . . if you get too close . . . it only gets worse. You know that. I know it too.'

She stayed silent.

'And the reason it pisses us both off,' he added, 'is we understand there's absolutely nothing we can do about it. Now. I found this new place. They do Kwak on draught. Do you think you can manage to drink it this time without breaking anything?'

Kwak was Belgian. They served it in a glass that was round at the bottom and had to be placed in a wooden stand to stay upright. She loved the beer, hated the way it was served. There'd been too many accidents with it before.

'I don't want Kwak,' she said.

'Then drink something else.'

'Is there a bar in Amsterdam you haven't taken me to?'

'Yes,' he insisted, starting the engine. 'There is. There always will be.'

19

There was a picture on the wall of Gert Brugman's living room. The Cupids twenty years before. He played bass with the band and sang, a tall smiling man in the photo, muscular bordering on corpulent with a friendly fisherman's face and a mane of well-combed black hair.

He didn't look like that any more.

Brugman lived in a first-floor apartment above a smart shop selling mushrooms, dope seed and other highs. It was a street behind the bustling tourist nexus of Muntplein. Not squalid. Not elegant either. He'd bought the place with the money they made from the last two albums. Brugman was born in Volendam and had once worked as a fisherman, something the publicists loved to push. Even before everything fell apart he was starting to grow weary of the place. Adulation was fine but in the town by the sea it could all get too close. Locals he hated patted him on the back and said, with a grin, the latest record was shit. Then he had to deal with the women. One-night stands were there aplenty but they weren't so much fun when you kept seeing the discards every time you set foot out of the door.

Not that women were a problem now. In the aftermath of the Timmers case he'd fled to the city – one bedroom, a window overlooking an alley. Six months later he'd had a stroke. Time had helped but he still walked with a noticeable limp. Beer and bad food had made him fat. His hair remained long but rarely combed, grey and thin. Brugman didn't change clothes much unless he got a gig singing old songs in one of the Jordaan bars. The old bastard who ran the smart shop underneath owned the freehold to the building. And hated him. Like most of his neighbours who scuttled away the moment Brugman appeared.

Lately he'd started to get letters from the building management promising the smart shop bastard would take legal action if he didn't pay all his back maintenance fees. They could go hang. He didn't have money to waste on that crap. The royalties from The Cupids had been locked up in legal disputes ever since Rogier Glas died and Frans Lambert vanished. They'd written the songs between them. He was just the singer so they took the lion's share. Eight years before he'd nagged the lawyers and discovered something like three million euros in royalties was locked up in a legal thicket so complex Brugman couldn't begin to understand it.

That was when Jaap Blom, their manager, had pulled himself out of politics for an afternoon, turned up smiling, got Brugman stinking drunk and offered to buy him out of The Cupids entirely for a quarter of a million.

It was a rip-off. Everything to do with Blom was. But Gert Brugman needed money so he signed, took the cheque, banked some, invested the rest and hoped to live as best he could on the proceeds. Not long after the financial crisis hit. Most of the investments plummeted or vanished altogether. The interest on the remainder wasn't enough to pay his bar bills. Brugman did what came naturally, dipped into the capital month after month. And now . . .

Most of the memorabilia was gone already . . . the golden discs, the original outfits from the Eighties, the stupid glitzy crap Blom had forced on them in the Nineties when their popularity began to fade. All that was left was his instrument, a 1960 Fender Precision Bass he'd bought in New York when they were wealthy enough to record there.

The thing had sat in its case for the last three years. He wasn't sure he could remember any of the bass lines any more. They didn't want that when he sang in the Jordaan. They just wanted to look at the last of The Cupids, Gert Brugman, a wreck of a man, reduced to singing cheesy folk songs for small change, strumming a cheap Korean electric guitar run through a puny battery-powered amp.

He hadn't let go of the bass out of pride. It was the last thing he had that connected him to the past. To the time when the three of them had been kings of Waterland. Of the Netherlands too for a while.

Brugman rolled himself a cigarette, lit it, closed his eyes. Then he swore, walked over to the black flight case and lifted the lid.

He blew the dust off the cherry red Fender, cradled it on his lap and felt his fingers struggle for the places they'd once found so easily. The strings were old and worn. He didn't have a bass amp any more. So he just hugged the thing and tried to play a few notes with his fat, aching fingers.

'This is shit,' Brugman said, listening to the feeble rattle of the dead and dirty Ernie Ball strings.

The sound was gone. The action was too low. Nothing worked. And he needed beer.

He picked up his shopping bag and went downstairs.

The narrow lane outside his house was deserted. Just two odd-looking kids, a girl with purple hair, another in black, fidgeting in ill-fitting clothes across from his front door.

Brugman used to wind up the jerk who ran the shop with a simple, repetitive joke: if it was so smart why did the people coming and going always look like idiots?

Seemed he had some more.

His phone buzzed. The email sound.

Brugman swore and checked the message.

From: LittleJo2006@gmail.com

To: DaNo1bassmann@kpn.com

Remember us? The time has come. Little Jo.

Nothing else but a photo he opened out of boredom, checked it then stuffed the phone back in his pocket. The picture was of three young girls on the Volendam waterfront, all fair-haired, all pretty. He looked up. The two across the road were older but they'd turned blonde somehow. And that didn't seem possible at all.

Three words came straight into Brugman's head unbidden.

The Golden Angels.

The Timmers girls were part of the lost past not the desperate present. But now he looked and looked and two of them stared back at him across the quiet, cobbled street then shuffled off round the corner.

It'll all come back to haunt us one day.

Did he say that? Or was it someone else?

He didn't remember things as well as he used to. But it was true all the same.

20

By nine Vos was back in the bar opposite his houseboat on the Prinsengracht. Sofia looked happy. Sam was up to his tricks, playing catch and tug with a customer Vos didn't recognize, an American by the sound of it, perched on a rickety stool at the counter sipping at a beer.

She came over with a drink and some food.

'Take him home when you like. The little chap ought to be exhausted.' She looked at Vos. 'You are. Aren't you?'

He tried to smile. Something had been bugging him all the way back into the city. So he'd found his way into the admin office, talked to the lone officer on duty and got what he wanted transferred to one of the tablets the younger officers loved so much. The thing sat on the table now. Turned off. Vos didn't like technology. All too often it seemed to serve up distraction when what you wanted was focus.

'Long day,' he said and left it at that.

'I know you hate it when I say this, Pieter. But I do watch the news. Marken. Those two girls from that case years back. The Cupids. They said they were on the run or something.'

'I can't—'

'I know you can't talk about it. I was trying to tell you something.'

He pulled up a chair and she sat down. They talked like this so rarely. He took her for granted. She didn't seem to mind and he really couldn't work out why.

'Gert Brugman,' Sofia said. 'The singer. You know him?'

'Who doesn't? Has he been hanging round begging for work again?'

The Drie Vaten was too small to host musical evenings. There were better bars in the Jordaan for that. But it didn't stop some of the local bums trying to pick up money. Sofia Albers was a soft touch and everyone knew it.

She reached over and took a sip of his beer then retrieved a piece of the liver sausage on his plate.

'He was in here half an hour ago. Asking for you.'

The man at the counter threw a rubber ball down the bar. Sam watched it bounce on the worn timber planks, gauging its trajectory, then set off after it, racing up and down the floor skidding on his claws. Maybe he needed to be taken to the grooming shop for a clip, fur and nails.

'Gert Brugman doesn't know me.'

'Not by name. But he knows there's a police officer from Marnixstraat uses this place. A senior one. Everyone does. He seemed anxious to talk to you.' She pulled a piece of paper out of her pocket. 'He left this.'

A mobile number. She read his face and left him then. Vos tried to call but there was no answer, not even voicemail. Sam got bored with the game and did what he always did when he was tired and wanted to go home: came over and curled up in a ball beneath the table.

Vos tried the number again then gave up. His head hurt. The beer wasn't helping. Sofia came back with another one and he couldn't stop himself taking a swig.

'He looked worse than usual,' she said. 'Which is saying something. I think . . .'

He reached out and put his hand on hers. She fell silent instantly. They didn't touch like this.

'Not now,' Vos pleaded. 'I need . . .' Need what? 'I need a line. A dividing line between what I do and who I am. This place is that line. Without it . . .'

The terrier shuffled against his legs, sensing an awkward

moment as always. Vos had never spoken to her quite like this before. She seemed surprised. Embarrassed too.

The American at the counter finished his beer, threw some money on the bar and came over. He was a big man, built like a boxer but with a broad and genial face. He wore a suit without a tie. A businessman in town, Vos thought. Looking for a few quiet hours somewhere local.

'Got to go, sweetheart,' he said in good Dutch, with only the slightest accent. 'See you tomorrow. Dinner in that place I told you.' He glanced at Vos. 'That's still OK?'

Sofia got up and he kissed her cheek.

'Sure, Michael,' she said. He nodded at Vos then went out into the warm night, ambling along the canal like any other visitor. Whistling. Vos could hear that through the open door.

'I didn't realize . . .'

'He's here for one of the banks. A nice man. Fun. From New York.' She went to the bar and poured herself a small glass of wine. 'A month. Maybe longer. He says he's not married.' She laughed. 'Maybe he isn't.' She took a sip. 'But it's just a month. What the hell?'

'You deserve better,' he blurted out.

Sofia Albers glared at him and said, 'How would you know? Seriously, Pieter. How?'

He got up from the table, gently extricating himself from the half-slumbering dog. Sam stood too and yawned. A loud noise for such a small creature.

'You so want to fix things, don't you?' she said.

'Not really. Gave that up years ago. I just try . . . try to stop them getting worse.'

She came and picked up his glass and the empty plate.

'I'm sorry,' he said and couldn't think of anything else. 'Really. I just . . .'

There was a moment of self-knowledge then. One he didn't

know whether to welcome or hate. He could cope with his private life. He could cope with work. But he couldn't manage both. One part would always be falling to pieces somehow. He didn't have the strength, the commitment or the patience to hold them all together.

'Seven thirty in the morning, OK?' he asked. 'Breakfast? I can leave Sam then.'

'Fine,' she said and got her keys.

He watched her lock up as he crossed the road to the boat. It was a beautiful evening. The city was quiet under a starry sky and crescent moon. Half a kilometre away at the head of Elandsgracht the corpse of Simon Klerk would be lying on a table in the Marnixstraat morgue, ready to be examined by the duty pathologist. A night team of officers would be scouring Waterland and Volendam to try to locate the place where he died and work out how his body managed to wind up on a solitary shore in Marken. Others were looking throughout Amsterdam for some sign of two young sisters who'd never set foot in the outside world in their adult lives.

So many questions. So few answers.

Sam trotted down the gangplank, waited for him to open the door, then ambled inside and went straight to his basket in the bows.

'Good boy,' Vos whispered, watching the terrier turn round and round in his bed before settling down, curled up, nose to tail, to sleep. 'Lucky boy.'

He picked up the tablet the admin officer had given him and, with no small amount of reluctance, switched it on. File deletion records from five years before. The narrative they seemed to tell appeared both obvious and unbelievable.

There's more than one story here.

Dirk Van der Berg said that. One of the smartest, most honest men in Marnixstraat. He was usually right.

Vos wondered what the sceptical, ever-inquisitive detective

would make of the curious collection of records the office had come up with that evening.

'Jesus, Frank,' he whispered to no one in the half-dark. 'What in God's name were you thinking?'

And why?

21

Wednesday. Nine in the morning. A week getting worse by the hour. Henk Veerman sat at the desk in his office; he could think of no other place to be. A few months short of five years he'd been in this job, promoted from deputy after the death of his predecessor. Five worthwhile years he thought, spent trying to put the place in order. He was fifty-eight. Another twenty-one months – he'd been counting – and he'd be able to take retirement, spend time the way he loved, out on the water on his yacht.

His wife had succumbed to cancer two years earlier. There were no children, no real ties to keep him. In a sense there was nothing but the institution. Veerman lived in a wooden house in the village not far from the harbour where he kept his beloved twelve-metre yacht, a classic, built in the Arsenale of Venice three decades before. When retirement came he'd promised himself the dream he'd shared with his wife before she died. To sail the yacht across the Atlantic, all the way to the warm and sunny Caribbean. Perhaps they'd stay there for good, safe from bureaucracy and recriminations.

The fantasy still lived on somewhere, though he knew he was not a good enough sailor to contemplate the crossing on his own. She was always better. Her strength and determination kept him going.

Now, just when the light of release and freedom was due on the horizon, it seemed everything might be snatched from him. Veerman thought himself a good and decent man. He'd done his best with Marken. It wasn't easy. Hendriks, his late predecessor, had seen to that.

Stiff, feeling old and impotent, he got up and walked to the window. The spinney by the shore was still occupied by a small group from Marnixstraat's forensic section. In the morning light they were clearing up, dismantling the tent erected around the spot where Simon Klerk's body had been found. The wood had been searched meticulously. Before long, Veerman knew, Vos and his prying team would be back asking difficult questions, of staff and, at some stage, patients. There was a momentum to events. It felt as if a beast that had long slumbered was stirring. Marken was a juvenile establishment. That meant most of the patients Hendriks had dealt with were elsewhere, some in other institutions, a few back in the community. Only the Timmers sisters and one other young inmate had remained of late from the days of his predecessor.

He stared at the waving trees by the bare shore. Even now he could pinpoint the one where he first saw Hendriks' body swinging like a pendulum in the spring breeze. The police had come out and swiftly concluded the case was suicide. But that had been a different officer, quite unlike the sharp and persistent Vos. Ollie Haas, the one with local connections who'd handled the Timmers case five years earlier.

Veerman hadn't argued with the verdict. Hendriks, an aggressive, bad-tempered man, had been troubled, not that his deputy had fully understood why. Besides, he coveted the job. It paid more. There was real work to be done. Damaged adolescents to be . . . improved, if not entirely cured.

A sudden movement caught his eye and he knew straight away who it was: the last remaining girl from Hendriks' day. Kaatje Lammers, twenty years old now, incarcerated since she murdered her mother with a kitchen knife at the age of twelve. A short, dark-haired young woman, lean and athletic. Forever trying to start affairs with the other girls. Trouble in waiting. They let her roam the garden early in the morning, jogging, practising tai chi moves she'd learned from a book. The perimeter was safe. It was easier than keeping her cooped up. And even if she got out there was that long, solitary road across the dyke back to Waterland. The best protection Marken had.

She was walking towards the police. Veerman grabbed his jacket and strode quickly downstairs.

He caught her just before she reached the trees.

A striking kid in a ragged white T-shirt, blue sports bra beneath, cut-off denim shorts. She slashed her own hair punk-style. Two months before she'd managed to scrawl an amateurish tattoo of a dragon on her right forearm using ink from a ballpoint pen and something sharp stolen from the kitchen. Visser hadn't wanted her punished for that. It was, she said, a sign the girl was building her own identity.

'Mr Director,' Kaatje said, stopping, out of breath.

Veerman pulled out a pack of cigarettes and offered her one.

'Don't smoke,' she told him. 'Bad for you, isn't it? I'd have thought a doctor would know that.'

'I'm not a doctor, am I?'

'Just the man who runs the place. Who's responsible.'

'That's right.'

'Poor Simon, eh.' She glanced at the police in the woods. 'I wonder who was responsible for that.'

'So do I,' he answered.

'The police will find out, Director Veerman. They always do. They did when I stuck a knife into my mum. Mind you, it wasn't hard.'

'Violence is a solution to nothing,' Veerman told her and hated the words the moment they came out of his mouth.

She put her skinny arms out like bony wings, hands on hips, grinning at him.

'But that's not right, is it? I mean, countries fight wars and tell you they were doing the right thing. If someone screws you around and no one gives a shit . . . what else are you supposed to do? Ignore them? Walk away? Pretend it never happened?'

He wasn't going to be led down that blind alley.

'The police will be interviewing people here soon.'

'I know.' The grin got wider. 'I was about to save them some time.'

'Those people are from forensic. They're not the ones.'

She scowled and said nothing.

'They're bound to want to talk to you. About Klerk. About the sisters.'

She was beaming again, bright white teeth glinting at him.

'Mia and Kim have done a runner, haven't they? Did they kill dear old Simon?'

'I don't know. I don't think—'

'I don't think so either, Mr Director. They're a couple of butterflies. Daft in the head.' She tapped her skull. 'Kim's the daftest. She thinks that dead sister of theirs is still around somewhere. Did you know that? Kim can hear her. Mia . . .' She chuckled. 'I reckon she just goes along with it. Saves trouble. And we all like saving ourselves from that, don't we?'

No, Veerman admitted to himself. He didn't know about that. Visser, if she did, should have told him.

Kaatje bunched her right fist until the knuckles went white and said, 'If it was me out there with him . . . I could have done it.'

'Why?' He had to ask.

'You don't notice anything, do you? Sitting up in that office of yours. Turn up at nine every morning. On your way home at five. What do you reckon happens when you're not around?'

Veerman didn't want to think about that. He'd done his very best.

'Kaatje. What happened back when Hendriks was in charge . . . we stopped that. We put a halt to things. The visitors . . .'

'Oh.' She laughed, mocking him. 'It was just the visitors now, was it?'

'When they talk to you,' he went on, 'just stick to the facts. If you can help them . . . if you've any idea where Mia and Kim have gone . . .'

'Facts?' She looked around, glancing at the forensic team clearing up by the shore. 'When do I get out of here, Director Veerman?'

He knew this was coming. She asked every time.

'Your next review's in a year. If everything goes well—'

'A year?' she snapped. 'You want another year of my life for what I did? My mum was a heartless bitch. She never loved me. Any more than you lot.'

'There are rules. We don't make them. I've explained this before. I'm sorry.'

She cocked her head to one side and scratched at the amateur-ish tattoo.

'Sorry? I don't think so.'

'Everyone here has your best interests at heart.'

'Then let me out. Give me my life back. I'm owed one. Same as everybody else.'

Something moved on the water. A distant sail, a hull bending with the stiff lake breeze.

'A week, Director. I'd like that review in a week. You can fix that, can't you?'

She leered at him. He couldn't wait for the day he'd never have to deal with problems like Kaatje Lammers again. There was no redemption for some of them. They relished who and what they were.

'I'll see what I can do.'

'Not good enough. I want to hear it now.'

That bright smile stayed on him until he said, 'Fine. I'll talk to Dr Visser. I'm sure we can manage it somehow.'

'You do that,' she said, then brought up her arms, waggled them around in the morning air like a child, winked at him and started jogging again, back towards the car park and the patients' building.

Veerman couldn't take his eyes off the lake. It was one of his neighbour's boats from the Marken harbour leaning into the wind. A beautiful day for sailing. It looked as if it was heading for Lelystad. In this weather it could be moored at Texel by the North Sea for lunch.

A police radio chanted something from the spinney. Kaatje Lammers waved at him from the porch by the residential block.

Freedom.

That was all she craved. So they did have something in common.

His phone beeped with a message. Veerman closed his eyes and steeled himself. The damned texts had been coming in for more than day now. He knew he ought to call the number. Get this straight. Tell the bitches – it had to be them – to leave him alone. Go to the police. Wait for some other unfortunate to take responsibility for their sad and wasted lives.

But he didn't have the courage and perhaps they knew.

He pulled the phone out of his pocket and looked at the text. The same as before. There were thirteen of them all told. Every crowing word identical.

> Good Day, Director Veerman. How are you? Well I hope. We must speak soon. Little Jo.

He spat out a curse and called Visser. She should have been in work by now.

Her home phone rang and rang. No answer. Then he tried her mobile and just got voicemail.

'Jesus,' Veerman whispered. 'Where are you, Irene?'

22

Vos had made his mind up about the morning before he set foot inside Marnixstraat. Van der Berg set off for Volendam to do what he did so well: sniff and fish around. Bakker was set to work going through the details of the night team reports. He made a few calls of his own.

After an hour he was summoned to De Groot's office. The commissaris was a tall, imposing man with a jowly face, a full head of black hair and a heavy moustache. They'd known each other for almost twenty years since Vos joined as a cadet in his late teens. Mostly the relationship had been amicable. Vos and Liesbeth used to go round to the De Groot family home in De Pijp for dinner when they were still a couple. It was De Groot who'd engineered Vos's return to the police after the doll's house case that led to the rescue of their daughter. There was a long history here. Friendship too, though one occasionally tempered by a sense of distance. De Groot was upright, predictable, a man built for management. Vos none of these things.

The commissaris ushered him into his plush office overlooking the canal and proudly took out his phone to show him some photos from the previous day's wedding. Vos remembered Sandra, De Groot's daughter, as a girl of ten, gangly legs, a silly laugh, thick spectacles. Now she looked lovely in a white wedding dress posing next to a handsome groom. Even on the small screen it seemed she'd been photographed like a fashion feature out of a glossy magazine.

'I'll be paying for this until I retire,' De Groot noted with a shrug. 'But she's happy. He seems a nice enough fellow. Got a steady job. Insurance or something. It's the happiness that counts. That's all.'

Vos said the first thing that came into his head. It sounded bland and predictable but that seemed to be expected on these occasions.

'You could have called me,' the commissaris added. 'Those Timmers girls missing. Now we have a murder.'

He took a seat, thought for a moment then said, 'I didn't want to disturb you. We all deserve time off. Besides . . .' He gave De Groot a run-through of the briefing he'd got from the night people. Forensic hadn't needed long to decide how Simon Klerk had died: a single shotgun blast to the head. They'd got nowhere with working out where he was killed or how his body was shipped to Marken. No one had seen any sign of the Timmers sisters.

'Early days,' the commissaris said. 'Keep me informed.'

'Of course I will.'

De Groot seemed deeply uncomfortable, which was not something Vos saw often.

'Let's put everything we can into finding those two girls. The sooner we get them back in custody the sooner we can all sleep at night.'

'It's not as straightforward as that.'

'Why?'

'Mia and Kim Timmers have spent the last decade of their lives, since they were eleven, locked in an institution. They can't know how to drive. I doubt they have a clue how to handle a boat. Where would they get a shotgun? How would they know what to do with it?'

De Groot's face fell.

'Those two killed that musician. Did some pretty disgusting things to him. If—'

'Ten years ago. That's irrelevant to the present case.'

'Is it?'

'Whatever happened there—'

'We know what happened,' De Groot cut in.

There was an important point here, Vos thought. It needed to be made.

'Whatever it was we failed them. They were children. Kids aren't born bad. We make them that way.'

De Groot scowled.

'Please. You sound like a social worker.'

'Perhaps I do,' Vos agreed. 'It doesn't matter. They left Marken with Simon Klerk. Three hours later they turned up in Amsterdam alone and then they vanished. I can't believe Klerk was dumped on the beach in daylight. So whoever took him there did it in the dark.'

De Groot said, 'They could have gone back.'

'They could. But how? Not by bus. We've checked the CCTV with the company. Someone would have to drive them. Any way you look at it there must be a third party involved. They couldn't do all this themselves. They can't be hiding out in the city on their own either, if that's what they're doing.'

The commissaris didn't like what he was hearing but he kept quiet.

'I want to pull in Ollie Haas for questioning at some stage,' Vos went on. 'We ought to talk to Jaap Blom too.'

'The politician? What the hell's he got to do with it?'

'Maybe nothing. He was the manager of The Cupids. He was there the night those people were murdered. It was his evidence that said Rogier Glas was innocent. Any objections?'

A big man, De Groot had a distinct way of signalling his disapproval without saying a word. Vos witnessed it now. That long pained sigh, a folding of arms.

'I thought you said that Volendam nightmare wasn't a part of this.'

'I said I doubt those girls murdered Simon Klerk. I've still got questions.'

Vos told him the truth. There were aspects of the Timmers murders that were unclear and he felt they might be relevant to the case. Perhaps Haas could clear up a few.

'Haven't you got enough on your hands?' the commissaris asked. 'A murder. Two missing killers. I gather Klerk's wife has been in an interview room downstairs since the crack of dawn shouting the place down. She's demanding to know what's going on. I'd like you to tell her.'

'I can't fix what I don't understand. I'm not asking for Haas and the politician in here now. Just giving you notice that at some stage. Probably—'

De Groot's temper snapped.

'What the hell is this? The nurse was killed two days ago. When those sisters went missing. That's the case. Not Volendam a decade past. This is about now. Not then.'

There was no good time to introduce this. So Vos brought up the missing records.

The commissaris just shrugged and said, 'Old files do get archived.'

'These weren't archived. They were deleted. For good, as far as we can see. Your name's on the register. It says you asked for it.' He passed over the tablet he'd got from records. 'Just after you became commissaris. That's your signature, isn't it?'

De Groot looked puzzled as he took the device and went through the documents with a nonchalant sweep of his fingers.

'You'd be amazed how much stupid paperwork I deal with in a week. None of this rings a bell. Why would I ask for records to be deleted?'

'I've no idea. The Timmers case was dormant. Ollie Haas had just retired. That doesn't mean it deserved a burial. It is your signature, isn't it?'

'This was years ago,' De Groot said with a frown.

'Five.'

'You can't expect me to remember every damned form that

comes across this desk.' He pushed the tablet to one side. 'I'll look into it. I'll talk to Blom's office. You talk to Mrs Klerk.'

'The files—'

'I told you,' De Groot retorted. 'I'll look into it. I'll deal with Ollie Haas as well. These are side issues. Track down those girls and you'll find who killed that nurse. One way or another. It's simple, isn't it?'

No, Vos thought. Anything but.

Still, he left the room and went back to the office. Laura Bakker had been busy. The walls were papered with photos, some recent, some old. Young girls in skimpy costumes on the seafront in Volendam. Big men, confident men bustling round them near a stage. More photos of The Cupids from their formation in the early Seventies, through their rise and steady fall. Hair. Clothes. The changing expressions, from bright youth to forced middle-aged smiles. They all told a story.

There was no news yet from Van der Berg. In the office Vos had ten detectives, six men, four women, working away at the back of the room, chasing up information from the night team, making calls.

He walked over and joined them. He'd never liked any of the music The Cupids made. It was too bland, too conformist and popular for him. But he'd always thought they served a purpose. Working-class men from a modest town by the water. Fishermen turned musicians. They made a statement: we can compete with the British and the Americans when it comes to selling records. Even if it's just predictable pap.

Now these men – Rogier Glas with his Zapata moustache and pockets full of sweets, Gert Brugman grinning as he hugged his Fender bass, Frans Lambert, a tall and muscular man holding a pair of drumsticks as if they were weapons – looked odd. Anachronistic. Out of place. Vos had a private theory that rock musicians ought to hang up their spurs when they turned thirty-five. Mostly it just got demeaning after that. These three looked as if they could handle the embarrassment. Perhaps even welcome it.

Bakker pinned up another photo. Ollie Haas, an officer no one had ever liked, not least because he always seemed to get out from under his many failed investigations. Then, next to him, two pictures of someone who didn't seem to fit at all. Jaap Blom a decade before outside his cafe and recording studio in Volendam. More recently taking his deputy's seat in The Hague.

She stuck up the last of the photos. Taken the day before on the strand at Marken, a naked body, head shot away, half-buried in the shingle.

'More than one story here,' Vos murmured, remembering what Dirk Van der Berg had said the previous day.

A sound behind and then a scream. Vos turned as Sara Klerk pushed past him, jabbing a finger at the pictures of her dead and bloodied husband. She began to shriek, no words, only fear and anger.

'Oh God,' Bakker muttered. 'I'm sorry . . .'

Vos said nothing, just got an arm in front of the woman, looked her in the eye.

'Mrs Klerk . . . We need to talk. Please.'

She wasn't crying. More mad than grieving.

'I said I'm sorry,' Bakker repeated.

'You did,' he agreed and coaxed the woman back into the interview room next door. There he sat her down and asked one of the uniformed officers to get her a coffee and anything she wanted to eat.

'I'll be with you as soon as I can.'

'Now—' the woman demanded.

'As soon as I can,' he repeated.

23

Hour after hour they'd spent in Marken, hogging one of the two computers in the community room, hunting, hunting, hunting. That bright morning after breakfast they begged Vera to let them try her old PC. They were bored. They wouldn't do anything wrong. They needed some release.

She glanced at them over the bacon and eggs then said OK, once she'd put a few filters in place. The thing wasn't broken at all.

They went upstairs while she did it. After fifteen minutes she called them down, told them to be good girls because that was in their nature. She had to go out for an hour or two. An appointment with the doctor, she said with a scowl. She didn't seem quite as stern. Or perhaps something worried her.

All the same she locked the front door when she left.

Straight away they went to the computer to see what was there. Mia typed, Kim gave the orders, same as she did in Marken. Lots of things seemed blocked as they had been there too. But they could get to Wikipedia and for Kim, locked in the institution, that vast and rambling universe had become as real as the world itself.

'Me,' she said and ordered her sister out of the chair. Mia moved to the adjoining seat and watched her take the keyboard, knowing what she'd soon be searching for.

'We've done all that,' she complained.

Kim wasn't listening. Searching, stumbling from link upon link, meandering byway followed by pointless dead end, only to retrace her steps once more and find somewhere new to become lost in all that useless ocean of information.

She'd started the way she always did, by typing 'three' then seeing where serendipity took them.

Three blind mice.

Three primary colours.

The Rule of Thirds that gave a painting its perfect, pleasing visual form.

The trinity of three, Father, Son and Holy Ghost.

Jesus was visited by three wise men. He was thirty-three when he died and rose again on the third day.

There were twenty-seven books in the New Testament which is three times three times three. Three times Jesus prayed in Gethsemane before he was seized.

The pagans followed the three-fold law that stipulated everything a person put into the world, good or evil, positive or negative, would be returned to them three times over.

'There,' Kim said, catching sight of another link, pointing at it. 'That's new.'

'Nothing's new,' Mia said with a sigh. 'It's all just . . . stuff.'

Kim's busy fingers ran across the keys. Another entry. A form of poetry now, the tercet. Three lines of verse, rhyming in a triplet.

'And this,' she said, placing a pale, thin finger on the screen.

> The wrinkled sea beneath him crawls;
> He watches from his mountain walls,
> And like a thunderbolt he falls.

They read the text beneath. Alfred, Lord Tennyson. 'The Eagle'.

'And like a thunderbolt he falls,' Kim whispered. '"He". Why's it always a "he"?'

'It's just a stupid poem,' Mia said.

Kim gazed at her and there was something new between them at that moment. Something hostile.

'Are you done?' Mia asked. 'Can I try now?'

Kim got up. They swapped seats. Not a word spoken.

Mia sat down, closed Wikipedia, opened a new window. She wanted to know how far Vera's filters worked and whether they could circumvent them.

'What are you looking for?' Kim asked.

'Some news.' They never followed that in Marken. There didn't seem any point. That world ended at the pebble shore, the high wire fence, the guarded gate. Nothing outside mattered.

Kim put her hands on the keyboard and stopped her sister typing.

'Why?' she asked. 'What's that to us?'

In Marken it was easy to pretend there were no differences between them. Two sisters, a third still alive in Kim's head. In a way Little Jo had grown up while they stayed young. Not innocent. Not quite.

'Because we need to know,' Mia said and forced her hands away.

Before Kim could object, Mia found what she wanted. A new site. Familiar pictures there.

Simon Klerk, smiling in his nurse's uniform. A picture of them, ten years old. Perhaps Director Veerman had nothing better.

'Dead,' Mia whispered.

'Best thing for him.'

Kim cocked her head, smiled the innocent, smug, cheeky smile of an eleven-year-old then said, in a high and childish voice, 'Now we can do more than sing, big sister. Once we get rid of Vera we can go where we like. Do what we like. The three of us. Together.'

Then she sang two lines from a long-lost hymn. Faltering soprano, so much higher than her customary range. The way Little Jo would have sung it once upon a time.

Praise the Lord through Sister Death,
From whose kiss no man may flee.

Again, even higher.

Praise the Lord through Sister Death . . .

Mia reached forward and gently placed her palm over her sister's mouth.

The singing stopped.

'Please,' Mia begged. 'No . . .'

With one wild jerk of her arm Kim swept her hand away.

'Don't do that again, Sister,' she snarled. 'Not to me.'

24

Go fishing, Vos had told him. So that's what Dirk Van der Berg did. First thing that hot summer morning he drove out of the city into Waterland, following the Marken bus all the way until it veered off to the right and left him with a clear run for Volendam.

Like most Amsterdammers he knew the place more through reputation than experience. It was somewhere for tourists and the fans who followed the Palingsound bands. Sometimes, if he and his wife had visitors, they'd take them out to the quiet green pastures around the town and treat them to some cheese in its quieter, posher neighbour, Edam. But mostly it was a foreign spot. A place where city police rarely ventured. There was reason enough, he guessed. Plenty of dope and the odd outbreak of violence from time to time. Some of the locals had a reputation for dealing with trouble themselves, not leaving it to the authorities.

That suited both parties usually. But not now.

He parked his car as close to the waterfront as he could and read the file he'd brought with him. Since Marnixstraat's documentation on the Timmers case was almost non-existent he'd pulled out photocopies of the press coverage. It was wild. A well-known musician had been murdered. For a few days he was suspected of killing father, mother and daughter of a local fishing family. Then that case petered out under Ollie Haas's clumsy leadership. The only certainty that seemed to remain afterwards had to do with the two surviving triplets, Mia and Kim. Just eleven years old and they'd murdered a fading pop star called Rogier Glas with a savagery that seemed impossible in children.

The paper said The Cupids were known throughout Waterland for their kindness, their support of local charities, the way they played for free at old people's homes and hospitals. How Rogier Glas was always helping at youth clubs and schools, pockets brimming with sweets, always ready with a kind donation. Their international careers may have vanished, but in Volendam they remained local heroes. Not a sniff of scandal about them.

Van der Berg read that part and took it with a pinch of salt. Show business had a few saints in his experience, but they were rare. The idea three of them might be former fishermen from Volendam . . .

He wasn't a cynical man by nature. Still the idea seemed plain wrong.

A woman went past in traditional costume, clogs and hat, long black-and-white dress, headed for the photo station where the tourists were now assembling near the harbour. The locals here seemed ordinary people. Bored people, the way they often were in areas that depended on the tourist dollar for survival. The only ones who got rich off the visitors were those who owned the hotels and restaurants and controlled the local economy. The workers struggled by on minimum wage mostly, and benefits during the long, sparse winter.

'All the same . . . You don't get kids who kill people. Not like . . .'

The remaining scraps of files in Marnixstraat told the grim tale of Glas's death. The man's throat had been cut then, post-mortem, his penis had been hacked off and stuffed down his throat.

'Not like that,' he finished. He'd felt this way at the time and for some reason believed it more strongly now.

There was a cafe just opening up down the road. He wandered in, ordered a coffee and a pastry, and tried to converse with the youth behind the counter. All earrings and tattoos, the kid didn't seem interested in much except the music videos on the TV. If he knew about the Timmers case he wasn't going to talk about it.

That was obvious after the briefest of conversations. Then a figure flitted past the door, a familiar one, a large dog by her side.

Bea Arends.

He was always good with names. Especially when they came with giant German shepherds who dug up corpses on the Marken shoreline. Van der Berg rushed outside, catching up with her as she fiddled with her keys by a bedraggled old Hyundai.

'We meet again,' he said brightly.

She stared at him. An earnest middle-aged woman who worked as a cook in the institution. People in kitchens got to know everything about a place.

'Found those girls yet?' she asked.

'Not yet.'

'Any idea where they are?'

He smiled. She knew he couldn't go there.

'Oh well.' She opened her door. He came closer and leaned against the front of the car. 'Is there something you want, Sherlock?'

'Just the usual. Answers.'

'What's the question?'

He laughed and said, 'Lots. Did Mia and Kim really kill Rogier Glas?'

She scowled and looked more fierce when she did that.

'Why ask someone like me? You lot said so. The courts did. Them doctors in Marken. Must be true, mustn't it?'

'People make mistakes,' he said with a sigh.

'They were just infants. I think that mother of theirs reckoned they'd be stars one day. Hoped that, anyway. Freya was a nice enough woman but a bit flighty. Pushy too. Pestered everyone to help her. The boys in the band. That manager of theirs. None of what happened made a lot of sense to me. You got paid to sort that out. Are you saying you didn't?'

'I'm not sure what I'm saying,' he admitted.

'Are you going to look at it all again?'

He shrugged.

'Got to find the girls first, haven't we? You must have seen them in Marken.'

She closed the car door.

'Course I did.'

'What were they like?'

Without much thought she said, 'Like . . . two kids who'd been kept in a kind of jail for most of their lives. No parents. No friends. So they were a bit weird. What do you expect? They love one another. I know that. Close as peas in a pod. Sing like angels too.' She hesitated. 'Kim's the awkward one. She thinks that dead sister of hers is still around. Or pretends she does.'

'And the other one?'

'Mia? She has a name you know. She's . . . kind. Thoughtful. A bit melancholy, I'd say. Who can blame her? I think she indulges her sister. I'm guessing mostly though.'

She stared at him.

'You haven't asked me about Simon Klerk.'

'No,' he said. 'I haven't.'

'Did they really do that?'

'We just need to find them.' He looked down the street, towards the steps that led to the waterfront. 'Is there anyone here who can help?'

'Not that I can think of. Good luck,' she said then climbed in without another word and got behind the wheel.

Van der Berg saluted and doffed an imaginary hat. He called Marnixstraat. Vos was in a meeting. Laura Bakker managed to tell him what he half-suspected: no one was any the wiser about any-thing two days after the Timmers girls went missing, apparently after leaving the naked body of their nurse half-buried on the Marken shore.

'You got anyone else to talk to out there?' she asked.

Ollie Haas, he thought. He'd driven past the former cop's house on the edge of the town. Vos had warned him off that

LITTLE SISTER

encounter, but Van der Berg had stopped by all the same. It didn't matter. The house was empty. No car in the drive.

'Not really. I suppose I might as well come back.'

'What about the brothers? What were they called?'

'Tonny and Willy Kok. Why would I want to talk to them?'

She laughed and he realized he was starting to appreciate the way this gangly young woman from the north saw things so differently sometimes.

'You townies. You really don't know how it works anywhere else, do you?'

'Tell me.'

She did and it seemed so simple. A couple of brothers like the Koks had lived in Volendam all their lives. They'd know everyone. Hold every last piece of gossip. They wouldn't give it up easily, especially to a man from the city. But it was worth a try.

'Give me an address,' he asked.

It was a farm on the way back to the city.

'Remember you're a stranger, Dirk,' she said after she looked it up on the system. 'They won't give you anything on a plate.'

'Learned that already,' Van der Berg grumbled.

Fifteen minutes later he was in the yard of a dilapidated smallholding. The place looked more like a cemetery for dead farm equipment than a working business. Tractors and trailers and pieces of machinery he couldn't even name lay rusting everywhere.

The ramshackle house behind the junkyard looked empty. He was ringing the bell for a third time when an ancient and muddy Ford tractor pulled into the drive, Tonny Kok at the wheel, his brother standing in a trailer behind.

Tonny jumped off, marched straight over and said, 'I reckon you must be psychic.'

'Why—'

''Cos you're just the man we're looking for. Hop on the back. We'll show you.'

Van der Berg looked at the rusted trailer sitting crookedly on barely inflated tyres. Tonny seemed the least grubby of the two, not by much.

'Tell you what. You get in the car. I'll follow your brother. OK?'

Tonny lifted his boots. They were covered in thick mud.

'It's not mine. It belongs to the police,' Van der Berg pointed out.

'In that case it'll be a pleasure,' Tonny said and climbed in, taking care to wipe his boots on the floor mat along the way.

25

Irene Visser didn't show up at Marken until gone eleven. Veerman had been waiting to talk to her all morning, getting more and more furious by the minute.

He followed her into her office, slammed the door shut and took a seat as she went to the filing cabinets and started to go through some papers there.

'You can take your coat off, Irene. You do work here, remember?'

She looked thinner, nervier than ever. Black coat. Skinny jeans. Hair still wet from the shower. She lived in a cottage in Marken, half a kilometre from him, close to the dyke road that led back to Waterland. Veerman had been there once only, a year before. A man had just left. There was cigar smoke in the air and dirty glasses on the table smelling of gin. Veerman had been shocked somehow. After his wife's death he didn't have a private life. He never guessed Visser possessed one at all. She never spoke of men. Of anything but work.

'I'm doing my job,' she said.

'Which means what? We didn't do anything wrong here, remember? We were the ones trying to fix things. So stop running round as if we're the guilty ones, will you?'

'I suppose that depends how you define guilt, doesn't it? Does an act of omission count?'

'For God's sake stop being cryptic, Irene. Say what you mean.'

Visser had worked at Marken for more than a decade. She was well entrenched when he arrived from Amsterdam. Veerman's spell with the institution was much shorter, eight years in all, three as deputy, five in charge.

She didn't answer.

'We aren't the guilty ones, are we?' he asked in a worried, quiet tone. 'Is there something I don't know here? Should I—'

'Will you shut up for once?' she screeched. 'I'm trying to think. I put my life into this place, you know. I didn't clock off every day at five o'clock and shove it straight out of my head.'

'Perhaps you should. Helps me stay sane.'

He was back to where he'd been with the Lammers kid outside that morning. Cold and scared.

'I had that nasty cow Kaatje on my back earlier. She wants an early review. I said she could have one.'

She stopped rifling through the papers and stared at him.

'Why?'

'Why not?'

'Because she's not ready.'

He nodded then said, 'If we don't give her that she's going to talk to the police.'

'And tell them what?'

'I don't know. I wish I did. I'm starting to think I'm the last person to understand anything here—'

'You can't let her out. She's not ready. She could be a danger to herself. And others.'

'We set the Timmers girls free, didn't we? That was smart.'

She grimaced, put the papers on the desk and came to face him.

'Why don't you just . . . go back to your office and add up some numbers or something? That's all you do here, Henk. You've no clinical knowledge. No . . . insight.'

'Seems not,' he agreed. 'But I am the director. I answer to the department. I answer for you.'

'Take the day off. Go out on your boat. Drink a few beers. Forget about here for a while. Leave this to me.'

'Are you serious?'

'Yes.' She nodded, picking up the papers again. 'I am.'

Visser walked to the door.

'Irene. *Irene.* Where the hell do you think you're going? Get back here. I order it. *Get back here.*'

He watched her walk down the corridor, stiff-limbed, tight-arsed. Then she went downstairs. He strode to the window and saw her go into the car park.

Kaatje Lammers was across the way, exercising next to a picnic table beneath the trees. A police van was close by. Two bored officers were chatting by the back doors.

Visser caught sight of the girl, went over and led her into the spinney where they talked close up in the shadows. The police didn't even notice.

This mess was going to end up in his lap, just like the last one wound up with Hendriks. He should never have let the Timmers sisters go. They ought to have been shipped off to an adult facility and become someone else's problem.

Visser walked towards her car, taking out her phone along the way. The girl called something after her, laughing.

His mobile rang.

'I've changed my mind,' Visser said. 'I'm recommending Kaatje for an early hearing and immediate release after that. She poses no threat to anyone.'

'You just said—'

'Did you hear me? She poses no threat to anyone. Not if we can get her away from here as soon as possible. Do it, Henk. Set the wheels in motion. You can get her out into the safe house in Amsterdam tomorrow ahead of the hearing if you pull your finger out.'

'You mean the safe house the Timmers were supposed to go to?'

'That's the one,' she agreed. 'See to it. One less problem to worry about.'

The line went dead. She climbed into her scarlet Alfa Romeo and edged out into the long drive. He watched the security gate rise as she spoke briefly to the guard. Then looked back at the car park. Kaatje Lammers was there, hands on hips, staring up at him.

As he watched she grinned and waved.

26

Out in the green fields of Waterland Van der Berg found himself chugging slowly along behind the tractor, trying to pump Tonny Kok for information. As Laura Bakker had predicted it was a delicate, difficult job. The man insisted he knew no more about the Timmers murders than he'd read in the papers. The family were local but didn't mix much. The mother, Freya, had something of a reputation from what Van der Berg could gather. A singer with the local bands. A lover of the nightlife.

The father, Gus, was a fisherman. Didn't go out much. Certainly didn't hang around the small round of bars where the Koks liked to drink nightly, when they weren't barred.

'Could two kids murder someone like that?' the detective wondered as the tractor veered off to a narrow lane somewhere close to the Marken road. Tonny Kok had been as evasive about what they were going to see as he was about the Timmers. Just something they felt the police ought to know about. That was all he'd say.

He found Tonny Kok was staring at him, a look on his craggy, stubbly face that was impossible to interpret. The man had the outward appearance of a yokel. But he didn't think these two were stupid. Far from it.

'You saying they didn't?' Tonny asked.

'I'm not sure. The brigadier who looked into it . . .'

'Mr Haas. Lives in that big place all on his own. We done his hedges one time. He didn't like the work. Didn't want to pay. Not a man I'd like to deal with again.'

'I just don't know, Tonny. And I'd like to. Those two girls . . .

whatever they did . . . whatever they've done . . . it's been a hell of a life, hasn't it? Locked up in that jail in Marken.'

Tonny Kok was pointing to a spinney ahead. There was a decrepit building behind.

'Family that lived there left the place ten, fifteen years ago. Drove past this morning doing more drains. Gate was off. That seemed funny.'

Van der Berg drew to a halt behind the tractor. He turned to Tonny Kok and asked, 'A family dead ten years ago. Now this nurse—'

'That stuff's your job. Not ours.'

It was said with such vehemence Van der Berg went quiet for a moment. Then he said, 'Quite. Asking people questions they don't want to answer. That's my job too.' He nodded at the farm-house. 'Have you taken a look?'

Tonny Kok shook his head vigorously.

'No we haven't. We don't want no trouble with you lot. Or with anyone. I thought we were doing you a favour, mister.'

Van der Berg got out and thought about the place. They were perhaps five kilometres from where Klerk's car was dumped in the ditch.

'Aren't you even curious?'

'Curious gets you trouble. Round here anyway.'

The drive was covered in mud hardened by the summer sun. Clouds of mosquitoes were rising like wisps of mist from the stagnant green channels on both sides of the lane. Ahead he could see tyre tracks had cut up fresh earth through the grass verge.

'Someone's been here, Mr Policeman,' Tonny Kok said. 'Maybe just a couple of toe-rag kids looking for somewhere to smoke and shag. But anyways . . . we thought you ought to know.'

Then he went and stood by the gate. It was off its rusty hinges as if someone had tried to close the thing and it had failed through the unfamiliar effort.

'All yours,' Willy Kok said, waving an inviting hand towards the decrepit building.

The back door was half open. Van der Berg found himself pulling a pair of latex gloves from his pocket as he walked. They were on his hands by the time he got there.

For a moment he wished he wasn't on his own. That Vos or Laura Bakker had accompanied him to this deserted house in the wide green fields of Waterland. Not two tough, impenetrable brothers for company, men he wasn't sure he could trust at all.

Then he pushed open the door and a buzzing cloud of flies came to greet him. Sweeping them away he saw what must once have been a family kitchen. Now there were cobwebs and grime everywhere. An overturned wooden chair next to a battered dining table. Plates and pots on the floor. They looked as if they'd been there for years.

Van der Berg had worked enough murders to recognize the signs. The bloodstain was on the limewashed wall, stretched out like a gory Rorschach ink blot, pellet marks biting into the stone. Forensic would spend hours on this fatal mark but he knew straight away the conclusion they'd reach: Simon Klerk was here and someone blasted a shotgun in his face from close quarters.

He walked outside. The brothers were standing by the gate idly smoking roll-ups. Van der Berg pulled out his phone. No signal. The world he knew was absent here. He was a stranger. An unwelcome one, perhaps.

'Got a phone that works?' he asked the brothers. 'Mine doesn't.'

'Lots of them city ones don't,' Tonny replied. 'Got to know your way round places like ours. That lanky girl of yours. She could tell you that.'

The detective held out his hand and waited. Something still bugged him.

The flies.

Too many for a dried-up bloodstain that was two days old.

He turned his back on the Kok brothers and returned to the house. The door that led out of the kitchen was closed, a chair set tight and diagonal against it, as if to trap whoever was on the other side.

Gloves on, Van der Berg removed it and gingerly started to pull back the handle. What came next he'd never forget. It wasn't a cloud of flies. It was a black, buzzing, fetid storm, a million tiny wings seeking escape from the dark inside.

He knew the smell too. With a resigned sigh the detective took out a handkerchief and put it to his nose and mouth then retrieved the police torch from his pocket and shone it into the gloom ahead.

Yet more flies, the smell of blood and flesh. Van der Berg tripped over something, shone his torch on the thing, tried to work out what it was.

After that . . .

He thought he had a strong stomach but he was wrong. He turned on his heels, went outside, gagged then threw up by the back door.

The Kok brothers stood by the gate watching him. He wondered if one of them was laughing.

Then he walked over, held out his hand again, breathing heavily.

'The phone,' he said.

27

Sara Klerk was looking for an argument. It didn't help that she'd waited an hour for Vos to find the time to talk to her.

'Busy,' he said by way of apology when she objected.

'You mean you've found something?'

Vos told her what he wanted. It wasn't much.

'So you know nothing?' Klerk's wife threw at them after listening to his broad and general answers to her questions. 'My husband was killed by those two evil bitches and you haven't a clue where they are.'

'We didn't say the Timmers sisters murdered him,' Bakker told her. 'Did we?'

'Who else then? He left with them, didn't he? Who else?'

Vos didn't answer that one. Instead he did what he could to extract some information from her about the dead nurse. They'd been married at nineteen. Childhood sweethearts in Volendam. No children. They didn't want them. Klerk had been a psychiatric nurse in the Marken institution for a decade since he left college when he was twenty-one. His wife worked part-time for one of the food companies making fish specialities, mostly for the tourists.

'What did he tell you about the sisters?' Bakker wondered.

She grunted something underneath her breath.

Then, 'Not much.'

'Not much? They were local. Surely people talked about them. Wouldn't they be curious?'

'Maybe they were,' Sara Klerk retorted. 'I wasn't. Simon . . . if I asked him, he'd just say how clever, how lovely they were. That pair understood they were Marken's star inmates. Everyone in town knew they were there.'

'Did they have any relatives?' Vos asked. 'Any visitors?'

'Jesus! You're the police. Aren't you supposed to know these things?'

'Only if people tell us, Mrs Klerk.'

She sighed and said, 'No one wanted to go near that pair. After what they did?' She shuddered. 'The thought of it's enough to give you nightmares.'

Bakker asked her about the sequence of events the evening her husband went missing. It seemed simple enough. Around five thirty he texted to say he'd be working late.

'What did you do?'

'I stayed in and watched the television. What do you think?'

She thought for a moment then said, 'I got a call. Around eight thirty. But it wasn't him.'

'How do you know?' Bakker asked.

'They rang off before I answered. I tried to get the number. It was blocked. It wasn't Simon's. He doesn't do that.' She hesitated, then added, 'Have you found his phone?'

Bakker checked her notes.

'Not yet.'

'Must have been a wrong number. When it got to eleven I phoned that Visser woman he works with. She said she'd look into it. Didn't want me to call you lot. An internal matter, she reckoned.'

'Did he work late often?' Bakker asked.

'He'd been on nights until a few months back. Now, not often. When he was on days it was never later than nine or so.'

'And he'd always call?'

'Usually.'

'Were you happy?'

'About what in particular?'

'I mean . . . were you happy as a couple?'

Vos closed his eyes and groaned quietly. Sara Klerk glowered at her and said, 'That's a hell of a question in the circumstances, isn't it?'

Bakker brazened it out.

'Not really. Your husband should have dropped those girls off in the city around six in the evening. He could have been back in Volendam before seven. That's not so late.'

The woman's full cheeks were starting to flush.

'He texted me. That's all I know. Then those evil bitches killed him. When are you going to find them?'

'We're working on it,' Vos insisted. 'Unless there's something else you have to tell us.'

'I was rather hoping you'd have something to tell me.'

'Nothing you haven't heard,' he admitted. 'I'll be in touch if I have something.'

She snatched up her bag and stormed out. Bakker watched her leave and said, 'If I were Simon Klerk I think I would have been working late a lot. She doesn't do charm.'

'People rarely do in those circumstances,' Vos told her.

The door opened. It was Koeman. He looked animated.

'Van der Berg just phoned in. He's out in Waterland somewhere. He thinks he's found the place they killed the nurse.'

Vos got his jacket. Bakker grabbed hers.

'There's more,' Koeman added.

'Like what?' Bakker asked, checking her bag.

'Like another body.'

They stared at him.

'The same place Klerk was killed?' Bakker asked.

'Looks like it. Male, Dirk says.'

Vos asked Koeman to organize a homicide team from forensic. Downstairs in reception they waited for a car from the pool. A short, muscular man in a bright blue shirt and red trousers walked through the door, pulling his baseball cap down over his face as he marched for the lift.

Vos had to run to catch him. Bakker, intrigued, followed.

The lift was arriving as they got there. Vos moved forward and stood to block the door.

'Ollie Haas,' he said, taking off the cap.

A man in his late fifties, totally bald, with a blank face, stubble, dark eyes flitting from side to side, looking for an escape route.

'Vos. Been a while.'

'A long while. We need to talk.'

Haas grabbed the cap back and said, 'No we don't. I got a call from your boss. It seems there's a problem with some of the paperwork here. We can sort it out.'

'Why did you bury the Timmers case?' Bakker asked.

He gazed at her.

'So this is the mouthy kid from Friesland? Frank mentioned her. You've found someone to look up to you at last, Vos. Congratulations.'

'I'd like to know that too.'

Haas held out a stubby finger and poked him in the chest.

'I didn't bury anything. It wasn't the easiest of cases. You wouldn't have fared any better. Those two sisters you've got loose killed that musician.'

'Who murdered their family?' Bakker asked.

'I don't know,' Haas replied, pushing his way into the lift. He pressed a button for De Groot's floor. As the door closed he grinned and asked, 'Do you?'

28

After the argument the sisters didn't speak much. If that was what it was. To Mia it seemed more like a kind of parting. A moment in which the closeness between the two of them, so old it seemed as real as shared skin or blood or bone, began to fracture.

She had wanted out of Marken just as much as her sister. But that was because she sought release from their haunted past. Klerk and the mysterious messages they'd received – the map, the note, the money – had seemed to offer that. For Kim what happened before was not a black time, a nightmare to be forgotten. It was still real, still alive. So fascinating she wanted to meet it, to get near the distant hazy truth, and follow wherever that knowledge led. The difference was simple. Kim wanted to race towards that dark night. Her sister knew they had to run away from it or risk paying a dreadful price.

Before Mia could raise the subject the Englishwoman came back and sat them down at the table for coffee. She'd bought waffles and sandwiches, along with some more stupid juvenile magazines about pop stars and fashion. In her way Vera was doing her best. Mia understood this. But the older woman seemed lost too, as uncertain of her role as she was about her charges.

After the curious interlude in the street the previous night, wearing the uncomfortable blonde wigs, staring at a tubby, middle-aged man they barely recognized, Vera had brought them home, left them locked in the house with two cans of beer and vanished for the evening. It was gone eleven when she returned. Kim said she'd heard the nearby church clock sound the time. She was counting everything again, trying to find the number three inside the passing hours. Mia had given up trying to talk her out of that particular obsession.

'When do we go out again?' Kim asked, barely touching the food.

'You don't,' Vera said. 'Not until I say so.'

The previous day's warmth seemed to have dissipated. They were back to being prisoners.

'We can't stay here forever,' Mia pointed out.

'Where you going to go then?' the Englishwoman asked with a sarcastic grin. 'What you going to do?'

'I don't know.'

'Exactly. Without me . . . without some money . . . you're stuffed, aren't you?'

'We can't stay here forever,' Kim repeated.

Vera went and fetched herself a can of beer, opened it, took a swig, looked at them and said, 'You are a pair, aren't you? Like two parakeets squawking the same tune. No wonder they all said you were crazy. Are you?' She puffed at her cigarette, started to cough, then choke. When she finally got that under control she asked again. 'Are you? As mad as they say?'

'If we are you ought to be scared, oughtn't you?' Kim replied in a low and truculent tone.

Mia's heart sank. They needed a way out of this. Even if it came down to fleeing Vera and finding the nearest police station.

The Englishwoman slammed her beer can on the table, so hard froth came out of the top.

'I won't take any mouth from the likes of you, child. Don't need to. You don't even remember me, do you?'

Mia blinked. Kim was staring at Vera. There had been something familiar about the woman from the start. But it was an old memory, back from the time just after the killings, when everything seemed a blur.

'Should we?' Mia asked gently.

Vera went to the sideboard and returned with a photo album.

Pictures of relatives back in England they assumed. People at the seaside. Eating fish and chips. On rides at an amusement park.

Then just one photo they recognized and it made Mia's blood run cold. It was the pebble shore in Marken, the institution behind. A staff photo probably. Simon Klerk was there looking thinner, younger, longer hair. So . . . enthusiastic.

It was hard to recognize the Englishwoman. Perhaps it was the uniform. That of a nurse or someone from the kitchen. It made her look bigger, fuller, healthier. Mia stole a glance at Vera now. The woman was sharp and caught that.

'Yeah right, clever one. I'm not what I was. Got cancer eating at me, haven't I? Had to give up work when they started hacking it away.'

She slammed the album shut just as Kim's fingers crept towards the picture.

'That's enough. I remember the pair of you when you turned up. Old man Hendriks rubbing his hands with glee. Two sisters he had to keep hidden until they were grown-ups.' She grabbed the album and tucked it underneath her bony arms. 'Determined that was going to happen, wasn't he? Didn't want any of his secrets leaking out?'

'What did you do to us?' Kim asked.

'I didn't do nothing, you silly cow! It was me and a couple of others trying to protect you. Not that it helped. Them sticking needles in you every time you got uppity.' She snorted. 'You didn't do yourself any favours either. Going on and on about your dead sister when you finally got around to saying something.'

Vera grinned then, in a high-pitched sing-song voice, said, 'Little Jo. Little Jo. Little Jo's come with us, missus, hasn't she?' Her old sour tone came back then. 'Remember that? I do. God . . . the crap we had to put up with.'

'We were children then,' Mia told her. 'Alone. Confused.'

'Not much different to now then.' A bony finger jabbed at them. 'You two need me. For everything. Don't forget it.'

'We can't stay here—'

'Think I want this? Any of it?' Her voice was close to a shriek. There was something wild and frightened in her eyes. 'I'm doing folks favours here. Not just you. Got no choice. Any of us. So shut up moaning and do as you're told.'

She got up from the table. Stiff and old, nothing like the plump woman in the photo. Vera rubbed her back and chuckled to herself.

'Some of those bloody songs you sang. Over and over again.' The mocking voice came back. 'Can you hear Little Jo with us? Can you?' A laugh. 'Yeah. Dead right. Come on then. Let's have it again. Sing us a tune, eh.'

Mia folded her arms, furious, silent.

The words and the melody came perfect from her sister's throat.

Praise the Lord through Sister Death,
From whose kiss no man may flee.

Higher and higher.

Praise the Lord through Sister Death . . .

'Enough of that,' Vera barked. 'You two stay here and behave yourselves. I'll be back middle of the afternoon. If you're lucky maybe I'll get you a video or something.'

'Thank you,' Mia said softly, trying to block her sister's faultless singing from her mind.

The woman got up. The front door slammed. They heard the key turn in the lock from the outside.

Kim fell silent and glared at the locked door.

'We need to be patient,' Mia suggested.

'Patient?' Kim laughed. 'Ten years. Half our lives. How patient can you be?'

29

When Vos and Bakker got to the farmhouse in Waterland Van der Berg was waiting outside smoking with the Kok brothers next to their tractor.

'Miss,' Tonny said, lifting his flat cap as they turned up. 'Lovely to see you again. I think you'd best not be going inside that place. Another dead man there, your friend reckons.'

'He won't let us in neither,' Willy added. 'And we seen lots of dead things out here over the years.'

'It's a crime scene, for God's sake,' Van der Berg muttered.

Two forensic vans turned up as he spoke. This was their show for the time being. They erected 'don't cross' tape and started to hand out white bunny suits. Vos, Bakker and Van der Berg climbed into theirs. The Kok brothers watched, still amused.

Then the detective told them what he knew. Someone had been killed in the kitchen. There was evidence of a single shotgun blast, blood spatter on the walls and floor. A body in the room beyond.

Vos zipped up his suit and asked the brothers why they were here.

'We went dredging up the lane,' Willy told him. 'Everyone said you were still looking for the place someone killed that nurse. Well.'

He stuck his big hands in his pockets and looked at his brother.

'No one's been in this dump for years,' Tonny continued. 'Last family went bust trying to flog bad cheese to the tourists. Even they knew it was rotten stuff.'

'Gate was open when we went past,' Willy added. 'Looked like somebody had been messing round. So we drove back home to get our phone. And Mr Detective was there already sniffing round.'

'Any idea who it is?' Bakker asked.

Van der Berg shrugged.

They followed the forensic team inside. The Kok twins stayed by their tractor.

'That pair are around a lot,' Van der Berg grumbled.

'They dredge the dykes,' Bakker replied. 'What do you expect?'

'I don't know. So we've no idea where those two girls are? Still?'

'None,' Vos agreed. 'Did you find anything in Volendam?'

'Just what I knew already. People there don't want to speak to the likes of us. The Kok boys aren't exactly helpful cither.'

Aisha Refai, the young forensic officer Vos knew and liked of old, was setting up her cases on the kitchen table. Bright and outspoken, she wore her usual colourful headscarf, green today, a fawn cotton shirt and jeans. The tall, middle-aged man, pale with a craggy face and a neat moustache, next to her looked plain by comparison. He was busy giving out orders while swatting away flies.

'Who's that?' Bakker wondered.

Vos went over and introduced himself.

'Snyder,' the man said. 'I got seconded here from Rotterdam first thing this morning.'

'What happened to Schuurman?' Vos asked. 'I usually get him.'

'He's on a course, isn't he? Any more questions, or can we get on with our work?'

Bakker was wandering towards the door to the hall, the source of the flies.

'Leave that!' Snyder ordered. 'We go first.'

'I'd like to know who he is,' Vos pointed out. 'Just a look.'

'It's my job to preserve evidence,' the forensic officer said.

'I know what your job is,' Vos said then pushed past, ignoring the protests, waved away the cloud of flies at the door and took a good look.

'This is outrageous,' Snyder objected. 'I'll have to raise it with De Groot.'

'Feel free,' Vos told him. 'I never have these problems with Schuurman.'

The body of a stocky man lay half-turned in front of him, face cast in a shaft of summer sunlight streaming from the cobwebbed window by the front door. A staircase ran up behind. The dust on the ancient wooden steps indicated there wasn't much point in venturing up there. No one had for a long time.

Vos took two steps forward into the hall.

'Cut that out!' Snyder cried. 'We haven't even started yet. I don't want a bunch of clodhopping detectives trampling on the evidence.'

Barely listening Vos crouched down and stared at the dead face in front of him. Weather-beaten, stubbly, grubby dark-brown hair turning grey. Between fifty and sixty. The same age as the two remaining Cupids, Gert Brugman and the vanished drummer Frans Lambert. But this man had a tattoo on his forearm. An old-fashioned anchor entwined with snakes, the blue and red ink merging into the skin with age. Before he interviewed Sara Klerk that morning he'd taken a good look at the pictures of Brugman and Lambert in the newspaper cuttings Laura Bakker had found. They were rough and ready men, solid Volendam stock. But if they'd had tattoos he'd have seen them in some of those publicity photos the papers ran.

'Any ideas?' he asked.

'There's no ID on him,' Van der Berg said. 'Not that I could find.'

'Jesus,' Snyder bawled. 'What am I dealing with here? You don't touch a damned thing—'

'There are two young women out there,' Vos said, getting to

his feet. 'Sick. Scared. Maybe dangerous to others. Maybe in danger themselves.' He pointed a gloved finger in Snyder's face. 'Don't get in my way. And don't even think of whining to De Groot either. That won't work.'

Snyder glared at him.

'Won't it? You sure?'

Vos walked outside, beyond the clouds of flies and the team of forensic officers, trying to find fresh air. Aisha Refai was by the door, glaring in the direction of Snyder. She followed the three of them as they left.

'What's going on, Vos?'

'You tell me,' he said, checking the pictures on his phone.

'I was off yesterday. Come in this morning. They say Schuurman's away on some course I never knew about.' She nodded back at the farmhouse. 'And here's this stuck-up prick from Rotterdam throwing his weight around. De Groot brought him in apparently. Wasn't sure we could cope on our own.'

Van der Berg shifted on his big feet. Laura Bakker started clucking too.

'Stop it,' Vos said, holding up his hand. 'If that's what the commissaris wants it's his prerogative.' He nodded at the farmhouse. 'Do your job, Aisha. It's important. If you find anything . . .'

'You'll know,' she muttered and tramped back in her suit.

'I'm no expert, as that charmer from Rotterdam will doubtless confirm, but I'd guess whoever our man is he got killed around the same time as the nurse,' Van der Berg suggested. 'The flies. The state of him. It is hot.'

Bakker looked at Vos, who said nothing.

'Is he right?' she asked.

Vos shrugged and stayed silent.

'Which raises the question,' Van der Berg continued, 'why strip Klerk naked and dump him in Marken? And leave the other one dead in his work clothes on the floor in there? I mean—'

Another van turned up. Three more forensic officers got out.

Vos didn't recognize any of them. He stopped one and asked where they came from.

'Rotterdam,' the man said. 'Snyder called us.'

Then they went off to the crime scene.

'So just because Schuurman's away we have to bring in a bunch of strangers?'

'People do go on courses, Laura,' Vos told her. 'It's August. Holiday time. There's quite a workload. Getting bigger all the time.'

'But—'

Aisha Refai wandered over. She looked sheepish.

'Progress?' she asked.

'Not really,' Vos replied. 'You?'

She glanced back at the farmhouse. The teams there seemed intent on setting up their gear. Sheets, lights, cameras.

'I seem to be peripheral to their plans at the moment. I found these in there. I'm guessing they got dropped by accident.'

She held up a plastic evidence bag. Inside was a Samsung smart phone. Recent. Expensive. It had a faux leather case, red crocodile. And an old, worn ID card.

The picture looked like the dead man inside. It gave his name as Stefan Timmers, age fifty-four.

'Timmers?' Van der Berg said, then got on the phone.

'Snyder's too busy poking round the bloodstains and the body,' she went on. 'He doesn't seem much interested in my ideas. What's the betting this is your man's phone too?'

Vos touched the case through the clear plastic.

'Well done.'

'Why do you say it like that?' Aisha asked.

'Nothing,' he told her. 'Can you check it out?'

She glanced back at the team at the house.

'Probably best if I sat in your car.'

They ushered her to the unmarked Volvo. The Kok brothers

watched closely then came over and asked if it was OK for them to leave. They looked Laura up and down before they did.

'Wish there were more like you around,' Tonny said with a cheery leer.

'Bye, bye.' She gave them a wave.

After a while Van der Berg returned with some news from Marnixstraat. Stefan Timmers was older brother to Gus. The triplets' uncle. He lived in a cottage in Volendam and had a string of convictions for theft, assault, drunk driving, threatening behaviour. At least one term in jail.

'Nice man, by all accounts,' he added. 'Kind of puts those girls here, doesn't it?'

'Take a look round his place,' Vos said. 'Call if you need any help.'

Van der Berg headed for his car. They watched him drive carefully down the narrow lane, not far behind the rusty tractor belonging to the Kok brothers.

'What are we looking for?' Bakker asked.

'Something . . . small. Something that's probably not here. A million miles away for all I know.'

The old Ford tractor was belching black diesel as it chugged slowly away. Bakker's sharp eyes followed it. She was thinking as always.

'You don't like the way those two look at you, Laura. I'm sorry. I should have said—'

'I can watch out for myself, thank you very much. You get used to it. God knows what it must be like if you're beautiful. Those two Timmers girls. Did you see the pictures? When they were kids? They were lovely. That . . . I can't imagine.'

He wanted to say something but knew it could so easily be taken the wrong way.

'If anyone ever tries that in Marnixstraat let me know. I won't stand for it.'

She threw back her head and laughed out loud.

'You're a bit late.'

He realized he was blushing.

'What? I mean it. I won't stand—'

'You really are an innocent sometimes.'

'This job screws you up,' Vos moaned. 'You just notice all the wrong things. Never look at what's right in front of your nose.'

'An innocent,' she repeated.

Something grey and heavy flapped above them. It was a heron coming in to land by the dyke. They hung around the city too. One was fond of standing on the back wall behind Marnixstraat, eyeing the canal in the busy heart of Amsterdam, hour after hour. In the vast green wilderness of Waterland, the bird looked different. At home. Unfeeling with its great spear of a beak. Malevolent, if Vos was feeling imaginative.

'We all are out here,' he said.

There was a shriek of delight from the back of the Volvo. Aisha Refai had found something.

30

Kim crooned the words of another song. This time her sister didn't follow.

They were back in their room, up the steep narrow stairs, silent for the most part after the confrontation with Vera. Pigeons seemed to be congregating outside the window. The smell of dope from the back of the coffee shop in Haarlemmerstraat was stronger than ever.

Sniffing it through the window, Kim laughed then reached up and stroked her sister's short black hair.

'We're different now. Aren't we?'

'Weren't we always?' Mia answered.

They never talked about this. It was awkward, unnecessary. That had been the case ever since the black night, a decade before, when the police came out of the dark screaming at them, staring at their bloodied fingers as they stood by Rogier Glas's van waiting to see what happened next.

Something then had joined the two of them, trapped them inside the same shell. But it was all an illusion. As the girls grew the differences became apparent. Physically Kim was a touch heavier, in the face, in the body. Quicker, stronger, bolder too while Mia sat back and watched, waiting for her moment.

Until now they'd barely quarrelled. It was rare they even disagreed. Decisions came jointly out of nothing. In the first instance from Kim usually and then Mia simply nodded.

But they *were* unalike in many ways. Even in the music – Kim the low notes, Mia the middle – the subtle shifts were there.

Mia thought about this and sang a snatch of an old hymn.

Kim listened, nodded, waited for her moment and came in with a deeper harmony. Just one line and then in unison they finished.

The pigeons cooed outside the window as if in appreciation. Someone in the kebab-bar kitchen clapped very slowly.

'Did you hear her too?' Kim asked in a whisper.

'No. Not really. We left that behind in Marken.'

With the madness, she thought.

Her sister frowned and stayed silent. Mia gazed at her more intently, more seriously than she would ever have dared before.

'We have to be careful. We both want to be free of this place. But we don't know where we're going.' She shrugged. 'Or why, really?'

'Because we're owed,' Kim muttered.

'We are,' Mia agreed. 'I'm going to mess with the computer. Want to come?'

Kim just shook her head and stared out of the window at the back of the kebab bar and the dope cafe in the street behind. One of the waiters there was waving at them.

Down the long steep stairs. Three flights of them. Mia sat and idly wasted half an hour looking through the limited pages Vera allowed. The child filter was on. She couldn't work out how to remove it. The news sites had nothing fresh to say about Simon Klerk. Or them.

Towards the end of the afternoon Vera returned from the doctor's. She looked as if she'd been crying.

'What you two been up to?' she demanded, in an obvious foul temper.

'Nothing,' Mia replied.

'Where's your sister?'

'Sleeping, I think.'

The Englishwoman placed her shopping bag on the grubby carpet at the foot of the steps.

'Keep your nose out of that,' she ordered, and set off up the flight of stairs.

Kim wasn't sleeping. She was waiting, hidden in the doorway of Vera's first-floor room. She listened as Vera marched up to the top of the house calling out her name. Then the woman marched down, a heavy, angry tread for one so skinny.

The Dutch liked steep staircases and narrow steps. Some were almost like cliffs or ladders into distant attics.

Hiding behind Vera's bedroom door Kim held on to the cord she'd unwound from the curtains. It ran across the shallow landing, tied to a radiator pipe at the other side. When Vera came storming down the familiar steps calling out her name Kim waited, saw a leg, then another, and pulled the rope tight.

One hand up, stifling a giggle, as the Englishwoman's shin connected with the trap.

Vera screamed then, falling head first down the steep incline, arms out waving frantically.

In front of the crippled computer Mia heard her cries. Then a shocking, physical impact as body met first wood and next hard tiles.

She raced to the hall. Weeping, looking like a deformed mannequin, Vera lay there. A crumpled, misshapen heap.

Kim on the steps above, laughing, curtain rope in her hand, snapping it like a whip.

31

Aisha marched out of the Volvo, proudly holding up the phone.

'It's not Klerk's,' Bakker said before the young forensic officer could speak.

'I was going to say that,' Vos objected.

She grinned.

'The case. I knew that was what you'd spotted when I thought about it. A man wouldn't have one like that. Not hard, you know.'

'Not hard,' Vos agreed. 'So?'

There was a shout. Snyder had emerged from the farmhouse, pulled down the hood of his bunny suit and started yelling for her.

'I thought the good times couldn't last,' Aisha said. 'I'd better get back to doing what the new boss asks.' She held up a bag with the phone and the ID card. 'And give him this. Sorry folks. Happy to help. Don't want to lose my job.'

'What—' Vos began.

'There are no prints. Maybe they wore gloves. Or wiped it. Dropped it . . .'

Aisha pulled out her notepad and handed over a name and address.

'Damn,' Vos muttered. 'That can't be right.'

Snyder's shouts were too loud to ignore. She shrugged and went back to the farmhouse, pocketing the plastic bag along the way. Only, Vos guessed, to be found again later when she could slip it in front of Snyder as something new.

'May I?' Bakker asked when he kept staring at the page.

He passed over the note.

Irene Visser. A street name: Kerkbuurt. Marken.

'But . . .'

147

By the time she looked up he was already climbing into the Volvo. The car was moving when she reached it. Bakker opened the passenger door and leapt in.

'Thanks for waiting for me!'

'Call in to Marnixstraat,' he ordered. 'Get me an update on the Timmers girls. Say nothing else.'

'You wanted to know how they could have moved the body,' she pointed out. 'It's obvious, isn't it? They roped in their uncle.'

'Nothing's obvious here.'

Bakker didn't argue. There was a look on his face that stopped her.

Koeman answered straight away. The conversation was brief and finished just as Vos drove the Volvo onto the main road, fighting to get ahead of a bus crawling towards the long stretch of dyke that separated Marken from the mainland.

'Sorry,' she said. 'Not a thing.'

The white tower of the lighthouse rose ahead. Then, like a low forest appearing out of the ground, the timbered houses of the island. Vos asked her to call ahead to the institution and see if Dr Visser was still at work.

It took less than a minute for her to get through to Veerman. He sounded more miserable than ever.

'She went home early. Didn't feel well.'

They reached the edge of the village. Kerkbuurt. The close near the church. It wouldn't be hard to find.

Vos thought of something and pulled in by the side of the road.

'What now?' she asked.

He took out his phone and switched it off.

'You too.'

'Sorry?' she asked.

'I want some privacy for a while.'

'We're supposed to leave them on, Pieter. At all times.'

He folded his arms, leaned back in the driving seat, looked at her.

'So Marnixstraat aren't supposed to know we're here. Fine,' she said and did it.

32

Vera was still crying at the foot of the stairs, a miserable bundle of pain. Her right foot was turned at an angle. Furious, scared and in agony, she writhed on the carpet, spitting out curses, pleading for help.

Kim bounced down from the last step.

'Who's boss now, Vera? Who's telling us what to do?'

In a flash she crouched down and retrieved the house keys from the woman's tatty grey jacket.

'I need a doctor! Christ . . .' She tried to get up, screamed the moment she put any weight on her foot. 'You broke my bloody leg.'

'Serves you right,' Kim spat at her. 'Asked for it.'

Mia went and fetched one of the chairs from the kitchen table, helped her up from the floor then held her arm as she sat down. Gently she rolled down the threadbare black sock on the woman's injured leg. The skin was going livid from a bruise. Gingerly she probed the swelling ankle.

'I don't think it's broken,' she said as Vera squealed. 'Honestly.'

The woman's fingers crept to the purple bruise.

'Bloody painful anyway.' She shot a savage look at Kim. 'You could have killed me.'

'Shouldn't have tried to make us your slaves, should you?'

'Don't be stupid! I was doing what I was told. What I was paid for. I said. A million times. You two aren't ready to go out there on your own. Not yet.'

'Who told you? Who paid you?' Mia asked.

'Not talking about this now.'

Some items had fallen from her jacket as she tumbled down the stairs. Mia walked over and recovered them. Two bottles of pills and a cardboard box of tablets. She held them out.

'Those are no bloody good,' Vera yelled. 'I want painkillers. I want a doctor.'

She took the medication anyway and stuffed it in her jacket.

'You really are what they said, aren't you? Couple of monsters that look like little angels.'

'Not little,' Mia pointed out, trying to stop herself getting angry. 'Not any more.'

'A doctor . . .'

Mia said, 'You just twisted your ankle. It'll be better in a day. I want you to hold on to the chair very tightly. That way it won't hurt.'

'What?'

'Hold on to the chair. We'll pull you upstairs. You can lie down in the bedroom. We won't hurt you.'

'I need a bloody doctor!'

'No you don't,' Mia insisted and nodded at her sister.

The two of them positioned themselves around the chair.

'We're tugging you up here,' Mia continued. 'Either you hang on and stay safe until we're in your room. Or you let go and fall down the stairs again. You choose.'

She took hold of the back, Kim the side, and together they started to heave.

Vera screamed to start with. Then holding on became more important than yelling. Step by step they lugged her up the stairs. On the landing Mia helped her out of the chair, let her lean on her as the two of them struggled towards the bed.

It was only when she got there that Vera realized what they'd done.

'I can't get down from here now,' she moaned, collapsing on the duvet. 'Not with this leg.'

'No,' Mia agreed. 'Where do you keep the painkillers?'

The woman leaned back on the bed, dragged a pillow behind her so she could sit upright, and stared at them. Defeated.

'Kitchen cabinet.'

Without a second thought Mia went downstairs to get them. Kim stayed in the room, grinning.

'You're stuffed without me,' Vera told her. 'You don't know how much.'

She retrieved the bottles and the box from her jacket and, with unsteady fingers, started to shake out some tablets. Kim was there in a flash, seizing the pills, everything.

'I need those, kiddo! I'm sick in case you hadn't noticed.'

'Drugs are bad for you,' Kim said lightly. 'We learned that in Marken. They're there to keep you down. To make you something you're not.'

'I'm sick!'

Footsteps coming up the stairs. Kim walked quickly to the front, opened the window then lobbed everything out into the street. Vera started to scream. Kim closed the window and told her to shut up.

Mia came in with some paracetamol and a cup of water.

'What happened?'

'That bitch only chucked my prescription away. I need that stuff. More than an aspirin . . .'

Kim threw up her arms and laughed.

'Oh for God's sake. If they're that important I'll get them back.'

She headed down the stairs, Vera's keys in her hand. The door opened and then was slammed shut.

The woman in the bed was staring at Mia, pleading.

'I know you're not as bad as her, love. I know she's the wicked one.'

Mia sat on the bed and gave her the water and the pills. So many people had done this same thing to them in Marken. Not with painkillers either. It felt odd to be on the other side of the transaction. Good in a way.

'No, Vera. We're both the same. You'd best believe it.'

'I can help you. You need me.'

'And now you need us.'

'That I do. So where do we start?'

'By telling us the truth. Someone got us out of that place. Someone told us to run the moment we could.'

'And how did they do that?' Vera asked.

'They left us messages. Inside Marken. A map. Some money. They said . . .' This was crazy. Wrong. She knew, but Kim . . . she wasn't sure. 'They said we had to run. It was the only way we'd be safe.'

'And that nurse of yours? The police think you killed him.'

Simon Klerk was a bitter memory.

'He said . . . he said he wanted his reward. We never hurt him. Just made him look a fool.'

'Think they'll believe that, girl?'

'I'm not a child!' Mia cried. 'I don't care what they believe. It's true.' And something else was more important. 'The messages in Marken . . . they said they were from Little Jo.'

A grim laugh came from the woman on the bed.

'Snap,' she said.

'What?'

'Same here. Don't you get it? I just got messages. I thought they were daft nonsense to begin with. Then money started to turn up, and you don't ignore money, do you? I don't—'

'They must have found you somehow!' Mia cried. 'Nothing happens by accident. I may be stupid but even I know that.'

'Search me . . .' Vera glanced at the door. There'd been no sound from downstairs. 'I got cash through the post. Those texts telling me to look after you for a while. Get you them wigs. Go and look at that bloke last night.'

'And you just did it—'

A sudden vicious look then.

'I'm sick. Don't have two pennies to rub together. I never meant you no harm. Oh . . .'

She grimaced with pain and it might have been the ankle or something else.

Mia got up and paid no notice.

'Where are you going?'

'Wherever I like,' she said. 'You can't stop us now, can you?'

'It was for your own good!'

She could have been Kim at that moment, ready to hit the stricken woman in front of her.

'Really? Do you know how many people have told us that over the years? Keep quiet. Do as you're told. Tell no one. It's all going to be fine in the end.' A pause, then softly she added, 'It won't hurt really.'

Vera screwed up her eyes in pain and gulped at the water.

'All I can think of is . . . someone remembers me from Marken. I can't imagine how else they got hold of me.'

'Is that the truth?' Mia demanded.

'Yes, missy. It is.'

Still no sound from downstairs. Mia left the room, ignoring the Englishwoman's squawks, and went down to the hall. Kim had to be still looking for the tablets.

The front door was unlocked. Opening it, stepping outside, felt like coming out of prison. Daunting, liberating. Scary.

In the street she looked around. People on bikes. A woman pushing a pram. A couple of youths jogging to the music on their phones.

Vera's pill bottles were on the pavement. The box was nowhere to be seen.

Nor was Kim.

33

It was close to five by the time they pulled into the lane by Irene Visser's compact, white-painted wooden cottage near the church. The summer sun had lost its power. The salt tang of the lake hung over the town, fanned by a light breeze. A gull perched on her roof, staring at them with beady yellow eyes as they drew up.

A red Alfa Romeo stood in the drive. The curtains were closed. Vos parked in the road and went to ring the bell, Bakker at his heels.

He wasn't hopeful. But then hope had been elusive in this case ever since the Timmers girls went missing. He'd spent long enough in this job to know when – and how – investigations turned intractable. Sometimes it was through a simple mistake. Too often, if he was honest. On other occasions they were quite deliberately misled. The police had an odd and uncomfortable job in the complex, morally ambiguous modern world. They were supposed to deliver justice to a society that often cared for it in principle only. To detect wickedness within a community that decried evil in public but was motivated largely by self-interest in private.

He kept his finger on the bell and waited, consumed by a single, depressing thought, a reminder of that awkward conversation with De Groot earlier. Whatever had happened to the Timmers sisters – whether they were guilty of murder or not – the fault lay elsewhere. Innocence was the natural state of humanity and it did not poison itself. Mostly the search for justice was defeated in the end by lies and silence. By people who cared more for themselves than the injured and the blameless around them.

A face behind the frosted glass. Irene Visser answered and immediately he was pulled out of his reverie. Something was different here. Very.

Then he smelled it. The floral aroma of gin, the English kind.

An observant woman, she spotted this and raised a tumbler to him. Full almost to the brim with ice and a piece of lemon.

'I always wondered what psychiatrists did when they weren't on the job,' Bakker observed with her usual tact.

'If you people ever stopped working you ought to give it a try.'

'Can we come in?' Vos asked.

She leaned on the door frame.

'No. Busy.'

'We need to know where you were the night before last,' Bakker said.

Irene Visser groaned, closed her bleary eyes and sighed.

'Why?'

'Because that's when Simon Klerk was murdered,' Vos said. 'Along with the sisters' uncle. Stefan.'

To Vos's surprise she laughed then said, 'What?'

'We found the place where Klerk was killed,' Bakker told her. 'Stefan Timmers was there too. Shot. We really need to talk to you.'

'I didn't even know the uncle. He never came to Marken.'

'We can talk here,' Vos said. 'Or I can take you into Marnixstraat. Long journey.' He nodded at the glass. 'No time to finish your drink.'

She swore then took a long look back at the hallway behind her.

'Fine,' Irene Visser said in the end. 'Come in.'

34

Back in Marnixstraat Frank de Groot wandered out of his office and went downstairs into the serious crimes unit. Koeman, a biddable man, seemed to be in charge. The commissaris asked what news there was from Waterland and tried, with no great success, to hide his anger when he heard.

'Where's Vos?' he demanded.

'I don't know. Bakker called in from that farmhouse to ask if we'd got anything on the sisters. That was almost an hour ago. Haven't heard from him since. He'll be there, won't he?'

De Groot leaned down and grumbled, 'I don't know. Call him.'

With stumbling fingers Koeman did.

'Voicemail,' he said. 'Bakker too.'

Force handsets had GPS switched on permanently. It showed Control where officers were.

'Get a location for them,' De Groot ordered.

Koeman pulled up the map app and typed in their numbers. Two stars, stationary outside Marken. The colour indicated the position was thirty minutes old and the phones were currently turned off.

'I'm sick of his bloody tricks,' De Groot moaned. 'Keep trying. Tell him I want to talk to him. Now.'

Then he walked back to his office. Ollie Haas was there, grim-faced and angry.

'This pisses me off no end,' he muttered as the commissaris returned. 'My pension—'

'I told you! You keep your damned pension. We didn't take it off you for screwing up the Timmers case, did we? Or that . . . that other thing.'

Haas laughed.

'After that . . . other thing . . . you couldn't, could you?'

De Groot printed out the statement they'd agreed and pushed it over the desk for him to sign. Haas went through it word by word.

'Maybe I'll think about it overnight,' he said, dropping the pen.

'Nothing to think about. If you sign that now you keep your pension, you don't get a criminal conviction . . . don't go to jail. Don't hear from us again.'

The old cop's grin got bigger.

'It's not my fault some idiot let those Timmers kids out.'

'Sign it, damn you!' De Groot roared. 'Or I swear I'll bring this whole place down around our heads. If that happens you'll be buried deepest beneath the rubble. That I promise.'

Haas mumbled a curse then picked up the statement and started reading it again.

'Lacks my style,' he complained.

'You mean it's precise, clear and competent.'

'You were always a very neat man, Frank. That's what matters today, isn't it? Being tidy.'

De Groot found the pen and held it out. Haas waited a moment and took it.

The statement seemed simple enough. An admission that he'd accessed old files on the Timmers cases over the network and deleted them.

'It doesn't say why I did it,' he pointed out.

'I can handle that,' De Groot said. 'You were covering up your tracks. Making sure we didn't kick you out without a penny.'

'And I did this five years later? Why exactly?'

De Groot took a deep breath.

'We both know why.'

Haas pointed to the glass door, smiled and said, 'But they don't.'

'You deleted the files. Then you came in here and put my signature on the records. That's the story. You get an internal caution and a black mark against your file. No further investigation. No financial penalty. If you know what's best you'll put your name to it and never set foot in this place again.'

'What's best for me?' Haas asked. 'Just me is it? Does Jaap know—'

De Groot slammed his big fist on the desk.

'Sign it before I pick you up and throw you out of the bloody window.'

'That was uncalled for,' Ollie Haas noted then shrugged, picked up the blue ballpoint and scribbled his name.

35

Summer nights in Marken were quiet. Insects buzzing along the shoreline and through the woods. Boats on the lake, uttering the occasional hoot. A radio from the patient quarters. The yammer of the single communal TV.

Amsterdam could not be more different. People, people, everywhere. Bikes coming at you from all directions, on the pavements, along the cobbled streets, by the broad canals.

Mia had no idea where Kim might be headed. Turn after turn she took and soon found herself confused. Was this really the canal corner where they'd stood with Vera the day before watching a battered bike getting pulled out of the grubby water?

She went to a street stall and bought herself a coffee in a paper cup. The girl who served it looked at her, curious.

Black hair, not blonde. They couldn't know. And even if they did? What crime, exactly, had they committed?

A bad one they said. But that was half a lifetime ago. The two of them, sisters, blood on their hands. Mia closed her eyes and tried to stop the memories coming back. The trouble was they were always there, formless, flitting between the real and the imagined.

A performance on the waterfront, fading evening sun the colour of their mother's golden wedding ring.

A moment out in the green fields of Waterland watching a bird and her chicks navigate the road.

'After you, Mother Duck,' Mia whispered, staring at the black waters of a city canal she couldn't name. 'Take care of your young ones.'

Was that real? It felt it. But then she wasn't sure of anything much now. There had been a time, the beautiful time as she thought of it, when they were complete: Kim, Mia, Little Jo. The Golden Angels of Volendam singing like larks, all in perfect harmony. Their mother watched and smiled. Their father . . .

A boat went by on the water. A man at the helm, a pretty woman in front. A picnic set out in front of them: water, wine, sausage, bread, cheese. Theirs was a life so distant Mia Timmers could not begin to imagine it.

Their father . . . she couldn't in all honesty remember.

Life had appeared good but then it was the only life they knew. And one hot summer night much like this the blackness fell.

Bad girls. Bad girls. What have you done?

Whatever you tell us, mister.

They were frightened, lost, so young. What else were they supposed to say?

Guilt.

That was real enough. A dark and shameful ache at the back of her head. A stain that wouldn't shift. A relentless whisper that hid away and murmured . . . your fault . . . *your fault, girl, it has been all along.* Then laughed and scuttled back into the shadows.

Whatever else had happened, they were, they knew, to blame. So many people said so. It had to be true.

A noise distracted her, a familiar one, out of context here. Mia looked down and saw a flap of wings on the grubby water. A bird came out from beneath the bridge. A duck, darker, dirtier than the ones in Waterland. Behind her four or five fluffy chicks struggled to keep up. The swimming mother never turned, never slowed for them; she just kept on and on. This was the city. The tiny ones had to follow, to obey, or fail. To do otherwise was to jeopardize your survival.

Your fault, your fault.

It always was. The unbreakable rule.

'Where in God's name are you, Sister?' she whispered, looking round the alien, hostile streets.

And what on earth are you doing?

This wasn't Marken. Kim didn't rule any more. The future, whatever it held, was up to her as much as anyone. If she wanted she could find the nearest policeman and throw the pair of them at the mercy of the authorities.

Just the thought of that made her want to laugh and shriek and cry.

Instead she walked over to a tourist booth selling canal boat tickets, begged a map and a cross on it for where she was, then worked out the way back to Vera's house in Vinkenstraat.

Kim had to return some time.

Had to.

36

Visser's house was as clean and bare as a hospital clinic. A few modern paintings on the pale wall. A dishwasher chugging away in the kitchen. The faintest aroma of a cat, not that there was one to be seen. Drink in hand she led them straight into the front room and pointed at the steel-and-leather sofa. Then she went to the sideboard and topped up the glass from a bottle of export Gordon's.

'Isn't it a bit early for that?' said Bakker.

'I didn't realize the police had jurisdiction over my alcohol intake.' She took a swig. 'Cheers. Hell of a day.'

'Why?' Vos asked.

She took a seat and glared at him.

'Why? One of our colleagues murdered? Apparently by two young women I signed off for release. I emailed my resignation to Veerman this afternoon.' The glass went up again. 'I've got an excuse.'

Before Bakker could chip in, Vos asked, 'What will you do?'

'Take a holiday. My brother's a surgeon. He's doing some voluntary work in Sierra Leone. I thought I might go and help out.' Another sip. 'Re-establish my credentials as someone who can actually get things right for a change. Contribute something worthwhile to this shitty world. I need some time away from this place. It gets to you after a while.'

Vos decided his phone had been off long enough. When he turned it back on the handset rang straight away. He looked at the number: De Groot. Then he handed it to Bakker and told her to take the call outside.

'Busy time for you too, I suppose,' she said when they were

alone. 'Sorry. I'm being . . . pathetic. It's not like me. I've spent most of my working life trying to fix things here. I should have moved on long ago.'

'Why didn't you?'

The question surprised her.

'What's it to you?'

'Just curious,' Vos said with a shrug.

'Sloth, I guess. Timidity. I quite liked it sometimes. Where else do you get the opportunity to meet that kind of patient? Kids. The worst we have, supposedly. You wouldn't take a second glance at most of them if you saw them in the street.'

He frowned. 'But people always looked at the Timmers girls, didn't they? They were beautiful.'

'True,' she agreed, nothing more.

'I don't think they murdered Simon Klerk. Or their uncle. That's impossible.'

He couldn't make out her reaction.

'The uncle?' She put the drink down for a moment. 'I don't remember them mentioning him. It was hard to get them to talk about their family at all. Very.'

Vos was struggling to get the chronology right.

'So you were there when they were first sent to Marken? Right after the hearing?'

She nodded and looked professional again.

'Correct. They were my . . . project. From day one. I thought I'd done a decent enough job. Seems I was wrong.'

The absence of papers from Ollie Haas's investigation was infuriating. Vos wanted a grip on what had happened then. There seemed no way to gain it.

'Do you think they killed the musician?' he asked. 'What was his name?'

'Rogier Glas,' she said straight away. Then she reached for the drink again. 'What makes you think they didn't? The police—'

'Forget about what the police told you. What did the girls say?'

There was a hard and sceptical look in her eyes.

'You want the truth? For the first eighteen months I worked with them they said nothing at all. Not a word. Not to me. Or anyone else.'

'Nothing—'

'Nothing. They were the most traumatized kids I've ever dealt with. They'd hold hands all the time, whisper to one another. Eat together. Sleep in the same bed. Go to the showers, the bathroom, walk . . . everything, just the two of them. And they'd sing. At times you'd see them stand around as if . . .'

A long sigh. She closed her eyes and rolled her head back.

'It was as if they really believed they were talking to their dead sister. Little Jo. They thought she was there. It wasn't pretending. It was real for them.' She shuddered. 'Sometimes they'd behave as if she was in the room and I wasn't. It scared me for a while, to be honest. *They* scared me.'

He tried to take this in.

'What made them talk in the end?'

'Patience. Sympathy. Persistence. And when they did, the last thing I ever asked them about was Rogier Glas and what happened that night. Why? What was the point? They'd been to court. They'd been handed down their sentence. If they wanted to talk it was their choice. And they never exercised it. Of course bloody Veerman brought it all up when we interviewed them for release on Monday. He wanted to hear them admit they'd killed him. Fool . . .'

'Why?'

The look again. Sour and disappointed.

'Isn't it obvious? Because we had to let them put all that behind them. It was their challenge. Their choice. I couldn't counsel those kids. They had to release whatever it was hanging around inside. Not that—'

Bakker appeared at the door, gesturing for him. He got up and she whispered, 'You're going to have to talk to De Groot.'

Vos nodded at her to stay with Visser then grabbed the phone and parked himself out of earshot in a small side room with a desk and a computer.

'I'm in the middle of an interview—'

'One that answers a few questions, I hope.'

'We'll see.'

'Jesus, Pieter. Don't go all smart on me now. Just find those girls. Nail this murder . . . murders. Christ – their uncle too?'

'It's too early to jump to conclusions.'

A long pause and then De Groot started on what he really wanted to say. He'd spoken to Ollie Haas. The former brigadier had admitted deleting the Timmers files using De Groot's name. He was scared that if someone came back to check them he'd lose his pension.

'How?' Vos asked.

'What do you mean how?'

'How did he get into the system, forge your signature . . . do all that?'

De Groot groaned.

'He's made a statement admitting it. That's good enough for me. You don't need to involve him. Jaap Blom's got nothing to do with this. I'm telling you . . . *telling* you. Find those girls. Bring them in. Close the case.'

'I don't think it's that simple—'

'If you tell me that one more time I'll hand this over to some-one who gets it. Do I make myself clear?'

The records were on the network. Someone with the right clearance could organize for them to be deleted. Perhaps even put De Groot's signature there. He still wondered: how exactly?

'Perfectly,' Vos agreed. 'I'll be back in an hour or so. We can talk—'

'Not tonight. I have other plans. Just do what I asked, will you? For once.'

Visser's voice was rising in the next room. Vos ended the call and went in. Bakker had told the woman about her phone being found in the house where Klerk and Stefan Timmers died. The psychiatrist was back at the gin, starting to shriek.

'We need to know,' Bakker yelled at her. 'Just tell us. Your phone was there. Where were you?'

He took a seat and asked Visser to sit down.

'We do need to know,' he agreed. 'We're not leaving until we do.'

37

On the way out of the house Kim had gone through Vera's bag and stolen her phone. There was no lock on it, no password. So, seated in a small park next to a busy kids' playground, she played around with the thing.

Her sister was the clever one, not that Kim ever acknowledged it. Mia would quietly, cautiously think through the few decisions they'd faced in Marken. What to do of an evening, which shampoo to use, the right girls to befriend. Few in Mia's case, though Kim was more garrulous and open. She'd teamed up with Kaatje Lammers a couple of times, got into plenty of trouble that way too.

Mia disapproved of Kaatje. But it never came to an argument. They were the same. They were different. That was how sisters were. If Kim was headstrong and unpredictable at times, Mia's common sense and careful judgement brought equilibrium to their lives.

And now . . .

Now Mia would be looking for her somewhere in this vast and unknown city. Kim felt guilty for putting her through that ordeal. She'd make up for it before long.

Vera's phone was cheap but recent. Plenty of texts. They all seemed to be from the same number.

Every message was terse and to the point.

The money will be there as promised.

The girls should arrive on Monday night.

Buy blonde wigs. Let them wear them only when I say.

Always the one short name at the end: Jo.

What memories she had of her dead sister were now so insubstantial she wasn't sure they were real at all. Little Jo was small, so short she looked more like a younger sister next to her and Mia. But she made up for her size in character. Always arguing, always pushing. Mia did as she was told mostly. But Kim, that child Kim, was always the first to give in, the one to do whatever they wanted because that way came love and affection, and sometimes a trifling reward.

But Jo took every last thing their mother and father said as a challenge to be tested. Ignored, for the most part. And if a row ensued she'd try to win it by setting one against the other. Freya Timmers being the victor usually since she was the real boss.

Little Jo had her mother's fire. The voice too, pitch-perfect on every note. It was possible . . .

Kim closed her eyes with a sudden stab of pain just recollecting how things were.

It was possible, perhaps even probable, that Little Jo would have bossed them all in the end. And perhaps now did somehow.

She read the texts again. All so short and practical. Like a general issuing orders to the troops.

Then Kim pressed the phone button next to the message, held the handset to her ear and listened to it ring.

The line was poor. A hesitant female voice said, '*Ja?*' Or maybe, 'Jo.'

One word. Spoken so quickly she couldn't begin to put a face to it, an age, anything.

Shaking, eyes beginning to fill with tears, Kim tried to speak.

The line stayed silent.

Then finally the words came.

'Jo. This is Kim.' The words felt heavy and awkward in her mouth. 'Kim. Your sister. Kim.'

She thought she could hear someone breathing. After that there was a click and the line went dead.

Kim stared at the handset. Shouted at it. Screamed.

Here was something that separated her from her sister. A temper, bright red and violent at times.

Kids were watching from the playground, legs dangling idly on swings, leaning against the slides and rides.

She didn't care. Jo, Little Jo, was a bitch at times. They never said that, not after the black night. But it was true. She was no Golden Angel. None of them were.

There was a girl there, small, blonde-haired, on her own, no one talking to her, bored, kicking at thin air on a bench. No more than ten or eleven. Skinny arms, skinny legs, pale, sour face that stared at her with a look that seemed to say she never smiled at all.

Like Jo.

Just like her, Kim thought.

38

Where were you?

It was the simplest of questions and prompted the simplest of answers.

Irene Visser sat in a chair nursing her gin and tonic in one hand, toying with her thin fair hair with the other, not looking at them directly, then said, 'I was here. At home. On my own. Reading. Watching TV.' The glass went up. 'Probably had a drink too.'

'Can anyone corroborate that?' Bakker wondered.

'Did I not say I was on my own?'

'No phone calls? No visitors?'

Visser sighed.

'This is very tedious, you know.'

Vos said there was no doubt. They'd found her phone at the farmhouse. Not far from the kitchen where Simon Klerk and Stefan Timmers were killed.

She paused for a while, thinking, then said, 'Not possible.'

'Your phone,' Bakker repeated. 'We checked—'

'No.' The woman looked baffled. 'My phone's here. I haven't been out to . . . where is this place?'

'Waterland,' Vos said. 'The middle of nowhere.'

'I have not been to the middle of nowhere. The phone's in my bag in the other room. Whatever you found . . .'

There was a sound in Vos's pocket. He pulled out his mobile, determined to kill the call if it was De Groot again. Instead it was Koeman so he got up and went into the adjoining kitchen to answer.

'I can show you,' Visser said from behind. 'If you don't believe me.'

She was headed for the door when Koeman's voice came on the line.

'Gert Brugman keeps calling,' Koeman said. 'The Cupids guy. He thinks the sisters are pestering him.'

'Wonderful. Anything from the farmhouse?'

Koeman growled.

'I don't know half the forensic out there. They're from Rotterdam, aren't they? What do I do about this Brugman idiot?'

Vos asked what the musician had to say.

'Lots, not that much of it makes sense. He reckons the Timmers girls came and stood outside his house last night. Then they walked off.'

'That's it? Does he know where they went?'

'No. He was very keen to give us a description. Blonde hair. Like they were as kids. Just grown up, he reckons.'

'Tell him someone will be in touch in the morning.'

'He won't like it.'

'Jesus . . . we've got two murders! All he's saying is two young women stood outside his house? That's it?'

'That's it,' Koeman agreed.

'I don't have time for this,' Vos told him and cut the call.

Bakker was still checking her notes, pretending she hadn't been listening.

'Lots of people have more than one phone,' she said. 'I just talked to Aisha and asked her to check the call log on the one she found.' Bakker looked up at him, bafflement on her pale face. 'There's a gap of almost two weeks. Up until then it was being used on a daily basis. After that nothing until one call two nights ago. Odd . . .'

'No it isn't,' Vos said with a sigh. 'Where is she?'

Bakker looked puzzled.

'Why not?'

'Because clearly Visser either lost the damned phone. Or someone . . . the sisters . . . stole it.'

'You'd report a stolen phone.'

'Where—'

A sudden recollection then. When they walked in he'd seen a small leather suitcase, expensive and bulging at the seams, parked in a side room by the door.

'God I'm getting stupid—'

Outside an engine revved wildly.

Vos raced to the hall.

The case was gone. As Vos snatched open the door they saw her Alfa vanishing down the road.

Vos strode to the car. Bakker fell in the passenger seat.

'Can we catch her?' she asked.

'We don't need to. It's Marken. Call ahead to the farmhouse. Get a squad car positioned at the end of the dyke road. They put that institution here for a reason. You can't escape an island easily.'

39

It was getting dark. A dying evening sun was casting the last of its golden stain across the lake. Vos drove through the winding streets of Marken, Bakker clung to the door handle as they sped after Irene Visser.

The psychiatrist knew the way out of this warren of medieval lanes. Vos didn't and he'd lost her already. This didn't worry him. As he'd told Bakker, there was just one way out, along the narrow road that sat atop the thin finger of dyke linking it to Waterland.

'Call Dirk,' he ordered. 'See what he's got at Stefan's place.'

'I will if you keep your eyes on where we're going—'

The car swerved past a line of tiny terrace houses and then hit a broader thoroughfare. There were street lights running in a line ahead. The dyke road.

In another timbered terrace across the water in Volendam Van der Berg's phone rang.

'You sound busy,' Van der Berg said.

'Vos wants to know what you've got.'

The detective looked around him. The place had bachelor written all over it. Unkempt, grubby, chaotic. He was in the low dining room trying to ignore the stale smell there. There were what Van der Berg took to be dusty eel or crab pots on the walls. Old photos of men by fishing boats. None of them smiling.

Van der Berg was getting a feel for Stefan Timmers already.

'A grotty dump belonging to a sad and lonely man, I'd guess. Give me some time. A bit of help would be nice. Can you get Aisha over here?'

Vos accelerated. There were red lights up ahead, travelling very quickly. Bakker called Aisha Refai, hooked her in to the call

with Van der Berg and said, 'If you can pull yourself out of Waterland, Dirk needs you over in Volendam.'

The forensic officer's answer took her breath away. Most of
the team were back at Marnixstraat. They'd taken Stefan Timmers' body out of the farmhouse and left a skeleton crew there to
await a fresh look in the morning.

'That was quick,' Bakker said.

'It was what the new boss wanted,' Aisha answered. 'Give me
an address in Volendam. Anything to get out of this place.'

Van der Berg passed on the location of the house and Bakker
left them to it.

'They've taken the body away,' she said as Vos closed on the
Alfa ahead.

'Already?'

'Sounds as if most of the team are back at base.'

He wasn't interested and told her to check there was a squad
car blocking the road as it came off the dyke.

'I did ask for that!'

'I know, Laura. Make sure it's there. And visible. She's drunk,
remember?'

Dead drunk, Vos thought. The words just came into his head.

40

Straight after Van der Berg came off the call with Laura Bakker his phone rang again.

'Dirk?' It was Aisha Refai. 'I'm on the way. Where is this place exactly? I don't get it on the satnav.'

He listened to her talk to whoever was driving the car then told her: a tiny black-timbered cottage behind the waterfront. Not easy to park near. She'd have to find space in the centre of the town.

'Do you have anything for me?'

He looked round the living room and thought: not much. At the end of the room there was a narrow eave and a tiny door. Once upon a time it probably gave onto a storeroom or a smoke-house. The fishermen here were famous for catching eels. Lots of them used to smoke them at home and sell direct on the street. But those days were gone. The eels were fast disappearing. Big companies had come in to catch the tourist trade, importing their fish from all over Europe.

'I'm sure we'll find something when you get here,' he said.

'You mean . . . no.'

He opened the old storeroom door. Van der Berg could still smell the smoke, an old woody tang. He found the light switch. A small fluorescent tube illuminated a low space no more than five metres long and three wide.

Walking in he saw it was a smokehouse no more. There was a desk at the end, a recent TV set with a DVD slot on the side and a modern laptop next to it. A strange place to come and watch television.

By the computer was a gadget he didn't recognize. A video

camera was docked inside it and beneath was a deep slot for what looked like old-fashioned VHS cassettes.

'Can you buy stuff that digitizes old video tapes?' he asked. 'The kind old people like me used to use. The big ones.'

'Of course,' Aisha said down the line. 'If you still have tapes to convert. Who has?'

Van der Berg opened the deep drawer beneath the desk and thought: Stefan Timmers for one. There were cassettes galore neatly stacked on one side and on the other a collection of plastic DVD cases.

'I think our man here likes to take pictures. Moving ones especially.'

Curious, he turned on the laptop, picked up the first DVD he found and slotted it into the drive. A few moments later the screen came to life.

Van der Berg shivered. It was an old home movie. Freya Timmers, an attractive woman, with too much make-up and a slur to her voice, was getting ready to sing. Karaoke by the looks of it.

She began to croon an old jazz number. Lena Horne if he recalled correctly.

'What's that?' Aisha asked. 'It sounds nice.'

'A home movie,' Van der Berg said, ejecting the disk and sorting through the rest in the drawer. He was glad to get the dead face off the screen. 'Wait a second.'

Then he sifted through the collection until he got the one he wanted. The label was for the year of the Timmers murders.

He turned on the TV and slotted the DVD into the drive. Some titles came up. After them came a very amateur musical act, a middle-aged woman plastered in thick make-up trying to sing an old Abba tune. Finally something that sent a shock of cold up and down his spine again, worse this time because now life and death ran together, no easy line between the two.

Three kids, sisters obviously. All dressed alike, scarlet shirts, blue shorts, red patent shoes. Everything too tight. Too . . . adult.

They started to sing and Van der Berg found himself rushing to find the remote and hit pause.

'I need you here,' he said. 'Aisha?'

There was a sound back in the living room. That was quick, he thought. Then he went to look, trying to erase the image of those three children, dressed and made up like showgirls. It all seemed so wrong.

Van der Berg stepped into the front room and said again, 'Aisha?'

The light went out and in that brief moment he realized he was scared. Then something hard came out of the shadows. A coward's blow. The sucker punch caught him on the cheek. Something else crashed into the back of his head.

A big man, he went down like a stone.

41

Near the end of the dyke a line of bright street lamps was emerging along the mainland running off to the right. They had to be getting close to the broader highway by the lake. To her relief Vos had eased off on the speed. He was right. Irene Visser was drunk. And she couldn't get away in the end. There was no need to turn this into any kind of chase.

'I can't see any sign of a roadblock up ahead.'

She called Control before he asked. A woman there went silent while she checked the status of the request.

'They're there,' the officer said eventually. 'Just turned up.'

'We can't see them,' Bakker told her.

The car went over a ridge in the road. The phone bounced straight out of her hand into the footwell.

Vos groaned.

'I'm trying,' she said. 'Sorry. If you drove a bit more carefully maybe. Oh my God—'

Afterwards it was simple enough to work out what had happened. The squad car had arrived at the tight bend where the dyke lane from Marken met the wide road back to the city. The men inside, two young and inexperienced officers, parked straight across the asphalt, side on to coming traffic. They were out of the car, one of them trying to position lights and a sign, the other spreading a spike strip over the road to take out the tyres of any incoming vehicle.

Drunk or not, Irene Visser spotted them early. She was probably doing a hundred and twenty at the time.

'Jesus,' Bakker whispered, watching the Alfa lurch sideways, tyres shrieking, brake lights flashing bright red, nose twitching into the skid.

'Call an ambulance,' Vos ordered, throwing her his phone.

The sports car was down to eighty when the front nearside caught the tail of the police car, flipping the vehicle onto its side in an instant. As Vos and Bakker watched the Alfa turned somersaults and rolled straight off the bend, over the low grass bank, down towards the bare shoreline ten metres or more below.

The two uniformed cops had retreated to stand on the opposite high dyke wall, the beams of their two torches following the doomed car as it twisted towards the pebble margin by the water.

The thing hit with a loud, explosive crash. Vos slewed his Volvo to a halt, leapt out and raced to the top of the dyke, Bakker behind him.

Thirty metres away Irene Visser's vehicle rolled over twice on the pebble beach then exploded in a burst of orange and red flame. Vos was trying to scrabble down the bank. Bakker came and held him back, then the two uniformed men.

'Pieter,' she begged. 'You can't get—'

A second explosion then. The bonnet of the Alfa flew into the air and the windows blew out on all sides. Up to the velvet sky sparks shot like crazed fireworks. The smell of burning diesel reached them.

Breathless, head shaking, furious with himself, Vos watched.

'She wasn't there. Irene Visser was never near that farmhouse.'

Bakker nodded.

'No,' she agreed. 'She wasn't.'

The car was consuming itself in a fiery burst of flames and smoke, rising to the night sky.

'So why,' he wondered, 'did she run?'

42

It was dark by the time Mia Timmers arrived back at Vera's house. There were lights on inside.

The door was locked. Kim answered it.

'Where've you been?' Mia asked.

'Where've *you* been, Sister?' Kim replied, then wandered back into the kitchen.

Mia didn't want to push things so she went upstairs to see Vera and give her the pills Kim had thrown out of the window. To her relief the Englishwoman looked a bit less sick, though she still complained she couldn't move.

'That's not all my medication,' she moaned, looking at the bottles.

'It's all I could find.'

'I need a doctor! I was a nurse, remember? This ankle's broken.'

Mia had thought about this when she was walking home.

'You can have a doctor when you tell us the truth. About who paid you. What we're supposed to be doing.'

Vera's narrow face was set in an angry scowl.

'I told you the bloody truth. I don't know. That's it.'

'But you must know something. How they found you. How—'

She froze. There was a sound from downstairs. Singing. Kim's voice. And then another, faint, high and faltering.

Vera swore and started to struggle with the caps of the pill bottles. Mia walked slowly down the steep steps. The singing had stopped. Then it began again, one voice this time. Kim's. An old folk song they used to perform when the three of them were being groomed for stardom by the men who hung around the recording studio above the waterfront cafe.

There was a smell from the kitchen. Kim had been frying eggs, she guessed. Probably burnt them from the acrid stink.

No arguments, Mia thought. That would be the worst thing.

Then she walked in and saw them. Kim at the table. Next to her a girl of ten or eleven. Shiny blonde hair, freshly washed, falling around her shoulders. Blue patterned dress with short sleeves. Narrow pale face, scared and puzzled at the same time.

Kim had a serrated steak knife in her hand. They'd had that sort at home but never got allowed things like it in Marken.

'Sing!' She stabbed the sharp pointed end into the old table. The girl stared at the wooden handle quivering in front of her. 'You can sing, can't you?'

Then Kim grabbed the kid by her skinny bare arm and squeezed, hard.

Mia whispered, 'This isn't us. She's not . . .'

A high, uncertain note, barely soprano, emerged from the girl's trembling throat, veering from tone to tone.

Wrong. All wrong.

43

Floodlights by the water. Medics on the shore. Unseen nightbirds hooting and rustling in the dark wetlands behind them. There was nothing for Vos and Bakker to do at that moment. Irene Visser was dead, the Timmers case in limbo, a mystery that seemed determined never to reveal itself.

He responded the way he usually did to such situations, shrinking inside his shell, silent, reflective. Bakker now had the routine set for these moments. Not nagging. She was aware that didn't work. Instead, carefully, without the least attempt to apportion blame, she tried to prod Vos into thinking about what had happened, retracing the steps that led them here, trying to see something, a fact, a marker by the road, that had eluded them on the way.

Seated in the car, both doors open, smelling the burnt fuel on the hot night air, he listened and did his best. Then shook his head and said, 'We need to step back from this. It's all too close. Maybe—'

'Don't say it.'

He frowned.

'Say what?'

'You don't want me near the case. It's getting too awkward. I should go back to Dokkum and see my aunt.'

'I'd never say that—'

'Oh no? What about when that Georgian woman's kid went missing?'

'That was different,' he objected.

'How?'

'You were different. Still a bit raw. Vulnerable. Not that you'd ever admit it.'

That seemed to ruffle her feathers.

'I'm not sure I'd agree.'

'I'd never expect you to,' Vos replied. 'But now. You're . . . fine.'

The medics were lugging a gurney up the incline from the burned-out car. Neither of them felt the need to witness that particular event.

'Thanks,' she replied. 'Don't overdo the compliments.'

'I don't need to. You're a part of Marnixstraat now. Most of the time anyway. And when you get . . . rebellious. Well.' He laughed, just for a second. 'We probably need it.'

'So if it's not me you were thinking about . . . it's . . . ?'

She didn't finish. They both knew what she was going to say.

'I didn't ask to come back to this job,' he said. 'I never planned it. I'm glad you found me. Sort of. But I don't know . . .'

The ambulance started up. People were dragging floodlights down the grassy dyke bank. When they turned them on they cast reflections on the water like miniature moons.

'I doubt myself,' he said quietly. 'Every day. I get up and think . . . why didn't I do this better? What makes me miss things that should be so damned obvious?'

She shuffled around in the seat.

'It's called being human, Pieter. You're not exactly alone in all this.'

'No.' He was glad of the conversation. 'I'm not, am I?'

'My old dad used to say a wise man always learns more from his failures than his successes. Maybe we should spend more time looking at our doubts and less with what we know.'

They were in the wrong place out here in Waterland. Strangers in an alien land. It was so obvious and he'd no idea how to address that problem.

'That's what worries me.'

His phone rang. He prayed it wouldn't be De Groot. Instead he heard the anxious voice of Aisha Refai.

'I'm in Volendam,' she said. 'The place Dirk was looking at. I think you should come here. Someone's attacked him. He's not too bad but—'

He passed the phone straight to Bakker and told her to get more details. Then started up the car and pulled away from the grim scene by the water.

44

Money. The sisters had some of their own, stolen in Marken. More left in the envelope with the map. And Vera's now too. It was time to use it.

Mia listened to the blonde girl's pathetic efforts at singing then stood up, smiled at her and said, 'It's late. Time you went home. Isn't it . . . ?'

She waited, still forcing the smile. Finally the kid said, 'Iris.'

'Iris,' Mia repeated. 'Come on then.'

Kim didn't move. Didn't speak. Didn't look at them. God knows what she might have done if Iris really could sing, a fine soprano, just like Little Jo. But all they got was that tuneless croak and perhaps that saved them all.

Mia took the girl outside, into the dark street. Amsterdam came alive at night, people everywhere. The girl knew where she lived, which was a blessing. Five streets away, back towards Dam Square.

They walked there and they talked. Mia told her how her sister was sad and confused. Because once upon a time, years ago, they'd had another sister, one who died. That loss never ceased to ache, especially for Kim. Sometimes she did things, silly things. Things they both regretted.

'Did she sing?' Iris asked.

'Yes,' Mia said, remembering.

'I can't, can I?'

'Have you tried much?'

'I did my best,' the girl said in a hurt voice.

'No. I mean . . . did your mum teach you? Anyone? Did they help?'

'Mum works.'

'What about your dad?'

'He's gone. Went years ago.'

'Brother? Sister?'

'Just me,' Iris said in a low, dead tone.

And that, Mia thought, is why you walk off with a complete stranger. Because there's nothing left to do. Nowhere to go. No one to talk to.

In Marken, trapped, desperate to be free, they'd pictured the outside world as a perfect place. Somewhere happiness fell from the sky, rose up from the cobblestones like wild flowers ready to bloom, seeping into everyone's life because that was what they were owed and all they had to do was wait. It was just another illusion. How many more?

Finally they found the place. The ground floor was a tacky-looking mobile phone shop. There was a stack of bells by the door. So many apartments tucked into such a narrow grimy building. Vera, with her tiny terrace house, was lucky to have such space to herself. Which was, perhaps, why she was chosen.

'Here,' Mia said and took out a fifty-euro note.

Iris stared at the money, puzzled. Scared perhaps.

'I want you to have this.'

'Why?'

'Because when you take it you're going to promise me two things.'

Mia waited. This was important. Iris had to be part of the deal, to volunteer herself.

'What things?' the kid asked.

'First . . . you won't tell your mum about us. About my sister. What happened. You won't tell her. You won't tell anyone. Kim's not . . . not well. It might make people . . . hurt her.'

'If she's not well she needs a doctor.'

'She's seeing one,' Mia insisted, the lies coming so easily.

'We're getting somewhere. But if there was trouble . . . it would set her back.'

''Kay.'

Iris put the money in the pocket of her jeans.

'You didn't ask what the second thing was.'

Two young eyes stared up at her. Surly. Not liking to be reminded she'd forgotten something. That awkward, cantankerous gaze might have been her sister now that they were free.

'You have to promise me,' Mia said. 'You won't walk off with someone like that again. You don't just go with anyone in the street. It's not good.'

'I didn't mean to.'

'But you did,' Mia said, trying to sound kindly. 'Doesn't matter what you mean to do. No one takes any notice of that. Only what they see. Or . . .' Her mind was racing back through the years. 'Or think they see.'

There wasn't a soul in the world who cared one whit for intentions. If that had been the case things might have turned out differently in Volendam. All that mattered really was appearance. The mask the world saw, not what lay beneath.

'Promise,' she said. 'Promise me now. Or I take the money back and I'll wait here and tell your mum.'

'I'd tell on you,' Iris replied with an unpleasant grin. 'And your sister.'

Mia folded her arms, leaned against the door and said, 'And then we all suffer. So which is it? Are we going to be smart? Or stupid?'

Kids. They were sweet in a way. But when the challenges came all they had was stubbornness when what they really needed was courage.

''Kay,' the girl said again and let herself in with a key.

On the walk back, through streets getting busier by the minute, Mia stopped and bought two pizzas, some beer, some pastries. She let herself into Vera's house. Kim was in the front room watching TV and didn't even look at her.

Upstairs the Englishwoman was a touch calmer. The ankle really was sprained, Mia thought. Not broken at all. Before long – and it would be difficult to gauge when – Vera would be mobile once more. And that would spell trouble.

'I bought some pizza. Plain. With salami. What do you want?'

'I want you two out of here,' Vera said. 'I want you gone.'

Mia found herself laughing.

'What's so funny, kiddo?' the woman asked.

'That's what I want too.'

After she'd divided up the food she served the rest on two plates, poured beer and brought it to Kim as she sat in front of the TV. It was a kids' channel, an old cartoon, full of bizarre mock-violence, scribbled blood, beheadings and beatings.

'If you ever steal someone off the street like that again,' Mia said quite calmly, 'this is over. I will walk to the nearest police station and . . . that's it.'

Kim reached for the remote and turned on the news. There was an update on the Marken case. Another body had been found. Stefan Timmers, their uncle, in the farmhouse where Simon Klerk had been shot dead.

Mia stared at the television, unable to think.

'Will you, Sister?' Kim asked.

'Yes,' she answered.

'And then they'll put us back inside somewhere. You one place. Me another. Forever and ever. World without end.'

'Amen,' Mia whispered.

It was hard to think of anything else to say.

Kim picked at the nearest slice of pizza and pulled a disappointed, childish face.

'Don't like salami,' she muttered. 'I thought you'd know by now.'

45

Dirk Van der Berg was seated on a chair in the grubby front room of the black-timbered cottage in Volendam when Vos and Bakker turned up, Aisha Refai fussing over him, checking his scalp. Tonny and Willy Kok lurked by the door whining to be released.

Vos told them straight: no one was going anywhere until he found out what had happened. Then he got the story. The Kok brothers had been on their way back from a few beers in one of the harbour bars. When they approached Stefan Timmers' place they saw a figure run through the open door and vanish down the street.

Van der Berg was inside, half-conscious on the floor.

'Someone biffed him,' Tonny said. 'I'm thinking maybe we should have gone chasing that fellow who skedaddled up the lane. But we were worried about the man here.'

'Moaning and groaning,' Willy added. 'Very strange. Don't get this kind of thing in these parts.'

Laura Bakker was with Aisha, checking on the injured detective.

'What do you mean?' Vos asked.

'Well, this is Stefan's place, isn't it?' Willy said as if it was obvious.

Close to exasperation, Vos asked Van der Berg if he was OK.

'I'm fine!' the detective cried. 'Will you stop these two women fussing over me as if I'm a bloody invalid?'

Aisha was demanding he go to hospital and see a doctor for concussion. Van der Berg hated hospitals and always had.

'You will have to get that looked at, Dirk,' Vos said. Something the brothers had said bothered him. 'Stefan's place? Why does that change things?'

The two of them chuckled. It was Tonny who spoke.

'Well I reckon you two have never looked at your files on Mr Timmers, have you? Try asking the local nick. They'll tell you. Best make some time.'

Vos waved his hands. 'Tell me what?'

'You'd need to be soft in the head to come in here burgling,' Willy told him. 'Stefan's not a man to mess with. I wouldn't. Not if it was the two of us up against him. Hard as nails and twice as nasty.'

Tonny nodded.

'Whoever it was hoofing down the street . . . he didn't know our Stefan. God . . . If he'd been at home he'd have given the daft sod the kicking of a lifetime. Get me?'

Van der Berg was on his feet, the women squawking at him.

'We get you, boys,' he said, keeping a hand to his head. 'I owe you a beer. But not now.' He glanced at Vos. 'We don't need to keep them. Do we?'

'I'll send someone round to take a statement in the morning,' Vos said. 'You can go now.'

'One thing—'

The brothers looked nervous.

'Hobbies?' Van der Berg said. 'Did Stefan have any?'

'Why are you asking us?' Tonny replied. 'He can tell you, can't he?'

'Stefan Timmers is dead,' Vos said, not taking his eyes off them for a second. 'So no. We can't.'

They shuffled on their big feet, scratching their heads, looking lost.

'Dead?' Tonny asked in the end. 'How?'

'Someone shot him. Out in that place you found.'

'The old farmhouse? Nothing to do with us!' Tonny cried. 'We just drove past—'

'It's OK,' Van der Berg said. 'We know it's nothing to do with you. But he's dead all the same. That's all we can say.'

Willy Kok looked close to tears.

'Bloody hell. What's going on? First that nurse. Now Stefan. This is what you people put up with in the city. Not here. Volendam's a quiet place. Quiet people who mind their own business. Why can't you let us be?'

'Hobbies,' Van der Berg said. 'What did he do?'

'Stefan?' Tonny cried. 'How many times do we have to tell you? He was a bad 'un. Fighting. Drinking. God knows what else. We steered well clear of him. So did anyone with some sense.'

Bakker didn't take her eyes off them.

'Those aren't hobbies, boys,' she said. 'They're just the way things are.'

Tonny Kok shook his grizzled head.

'I don't know what in God's name you're talking about. Jesus. He wasn't a man I cared for but all the same. You said we can leave. Well . . . can we?'

Van der Berg looked at Vos who said, 'Thanks for helping here. I appreciate it.'

He watched them shuffle out.

'Before we take you to hospital would you care to tell us what that was about, Dirk?'

Van der Berg led them through the door to what was once a tiny smokehouse, now a kind of video studio.

'I'd been in here when whoever hit me turned up,' he said, indicating to Aisha to put on some latex gloves. 'One man I'd say, from the footsteps. Didn't see him. Too interested in this stuff. You know when you get that buzz in your veins? Like you've found something? Well . . .'

He looked back at them and grinned.

'I had it then. Big. Stefan's been taking pictures here. For years. Pretty pictures. Some of it maybe porn. Some . . . just home movies. There's stuff going back a couple of decades, I reckon.'

The desk looked different. It took him a moment to realize why. The laptop was gone, along with the camera. The drawer was half open. Aisha pulled it all the way and Van der Berg looked in.

'There,' he said, pointing to a gap on the left. 'I found a stack of DVDs, all dated. Important I guess. That's what he came for. That and the computer and the camera. All gone.'

Aisha reached in and drew out a few old VCR cassettes, the tape ripped and snapped, a brown shiny mass of ribbons.

'Guess he didn't have time for these,' she said. 'So he just tore them to shreds.'

All the same she took out an evidence bag and started to tidy the remnants away.

'Get people in here,' Vos ordered. 'See if you can pick up something on whoever attacked Dirk.'

'It's not bad,' Van der Berg objected. 'I've had worse on a Saturday night in the Jordaan. I really don't need to go—'

'In the car,' Vos insisted. 'Laura can hold your hand if you like.'

He looked the way Sam did when Vos said no to him: down-in-the-mouth and fearful.

'What happened your end?' Van der Berg asked. 'Much?'

'Later,' Vos said, heading for the door.

46

One hour later, close to midnight, Vos picked up Sam from the Drie Vaten and took him for a walk along the Prinsengracht. To his surprise De Groot hadn't made one of his customary phone calls. Perhaps the commissaris was starting to feel as puzzled and depressed as he was by the bleak turn of events.

It was a warm night, even this late. Close to the old courthouse on the way to Leidseplein Vos stopped and sat down on a bench by the water. There was still traffic on the canal, tourist boats mostly, out with diners or party revellers dancing to music. Sam, gauging his owner's mood as always, was quiet and well behaved. Vos's hand strayed down to the dog's wiry fur, stroking his head, the soft ears. The terrier groaned with delight.

Then came a short bark, one of familiarity. A tall figure emerged along the canal from the direction of the Drie Vaten, walking with a stiff gait Vos knew only too well.

'Frank,' he said, surprised. 'You're out late.'

De Groot joined him on the seat, smiled at the dog and stroked him under the chin.

'I looked in the bar. Your boat. I may be a lousy detective but it's not hard to work out where you'd be if you weren't there.'

'You were a very good detective,' Vos said.

'Did my best,' De Groot replied. 'I can't imagine you without this little chap now, you know. You make quite a pair. Is Van der Berg OK?'

'Bang on the head – and it's a very hard head.'

'Don't minimize these things, Pieter. A bang on the head can turn serious.'

Vos ruffled Sam's fur.

'Sorry. It's been a shitty day all round. I imagine you heard.'

'The uncle. The Visser woman. Yes. We're going to have to suspend those uniformed men. It was stupid.'

Vos watched another glitzy boat cruise down the canal.

'I don't think that's a priority, is it? Apportioning blame.'

'The woman died.'

'I'm aware of that. I was there, remember? She was stinking drunk. Driving like a lunatic. Running away for some reason.'

De Groot didn't seem to be listening.

'There'll be an inquest. Publicity. I'll get questions from all directions. I can't pretend it was just an accident.'

'But it was.'

'All the same . . .'

Vos knew he was right. This was what management was about. Coping with unexpected situations. Dealing with problems others couldn't be bothered with. Someone had to do it and he was deeply grateful none of the drudgery fell to him.

'I'm tired, Frank. And grumpy.'

'Join the club,' De Groot bleated. 'I came to apologize. I've been biting everyone's heads off ever since I came back from that wedding. I don't know. You go to something lovely like that. Something as near as dammit perfect. And then . . . the next day . . .' He reached for the dog again. Sam yawned with pleasure. 'The Timmers case too. You get used to dealing with some shit in this job. Just occasionally it gets to you.'

'I tried to call.'

'Tell me now.'

So Vos gave him more detail on what he had, from the find in the farmhouse to Visser's death and Van der Berg being attacked in Volendam.

'Whoever it was came looking for pictures?'

'Seems so,' Vos agreed.

'Did they get them?'

Vos thought back to the smokehouse, what was gone, what was left.

'Dirk thought Timmers was in the process of transferring everything from tape to DVD. He had some kind of conversion kit.'

'What sort of pictures?' De Groot wondered.

'From what he saw . . . maybe porn. Some local stuff too. Family videos. We don't know.' He recalled the way Aisha carefully stashed the torn brown tape from the cassettes into the evidence bag. 'The laptop got taken. The DVDs. He ripped up the cassettes.'

'Not likely to know then?'

'I doubt it.'

'What next?'

Sam shuffled over and parked himself on Vos's shoes.

'Depends what your man from Rotterdam comes up with.'

'He's not my man from Rotterdam! Schuurman's on a course. The department's understaffed as it is. I didn't want any juniors sticking their oars in here. I get it from all directions, Pieter. Above. Below. Sideways. I need to think these things through.'

'Whereas I just get it from you,' Vos said with a smile.

'Right. You will focus on those girls now, won't you?'

Vos hadn't given the Timmers sisters much thought at all but still he said, 'Working on it.'

De Groot pulled out his phone and showed him a couple of emails. One was from Veerman in Marken confirming that Kim Timmers had been warned on several occasions for stealing items from staff and visitors. Money. Jewellery. Phones.

'Pretty obvious they stole her handset then used it that night. You wanted to know how they could do this. There's your answer. They called their uncle. A small-time hood by the way. I can send you his record too.'

But Irene Visser said Stefan never visited them in Marken. Not that he mentioned this to De Groot.

'Please.'

'The uncle picked them up. They murdered Klerk. Took his body to Marken. Came back to the farmhouse and maybe . . . maybe had an argument . . . I don't know. You'll work it out.'

Vos stayed silent.

'We need to find them, Pieter. Don't we?'

'We do.'

'And I don't want to hear about what happened ten years ago. The past's past. This is now.' De Groot got to his feet. He looked old and somewhat creaky. 'Well. It's late. I suspect we're in for a long day tomorrow.' He bent down and patted Sam one last time. 'I'll leave you now.'

Vos watched him go and so nearly said what was in his head . . . *But Irene Visser ran.*

Not from a farmhouse she'd never visited. It was something else and there were only two places the answer could lie: in Volendam or Marken.

He took out his phone and called the number Gert Brugman had left at the bar of the Drie Vaten two nights before. Brugman was the only person they knew who'd seen the sisters since they vanished into the city. He'd provided a description. Or rather the news they were still blonde-haired. Perhaps there was more.

No answer.

Rijnders was running the night team, a sound, inquisitive man.

'Frans Lambert,' Vos said when he got through.

'Is this a pub quiz?' Rijnders asked. 'Because if it is I should warn you. Bands of the Seventies and Eighties? My specialist subject.'

'Well you know then.'

Rijnders laughed.

'Drummer with The Cupids. Good musician. Serious guy. Big man. Could have been a professional footballer if he wanted. Ajax academy offered him a contract as a kid. Preferred music.

Played sessions with some big American and British bands. More rock than pop, but I guess with The Cupids he went where the money was for a while. He could have moved to the US and earned a fortune for session work, or so everyone reckoned. Except there were some contractual issues with his manager or something. Then came the Timmers thing . . .'

'Any idea why he vanished?'

There was a long sigh on the end of the phone.

'It's one of those great rock mysteries. Just before all that trouble broke he flew out to Asia somewhere. He was big into Eastern philosophy and stuff. No one's seen hide nor hair of him since. I'm not aware of any sightings of him running a frites joint in Utrecht but then he's not Elvis. Just the long-lost drummer of The Cupids, mostly forgotten except by pub quiz saddos like me. Anything else?'

'I want you to find him,' Vos said. 'I'll be in before eight. By then would be good.'

After that he thought long and hard. He meant what he'd said to Laura Bakker earlier that night. He did trust her now, and in truth he hadn't much before. She was young. Impetuous. Clumsy sometimes. But she was also dogged, curious and good with detail.

He called her. A sleepy voice answered the phone. Vos wondered if she was on her own. He knew nothing about her private life at all. It would have been impertinent to ask.

'I hope I didn't wake you.'

A drowsy yawn and then, 'It's late. What do you think?'

'I thought maybe . . . you'd still be up.'

'Well I wasn't.'

'Oops. Sorry.'

'Oops,' she repeated. 'You think you can get away with anything if you say that.'

'Mostly I can.'

She laughed and said, 'True. So what's happened?'

'Probably lots,' he said. 'It's just that no one's told me. Yet.'

'That was worth waking me up for?'

'First thing in the morning I need you to go to Marken.'

A pause.

'And . . . ?'

'A fishing expedition.'

'You sent Dirk on one of those today. He ended up getting bashed on the head.'

'I'd rather you avoided that. Tell the director there . . .'

'Veerman.'

'Tell him you need to see Irene Visser's office. Her papers. Talk to him. Talk to the staff. The patients.'

'Her neighbours?'

That was a good suggestion, he thought. Just a wrong one.

'Don't bother with the neighbours just yet. There's something in that place we don't get. I should have seen it before.'

'You mean the thing she was running from?'

Sam got up, yawned and stretched on the cobbles.

'Exactly,' he said. 'Is that OK?'

'Oh yes.' He could tell she was flattered, not that she was going to let on. 'Very.'

47

Thursday. Vos trudged into work at half past seven. De Groot had suspended the two young uniform officers whose clumsiness had led to Irene Visser's death. Given the interest the media were starting to take in the case it was probably inevitable. Nothing made a good story like a murder investigation going wrong.

Van der Berg was at his desk, brushing aside all inquiries about his head. Laura Bakker had gone to Marken. De Groot was nowhere to be seen. There was nothing from forensic Vos couldn't have guessed already. Both men died from single blasts of a shotgun. No sign of a weapon, no prints, no incriminating physical evidence so far.

The night team had found Stefan Timmers' decrepit Land Rover burned out near Volendam harbour. The blackened shell was downstairs being looked over.

'Going to take a while to get anything out of that,' Rijnders said as he got ready to knock off shift. 'If they can. The fact his shotgun case was in the farmhouse . . . Must have been his weapon that killed Klerk, don't you think?'

There was no sign of the weapon itself. Vos had wondered about setting up a fingertip search around the farmhouse. But it was August. De Groot would start moaning about stretched resources, with some justification. Waterland was a flat green wilderness. If it were simply fields a concerted search might reveal something. But the whole area was criss-crossed with a multitude of dykes and canals, some narrow, some broad. Anyone wanting to hide a firearm would surely throw it in the green, opaque water. Then it was as good as gone.

The file on Timmers was pretty damning too. A string of

convictions, including three for serious assault. He'd spent six months in jail for the last. Local intelligence suggested he worked as a runner for hire whenever the local gangs needed drugs or other contraband shifted.

'Just the man you'd want for dirty work,' Rijnders observed.

'He didn't visit the girls in Marken, though.' Vos still couldn't make the connection. 'And why . . . why come back to the place they shot Klerk? Why take the risk?'

Rijnders said cheerily, 'Well that's for the day team to discover, isn't it?'

He was about to leave when Vos reminded him about the drummer.

'Oh. Sorry. Frans Lambert. Yes.' He bent down and brought up something on the computer. 'Short of it is . . . he's dead. Surprise, surprise.'

It was a story from an English-language newspaper in Bali, five years before. Vos noted the date, around the time the Timmers files went missing.

The clipping was headlined, 'Expat Dutch Businessman Lost at Sea'. It was just six paragraphs accompanied by a photograph of a tall, fit-looking middle-aged man with a greying moustache standing next to some gym equipment. The caption read, 'Bram Engels, proprietor of Prinsen Health Club'.

'Bram Engels?'

'No. It's Frans Lambert,' Rijnders insisted.

He pulled up a series of earlier shots of The Cupids. The same man, same moustache and serious smile.

'I made a few calls to the police out there and our embassy. It seems Mr Engels turned up around the time Frans vanished. He had some money with him. Started a fitness and sauna club. Owned a small boat. Just like Frans did when he lived in Volendam. He played drums in one of the local nightclubs too. Everyone says he was really good. Went out with a girlfriend one day. Fishing. Swimming. Who knows?' He pulled up a photo of a small cruiser, seemingly adrift on a bright blue sea. 'They find the boat. They don't find Bram. Or Frans for that matter.'

'They didn't get a body?'

'The woman gave a statement to the police. He went for a swim. She had a nap. He never came back. A month later they found some remains. He's buried in a place called Seminyak. It seems he'd given up on the Netherlands. That was his new home.'

'You're happy with this?' Vos asked.

'The police say he's dead. The embassy say he's dead. The business went into liquidation after it happened. There's no trace of any financial activity. Nothing to suggest it wasn't him in the water.'

'What about the money? Royalties? The Cupids must have—'

'That would all go through the manager.' Rijnders scowled. 'Word was that Jaap Blom was a bit of a bastard. He kept his musicians on a basic wage, pocketed the rest, handed out some extras when they started to moan about talking to lawyers. Told them what to do, what to play, where. And if they even whispered about going solo . . .' The detective put a pretend gun to his head and said, 'Bang.' Then he thought for an instant and added, 'It's just gossip, and the music world's full of that, but people say Jaap could turn pretty nasty if anyone asked for too much. I know he's a nicer-than-nice politician now. But word was he'd threaten to cut your fingers off back then. If you pissed him off.'

Vos stared at the photos of Frans Lambert, in Volendam with the band, under a false name in Bali.

'Maybe you should ask him,' Rijnders said.

'Chance would be a fine thing.'

The night man scratched his chin.

'What do you mean? Didn't De Groot pass it on? Jaap Blom's coming in here at nine fifteen. He heard we were scratching around The Cupids. Offered to help. I thought—'

Vos picked up his phone and said, 'I haven't checked my messages yet. Thanks.'

If Rijnders realized that was a lie he didn't let on.

Nine fifteen. Blom had to come through reception.

Van der Berg was busy sifting through the thick file on Stefan Timmers. Vos called him off.

'I want you to go back in time,' he said.

'May I know why?'

'Not sure.'

Van der Berg nodded.

'I like it when we start this way. Let me guess. Ten years. Back to Volendam.'

'No. Five. And I don't know where.'

There was an awkward silence then Van der Berg said, 'Five. Well here's what I know for starters. Some guy who was director of Marken before Veerman killed himself.'

'What?'

'Threw a rope round a tree in that wood close to where we found Simon Klerk. Put his neck in it. Didn't I mention this?'

'No.'

'Sorry. I saw it when I was nosing through the files. It didn't seem relevant.'

Vos shrugged and said, 'Perhaps it isn't.'

'Perhaps,' Van der Berg agreed. 'Five years. Ollie Haas deleted those records.'

Vos said, 'The same month that missing drummer seems to have drowned in Bali. Under an assumed name.'

'Really?'

'Looks that way.'

Five years. There was one other thing and neither of them was keen to mention it.

'I think that's what Irene Visser was running from,' Vos said instead. 'Not us. Not what happened in that farmhouse. Something different altogether. Perhaps if we—'

He stopped. De Groot was marching through the office. Calm, relaxed, intent. Vos closed down the pages on Frans Lambert as the commissaris marched up to his desk. Then he related a summary of the case so far, the weapons, Klerk and Stefan Timmers.

'Pretty obvious what happened,' De Groot said. 'They've got a thug for an uncle. If they wanted to kill that nurse . . .'

There was still no sign of the sisters, and not the least intelligence from the streets about two blonde girls aged around twenty, hiding somewhere in the city.

'Maybe they've upped sticks,' Rijnders suggested, grabbing his car keys. 'Gone back to Volendam—'

'No one could hide there,' De Groot said. 'It's too small. Too obvious. If you're going to hide you go somewhere big. Somewhere you can be anonymous.'

'They're managing that,' Vos agreed.

'They've murdered two people,' the commissaris added. 'They need to.'

Something bothered Vos. He couldn't understand why two young women on the run would advertise themselves by standing outside Gert Brugman's apartment, making sure they were seen looking just the way they were in Marken. Fugitives usually tried to disguise their appearance. They seemed to be flaunting it.

He made a note to tell the patrols they had to take the description of the sisters with a pinch of salt.

'I had a call from Jaap Blom,' De Groot added. 'He wants to come in with his wife and answer any questions we have. I told him it wasn't necessary but he's back up here for a while. I thought it would be polite.' He gave Vos a sharp look. 'My office, nine fifteen. Just the two of us. We don't need to record it. He's not making a statement.'

'Fine,' Vos said.

'And try not to piss him off.'

48

Laura Bakker drove carefully all the way to Marken and found herself at the institution gates just after nine. There was a TV news unit parked outside, one camera hard up against the barrier, the other filming a reporter talking about the second tragedy to hit the institution in a week.

She drew up, showed her police ID to security then went through to the car park. It was another perfect morning out by the water. Perhaps there'd come a time when she'd cycle out here. Even get Vos to join her. He needed the exercise. She craved the green open spaces of her childhood.

But not now. There was a job to be done. On her own for once. Finally he was extending an invitation to her, one she'd been waiting for, the chance to prove herself.

Climbing out of the car she found herself face to face with a short, ragged-haired girl with elfin features, beaming at her as if amused.

'You're a policewoman, aren't you?'

'I am,' Bakker agreed. 'Have we met?'

'Oh no. I just saw you the other day. I'm an inmate here. They won't let me talk to the likes of you.'

Bakker introduced herself and shook her sweaty hand. The girl had been running by the looks of it. There was sweat on her young face and under the arms of her T-shirt.

'Kaatje Lammers. Nutcase,' she said.

They were alone in the car park. Steam was coming from the ground-floor block she took to be the canteen. Veerman and the medical staff were nowhere to be seen.

'We're talking now, aren't we?'

The girl laughed and said, 'Well spotted.'

'Is there something—'

'Is it true Irene Visser's dead? You lot killed her last night? I heard the cooks talking. They won't let me see the news . . .'

'There was an accident. A car crash. No one killed her.'

'Running away, the cooks said. From what?'

Bakker's phone started ringing. She rejected the call.

'I don't know. I wish I did.'

'Did you ask her about Simon Klerk?'

We tried, Bakker thought. The woman was evasive from the outset. And the fast-moving cycle of events – the missing sisters, Klerk's death, the shocking scene in the farmhouse – meant the case had moved ahead of them, leaving everyone trying to catch up.

'Do you think she had something to tell us?'

'Everyone's got a story,' the girl said with a wink. 'Question is . . . why should they tell it? To you lot? I mean . . . what good is it?'

'I don't know. We could sit down here and talk if you want.'

Rapid footsteps sounded across the asphalt. Veerman was there, dark suit, dark face as usual. He looked furious.

'What is this?' he snapped. 'I'm trying to deal with Visser's death here. Talk to the staff. Try to explain the inexplicable. And you just march in . . . where's Vos?'

'Vos sent me,' Bakker said.

Kaatje Lammers was loving every moment of this.

'Why?' he wondered.

She glanced at the girl, who wasn't going anywhere.

'We've reason to believe Irene Visser was planning to leave Marken in a hurry. I want access to her office. Her computer. Her papers. To people who worked with her.'

'You can't just march in here the day after she died and start turning the place over.'

'I just want to have a look around. That's all. I'll do my best not to upset anyone. It's all . . . routine.'

Kaatje Lammers had her hand over her mouth, stifling a giggle.

'I could start with Kaatje here,' Bakker added. 'You were one of Dr Visser's patients, weren't you?'

'Star pupil. She had all sorts of people coming in to take a look at me. I'm special, you see. Genuine sociopath – I believe that's the expression. Isn't it, Director?'

'Not now,' Veerman said. 'There's no time.'

'I've got all the time in the world!' Kaatje cried. 'What you talking about? If she wants a chat—'

'Kaatje's being transferred,' Veerman broke in. 'To sheltered accommodation in the city. Dr Visser agreed this yesterday. I just need you . . .' He was struggling with something. 'We've got to go through some papers first.'

There was a brief silence. Then Kaatje Lammers slapped her cheek, opened her mouth wide and said, 'Stupid me! How could I forget something like that? See!' She tapped her skull, grinning. 'All wrong up here.'

'Then why are they letting you out?' Bakker asked.

Kaatje shrugged and looked at Veerman.

'These are clinical decisions,' he said. 'I don't intend to discuss individual cases with the police. Do I have to call your superiors and explain that?'

He summoned a uniformed guard walking out of the canteen and told him to show Bakker to Visser's office.

'You can interview who you want, but only with my permission,' he added. 'And I will be present. We'll get your things, Kaatje. Sign those papers. Then I'll find you a car.'

'Great.'

The girl wandered off with him, waving her fingers at Bakker as she walked.

Fifteen minutes later the gates of Marken opened. A black Mercedes took her beyond the iron barrier for the first time since her incarceration. She sat upright in the back, waving at the camera crew through the car window.

49

Back in the city Kim Timmers crouched in front of the TV set watching the live news, mind alive with possibilities.

She followed the black car as it edged out of the familiar Marken gates, saw the dark-haired grinning figure in the back. Mouthed one delighted word, 'Kaatje.'

Mia was upstairs trying to deal with Vera. The day ahead looked empty and boring.

Those trapped in Marken went to one of only three places: the outside world, another hospital, or the safe house in Amsterdam, the place they were headed when Simon Klerk drove his yellow SEAT up the lane with other ideas. She had to recall the timing now. It was early Monday evening that they left the island. Now it was Thursday morning and the world seemed no clearer at all.

Mia was no help. The Englishwoman was getting more awkward by the hour. Soon she'd be mobile and there'd be decisions to make.

She thought of Kaatje Lammers, smiling in the back of the car. When Kim got cold feet about anything in Marken Kaatje was always there to put some steel into her spine. She was more fearless, more ruthless than either of them. A sight more sneaky too.

An excellent ally. A partner in crime.

The world. A hospital. Or that house.

It was a guess but that was all Kim had. She found the bag they came with. Inside was the address Simon had given them. A quiet place near the museum. No locks on the doors. No bars on the gate.

The note went into her pocket then, quiet as a mouse, she let herself out, map in hand, working out the geography of the city as she walked.

Twenty minutes later she was there, a narrow curving road of tall houses not far from the Rijksmuseum. A black car that looked like a taxi turned up not long after. As Kim watched, a security guard from Marken got out of the passenger seat, went to the back door and helped Kaatje Lammers out. She had a bag like the one Simon Klerk had given them. A child's one with Disney characters on the side.

Kim stayed in the shadows of some bushes on the far side of the street. A friendly-looking man came down from the hostel and said hello to Kaatje, taking her bag. A complete stranger. A halfway house they called it. Somewhere you could be free some of the time.

Kaatje stopped on the steps of the red-brick building, turned, smiling, looking sweet the way she could. Kim walked out into the bright day and stared across the road. Their eyes met. It took a moment for the figure opposite to recognize her. Then Kaatje's smile grew bigger and she did that subtle wave with her fingers, a tiny gesture she used a lot.

She mouthed something and vanished inside.

One word, easy to read.

Later.

50

Jaap Blom looked every inch the politician. Trim, smart in a sleek grey suit, a full head of blond hair that almost didn't look dyed. He was at ease as he walked into De Groot's office and found a seat for his wife. Lotte Blom fitted the picture too. An elegant woman, more casually dressed than her husband in black trousers and a white silk shirt. She was perhaps a good ten years younger than him though both possessed the timeless, suntanned look of the wealthy so Vos found it hard to tell. Politics was Blom's world now but there remained a patina of show business glamour about the couple, Jaap with his yellow locks and masterful manner, Lotte with her perfect black hair set in a Loren cut to match her dark Mediterranean features.

Vos recalled the last time he'd seen Gert Brugman, trying to entertain a bored and rowdy audience in one of the Jordaan music bars. Time had been kind to this pair in a way it had never reserved for one of the musicians who surely helped put them where they were now. He recalled Rijnders' words about Blom's management style and reputation. It wasn't difficult to see a powerful, controlling individual behind the politician's mask. Perhaps intimidating if the occasion warranted it.

Lotte Blom said, 'I told Jaap you people had been around in Volendam asking questions about The Cupids. And that horrible thing that happened. After all these years. I thought you might want to talk to us.'

'Where did you hear that?' Vos asked.

Blom took a seat next to his wife and nodded at De Groot.

'All that stuff on the TV,' Lotte Blom went on. 'About the Timmers girls. How you idiots set them free—'

'That wasn't us,' De Groot intervened. 'We knew nothing about their release. Had we been asked—'

'It was a medical decision,' Vos said. 'They wouldn't have consulted us anyway. I don't understand, Mrs Blom. Why are you here?'

'Did I not say?' she asked with a wave of her tanned and neatly manicured hand. 'Jaap's in The Hague most of the time. Working all hours, not that anyone appreciates it. I prefer to keep house for him in Edam. It's quieter. So I hear what you're up to.'

Only a few kilometres separated the elegant and upper-class town the Bloms made home from the more rowdy and working-class Volendam. Vos could appreciate word would get around. He still didn't think they'd made that much noise.

'My wife heard you were reopening the case,' Jaap Blom cut in. 'The family. Poor Rogier's death. All that crap the papers tried to push his way. He just loved kids. That was all. I don't spend as much time up here as I'd like. So we thought . . . while I'm here I'd make myself available. In case I can help. So?' He gestured with his open hands. 'Any questions?'

'We're not reopening the case,' De Groot told him.

'In the sense that it was never closed,' Vos added. 'We still don't know who murdered Gus, Freya and Jo Timmers.'

'Do you have new information?' Blom asked.

'We're trying to find the surviving Timmers girls,' he said very carefully. 'It wouldn't be proper for me to discuss an investigation in progress—'

De Groot leapt in quickly.

'Mr Blom has some responsibility for justice issues within the House of Representatives. He's not someone who's just walked in off the street.'

'All the same . . .'

Blom stared at Vos and said, 'A good friend of mine died that night. Another vanished and I still don't understand why. As for Gert . . . he was a mess anyway. But what happened then marked us all. Cost me a damned lot of money too.' He checked himself at that. 'Not that money's important. I made that band. Put them together. Told them what to play and fixed it so it sounded good. Kept them in the charts longer than they deserved, too, when we shifted the sound a bit.' He winced and pulled at his hair. 'Not that you hear some of that later shit on the radio any more, thank God. Just the old stuff. The originals.'

'As I said,' Vos replied, 'our focus is on finding Mia and Kim Timmers. And trying to understand what happened to Simon Klerk. And their uncle.'

Lotte Blom snorted.

'Huh! Stefan Timmers? I grew up in Volendam. I can tell you about him. An out-and-out criminal. A thug for hire. Gus was scared of him. Everyone was. As for Freya . . .'

Her husband was squirming in his seat.

'What about her?' Vos asked.

'She'd do anything men wanted to get her own way. As for what happened—'

'Love, love,' Jaap Blom said, putting a hand on her arm. 'Enough. They're dead. Whatever they were like—'

'And to think those she-devils of hers murdered poor Rogier.' She stared at Vos and asked, 'They did, didn't they?'

'So it would seem,' he replied. 'I didn't handle the case.'

'Do you not have an opinion?'

De Groot intervened and said, 'We're dealing with today. Not what happened ten years ago.'

Blom shrugged.

'As you can see, gentlemen, it was my wife's idea to come here. I think she's probably said what she wanted. Can I help in some way? If so—'

'What happened?' Vos asked before De Groot could stop him. 'That day in Volendam? The talent contest?'

Blom laughed and said, 'Surely you know. Brigadier Haas investigated everything very thoroughly as far as I recall.'

'I'd just like to hear it.'

What followed was short and plain. Freya Timmers took her three daughters to sing on the stage by the harbour during the summer fair. All three Cupids, Glas, Brugman and Lambert, were the judges, though most people thought Blom would tell them which way to vote. As soon as the contest was over and the prizes handed out Lambert caught a cab to Schiphol to go on holiday in the Far East, never to return. Rogier Glas and Blom went to the recording studio to work on some new songs. Gert Brugman stayed around the waterfront drinking with the locals.

'What time did Glas leave?' Vos asked.

The politician frowned.

'I went through all this with Haas. We packed in about eight. I drove home to Edam. Rogier went to pick up his van. He had a cottage out of town. Next thing I hear . . .'

'Haas told us,' Lotte Blom said firmly. 'That Timmers girl and their parents got killed the moment they set foot in the house. Someone was waiting for them. One of the neighbours heard some screams.' The memory seemed to amuse her. 'Did nothing of course.'

'Why not?' Vos wondered.

She stared at him as if the answer was obvious.

'Gus Timmers was an animal. Like his brother. There were always lots of screams. Him. Her. Those kids of theirs. I doubt you people would even have turned up if someone had called.'

Freya was furious the girls had only won a runner-up prize, Blom said. She'd gone home with Jo and her husband, leaving Mia and Kim to pick up whatever bauble they got. They'd left just before eight, found the door to their home open, walked inside . . .

Vos asked, 'Why did Mia and Kim think Rogier Glas was responsible?'

Lotte Blom laughed in his face and said, 'I can't believe you're asking us that. I don't know why we came here. Truly.'

De Groot huffed and puffed and then said, 'Freya Timmers

had tried to lodge a complaint with Haas the previous week. She said someone connected with The Cupids had . . . abused the girls' trust.'

'Who?'

Blom shook his head.

'Haas took this up with me. It was all a fairy story. She was trying to get me to sign up the girls. A recording contract. Everyone knew The Cupids were finished. Except them. The best I could fix them up with by then were a few holiday camp gigs. Maybe an Eighties revival tour. She thought those kids could take their place. I might have signed them, but not for the kind of money she was after. It was ridiculous. I assumed going to Haas was her way of trying to force things. Maybe she talked those kids into believing it too. They adored her. She was the loving mother. They were her three darling angels. There wasn't anything they wouldn't have done for Freya.'

'That bitch slept with half the men in Volendam trying to get what she wanted,' Lotte Blom muttered.

'No, no.' Her husband tried to calm her down. 'It wasn't that bad. She just . . . liked to get around. And they're dead. Whatever we think of them . . .'

'I still don't understand why the girls thought it was Rogier Glas,' Vos pointed out.

De Groot glanced at his watch. Jaap Blom did the same.

'The truth is we don't know,' the commissaris said. 'When they were taken into custody they wouldn't talk at all. Not that it mattered. They were there. They had the knife. There was no one else around.'

Vos considered his options then looked at Blom and asked, 'Where were you on Monday night?'

'At home. With Lotte.'

'Doing what?'

'I was watching TV,' she said. 'Jaap spent the evening dealing with government papers. Ministry papers. As he usually does. No time off—'

'What are you suggesting?' Blom snapped.

Vos sighed.

'I'm not suggesting anything. I'm just asking the questions police officers always ask.' He smiled. 'If we didn't I expect we'd be in trouble with the ministry. Wouldn't we?'

No answer to that.

'You didn't go—?'

'I drove back from The Hague in the morning. We had lunch at a restaurant in the town. We never set foot out of the house after—'

'Where were you last night?'

Blom was getting mad.

'This is ridiculous! The same! At home! Why—'

'That's enough,' De Groot barked.

'Last night someone assaulted an officer of mine,' Vos continued. 'In Volendam. And stole what I believe to be crucial evidence from Stefan Timmers' cottage.'

There was a steely, arrogant glint in Jaap Blom's eyes at that moment.

'I am an elected member of the House of Representatives. Not a common criminal.'

'We're done here,' De Groot announced.

'Have you ever been to Marken?' Vos asked.

A long silence. Lotte Blom muttered something inaudible under her breath. Then her husband said, 'I'm a politician. I live in Edam. I visit lots of places all the time. Of course I've been to Marken—'

'I meant the institution. Not the village. Did you ever visit there? In an official or a private capacity? Have you ever met Kim and Mia Timmers since that night ten years ago?'

'This is ridiculous,' Lotte Blom complained. 'And insulting.'

De Groot was growling.

'No,' her husband said. 'To all those questions.' He turned to his wife. 'Are we done here? Do you think this was worth it?'

Lotte Blom uttered a long sigh then opened her bag and played with her phone.

'Thanks for coming,' the commissaris said and got to his feet. They shook hands, all of them, and the Bloms left.

'I had to ask, Frank,' Vos pleaded.

'You really shouldn't call me by my first name.'

'I don't when people are here.'

'But you do.'

'Sorry.'

Vos stood up and looked around the office.

It was sunny out by the canal. If it was his day off he'd be spending it lazing on the boat with Sam, heading for an afternoon beer across the road in the Drie Vaten. That thought was tantalizing.

'I really don't mind if you'd rather someone else took over this case. I won't object. Honestly.'

Not that he meant it. He just wanted to hear the response.

'I don't have anyone else, do I? It's August. Every sane man out there's on holiday.'

He played with a photo frame on the desk. It was of his daughter's wedding. De Groot looked as if he wished he were back there in the church.

'What next?' he asked.

'I track down those girls. That's what you want, isn't it?'

De Groot nodded.

Vos left.

51

Veerman asked Aartsen, a ginger-haired day nurse, to stay with Bakker every inch of the way around Marken. He was about thirty-five, a timid, tubby man. It was clear he'd rather be anywhere else in the world.

She started in Visser's office, a tidy room that overlooked the wood next to the lake. The tents of the forensic team that had handled Klerk's body were still there, as if someone had forgotten about them. Aartsen started moaning about how he had work to do.

'Me too,' Bakker replied and went to Visser's desktop computer first. 'How do I get the password?'

He didn't know. He was a nurse, he said. She called Veerman. He didn't have a clue either. The network was handled externally, by an outsourcing outfit in the city. He could put in a request for a password retrieval, but it normally took a day or so.

She turned to the filing cabinet, three drawers deep by the window. It was locked. Aartsen didn't know where the key was. Neither did Veerman.

'Do you do your own maintenance?' she asked. 'Or is that outsourced too?'

There was a handyman employed part-time. He had a workshop near the canteen. She got Aartsen to take her there. It was the handyman's day off but the place was open so she could wander in, check through the tools and then walk off with a decent-sized, shiny new crowbar in her hand.

Aartsen was on the phone to Veerman before she even got to the stairs back to Visser's office.

'You can't damage institution property,' the nurse insisted, trying to push ahead and block her way.

'I'm just going to pick the lock,' Bakker said cheerily, waving the crowbar in his face. 'It's a technical trick we learn in the police. You should watch and learn.'

Veerman turned up just as she got the crowbar inside the lip of the top drawer. Bakker heaved. The drawer flew open. The director stood at the door, arms folded, not saying a word as Aartsen stuttered his way through a series of excuses and apologies.

The cabinet came away easily under the pressure. Laura Bakker pushed it to one side with her hand. The thing toppled over almost immediately. She dragged open the drawers. Empty files in the top one. Nothing in the middle. A red leather handbag in the bottom.

Veerman watched in silence. Aartsen quietened down. She put on a pair of gloves and opened up the handbag. There was a rip in the side. It was obviously an old one, discarded because it was damaged, nothing inside but fluff and dust.

'You don't seem surprised, Director,' she said.

'Most of our work's computerized these days. Why would I be?'

'What's the point of keeping a filing cabinet then?'

She looked at the drawers more closely. There was no dust in them. The runners had been used. This had been a place Visser stored things until recently.

'Irene did things her own way,' he replied. 'I don't know how exactly. She was clinical staff. I was admin. It wasn't my job to tell her what to do. And now she's dead.'

Bakker wondered whether it was worth going to her home and taking a poke around.

'What was she trying to hide?' she asked, half to herself.

'I'm not aware she was trying to hide anything.'

'She fled the house when we went to question her. We thought it was because she was connected to Klerk's death. But she wasn't. The phone was stolen. Lots of things get pinched here, don't they?'

Aartsen stared at his shoes. Veerman said, 'Our patients are very disturbed. We have to put up with things that might result in disciplinary action in prison. Turn a blind eye to them.'

'Did you do that? Did you know Visser was ignoring things? The theft of her phone?'

He was getting tetchy.

'I didn't sit over her every minute of the day. That's not my job. And it's not my style. Now . . .' He walked over and set the broken filing cabinet upright. 'Unless you want to damage some more of our property perhaps you could find something else to do. I've business to attend to.' He looked at Aartsen. 'See her out, will you?'

Bakker couldn't think of anything else to say, anywhere new to look. This was her first big individual test and it was all going so wrong.

They went downstairs and crossed the car park to take the crowbar back. By the workshop was another door marked 'Staff Only'.

'What's that?'

'It's the staff cloakroom,' Aartsen said.

'What's there?'

He groaned.

'Coat hangers. Toilets. Showers. Lockers.'

He looked glum as if he'd said too much. She pushed her way in. At the end of the room was a ceiling-to-floor set of metal lockers with the same institutional look as Visser's filing cabinet. She walked along until she found one labelled 'S. Klerk'.

'I take it you've cleared this out?'

Aartsen didn't look at her as he said, 'I don't know. It's all gone crazy this week. Why would—? No. *No. Please.*'

The door was locked so she pushed the crowbar under the lip

before he could finish. One heave, harder than the pressure she'd needed for the filing cabinet, and the locker was open. Bakker pulled on a pair of latex gloves then took out her pocket torch and shone it inside.

'Director Veerman needs to see this,' the nurse announced.

'The more the merrier,' she said.

52

Laura Bakker's nervous hand reached inside Simon Klerk's locker and retrieved the first thing it found. A hand towel, crumpled and worse for wear. She knew what to do straight away: sniff it.

Veerman marched in at that moment and demanded to know what was going on.

Two months earlier Bakker had been on the team for a particularly nasty rape in the red-light district. A street woman attacked by a group of drunks on the way home. They'd nailed the leader of the culprits through a towel in a coffee shop he'd visited afterwards. She'd found that. Vos had been proud.

Three rapid strides then Veerman came up close and told her to leave. Bakker held out the towel and said, 'What does that smell like to you?' She pointed to one of several stains on the white-and-red-striped fabric. 'There's a clue.'

He stared at her as if she were crazy. She sighed, got an evidence bag out of her pocket and popped the towel inside.

'Well we'll soon find out. Why didn't you tell me about the lockers?'

'Why would I?' he asked.

'Did Irene Visser have one?'

'No. She had an office. Why would she need a locker? What are you doing?'

'This . . .'

Filthy jeans and a pair of mud-caked short galoshes came out next. There was a different smell to them. Diesel, she thought, and salt water. Then came something that prompted a memory: Sara Klerk in Marnixstraat asking out of nowhere if they'd found her husband's phone.

Here it was, a fancy Sony, the waterproof kind. She pressed the power button. Nothing happened. Flat battery she hoped. Perhaps that was why he left it when he took the sisters out of Marken. Or he didn't want to be disturbed. The phone went into another evidence bag. After that there was one thing left. A set of keys on a fob that bore the name 'Evinrude'.

Back in Friesland Bakker had an uncle who liked to go fishing. He owned a small boat. The outboard motor on the back was the same American brand.

There were three keys on the ring. One was small and had the Evinrude logo too. The other two looked like standard modern door keys. She turned the fob over. Scrawled in blue ink, a few years old she guessed, were the words 'Flamingo Club: Spare Set'. Above those, held down with old sticky tape, was a paper cut-out of a pink bird flapping its wings, grinning with its odd-shaped beak.

'So Simon Klerk kept a boat?' she asked, looking at Veerman.

'I've no idea.'

She waited and wondered: was that it?

'He kept this stuff here, Veerman. Not at home.'

'He never mentioned anything about a boat.'

'Not to me either,' the nurse chipped in.

'These are a spare set of keys for somewhere called the Flamingo Club—'

'Never heard of it,' Veerman interrupted. Aartsen said the same.

Bakker stuck her head inside the locker. There was nothing else.

'Don't touch anything,' she told them. 'I'm going to talk to Marnixstraat—'

'What Simon Klerk did in his spare time was nothing to do with us,' Veerman insisted.

'You must have talked to the man!'

He shook his head.

'Not much. I work days. Until a few weeks ago he was always on night shift. There was no need for me to be here. I barely saw him.'

'I'm days too,' the nurse said, putting his hand up like a child in class. 'I didn't know the guy.'

Bakker tried to picture this. The institution wasn't big. It didn't need many people. There still had to be some kind of hierarchy.

'So who was in charge?' she asked.

'Klerk when he was on duty.' Veerman checked his watch. 'Irene would come in if there was a medical issue. But we don't have many of those. Klerk was a trusted man. One of the longest-standing members of staff we had. He'd be here with the night security staff. This is a remote secure facility. Not a prison.'

'I can see that.'

'Are you leaving now?' he asked. 'Or do I call De Groot?'

Bakker went to the car and put the evidence bags in the boot. After that she pulled out the USB charger for her own phone, attached the cable to Klerk's Sony and plugged it into the cigarette lighter.

Sara Klerk's phone number she got from the office system.

The woman worked in one of the local food factories. Casual labour in all probability. But she wasn't at work then. There were street sounds: cars and voices.

'It's Officer Bakker,' she said when the call got through. 'I need to know where your husband kept his boat.'

There was a long pause then, 'What boat? We don't have a boat.'

'Are you sure?'

'Of course I'm sure. What would we do with a boat?'

'I don't know. Go fishing. Pleasure trips—'

'We've never owned a boat.'

'OK. What about a place called the Flamingo Club? Do you know where that is?'

There was a curse on the line.

'Have you found those bitches yet? They killed my husband.'

'We're looking,' she said. 'Making steady progress.'

'Those cows—'

'The Flamingo Club, Mrs Klerk.'

'I don't know what the hell you're talking about.'

'Simon never mentioned it to you? He didn't belong to any associations? Men's clubs? Drinking? Fishing? Football—'

'He worked. He came home. We got on with our lives. Then those two devils took him from me. Why don't you do something about them?'

The line went dead. Bakker stared at the phone, puzzled. Too many questions. Too few answers. Then she called Vos and filled him in.

'Good work,' he told her. 'Get back here with those things. Let's see what they add up to.'

'I think they add up to Simon Klerk having sex with someone,' she said. 'In Marken. Or close by. On a boat. This Flamingo Club.' That last irked her more than anything. 'What kind of thing can that be? I tried Googling it. There's nothing . . .'

Vos took a look on the police system and couldn't find anything there.

'Just come back, Laura. Then we'll work out where to go next.'

'Where we go next will be here, won't it? It'll be in Waterland. Where I am now. If this thing's to do with boats how far away can it be?'

He was hesitating, which meant she could win this one.

'Tell you what,' she said before he could butt in. 'I'll take a drive along the dyke. Marken to Volendam. See if there's anything promising.'

'Well—'

'I'll try and track down Sara Klerk too. She's not the kind of woman you can talk to over the phone.'

There were voices in the background. She could hear Van der Berg trying to say something.

'Fine,' Vos agreed, suddenly distracted. 'Do that. Then come home.'

Laura Bakker wanted to laugh but didn't. Vos sounded ill at ease.

'Home,' she said. 'Right. Will do.'

53

Van der Berg had a twinkle in his eye. Vos recognized that. They went to Vos's desk, out of earshot of everyone, and he laid out what he'd found.

What happened five years before? In Marken two things. On May the 20th that year a thirteen-year-old female inmate at the institution had been found drowned in the Markermeer, half a kilometre offshore. Ollie Haas had investigated. The death had been recorded as accidental, probably suicide.

'What had the kid done?' Vos asked.

'Damn all from what I can see. She was in care at a kids' home in the area. There'd been a row. She'd flown at a visitor she said had tried to molest her.'

Vos reached for the file under Van der Berg's arm. The detective retreated, wagged a finger and smiled.

'Not done yet. I got the autopsy report. The files didn't get canned for her. She was recovered by a fishing boat at nine in the morning, face down in the water. She'd had sex not long before she died.'

'DNA?' Vos asked.

Van der Berg sighed.

'Haas's report said she'd been threatening suicide for some time. The kid had been kept in secure accommodation inside Marken. Somehow she'd got out.'

'You still try to find out who she'd been with.'

'Yes, well. He didn't.'

Vos waited.

'Two weeks later the director of the place, Kees Hendriks, was found in the woods. Not far from where Simon Klerk was buried. Hanging from a tree. Haas handled the case. Suicide. Again.'

Van der Berg put the file on the desk and pulled out a photo. A girl who looked no more than twelve. Sad plain face, straight blonde hair, long and tousled as if she didn't care. There was a cut above her right eye and a bruise on her temple.

'That was taken after she had the fight in the kids' home. There's no record of who she was accusing. If it got to the police . . .'

'Wait,' Vos cut in. 'They put her in Marken and never even went to court.'

'Protective custody,' Van der Berg explained. 'All legal and above board. Kees Hendriks had signed off the papers personally. Her name was Maria Koops.'

Vos checked the dates against his notes. On May the 20th the girl was found drowned. Two weeks later the director of Marken seemingly killed himself. Fourteen days after that most of the files on the Timmers case were deleted from the Marnixstraat system, by Ollie Haas according to his confession, covering his tracks in order to keep his pension. Two weeks later in Bali the missing drummer for The Cupids, Frans Lambert, living under an assumed name, drowned in a boating accident.

One other thing. He checked this on the system and didn't mind if Van der Berg saw. Frank de Groot was made commissaris just after the Koops girl was found dead.

'They didn't keep any of her clothes. Anything that belonged to her. Just these . . .'

A series of photos from the time. The dead girl on the pebble beach at Marken, stiff, arms by her side, next to a police boat. Eyes closed, blonde hair drenched. Around her the boots of men. Then another shot. Haas directing some of the officers. A middle-aged man in a grey suit talking to him. He looked worried.

'That,' Van der Berg said, 'is Kees Hendriks. His picture's in the cuttings from the paper after he killed himself. But here's something that really baffles me.'

He placed a photo on the desk. A recent headstone. Date of birth, date of death. A name, Maria Koops. And two lines chiselled in the grey stone.

> *Love is like a chain that binds me.*
> *Love is like a last goodbye.*

'That's from a Cupids song,' Van der Berg explained. 'Apparently quite a few people in Waterland like it played at their funeral. If—'

'Wait.'

Burials cost money. The state certainly didn't want to foot the bill. Prisoners who died in jail were cremated unless their relatives took over the cost of interment.

'Who paid for all this? The parents?'

'She had a single mother. Couldn't be traced. The father was never named. I called the church in Volendam. Nice guy there, the caretaker. He went out into the graveyard and took that picture on his phone. That's her. He looked up the records. An anonymous donation put that kid in the cemetery. Someone still puts flowers on her grave—'

'Get the girl exhumed,' Vos ordered. 'Don't let De Groot know. Leave that to me.'

'Are you serious? We can't just exhume someone like that. On a whim.'

'It's not a whim,' Vos replied, sounding a touch fractious. 'Get on it . . .'

'We need forensic on side, Pieter. If Schuurman was around maybe he'd be willing. But this new guy? And really . . . why? It won't help us find the Timmers girls. Or who biffed me on the head in Stefan's place last night. Will it?'

'More than one story,' Vos said. 'Maybe you're right. It doesn't mean there's more than one answer.'

Van der Berg was thinking about that when Aisha Refai marched across the office, sheets of paper in her hand, a big smile on her face.

'I need a favour from you,' Vos said when she turned up.

She slapped the pages on his desk.

'Something interesting?' she asked.

'Exhumation. Female. Five years in the ground.'

Aisha grimaced and said, 'You do know how much paperwork that requires? We have to go to court. Get the relatives on side—'

'There are no relatives.'

'That makes it even more complicated. Put it in writing—'

Vos threw up his hands in despair.

'I don't have time for that.'

'Then you won't get your exhumation order. Do you want to look at what I brought you or not?'

They did. Preliminary reports on Simon Klerk and Stefan Timmers.

'A summary will do,' Vos suggested.

She grimaced.

'A summary? Right.'

54

Vera wasn't getting any better. The ankle was more swollen. It probably was broken, Mia thought when she brought her some coffee and a sandwich for lunch. She watched her pick out the ham and leave the bread to one side. There was a sly and calculating look to her now.

'How are you feeling?'

'Can't put any weight on this ankle. Going to be as big as a football by tomorrow. I need a doctor, sweetheart. How do I get the rest of my pills?'

'I don't know.'

'I'll tell you how. You get me out of here. Get me to the hospital. Let them fix up my ankle. We'll all be fine then.'

Mia kept quiet. They couldn't be fine. They never were. It was impossible now.

Trying to make conversation she asked about the past. The Englishwoman told her to look in the top of a set of drawers by the window. Another photo album. She brought it over, sitting on the bed just far enough away to maintain some distance.

Pictures of a younger, healthier woman. Smiling, happy in the city. A few close to the Volendam harbour. Mia could recognize that even though the reality was somewhat hazy and faded now.

'Don't suppose you have picture albums, you and your sister.'

'No,' she agreed. 'We don't.'

That black night a decade ago took everything. Mother, father, sister. The few possessions they valued. She and Kim went from the brink of a golden future, to ... what? Two wretches the world stared at in horror, afraid to touch, to approach.

'Does that mean you don't have memories?'

'No. Not exactly.'

Irene Visser was supposed to have conversations like this. Awkward, probing interviews where she pressed at the part of them that hurt. But that wouldn't happen now. She was dead, in a road accident. It was on the news. So was Uncle Stefan, not that they knew him as anything much but a name and an angry face, coming round the house from time to time, cajoling their father, sidling up to their mother in ways she didn't like and they hated.

'I was telling the truth, love. When I said I don't know who it was pretending to be that sister of yours.'

'Who said they were pretending?'

'Oh Christ.' Vera sighed. 'Jo's dead.'

'I know. What I meant was . . . perhaps it's someone else called Jo. Someone—'

The woman chuckled, a smoker's laugh, sick and old.

'Yeah. Someone who just happens to want you out of Marken. Living here with me. Waiting on God knows what. Sending them messages.'

Mia said nothing.

'Where's your sister? I heard her go out. I didn't hear you two talking.'

'She just left.'

'Think she's all right? In the head I mean. Don't doubt you are. Not so sure about her.' Vera waggled her hurt leg and winced with the pain. 'Hurts like mad if I just move it an inch or so. Got good reason, haven't I?'

'I'm sorry, Vera. Really I am. I won't let it happen again. When—'

'Say someone found him. The bloke who killed them. Your mum and dad and Little Jo. What would you do?'

Another question the dead Irene Visser had never dared ask.

'No idea,' Mia said straight away.

'I know what your sister would—'

'Kim's not well. I'll look after her. Like I did in Marken. I'll keep her out of trouble.'

Vera pushed the empty plate back across the bed.

'You're a good girl,' she said. 'It's a scandal they locked you two up in that place.' A long pause and then, 'You didn't kill him, did you? That man. Glas. I don't believe it. Not for one minute.'

'We said we did. What more do you want to hear?'

'But why?'

Mia Timmers closed her eyes.

A hot summer night. Music, loud and raucous, on the distant waterfront. Blood in the cottage, in the back alley where a man was cut to pieces in his van. A famous musician. Someone they revered. A few people anyway.

'Because we were to blame,' she said and took the plates downstairs.

There was no sign of Kim. No way she could get in touch with her. At some point the money would run out. Vera would be mobile. They'd have to think about what to do, where to go.

There was never a need to face those decisions before. Someone – their mother, their father, another adult – always made them for them.

'Not now,' Mia whispered, staring out of the kitchen window at the dark figures in the coffee shop and the busy men in the kebab-bar kitchen.

She closed her eyes again and heard that old, coarse music, saw the black night, the blood, the face, the mouth of Rogier Glas. Then she sat down at the table, alone for once, and did something she'd never managed when Kim was around.

Mia Timmers began to cry.

55

Laura Bakker's plan was simple. Get off Marken and drive along the lake road to Monnickendam. Then find the single-track lane called Hoogedijk that ran by the side of the Gouwzee, the inner stretch of the Markermeer, all the way to Volendam. Find Sara Klerk if she could. Talk to the woman. Go back to Marnixstraat.

There was scarcely any traffic along Zeedijk as it ran by the dyke north. She skirted the centre of Monnickendam, past modern housing estates and industrial units, then turned right for the minor road, by a large cheese farm packed with tourist buses. After that came the tiny harbour of Katwoude and a string of houses. According to the map this was the last sign of habitation she'd see until she pulled into the Marina Park at Volendam four kilometres away.

The lane was so narrow, with bike tracks on both sides, she wondered how the Kok brothers' tractor managed to do its job. Beyond Katwoude there was nothing except the odd jogger, a couple of cyclists, fields and fields of pasture and rising maize to the left, the low wall of the dyke on her right.

She came to a sharp left bend for the final stretch north to Volendam. The tiny entrance was so well hidden she drove past at first. Then, carefully in the narrow road, she reversed fifty metres to look again. There was a track wide enough for a car, a white barrier in front of it with a large sign, '*Toegang Verboden*'. No admittance. Next to it, crooked from age and the wind, was a plastic flamingo no higher than a child.

Bakker pulled up in front of the barrier, climbed out and looked at the keys from Klerk's spare set. They were inside a plastic evidence bag now. Someone might shriek at her for doing this.

But they weren't there. She was on her own. This was a chance to prove something.

One key looked too small. The other more promising. She tried it and unlocked the barrier, pushing at the white pole until it reared upright on the counterweight by the gate. Back in the car she looked at Klerk's phone. It had picked up some charge so she pulled out the cable and pressed the power button. It booted up quickly and came up with a no signal icon.

With the mildest of curses she took out her own police-issue phone. That was struggling for coverage too. She was at the edge of the lake, in a dip, a black spot perhaps. Nothing to do but drive on. After about a hundred and fifty metres the narrow shingle lane ended at a small car park, asphalt, well made. Though not, perhaps, well used. There was one set of recent muddy tyre tracks and nothing else.

A path wound through a small thicket of elder and bramble. She got out and made her way past the shrubs. This was natural land, not a man-made dyke. The ground rose a good few metres with bushes and vegetation quite unlike that of the flat, bare Waterland pasture behind. After a minute she could see the Gouwzee to her right, a good five metres below what seemed to be almost a cliff in miniature. This couldn't run for long. Further along she could see how the spur of land returned to dyke and the narrow coast lane, beyond that the forest of yacht masts that had to mark the Volendam marina.

Then the track veered sharply to the right and she saw it. A low building, set above the waterline. Green timber to match the vegetation. Two storeys with a single window to the south side. From the lake it would look almost like a large hut. From the road it was invisible.

There were steep steps leading down to a single door. Climbing down, Bakker realized what she was seeing. A small boathouse on stilts, with what looked like a timber landing stage at the foot beneath a top floor that might be used for storage.

Such a building wouldn't seem out of place anywhere near water in the Netherlands. Yet this seemed so well hidden. And as she drew closer she realized the windows in the top floor were closed to the outside world by dark, fully drawn curtains.

She reached the narrow wooden door on the land side of the building. Simon Klerk's key fitted perfectly. She turned the lock and pushed at the handle.

Getting nervous she checked the phone again. Still no signal.

'Well. Can't say I didn't try.'

Then she took out her torch and walked inside.

56

It was a narrative that Vos needed, a linear sequence of events that led from one place to the next. Without that he couldn't picture the crime in his head. The details that Aisha had brought out from forensic were like paint and brushes for an artist. It was his job to wield them and create, from the faint sketches they had, the bigger picture.

Aisha Refai set out the tools for the task.

From the autopsy that Snyder, the man from Rotterdam, had overseen it was clear that Simon Klerk had been tied naked to a chair in the Waterland farmhouse. For some time, she said. There were abrasion marks on his shins and arms, signs that he'd struggled against the ropes.

'You're sure of this?' Van der Berg asked. 'This Snyder guy knows his stuff?'

She looked bashful.

'Snyder's not the most charming man I've met. But he's OK. He does a good job. Honest. I've learned a few things. And . . .' She was a genial woman, mid-twenties with a scarlet headscarf that just about covered her dark hair. 'He thought it better this came from me. To be honest I think he might be a bit scared of you two. Who can blame him?'

Vos pooh-poohed that. She spread out a selection of photos on the table. Klerk's body in the pebbles on Marken. Laid out on the silver table in the morgue. The abrasion marks were obvious in some close-up photos. Then she showed them the rope. Heavy old sisal.

'It was in the farmhouse already,' she said. 'Lying around. We found more in one of the rooms.'

'So this is spontaneous?' Vos asked. 'Something happens. He drives them to a remote location. For whatever reason . . . sexual probably.'

'Seems a reasonable guess,' she agreed.

'How did they manage to overpower him? Klerk couldn't have been a pushover. A nurse working in an environment like that would be used to dealing with violent—'

'Marken was for juvenile girls,' Aisha cut in.

'All the same—'

'You're running ahead of yourself, Vos. Let me take this one step at a time.'

More photos. Tyre marks in the drive. Two sets, one narrower than the other.

'These are for Klerk's car,' she said, pointing at a series of tracks that stopped close to the back door. 'We're pretty sure the others are from Stefan Timmers' four by four. It got badly burned in the fire but I'd assume Timmers drove to the farmhouse in that.'

Van der Berg wanted to know when. Aisha thought for a moment, licked her finger, stuck it in the air, waited then shook her head. There was, she said, no way of putting a time to the tracks. They needed some independent verification. A witness. And that was unlikely out in the wild green pastures of Waterland.

'You want to know how two young women could subdue a grown man. Well . . .' She threw some more photos in front of them. 'There's this. We found it on the floor.'

A knife. Shiny, silver, very sharp from the looks of it, very plain in design. Not a speck of dust so it hadn't been there long.

'That looks like canteen cutlery to me,' Aisha continued. 'Wouldn't be hard for them to steal it in Marken. My guess is they drove to the farmhouse. Klerk wanted something. The girls overpowered him. Walked him inside. Made him strip naked. Tied him to that chair. It's a wild one but—'

'Why?' Van der Berg asked.

'We're forensic, Dirk. We do how. Not why. That's your call.'

He didn't like that answer.

'No need to get smart—'

'She isn't,' Vos interrupted. 'Aisha's right. Though . . .'

If you wanted to kill a man why make him strip first? To humiliate him. That seemed obvious. But the obvious was often wrong. It was what you wanted to hear. The solution you craved. The truth was usually more elusive, a teasing creature lurking in the shadows.

'Questions?' Aisha asked.

'Not yet,' Vos said. 'Let me get this straight. Klerk drove the girls to the farmhouse. They got him inside. Made him strip. Tied him to the chair.'

'Correct.'

'Then they shot him,' Van der Berg added.

She threw up her hands in despair.

'You're trying to spin this out!' he cried.

'No I'm not. I'm trying to understand. What we know. And what we don't know. Because—'

'Because what we don't know's more important than what we do,' Vos noted.

Aisha nodded and said, 'Up to a point.'

'The sisters called in their uncle and said bring along your shotgun. We've got someone we want dead,' Van der Berg guessed. 'And then they—'

'If he doesn't stop this I will go mad,' Aisha moaned.

'But—'

'Shut up, Dirk,' Vos ordered. 'And listen. The ropes.' He'd been staring at the pictures. Something didn't add up. 'The ropes are wrong. They're still tied.'

'The ropes are still tied,' she agreed. 'Which means—'

Vos placed a finger on the nearest picture.

'He freed himself. He wasn't tied to the chair when he was killed.'

'Exactly. From the wound and the spatter it's obvious he was standing up.'

Van der Berg shrugged.

'So what? He worked himself free. Went for them. Uncle Stefan got out his gun.'

Aisha nodded.

'Possibly. The trouble is . . .' She found the pictures of the abrasions again, red weals on Klerk's arms and shins. 'This went on for some time. An hour. Maybe two. Would they just watch a naked man wriggle his way free like that? I don't—'

'No. They wouldn't.' Vos was getting a picture now, a hazy image emerging from the fog. 'That doesn't work at all.'

'So what does?' Aisha wondered.

He ran his fingers over the pictures again.

'Klerk had to be left on his own for a while. Naked. Strapped to the chair. The girls left. They caught that bus. We can time it exactly.'

'Where they were picked up was a good twenty-five-minute walk from the farmhouse,' Aisha agreed. 'Judging by those abrasions . . . we'd have to do some more tests to check . . . but I don't think he could have worked his way out of them by then. Maybe the uncle got the girls later in Amsterdam and brought them back. They lugged the corpse over to Marken. Returned to the farmhouse. He got shot. Except . . .'

She was keeping something in reserve.

'You don't think that, Aisha,' he said.

'I don't know what I think.' She reached into the file and pulled out more photos and some documents. 'Here. Take a look at Uncle Stefan. Tell me what you see.'

57

Jaap Blom owned an apartment in Amsterdam, the mansion in Edam, and a penthouse in The Hague. The first gave him a resident's parking permit so he'd brought his soft-top Mercedes E-Class coupé into the city. The traffic was bad on the way back to their country house. Trapped in a sluggish line of cars trudging towards the IJtunnel Lotte Blom turned to him and asked, 'Did I do well?'

He tapped his fingers on the wheel. Most of the time he spent away from Edam. Work, he said. And for the most part that was true. What she did while he was away was her business. It had been like this for years. Perhaps children would have changed things but they never came along, and her suggestion of adoption was one he could never countenance. Blom was a self-made man, a Volendam caterer turned band manager. He'd created The Cupids, a product, a brand, just like the restaurants and hotels he'd sold, at a huge profit, in the wake of their success. He didn't want another man's cast-offs.

'In what sense?' he asked.

'In the sense that . . . was I believable?'

'You're always believable, Lotte. You say what you have to say with so little grace no one could ever accuse you of lying.'

She laughed at that then reached into her bag, took out a pack of cigarettes and lit one.

'I've asked you so many times not to smoke in the car,' he said. 'It stinks for ages afterwards. I have to get it valeted the moment I go back to The Hague.'

'True,' she said then leaned back in her seat and blew smoke up towards the roof.

Blom grunted and hit the soft-top button. The fabric retreated towards the boot with a metallic hum and whir.

'Wonderful,' she complained. 'Now we expire of pollution instead.'

'There are a couple of parliament dinners next week. I thought you might like to come.'

She turned, stared at him then started to laugh. The traffic was moving again.

'Just an idea,' he muttered.

'You still haven't answered my question.'

'You did fine!' he yelled. 'Thank you. It's in both our interests, you know.'

She sighed and relaxed in the soft leather seat.

'Must be awful.'

He didn't want to ask but he knew this wouldn't go away.

'What?'

'Thinking something's dead and buried. Then watching it crawl out of the grave.'

'We've nothing to worry about.'

She leaned against the car door and gazed at him.

'I never had anything to worry about in the first place.'

The car lurched forward as he misjudged the pedal. They almost hit the vehicle in front. The traffic picked up once more and they entered the incline towards the tunnel. Ten minutes to get through and then another thirty to Edam. After that he'd retire to the summer house at the end of the garden by the canal. Peace and solitude away from the world. Away from her.

'Once they find those kids this'll all blow over,' he insisted. 'We can go back to normal.'

The laugh again and she echoed, 'Normal?'

He bit his tongue then said, finally, 'As normal as it gets.'

'Marken.' She had a sarcastic, musical voice. 'I don't understand why you told Vos you never went there. Truly I don't. I mean . . . what if he checks?'

A long pause. The car moved, more steadily this time.

'There's no need to complicate things,' he answered. 'They're busy enough as—'

'It was weird enough you screwing that woman. What was her name?' She rapped her long nails on the dashboard. 'Don't remember. Don't really care. Sad in the end. But those . . . charity visits. Yes. That's what they were. Perhaps you should have mentioned them. I know they're unimportant, like you say. But they did ask.' She looked at him. 'Unless she got rid of those records for you? Was that it?'

'The past is past,' he said. 'Done with.'

'So you keep saying. Let's change the subject. I was reading in one of the Sunday papers how inexpensive property is down in Italy at the moment. Calabria. The Mezzogiorno. You can pick up a villa for maybe . . . three-quarters of a million. Tops.'

'Don't we have homes enough?'

'It's not for us. Me. I need a project. Something to get me out more.' She leaned over and kissed him on the cheek. The cigarette smell hung around on her breath. 'It won't be any trouble. Or work on your part. Just give me the money. I'll do the rest.'

He thought for a moment then said, 'I can't go above a half.'

'After all. You never know when a bolthole might come in handy.'

They entered the dark mouth of the tunnel. The car lights came on. Smog and smoke surrounded them. She reached out and hit the roof button, closing it over their heads.

'Fine,' he muttered.

'We can put the transfer through this afternoon, can't we? That would be *so* nice. You're such a sweetie.'

She leaned over to kiss him again. Blom shrank towards the window.

Lotte Blom reached into her bag for another cigarette.

'I do hope it wasn't something I said.'

58

When she turned on the lights the shack wasn't what Laura Bakker expected. Her uncle back in Friesland kept a place for his men friends. Fishing gear and stacks of beer cans. Cans of oil and fuel. Dank and smelly equipment on the walls.

The top floor of the Flamingo Club was furnished in scarlet, walls, curtains, furniture, like a sleazy nightclub in miniature. There was a small dining table next to a gas cooker, a refrigerator by the side. She opened it. Bottles of wine and beer. Soft drinks too. Recently bought, judging by the use-by dates.

On the sideboard sat a bowl full of sweets, a pile of chocolate bars next to it. Then a few pop and fashion magazines just a few months old.

A red velvet curtain marked off the end of the room. Bakker walked up, drew it to one side, and found herself wishing Vos or Van der Berg were there with her. Not for comfort. She just wanted someone with whom she could share her outrage.

Instead she whispered, 'Bastards.' Then took a closer look. A double bed with a pink satin coverlet and matching pillows, the kind favoured by the loucher Amsterdam sex clubs she'd raided. A door beyond that led to a tiny shower and toilet. Ranged behind the washbasin was a stack of condom packets, some gel, a few sex toys. She took out her latex gloves and pushed them to one side. Something else was hiding there. It took a moment for Bakker to appreciate what it was: a child's soft toy, a penguin, old and threadbare, which could only denote true love for the kid who'd once owned it. The thing sat next to a couple of shiny plastic vibrators and some other devices Bakker couldn't name, and didn't wish to.

'Bastards,' she muttered again and walked out, past the bed, closing the curtains.

The room was hot and stuffy. Flies and mosquitoes were rising from the lower floor, along with a smell of something else. She checked her phone and knew what to expect: out here, in the dead land between Volendam and Monnickendam, perched on a ledge of rock past the dyke, the outside world had receded. The Flamingo Club was in the perfect spot, visible only from the Gouwzee, private, undisturbed.

She'd forgotten about Marken and Sara Klerk. All that drove her was a growing red rage in her head and she knew what put it there: the sweets and the soft drinks, the battered penguin, the chocolates. Stuff for kids. Something to give them and say: now you're part of this. Don't tell a soul or they'll blame you. Because it's your fault really. You never said no. Which is as good as saying yes.

You let it all happen.

You made it so.

A steep line of wooden steps led down to the lower floor. She thought she heard a car somewhere as she took the first few but that was probably someone on the road. At the bottom she had to pull out her torch and fumble round for the light switch, half-reluctant to find it for fear of what it might reveal. In the end it was by a workbench with some tools scattered on the surface. A single fluorescent tube flickered to life and there was nothing here to scare her really. Just a set of double doors leading out to the sea, and beneath her on a slipway a small motor cruiser.

This was bigger than her uncle's boat. The Evinrude wasn't a simple outboard. It sat at the back of the vessel, driven from a wheelhouse amidships where a big shiny throttle sat begging for action. Toys for the boys, she thought. But which boys?

The phone came out again. Still no signal.

'Dammit,' Bakker snapped. Maybe she'd have to drive all the way back to Monnickendam to call in.

Then something buzzed in her pocket and she remembered. Simon Klerk's phone. It ought to have some charge now. Maybe it was on a different network. She took out the handset and sighed as she looked at the screen. The Sony was out of coverage too. The buzz was simply a reminder. A dead man's appointment with the dentist.

Bakker was always interested in the way people organized their phones. In particular what they put on their home screen. You could tell a lot about their personality from that. Men . . . often it was news, sports sites, email, messages, social media and games.

Not with Simon Klerk. Alongside the stock icons was one for video. That struck her as odd.

She opened up the app and clicked on the first file. It was home-made, from the phone. Bakker stared at it in fascinated horror. This was the girl she'd talked to, Kaatje Lammers, laughing, bent down beneath someone who had to be Klerk. Playing with him, all fingers, lips and saliva.

There was a noise from somewhere up the stairs.

Then a woman's voice in the shadows said, 'I thought you might come sniffing after that phone call. Having fun?'

When Laura Bakker looked up all she saw was the wooden stock of a shotgun coming straight at her in a fast and vicious swipe. The thing connected hard with the side of her head. In an instant she was falling, getting pushed down, into the hull of the cruiser below.

There she fell, legs crumpling beneath her, light fading. Flies rose all around and she knew now what they were feeding on. Blood, recent and sticky in the well of the boat.

The gun stock flew again. She rolled, avoided some of the pain. But then it was back, impossible to evade. Face down, half-conscious, unable to see anything except the gory, sticky deck, she was aware of hands on her, tying her wrists together, taking the issue handgun from her belt.

Light then, and not long after the low rumble of an engine.

Evinrude, she thought.

59

Aisha Refai shuffled her papers nervously.

'This is for certain.' More pictures. Now of Stefan Timmers, a bloody heap in the farmhouse, and on the morgue table. 'He left the place, presumably with Klerk's body. He went to Marken. We've found pebbles from the beach in the soles of his shoes. You have Stefan in the frame without a shadow of doubt. Though given he's dead—'

'Point taken,' Vos cut in. He stabbed a finger at the flabby corpse on the table, turned face down. 'He was shot in the back.'

'In the back. From close range.'

'And Simon Klerk . . .'

'Close up again. Straight in the face.' She thought about it and jerked up her arm, firing a pretend shotgun, her dark features briefly full of fury. 'Something angry about that. Almost personal. You look someone straight in the eye and take their life. The uncle though . . .'

'That was cowardly,' Vos suggested. 'The way you'd kill someone if you were scared of them.'

Plenty to be scared about, Van der Berg said. The man was a thug with a long criminal record. Prone to violence. Perhaps more than the local police knew.

Something was missing, Vos thought. And then he remembered. Irene Visser's phone. The sisters had stolen that and left it – or lost it – at the farmhouse.

He asked her if there was anything new on that. She sifted through her reports.

'Not much. Sorry. Oh. I know I said there were no prints on it. I was wrong. There were.'

She showed them a photo on her tablet. A bloody fingerprint on the back of the handset.

'One of the girls?' Van der Berg suggested.

'No. It's Simon Klerk. Maybe . . .' She was struggling. 'Maybe he stole it from her.'

They went quiet. Too many possibilities to handle. Then Vos said, 'How about this? The girls left Klerk tied up to teach him a lesson. He was there for an hour or two on his own, struggling against the ropes. He got free. He didn't have his phone with him. Laura found that in Marken. Maybe he forgot it.'

Van der Berg and Aisha nodded.

'So he finds Visser's phone one way or another. Where's he going to call first? Home. Maybe—'

'And before he gets through Uncle Stefan gets there,' Van der Berg chipped in. 'With the girls or not. He shoots Klerk. He takes the body over to Marken . . .'

'Wish we could find that boat,' Aisha grumbled.

'Then they all come back and they shoot Stefan.' Van der Berg didn't look convinced himself. 'But why?' A brief grim laugh. 'I mean . . . it's like leaving a sign up, isn't it? Look what we did. Here's our dead uncle to prove it.'

Vos stared at him and said, 'A sign?'

'Did I say something?' the detective asked.

60

The halfway house was nothing like Marken. The staff wore ordinary clothes. There were no locks on the doors, no obvious security.

No need, the man who introduced her to the place said. Did she understand why?

Oh yes, Kaatje Lammers told him earnestly. Very much so. It was all a question of trust.

They gave her new clothes and she put on the ones she liked best: blue jeans, black boots, a red patterned cotton shirt. Then she looked at herself in the mirror. All in a room of her own giving out onto the tree-lined street. A single bed, a tiny shower and toilet. The TV worked though the channels were limited. The Internet was downstairs, a single PC in a study with strict rules on where to roam and how much time to spend there.

The residents were all temporary, the man said. If things went well she'd be here a few weeks, no more.

'And after that?' she asked.

'After that you go back to your family,' he said too quickly. Then he apologized. He hadn't read the file. In the reception office he pulled up something on his laptop and went through it, murmuring to himself.

'My family?' she asked.

'Still reading,' he said and waved at her to be quiet.

She knew that look. Puzzlement. Something was wrong. It always turned out that way.

'Family,' she repeated.

'I need to look into this, Kaatje,' he said. 'Did Marken tell you why you were being released?'

'Should they?' she asked, trying to sound sweet.

He typed away on the laptop. Sending an email she guessed. Veerman was a stiff old bastard. Someone who always wanted to play by the rules. Perhaps just once he'd tried to bend them and discovered he didn't quite know how.

She waited. His face had turned grim.

'I will behave,' she promised. 'I'll do anything you ask. I'm . . .' It was a struggle not to laugh. 'I'm better. The doctors said so. All those things in the past. I was a kid—'

'We'll look into it,' the man cut in. 'Everything will be fine. Make yourself at home. Use the facilities. This is a liberal facility. We trust you to be responsible, Kaatje. Trust is important. Once broken . . .'

A wan smile then.

'Once broken?' she asked.

'Then things change,' he answered.

'Just the once?'

'Just the once. We'll know. You understand that?'

She nodded.

'I'll be on my very best behaviour then.'

A single small act of rebellion could bring this to an end. They'd said things like that in Marken. Did you clean your teeth? Did you muck out your room? Do you understand what privileges are? And how easy it is to lose them?

Most of all . . . did you go where the men told you and submit to what they wanted?

Sometimes. But not always. If you gave in completely you lost yourself in their wishes. What they stole from you wasn't just any precious innocence you still possessed. It was your identity. The thing that lived inside.

Kaatje went to the window and stared out across the tree-lined street. She was there in the shadows of the alley. Purple-red hair and a fake black leather jacket. They weren't allowed to look like that in Marken. Everything cool was banned.

Kim was looking up at her. Kaatje did her subtle finger wave. No locks. No obvious boundaries. Didn't need them, did they? And out there were the Timmers sisters free as birds. Life, as always, was innately unfair.

She went downstairs. The man was in his office typing away. Finding something wrong the way they always did. Not that it was needed. Somewhere, somehow Kaatje knew she'd fail the system, and when that happened the inevitable followed: incarceration, cruelty, despair.

He was right about one thing. The door was unlocked. She walked out into the quiet street. The girl across the way came and stood beneath a lime tree opposite, leaning against the trunk.

Kaatje wandered over, looked at her and felt her purple-red hair.

'You're beautiful,' she said and kissed her quickly on the cheek then, just for fun, nibbled at Kim's earlobe.

'Don't do that!' Kim giggled. 'We're not in Marken now.'

'No.' Kaatje looked back at the red-brick house. 'But I'm still in jail. They make me stay there.' She stared at Kim. 'Won't be long before it starts all over again.'

Breathless, excited, perhaps frightened, Kim took hold of her and whispered, 'We have a house. A place. You can come. You can stay.'

'For how long?'

'Who knows?' Kim answered. 'It's there now. It won't be forever. What is?'

'Nothing.'

She kissed Kim again, more gently this time. A lover's kiss. Soft and intimate.

'Don't do that,' Kim said and meant it.

'What'll Mia say? She hates me.'

'She doesn't hate you. Besides . . . she does as she's told.'

''Kay,' Kaatje said and off they walked, hand in hand, down the narrow street, across the busy canalside road, over the bridge to Leidseplein.

61

'What if it wasn't anything to do with the girls?' Vos asked. 'If they just left him there? Trussed up, naked. A kind of lesson. Then they went into the city and that was it.'

Van der Berg groaned and thumped his fist on the table.

'Because that's not possible. He was their uncle. He had the car. The knowledge. The gun. And also . . .' The detective waved his finger in the air as if he'd won the argument. 'How would someone else know? A naked man stuck out in the middle of nowhere?'

'Visser's phone—' Vos started.

'Made just the one call,' Van der Berg broke in. 'To the wife and he didn't get through. Strange number so she didn't twig. I'm sticking to my theory. He was doing that when the sisters and Stefan marched in. Then . . . bang.'

Vos was rifling anxiously through the documents.

'If you told me what you're looking for, Pieter,' Aisha said.

'The call log.'

It took a while but eventually she found it. He ran through the lines. No one had got round to looking at this closely. There didn't seem any good reason and they simply didn't have the time.

He found the entry, placed the sheet on the table, stamped his finger on it.

'That's the call. Made from Waterland at twenty-one minutes past eight in the evening.'

'And?' Van der Berg demanded.

'Bereaved wife. Upset. Angry. We just took her word. We never checked the duration.'

The call had connected for two minutes and thirteen seconds.

'Could that be wrong?' he asked Aisha. 'Or does it mean what I think it means? He found Visser's phone and called home. He got through. He talked to her.'

'He talked to her,' she agreed.

Van der Berg nodded, a big light coming on.

'If you wanted to kill your philandering husband and blame it on the Timmers girls what better way to do it than hire their uncle for the job? Then shoot him too.'

Vos was on the phone already.

'Laura's out there,' he said, listening to it ring. 'She was going to try and talk to Sara Klerk. I want her pulled back.'

They waited a moment then Van der Berg went to the computer and called up the location system. Vos gave up. There was no answer.

'Where is she?' he asked.

Van der Berg finished typing in Bakker's details, looked at the screen and mumbled, 'That can't be right.'

There was a map of Waterland, then the Gouwzee running out between Marken and Volendam. Laura Bakker's position showed up as a green dot moving slowly across the water, further and further from land.

Vos grabbed his jacket and told Aisha to order out a police boat from Volendam.

'Get a helicopter in the air too.'

'What are they looking for?' she asked.

Van der Berg was checking his gun, grabbing the car keys.

'A boat,' Vos said then ran for the stairs.

62

They were somewhere out on the water in the cruiser from the hideout called the Flamingo Club. Face down on the composite deck, hands tethered with nautical rope, feet still free, Laura Bakker tried to think.

No point in yelling. The lake would be empty on a weekday morning. All she could do was argue. When her head cleared enough she rolled over, looked up. Sara Klerk was at the wheel of the boat, hand on the shiny silver throttle, shotgun set against the cabin window to her side. The green jut of land on which the boathouse sat was receding faster than seemed possible. Soon they'd surely be beyond the Gouwzee in the vast and empty Markermeer.

Bakker shuffled upright against the wheelhouse and tried to make herself heard over the sound of the engine.

'Sara!'

The woman turned for a moment and shook her head.

'*Sara!*'

Think this through, she told herself. Most of all . . . stall.

'You can't do this,' Bakker shouted. 'Marnixstraat know where I went. A team was following me out there.'

The Klerk woman glared at her.

'You're lying. Sticks out a mile.'

'They'll find me.'

She laughed.

'Don't kid yourself. You know how big this lake is?'

'I know what your husband did,' Bakker yelled.

Sara Klerk eased the engine into a steady cruise.

'Do you?'

'I know he was abusing those girls.'

She notched the throttle back. The engine fell away more. This was bad.

'Everyone will sympathize—' Bakker began.

Furious, Sara Klerk grabbed the shotgun and pointed it straight in her face.

'Do you think I want your damned sympathy? What use is that to me?'

'Shoot a police officer and you'll never set foot out of jail. Kill a faithless abusive husband and—'

'Didn't just kill him, did I? That pig Stefan . . .' But she put the gun to one side and blipped the throttle up again. 'Point taken though.' She laughed. 'No need for a gun out here, is there?'

The cruiser picked up speed as Sara Klerk began to talk. A solitary gull swooped over the boat thinking maybe there were fish getting gutted. It made one low pass then left.

Soon the salt smell of the greater lake was all around them, nothing else at all.

63

Mia heard the front door, left Vera and went downstairs. Kim was there grinning. Kaatje Lammers by her side.

'What—?' she started to ask.

'I rescued her,' Kim said. 'I set her free.'

Kaatje started wandering round the ground floor, grinning at everything there: the computer, the cosy living room, the kitchen. She went to the fridge and took out a beer.

'You look different too, Mia,' she said, cracking the can.

'We have to look different. They're searching for us.'

Kaatje raised the can in a toast.

'And now they're searching for you,' she added in a quiet, worried voice.

'Not yet,' Kaatje added. 'Veerman sent me out to that place you were supposed to go. The halfway house. Near the museums. Daft idiot running it. He doesn't lock the doors. We can go wherever we like.'

This didn't ring true at all.

'I can pop back home tonight if you like, Mia. If you don't want me here.'

'We do,' Kim cut in. 'You can stay. As long as you want.'

'Vera—' Mia began.

'She's a bloody old bitch.'

'Who's Vera?' Kaatje wondered.

Before Mia could get in, Kim told her. Everything.

'Vera's getting better,' Mia said. 'We have to . . . we have to think this through.'

Kaatje laughed at that.

'What's there to think about? You've got a place. You've got money, haven't you? Make the most of it. They'll take it away soon enough.'

Mia couldn't think of anything to say. The two of them wandered off, Kim showing her around the house. Downstairs only. She was staying away from the upstairs floors, and that was good.

Something was wrong here. Mia went up the steep staircase to their room and found the bag they'd brought with them from Marken. There were papers about the halfway house Klerk was supposed to take them to. An address, details. And conditions. What would happen when they arrived.

Mia scrabbled through their clothes trying to find the envelope. It had to be there somewhere.

64

Out in the endless expanse of Waterland, blue light flashing, Van der Berg at the wheel, hooked through by voice to the helicopter about to get airborne and the police boat leaving Volendam, Vos struggled to picture what was happening.

She was in a boat. Sara Klerk was at the wheel. The green dot kept moving out from land. Now it was past the long finger of dyke stretching out from Marken, headed for the vast grey emptiness of the Markermeer.

'I should never have let her go out there on her own,' he grumbled.

'Oh for God's sake,' Van der Berg cried. 'Don't blame yourself for every damned thing that comes along.'

'She shouldn't—'

'It was a routine call. No need for two officers. No one had a clue—'

The helicopter crew called in. They were airborne. Control patched Vos through to the patrol boat. It was still in the Gouwzee, tracking the moving dot everyone could see on their screens.

'How long?' Vos demanded. A crackle across the radio. '*How long?*'

'Ten minutes,' the helicopter pilot said.

'Same here,' the boat replied.

Silence then.

'Where exactly am I going?' Van der Berg asked.

'The harbour,' Vos replied. 'They'll bring her back there.'

One way or another, he thought.

65

Kaatje had opened more beer. Kim was with her. The two of them looked ready to get drunk. Mia had found the letter and read it through, then checked on the computer just to make sure.

The house was too hot for comfort. The atmosphere was wrong. She walked into Vera's room and found the woman sleeping. Her ankle was barely swollen now. It wouldn't be more than a day before she could get around. Perhaps less. And then?

They had no plans, no ideas, no direction for the future. The simple promise of freedom was insufficient. If they could solve any one of the riddles surrounding them that might be different. But Mia had no idea how to approach that problem. She doubted the dilemma even occurred to her sister.

Still, a decision had to be made and if it meant a confrontation that was that.

She walked into the kitchen and looked at the two of them, the empty cans on the table. Kim was bleary-eyed, Kaatje mouthy and full of herself.

Mia thought about her clothes. The red shirt. Long blue jeans that almost reached the ground.

'What did they say?' she asked. 'When they took you to the safe house?'

'Just what I told you. I can do what I like now. They *trust* me.'

Kim giggled at that.

The letter they'd been given went on the table.

'They told us we'd have conditions,' Mia said. 'Times we could go out. Never more than an hour or there'd be trouble.'

'Said the same to me,' Kaatje agreed.

'They were sure they'd know,' Mia went on. 'They'd tag us. They could tell we'd gone. And where we were.'

Kaatje put down her beer.

'A tag? What's a tag?'

She crossed her legs then. Mia looked at her long blue jeans. Then she crouched down by the table and tried to roll up the bottom of the left leg. Kaatje snatched her feet away and snapped, 'What the hell do you think you're doing?'

Kim had put her beer down too.

'Just looking,' Mia said. 'I'd like to see.'

'See what?'

'What?' Kim added.

'See what's there, Kaatje. If they tagged you.'

The girl got up, stroked Kim's garish hair, grinned, went to the back window by the cutlery drawer and stared out at the kebab bar and the coffee shop behind. Summer in Amsterdam. Mosquitoes were rising everywhere. She squished one on the window, slowly, pulling off its wings while the creature struggled.

'You pair kill me,' she said, to the glass not them. 'Stuck up little cows. No better than me or anyone else. But you thought that . . .'

'We didn't,' Mia replied, going to Vera's handbag, emptying out all the money there, stuffing it into her pocket. She'd packed the case Simon Klerk had given them, the one with Disney characters on the side. It sat in the hall, near the front door.

Kaatje turned. There was a kitchen knife in her hand.

'You stopped playing their games, didn't you? Simon told me . . .'

'That was our choice,' Mia insisted.

'We thought we could use it. To get us out of there,' her sister added. 'A promise. Do that. Get this.'

'Yeah?' Kaatje came closer to the two of them, the blade shining under the bright sunlight. 'Well I'm just a born scrubber,

262

aren't I? Gave in every time. And where are we now? You two out here, doing what the hell you like. And me . . .'

She put her right leg up on the spare chair by the table then rolled up the jeans around the ankle. A grey plastic bracelet was locked there, what looked like a watch without a face stuck on the side.

'One hour,' Mia whispered. 'When did you walk out?'

'Bit more than that,' Kaatje said with a grin.

Mia stared at the knife and said, 'Kim. The bag's by the door. We're leaving. Just the two of us.'

'Leaving for where?' the girl screamed, waving the blade at them. 'If I'm getting banged up for good who the fuck gives you the right to walk away like nothing ever happened? Huh?'

'No one,' Mia murmured and didn't listen to her rants any more.

Head down, cowed for once, Kim did as she was told. They picked up the bag. Mia checked the money again. All told it was just over a thousand euros. Then she held open the front door and let her sister out.

Kaatje stood in the hall, wild-eyed, brandishing the knife.

'Good luck,' Mia said and noticed they didn't get the finger wave now.

Out in the narrow street she looked up and down. Left or right. It didn't really matter.

'This way.' Kim was pointing back towards the city centre. She put a hand to her sister's cheek. There were tears in her eyes. 'I'm sorry. I'm an idiot. You'd be better off without me.'

'No,' Mia said, starting to walk where Kim wanted. 'I wouldn't. I'd be as good as dead.'

Behind them the front door slammed.

66

Evinrude.

Her uncle's boat was nothing like this. But Laura Bakker had grown up on a farm. She was familiar with machinery, its capabilities and its dangers too.

All she required was an opportunity.

Sara Klerk cut the engine. To Bakker's relief the shotgun stayed where it was.

'You won't sink easily, will you?'

'No,' Bakker replied. 'I'm a witch. We float.'

'Not for long.'

Somewhere in the distance was the drone of an engine. High in the sky. Further off what sounded like the high-pitched whine of a speedboat. She wanted to think these were the sounds of hope. But you couldn't rely on anything except yourself in the end.

The cruiser slewed to a halt, bobbing gently on the Markermeer's steady waves. Sara Klerk looked at the back of the boat. Close to the transom was a modern anchor, two pivoting flukes around a long shank. Small, portable, convenient. And unattached to any chain. Maybe it came with the cruiser. But if the boat simply shuttled between Marken and the Flamingo Club's slipway it was never going to be needed.

Sara Klerk winked at her, and went for the thing.

The noises outside were still distant but Bakker thought she could make them out more clearly. The chop-chop of a helicopter. The frantic wail of a high-powered boat.

Still no time to waste.

Sara Klerk was by the outboard when Bakker moved. She

lunged to her feet and fell towards the wheel and the throttle. The cockpit was cramped. One attempt only and then the woman would be back.

Her elbow caught the throttle and opened it wide. Then she jabbed at the wheel and turned it fully to the left. The cruiser roared and bucked like a horse that had been kicked, rearing to one side.

Bakker found herself falling hard to the cockpit wall, banging against the shotgun, tumbling to the floor. Last chance now.

A scream. Not hers. She looked up and saw Sara Klerk fling away the anchor, struggle to hold onto the boat deck, lose her grip and fall head first over the side.

Visions of the outboard turning on the woman in the water, of blood in the grey waves, and opportunities lost. The noise from the sky was louder. Something else was getting near. She clambered to her feet, got her chin to the throttle, eased it back down. Winded, the boat lost its momentum and fell back into the waves.

There was a blue police speedboat approaching from the coast side. The blast of rotors deafened her as the helicopter came to hover overhead. Bakker lurched towards the stern, steeling herself for that red stain through the choppy foam wake she'd left behind.

It wasn't there. Just an angry desperate woman, flailing at the waves.

She looked up at the helicopter and nodded, mouthing, 'I'm fine.'

One minute later the boat came alongside. Three officers there, uniformed, two of them recovering a furious Sara Klerk from the water. Then the third leapt over onto the cruiser, looked Bakker up and down and said, 'Are you all right?'

'I will be when you get this stupid rope off me.'

He did that. She told him to take the cruiser and touch as little as possible. Then she climbed onto the police boat. The Klerk woman was sitting in the stern like a drowned rat, both terrified and furious.

She rushed over and said, 'Sara. *Sara.* Will you please look at me?'

A guilty look, regret and trepidation.

'I think we need to talk,' Bakker told her. 'Don't you?'

67

In the red-brick building behind the Rijksmuseum the administrator looked at the alert on the monitor system.

One hour and fifty minutes gone. They had to have some
leeway. Even this one. He'd been through the skimpy documentation Marken had sent. That alone was enough to recall the kid.

What bugged him was a simple truth. Calling the police was
an admission of failure. A step backwards. One that sometimes
was hard to reverse.

Her file was in front of him.

'Kaatje, Kaatje,' he whispered. 'Where are you? And what are
you doing?'

That wasn't his call now. It was down to Marnixstraat.

68

Vos stayed on the phone all the way into Volendam. The helicopter was heading back to the mainland. The police boat seemed busy.

Then he heard the news and it pushed him back into the seat, eyes closed, breathing deeply.

'For pity's sake, Pieter,' Van der Berg moaned, negotiating the labyrinth of narrow lanes that led to the waterfront.

There were lights flashing ahead. Police cars and vans lined the crowded waterfront. An ambulance was waiting, a stretcher out of the back.

'She's safe,' Vos whispered.

'Oh!' Van der Berg slapped the steering wheel. 'Boy do you know how to break things.'

'Park over there,' Vos ordered, pointing at a gap between the ambulance and a marked van.

'I thought for a moment . . .'

The words failed him. He found somewhere to dump the car.

'Perhaps we underestimate our young lady from Friesland,' Vos said, opening the door. 'Or I do.'

When they got out the harbourside was crowded: police officers, medics, locals gawping, most of them with their phones out ready to take pictures. Vos thought about trying to clear the area then realized this was impossible. It was a public event, like it or not. Ahead he could see the blue police boat manoeuvring past the outer wall. A small white cruiser was following close behind. It seemed such an ordinary scene set against the silver line of the lake. Then a figure stood up in the back of the police boat, tall and upright, red hair blowing in the wind.

Vos found himself waving, Van der Berg too. She seemed too busy to wave back.

He looked around. Volendam. He still hadn't got the measure of this place. It was a holiday town of sorts, made from fishing, now mostly built on tourism. A place apart from the city just thirty minutes away by car. They were strangers to these people and would remain that way. What he needed was some local insight.

A minute later the patrol boat moored at the quayside and the cruiser joined it moments after. Vos pushed his way through the crowd and got to the gangplank as a couple of dock workers were pushing it out to the craft.

Laura Bakker came off first, surprised to see Vos and Van der Berg standing there, holding their arms out wide.

'Are you all right?' she asked.

The big detective came up and gave her an awkward hug. Vos, unable to bring himself to do the same, dropped his arms and said, 'Actually we were wondering that about you.'

Her hands went to her hips.

'I'm fine, thank you. I was in control here, you know.'

'We sent out that patrol boat and helicopter to rescue—'

'Rescue?' she cried. '*Rescue?*'

Two of the officers from the boat led Sara Klerk, cuffed and despondent, to the custody van by the quay.

Bakker ticked points off on her fingers as she told them what she'd got out of her on the way back. The woman had long suspected that her husband was having sex with inmates at Marken. On Monday night he phoned her from the abandoned farmhouse. Kim and Mia Timmers had turned the tables on him when he took them there. They'd pulled a knife, stripped him naked, tied him to a chair.

When he got free he called home. A furious row ensued. She hired Stefan Timmers to take her out there and frighten the life out of her husband.

'She claims Klerk turned violent when they got there,' Bakker continued. 'It's bullshit. He was naked, for pity's sake. She hired Timmers to kill him. Then they buried the body in Marken to make it look like it had something to do with the girls and came back to the farmhouse to clean up.' She pushed aside her hair in the gentle marine breeze. 'Sara reckoned Stefan demanded more money and attacked her when she said no. There was a struggle. The gun went off.' She shrugged. 'I don't believe a word—'

'Stefan Timmers was shot in the back,' Van der Berg pointed out.

Bakker smiled.

'Well there you go.'

She told them about the Flamingo Club. Sara Klerk had got the original set of keys out of her husband at the farmhouse. He'd been planning to take the sisters there but decided they didn't have time.

'We need forensic in that shack,' Bakker added. 'Looks like a treasure trove to me. A fun palace for whoever was involved. And . . .'

Simon Klerk's phone came out, still inside the evidence bag. There was just enough charge for her to show them some of the video.

'We've got to talk to this kid. Her name's Kaatje Lammers. Nutcase. They let her out of Marken this morning.'

She closed her notebook.

'That's all I can think of for now. Can we go to a cafe? I need the loo. Could use a coffee too.' She beamed at them both. 'But thanks for thinking I needed rescuing. I appreciate that.'

Vos called Marnixstraat to order a team to the Flamingo Club then asked for an alert to be put out for Kaatje Lammers. Sara Klerk could find herself a lawyer and spend the night in a cell.

The three of them walked into the first cafe they found and ordered coffee. There was a smokehouse next door. The persistent aroma of oak and fish came through the open windows.

Bakker excused herself and went into the loos. There she stumbled into the first cubicle, sat on the toilet, let her head fall down, her hair all over her hands, wondered whether she was laughing or crying or something of both.

She'd no idea how long she'd been there. So many images ran through her head. Blood swilling through the grey waters of the Markermeer. A bed in a wooden cabin hidden from view. A battered penguin that must once have been a much-loved child's toy.

For a second she thought she might throw up. Then there was a sudden loud knock on the door.

'Are you OK, miss?' asked a female voice outside. 'Your friends are worried about you.'

'I'm fine,' she cried. 'I'll be there in a moment.'

She finished, went to the mirror, wiped her eyes, her face and combed her long red hair. When she got back to the table her coffee was cold so they ordered another one.

To her relief they didn't ask a single question. Van der Berg's big hand came out and grasped hers. Then Vos reached out and took her fingers too.

She smiled, laughed, couldn't think of a word to say.

Then it came to her.

'So now we go back to Marnixstraat?' she said. 'We can—'

'No, Laura,' Vos cut in. 'Now we take you home.'

69

The uniform patrols didn't take much interest when the halfway house phoned in a report about a missing girl who'd broken the rules. Then the call came in from Vos in Volendam and someone matched up the names.

Kaatje Lammers.

The tag showed the last place she'd been where a GPS signal was still visible. A location in Vinkenstraat.

Two officers cycled down there, one male, one female. They banged on the door of the nearest house. It fell open to their touch. Walking inside they found the place empty until they reached the kitchen. There sat a weeping young woman in a red shirt and long blue jeans.

'Kaatje?' the woman officer asked. 'Kaatje Lammers.'

Eyes streaming, pink with tears, she nodded from the table.

'You're over time on your tag, There are rules—'

'You don't get it, do you?' Kaatje cried, her thin voice breaking. 'Those two sisters. Kim and Mia. They're wicked. I wanted to come back but they wouldn't let me.'

'The Timmers girls?' the man asked. 'They're here?'

'They were. They're . . . monsters. They said I had to stay here. Or else. And then. And then . . .'

She closed her eyes. The woman officer came and put an arm around her.

'It's all right, Kaatje. You're safe. There's nothing wrong. Lots of people break the tag rules. It's not the end of the world. We'll just go back to the hostel. Our people will want to talk to you in the morning.'

The girl didn't move.

The woman tried to comfort her. Hands together across the tablecloth.

Kaatje sobbed and looked up. The puddle was growing, enough to form a scarlet drop that fell from the ceiling like a bloody tear, splashed on the white cotton, spreading out over the fabric.

The man was rushing for the steep staircase. The woman was recoiling from the table, staring above them, at a single red spot getting bigger by the minute.

'They did it,' Kaatje said through her tears. 'Kim and Mia. Monsters. They made me watch. They did it. Not me.'

70

When the Timmers sisters walked out of Vera's house they followed the direction the streets seemed to lead, straight into the centre of the city. Amsterdam was still strange to them and grew stranger with every footstep. They passed women in red-light cabin windows, writhing in their underwear, wriggling fingers at curious men wandering down the street. Dope smoke seemed to work its way out of coffee shops on every corner. There were windows full of sex gear and bar after bar.

Men got curious from time to time. They ignored them, wandered on. Though once, when a drunk got too persistent Kim turned on him with a sudden shocking violence. And that was that.

They bought chips and ate them by a canal. Everything here seemed unreal and distant. Threatening too. From time to time they saw police, stern figures in uniform watching everything, looking for reasons to intervene.

But they surely sought two golden-haired angels, not a pair of scruffy tramps, one black-haired, one red-purple, lugging a single bag between them.

Next to a coffee shop Kim tugged at her sister's arm and said, 'We could . . .'

'No,' Mia said. 'We can't. How can you even think of it?'

Three streets on and they realized they were in Chinatown. The smells, the garish windows, the foreign voices click-clacking on the street. They turned down a narrow alley, getting lost, getting confused.

Beneath a sign that said simply, 'Hostel', a man with an Oriental face came up and said, 'What you looking for, girls? You tell me.'

He was short, not much older than them. You had to trust someone, Mia thought. Just for a while.

'A bed for the night.'

He laughed.

'One bed? Two girls?' He winked. 'Just the two of you? Nobody else coming?'

'Just us,' Kim replied with a grunt and he didn't argue then.

Forty euros for the pair of them. He wouldn't bargain. The room was tiny and smelled of cigarettes and dope and sex.

Someone was screwing noisily along the landing. Drunks congregated outside a bar across the lane.

They didn't get undressed. Just crawled beneath the old bed-clothes and hugged one another. Mia had stolen Vera's phone. She hadn't quite known why but now it buzzed.

A message: *Where are you?*

Mia typed: *Who is this?*

You know who.

No. We don't.

Kim watched beneath the sheets, hands trembling alongside her sister's.

Little Jo.

Jo's dead.

Kim whimpered at that.

I'm a friend. Where are you? Where's Vera?

Vera's home. We're somewhere safe.

A long pause, then . . .

Nowhere's safe. Don't you know that yet?

'Screw this,' Mia cursed and phoned the number instead. It just rang and rang. Not even voicemail.

Then came another text.

We do it this way, sisters. No other. Where are you?

A moment it took her then with fumbling fingers she replied.

The same place you are. Everyone. Hell.

Mia turned off the phone. They hugged each other. They cried. Eventually, her damp face in her sister's neck, Kim whispered, 'There's nowhere left, is there? They'll keep us apart—'

'There's home. There's always home.'

Green fields. The smell of the Gouwzee. That recurring memory of the mother duck leading her chicks across the road.

Kim lifted her head and wiped her damp eyes with her sleeve. 'We can't go there.'

'We have to,' Mia said.

71

Sometimes the fog cleared.

Sometimes it got thicker.

Sometimes the world went both ways and then it was hard to know where to turn – and who to believe – at all.

It was the following morning and Frank de Groot was demanding to know where the Timmers case stood.

In a Marnixstraat interview room Sara Klerk had signed a confession. Three doors along Kaatje Lammers had tearfully told how Vera Sampson, a former Marken nurse from England, was murdered in her own home by the Timmers sisters while she watched in horror, unable to stop them.

Outside the window it just looked like another summer day. Traffic building up on the street, people wandering down Elands-gracht going shopping. A few people were walking their dogs. Vos had taken Sam for a stroll first thing, his head full of riddles and improbabilities. Thinking back now he'd no idea where the two of them had wandered. Along the Prinsengracht he guessed but he couldn't remember a thing about the route. Just that he'd dropped off the wire fox terrier at the Drie Vaten at the end, to Sofia Albers as usual. The American was there for breakfast. Maybe that relationship was going somewhere.

Then came the office and not long after the summons from upstairs.

'Bakker did well,' De Groot noted, pulling Vos out of his reverie.

'She went off on her own. Entered a dangerous situation with-out even alerting us to the possibility. Could have got herself killed. I don't call that doing well.'

De Groot leaned back in his chair and uttered a long, pained sigh.

'Going to be one of those days, is it?'

'Don't know what you mean.'

'I was trying to be positive. She's closed two murders.'

'There was nearly a third.'

The commissaris glanced at his computer screen.

'There is a third. This Englishwoman. You were right. Those Timmers kids didn't kill the nurse or their uncle. But they—'

'I doubt that.'

De Groot hesitated then said, 'What?'

'We only have Kaatje Lammers' word. I talked to your man Snyder this morning . . .'

'He's not my man.'

'Vera Sampson was stabbed to death. A violent, frenzied attack. We have the knife. It was wiped. No prints. There's blood on Lammers' clothes—'

'She says she was there. She tried to intervene.'

Vos had gone through the overnight interview. It was all so pat. So obvious. Lammers was about to be returned to a secure institution in the south later that morning. Out of the loop.

'A frenzied attack,' Vos repeated. 'If you intervened you'd at least have been cut. She's lying. I think she killed the woman. She just wants to lay the blame at their door. The way Sara Klerk did. Can't you see, Frank?'

'No,' De Groot muttered. 'Enlighten me.'

Vos wasn't sure he could but he tried anyway.

'They're scapegoats. Maybe they have been from the start. When Ollie Haas found them in Volendam next to that musician's van.'

'Wait, wait.' De Groot was getting louder. 'Are you now telling me they didn't do that either?'

'I don't know.'

'Then why are we pissing around like this? I've got the media chasing me about that doctor woman you ran off the road. I've got—'

Vos almost laughed.

'Are you serious?'

'There's an internal inquiry.'

'Yes. About two uniform traffic police who screwed up.'

'Another murder. Two convicted killers on the loose. And here you are trying to dig up a dormant case from ten years ago. If you want to prove those sisters innocent you're going to have to bring them in first.'

'I may need to talk to Jaap Blom again.'

De Groot went silent for a while then asked, 'Why?'

Vos told him. According to an anonymous tip-off left with the night team a black Mercedes coupé had been seen in Volendam not far from Stefan Timmers' cottage on the night Van der Berg was attacked.

'Someone stole what I can only assume was incriminating evidence that night—'

'An anonymous call?'

It was from a pay phone in a Volendam bar. De Groot was unimpressed.

'There are a few people out there who don't like Blom,' he said. 'He's successful. Not many are. It's probably just a malicious call. If it wasn't, why didn't they leave a name?'

It was a good question so Vos didn't answer it.

'I suspect there's been some kind of paedophile ring operating in that area. The Flamingo Club wasn't just for a nurse from Marken. He didn't have the money, for one thing.'

De Groot stabbed his finger on a sheet of paper on the desk.

'This is Snyder's prelim report from that place. It says the opposite. They've got Klerk's prints all over the spot. All the others are small. Girls probably. You've just got one pervert. No one else.'

Vos hadn't seen that document. Snyder must have sent it directly to De Groot. He picked up the paper and read it.

'This is all recent forensic,' he said when he was done. 'What's been going on there goes back years. I need to talk to Blom.'

'No.'

Vos asked, 'Why?'

'Because your priority is to find those girls. I don't see how bringing in a local politician who hasn't seen them for a decade takes that forward.'

It wasn't worth arguing with De Groot in circumstances like this.

'The director of Marken. Veerman—'

'The answer's no to that too.'

'Oh come on, Frank! He had a nurse abusing the patients there. Shipping them out at dead of night to entertain God knows who . . .'

De Groot closed his eyes and said with a pained impatience, 'We've been there already. Klerk was the only one using that place.'

'You can't bury this. Not possible.'

'I have no desire to bury anything and it offends me deeply you should even suggest it. If—'

'There are clear signs of historic sex abuse. On a scale—'

'I'm a family man!' De Groot roared. 'More than you'll ever be. Don't lecture me . . .'

He stopped and there was one of those awkward silences that occasionally fell between friends trapped by a sudden and unwanted outburst of candour.

'I'm sorry,' De Groot said finally. 'That was unfair and uncalled for. It's just . . . Christ . . . this kind of thing . . . it's disgusting.'

Vos shrugged.

'It's OK, Frank. You're right. I was never good at the family stuff. Work always seemed more compelling somehow.'

De Groot gathered himself.

'Don't think for one minute this will be swept under the carpet. But it is historic. We do have more pressing matters to deal with. Marken's a penal institution. It comes under the control of the ministry, not us. I talked to them last night and told them what we have. They're closing the place today and shipping the remaining inmates elsewhere. Veerman's suspended pending an investigation—'

'Who?' Vos cut in. 'Whose investigation?'

'Theirs.'

'We've got criminal offences here! Rape. Assault. Murder for all we know. That kid who died five years ago. Maria Koops. She'd had sex not long before—'

'And there wasn't the least sign of violence. She killed herself. Or just drowned. Then there's this.'

He slapped a printout on the desk. It was a report from one of the neighbourhood teams cleaning up after Vera Sampson's murder. A local girl told them she'd been abducted by a young woman living in the same house, forced to go inside and sing for them. She'd only escaped by talking her way out.

'This pair are dangerous.'

'It's clear—' Vos began.

'*Cut it out.* The ministry have their own investigations team. They're perfectly capable of handling the initial inquiry into Marken. If they uncover criminal activity by any individual still alive they can call us. If all they're doing is writing a history book I'm happy to leave it to them. We don't need to waste time trying to implicate dead men.'

Vos didn't know what to say.

'You do see the sense in this?'

'Will they exhume Maria Koops? Will they find out who paid for her burial?'

De Groot looked at him and shook his head.

'If it comes to it. Or I imagine they'd ask us to do it. I don't understand. Usually you're so good at focusing on what matters. Right now—'

'More than one story,' Vos muttered.

'What?'

'Nothing. What do you want me to do?'

'What I keep saying. Find the Timmers girls. Perhaps if you'd done that this Englishwoman would still be alive. Would you like to tell me where you plan to start?'

He'd been thinking about this ever since he woke up and checked the overnight logs. Kaatje Lammers said she'd no idea how Kim and Mia found their way to Vera Sampson's house in Vinkenstraat. There had to be some connection to Waterland. The strange phone call they'd received the previous Monday, supposedly from a former girlfriend of Ollie Haas, continued to bother him too. Who made it? Who attacked Van der Berg? What did they take?

'An answer would be nice,' the commissaris added.

In spite of what Gert Brugman had said they did look different now, according to Kaatje Lammers. Long blonde hair gone. Mia's was black. Kim's a kind of purple. All the same they were strangers in the city. Everything must have been alien to them. Someone had lured them there. Arranged the house. Paid for things. Now Vera Sampson was dead they'd be on their own for the first time in their adult lives.

'I think they'll go back to Volendam.'

'Why?' De Groot asked.

'Apart from Marken it's the only place they're familiar with. If we talk to people who knew the family—'

'Good. Focus on those two. If anything comes in from Marken I'll let you know.'

Vos got to his feet.

'Pieter?'

He stopped at the door.

'Yes?'

'We're in the spotlight here. From lots of angles. The press. Politicians. God knows who else. Let's not do anything that makes things worse. Get those two girls back where they belong. Inside. Then we can talk about the rest. If there's anything left to discuss.'

'Can you give me a name for who's handling the Marken inquiry?'

De Groot didn't need to check his notes for that.

'He's called Jonker. Leave him to me.'

Bakker was at her desk, staring at the computer. Van der Berg was two seats away doing the same. He pulled a chair between them. Sara Klerk had been charged with the murders of her husband and Stefan Timmers, along with the attempted murder of a police officer. She'd appear in court later that morning.

'I don't have to go, do I?' Bakker asked. 'Court's dead boring.'

He checked his messages. Nothing.

'Has anyone asked for you, Laura?'

'Not yet.'

'Well,' Van der Berg broke in, 'then the answer's . . . no.'

Vos reached over and called up one of the news websites. Vera Sampson's photo was there alongside a story that said the Timmers sisters were being hunted in connection with her murder. They had an old file picture of them as girls, blonde hair and smiling faces. The Golden Angels.

'That got out quick,' Van der Berg grumbled. 'We didn't give them a statement, did we?'

'Not that I know of,' Vos said. He looked at Bakker. 'Are you OK going back to Volendam?'

The question baffled her.

'Why wouldn't I be?'

'Just asking.'

'If you mean the Flamingo Club . . . Snyder's people are still crawling all over that. He left Aisha behind. She's not happy.'

'No,' Vos said. 'Not there.'

'And me?' Van der Berg asked, full of hope.

'I need a few addresses.'

He passed them over. Blom. Veerman. Ollie Haas's he had already.

'Just keep the fact I asked for them under your hat. Doesn't need to go on the file. Not yet.'

'My hat,' Van der Berg said with a nod. 'God that gets used a lot. Oh. Gert Brugman's been calling again. He's still eager to talk. Wants it to be you. Apparently he's heard you're . . .' Van der Berg scratched his chin. 'What was the word he used? Straight. That was it.'

Vos cursed himself. He should have spoken to Brugman before.

'You deal with it. Tell him I'm busy.' He glanced back at the office. 'Don't talk to him here. Go to a cafe. Or his place.'

'And remember my hat?'

'Hat weather all round,' Vos agreed.

72

They'd barely slept in the tiny flophouse in Chinatown. The night sounds were unlike any they'd ever heard. Fighting. Drunks yelling and shrieking in the street. Music blaring, loud rock, obscene punk.

Someone in the adjoining room must have shoved a bed up against the partition wall at some stage. They listened to it banging rhythmically, frantically, so hard the force shook the plaster. Behind it a man was screaming filth, a woman moaning.

Kim had held her harder during that and started to cry. So Mia kissed her forehead and whispered in her ear.

This will end.

It would too. She just didn't know when. Or how.

The banging stopped. Then started again twenty minutes later. Three times it happened and the last just ended in him screaming, frantically, about how he couldn't come. And that was what he'd paid for.

The sound of slaps, Kim hugging her more tightly. Then the slam of a door and a woman sobbed for a while. If her sister hadn't been there Kim would have walked out into the corridor and knocked on the room to see if she could help. But not now. They were fugitives. Lost somewhere they didn't know and couldn't begin to understand.

Finally the woman left too and the sisters understood what kind of place this was. Somewhere a room was bought by the hour, rarely for the night. It wasn't until three that the rows and racket ended. After that they slept for a while. When they woke Mia turned Vera's phone back on. It was close to nine. The sounds outside were different. The music quieter, people's voices more ordinary.

She checked the news headlines. What she saw there made her mad and scared all at the same time.

'What is it?' Kim asked in a quiet, frightened voice her sister hadn't heard before.

'Nothing.'

She turned off the phone. Kim reached for it.

'We don't need this any more,' Mia said and threw the handset in the bin. 'No one to call.'

There were such decisions in front of them. To run. To hide. To give up. To confess. And none had welcome outcomes.

'Kim,' she said, taking her sister's hands. 'You've got to listen to me. We have to do this together.'

'Can't go back. They'll find us. Maybe Vera—'

'The police are at Vera's. Kaatje took them there. Kaatje . . .'

The news had said the rest. And who was responsible. She didn't think Kim was ready to hear that.

'They're going to find us,' Kim muttered.

'Sooner or later.'

Kim thought about this and said, 'Do we let them? Or make them?'

'Make them,' Mia insisted. 'Timmers girls. Awkward little cows.'

That made her sister laugh.

There was a black void between them. Something they both recognized but never mentioned. Now that chasm had to be crossed.

'We never talk about it, do we?'

'No,' Kim agreed.

That night so long ago back when they were still the Golden Angels. Two girls walking home from a talent contest on the seafront. Discovering an unreal horror in their home. Then running, shrieking down the street and finding themselves in something even worse.

'Visser said we shouldn't,' Kim added. 'All those policemen too. They said . . .' Even this was somewhere new. An exciting place. A room they'd wanted to enter for years but never dared. 'They said we shouldn't. It would let out all the demons again.'

'That's because the demons were us.' Mia smiled. 'They said that too.'

Just those brief sentences felt good. Like a window opening in a darkened house to reveal a sunny day outside.

'They let us out though, didn't they?' Kim said.

'Visser had to. They couldn't stop her. We were too old. We were . . .'

There was a word they never used because they were always told they were the opposite.

Innocent.

Not yet. They weren't ready.

'Not quite as guilty as they . . . as we . . . supposed.'

She realized the phone had been on for part of the night anyway. Perhaps that was as good as wearing a tag.

'We've got to move. Right now.' She took Kim by the arms. 'You have to do what I say. Please. No arguments. No running away.'

One more thing too.

'No Little Jo. Or imaginary friends. It's just us. It always will be now.'

Kim looked at her, blank, dumb, as good as eleven years old and said, ''Kay.'

They picked up their things and got out of the place. In a nearby shop they bought hair dye and make-up. Then they found a cheap clothes outlet, rock gear, Goth stuff. Jeans with chains and ripped T-shirts, heavy boots, some face jewellery. In a public washroom they locked themselves in a cubicle.

Thirty minutes it took. After that they reappeared, old clothes dumped in the bags for the things they'd bought.

Chestnut hair, thick white face paint, black clothes, black boots, chains, rings in their noses. The Goth look. Identical almost.

There was a sign for Centraal station. They could catch the bus back to Waterland from there.

'Uncle Stefan—' Kim began.

'Uncle Stefan's dead,' Mia interrupted.

A long silence.

'Who then?'

Mia couldn't answer for a moment. Her head was full of memories of green fields, cows quietly grazing, dykes thickly weeded, herons standing sentry, ducks and chicks on the water. A decade they'd been kept away from the dreamy paradise they remembered as home.

How much of what she remembered was an illusion? How much real?

Two questions they could ask of everything if she was being honest. Not that honesty got them anywhere.

'Do you trust me?' Mia asked and gazed at her sister directly, in a way she'd never have dared before.

'Yes,' Kim answered.

'Then don't ask questions. Just do as I say.'

It was thirty minutes to the bus station. Another forty before the Waterland bus came in. No one gave them a second glance.

They sat on the hard seats at the back, the way people dressed like them did. Entering the black mouth of the IJtunnel Mia reached out and took her sister's hand, squeezing as they headed down into the dark.

73

The vans started to turn up at Marken at seven in the morning. Veerman had been there half an hour by then. The ministry was making a press announcement at nine thirty. The idea was to have everyone out and the place closed long before the media circus gathered outside the gates.

It was Jonker, the district administrator, who came to watch the final moments of an institution that had quietly gone about its business, unnoticed mostly, for eighteen years. He was a fat, short individual with the confident demeanour of a civil servant detached from the grubby detail of everyday life. Never given to openness. Always watching his back.

There were papers to be signed, he said, when he told Veerman to get inside and go to his office.

Three minibuses arrived to take away the remaining patients. They'd go into secure adult institutions for a few days until better places were found for them somewhere well away from Waterland. From the window looking back to the wood Veerman watched the familiar figures, none more than nineteen, shuffle in a puzzled line to the vehicles, each carrying the one small case they were allowed. He couldn't rid himself of the memory of the day they'd found Kees Hendriks swinging from a tree by the lake. Back then, five years ago, common sense had told him it was time to run too. To get out of Marken altogether and find a better job, somewhere that connected with the outside world.

But then Jonker turned up, waving temptation in his face. More money. Promotion. Probably above his talents. They had a way of knowing what you wanted without even having to ask. And so he acquiesced because nothing could have been simpler.

'Is there anything I should know?' the ministry man asked.

'Such as?'

'Such as . . . anything.'

'You need to be more specific.'

The tubby civil servant glared at him and said, 'That's precisely what I wish to avoid. We will be seizing your files. Visser's. Everything we can lay our hands on. Do I need to spell this out? Because if I do . . .'

He left it there. Veerman got the message. It was never said out loud.

'Irene cleared out her files before she died. There's nothing left here beyond the routine medical reports. Besides . . .' He wondered what Jonker thought might be lying around. 'There never was anything really. Unless she had it. I wasn't a party to any wrongdoing. If that's what you think.'

The man stared at him.

'You are the director—'

'I work days!' Veerman cried. 'Only days. That was the agreement from the beginning.'

Jonker walked to the familiar desk and took Veerman's chair. He revolved in it, fingers steepled together, thinking.

'What does suspension mean?' Veerman asked. 'Do I get paid?'

Outside the window the kitchen staff and security had lined up to watch the last of the girls climb into the minibuses. Two of the cooks were weeping. Some of the girls were too. Veerman felt dismal and guilty. The girls waved through the windows and the staff waved miserably back.

They'd all been told their jobs were gone. Statutory notice. Not much work in Waterland for them either. They'd probably have to swallow their pride and take the commuter bus into the city, fighting for whatever menial posts they could find.

'I haven't decided,' Jonker told him. 'What exactly are you planning to do?'

He hadn't even thought about it since the call came the previous night.

'The usual. Whatever you want,' Veerman said and hated himself even more.

'If I suspend you with pay you could take a holiday, couldn't you? Somewhere distant. You like boats. Go sailing somewhere. The Adriatic. The Caribbean. Anywhere a long way away.'

'I do like boats,' Veerman admitted, seeing his wife's face, knowing what she'd say right now.

'No contact with anyone. Not the police. Certainly not the media. Then I'll pay you. Three months while I mull over what to do next.'

Veerman couldn't think of a single place he wanted to go.

'And after that?'

Jonker blew out his chubby cheeks.

'You're not far off retirement. I can probably find some part-time admin work in headquarters. So long as you don't do anything stupid.'

'I only work days,' Veerman said softly, almost to himself.

'They may start asking questions about the Koops girl.'

Just the name made him close his eyes in pain and shame.

'It really might be best if you weren't around for that,' Jonker added. 'Go see a travel agent. Straight away.'

The kitchen people and the security staff were heading for their cars, a sorrowful troop, barely talking to one another. This was the end of Marken. He wondered if the place had helped anyone at all.

'Henk? Stop dreaming.'

Veerman looked at the corpulent, self-satisfied civil servant in front of him and realized how much he detested the man and what he stood for.

'Do they never haunt you?' he asked.

Jonker stared coldly at him for a moment and then burst out laughing.

'I don't know what you mean.'

'I mean—'

'No one can haunt you, can they? Ghosts come in the dark. You only worked days.'

Guilt and shame and regret dogged him. But there was fear too. That had been there from the start. From the moment they told him that Kees Hendriks, a man so intractably dour it was hard to bear an hour in his presence, had walked out of his office into the wood by the Markermeer, thrown a rope over one of the trees and hanged himself in the summer lake breeze.

'It's hurricane season in the Caribbean,' Veerman said.

'Could be hurricane season here too if you start squawking. Just go home. Pack your bags. Call me in a week or two from somewhere distant. I'll see what I can do.'

Veerman bowed his head. Defeated. Jonker looked at the laptop on the desk.

'Is that clean?' he asked.

'Of course it's clean.'

The man folded his arms and gazed at him.

'You can take it if you like. Old piece of crap anyway. I don't want the thing.'

Veerman did as he was told, got down on his hands and knees, pulled out the power cord, closed the lid, tucked the laptop under his arm.

'If there's anything else you want from this dump . . .' Jonker said, waving his hand around the office.

'No. There's nothing.'

'Good. Get some things from home. Find yourself a hotel somewhere. Keep in touch.'

'A hotel?'

'In case the media come asking questions. Or that bastard Vos. He's supposed to be finding those Timmers kids. I don't want him poking his nose in here.'

The brigadier was a scruffy individual with wayward dark

hair and a diffident yet persistent manner. An interesting and inquisitive man. Veerman could appreciate why they wouldn't want him around.

'I thought the investigation was internal,' he said. 'Historic sex abuse. The primary suspect dead.'

'Let's hope it stays that way. Are you ready?'

Veerman took one last look around the office and realized he wouldn't miss it for a moment.

'Good. Go home. Pack your bag. Make yourself scarce. I'll deal with this now.'

'You've got experience,' Veerman found himself saying automatically.

Jonker ushered him to the door.

Outside in the hot day, watching the staff leave, he checked his phone. There were no more messages from Little Jo. Three a day he'd been receiving. All along the same lines. And suddenly they'd stopped.

Aartsen, the ginger-haired nurse he'd told to watch Laura Bakker, slunk past carrying a holdall.

'Good luck,' Veerman called.

The nurse stopped and glowered at him, his fat face full of hatred.

'I never did anything wrong,' the man yapped. 'Not ever. Why's this happening to me?' He stabbed a finger at Veerman's face. 'Got a mortgage. A wife. Two kids. No job. Why? Can you tell me that?'

'No,' Veerman said quietly. 'I'm sorry. I can't.'

74

Van der Berg called Gert Brugman and arranged to meet him in a cafe they both knew in the Nieuwmarkt. It was good to get out of Marnixstraat. The place was gaining a febrile atmosphere, the kind that came from cases going wrong.

He was an experienced detective, older than Vos, so this sense of failure felt distinctly odd. The murders of Simon Klerk and Stefan Timmers had been solved. The dead nurse's wife had signed a confession. The best lawyer in Amsterdam couldn't save her now. All that seemed to remain was locating the Timmers sisters. Now they were out of the Englishwoman's house that ought to be easy. They were young, inexperienced on the street. If they thought things through they might simply give themselves up in the end.

And yet . . .

Someone had banged him over the head. Aisha was still working on the ribbons of old VCR tape they'd recovered from the Timmers place. Van der Berg was sufficiently immersed in the complex, unpredictable ways of criminal investigation to avoid all thoughts of hunches and intuition. Yet sometimes he recognized an awkward underlying feeling of discomfort in a case. The sense that there was a hidden gap in their knowledge just pleading to be filled. When that happened the surprises were rarely pleasant.

Brugman was waiting for him inside. It was a warm, sunny day. They should have taken a table on the pavement, opposite the market stalls in the square. But the musician wanted to stay hidden and Van der Berg was happy with that. He bought the coffee. Brugman looked like a man on the slide. Overweight, dishevelled in old clothes that still had the patina of show business about them – black shirt, shiny pearl and metal buttons, wild embroideries of a dragon front and back.

'How are things?' the detective asked. 'I mean . . . with the music. I have to ask. I guess everyone does.'

For a while The Cupids had been everywhere, on the TV, the radio, in theatres. They had been a part of Dutch life. Then they started to fade, almost visibly. They weren't on the screen so much, or in the charts, and when they were things were different. Playing music too young for them. Pretending time, the passing years, never existed. Van der Berg realized he felt uncomfortable seeing Gert Brugman like this. It was as if minor royalty had stumbled on hard times, a glittering god had fallen to earth and turned sadly human, all that stardust turned to nothing more than crumpled tinsel.

'The music?' Brugman nodded at the black instrument case at his feet, and the yellow amp with a dragon design, like the shirt, next to it. 'It's this now. I asked for Vos. Why didn't I get him?'

'Because Brigadier Vos is busy. You got me instead.'

He gestured towards Brugman's gear.

'Can I? I used to love that guitar of yours. Always wished it was me up there . . .'

He didn't object as Van der Berg opened the case. A shiny black instrument sat there. It looked cheap and new.

'Not the one I remember.'

'The one you remember was a bass. I can't busk or play the bars with a bass. And anyway . . .' Brugman scratched his skimpy beard. 'I may as well sell the thing. No use to me. Just memories. Could use the money.'

'Good memories?' Van der Berg asked.

'I didn't come here to talk about the past. Those two kids. I saw the news. They say they killed someone else last night. Is that true?'

'I don't know.'

Brugman took out his phone and found a message on it. Van der Berg shivered when he saw it and the pictures underneath.

Remember us? The time has come. Little Jo.

The photo was Jo Timmers, pretty as a picture, golden hair shining, beaming for the camera in her scarlet shirt and blue hot pants. Below was another image. Her grown-up sisters, tall, unsmiling, long blonde hair that looked suspiciously like wigs. Posing. Reluctantly, Van der Berg thought.

'I told your people before. They were outside my door on Tuesday night. They sent me this picture.'

The email address was just gibberish. Fake probably, and untraceable.

'What is this?' Brugman asked, picking up his coffee with shaking hands. 'They were just looking at me. Then they were gone.'

'"The time has come." What does that mean?'

'You tell me. Is there something going on I don't know about?'

It seemed an odd question.

'Like what?'

'Like you finding out what happened. With Rogier. Those kids' parents.'

'You don't think they killed him?'

Brugman glared at him and said, 'Do you?'

Van der Berg wasn't minded to answer that question so he asked if he could have the phone. The musician shrugged and handed it over. A quick reply to the email.

The time has come for what?

Straight away the phone beeped and came back with an error message: email undeliverable, unknown address.

Brugman was sweating. The day was getting hotter and there was a smell of drains leaking out from somewhere close.

'What were you really like, Gert? The Cupids. I mean as individuals. You. Rogier. Frans . . .'

'I drank. Frans went to the gym. Or one of those meditation places or something.'

'And Rogier?'

He didn't seem too keen to answer that question.

'Rogier was the talent. The one who wrote the songs. He never let us forget that. He didn't mix with us so much. Not after the money rolled in.'

'Women? He wasn't married.'

'He didn't need to be married. Of course there were women.'

'Kids?'

Brugman groaned.

'Not all that crap again. He just happened to like being around them. No crime in that, is there? Rogier nagged us all the time. Let's go and see some sick kids in hospital. Make guest appearances for charities. Those sweets.' He shrugged. 'It was a bit of a gimmick I think. Genuine. But not bad publicity either. There was nothing more to it than that. Jesus, if he'd been some kind of pervert don't you think I'd have known?'

'People always say that. They don't wear a monster outfit and a badge.'

He thought about what Vos had told him of the interview with Jaap Blom.

'Freya Timmers thought you guys were on the way out. She wanted a recording contract for those kids to take your place. She was trying to pressure Blom into giving her one. Said that if he didn't she'd go running to the police and tell them one of you had been abusing her girls.'

Brugman put down the coffee. There was a red blush building behind the stubble.

'Who in God's name told you that?'

'Doesn't matter.'

'Jesus! We'd been on the way out for years. But we were still gods in Volendam. We could walk into any bar, snap our fingers, walk home with who we liked. Why piss around with kids?'

'I guess some people like it.'

'Well not me. Not us. Are you going to do anything to find those girls? They were local. Cuties. They deserved better than they got.'

'And they sent you a message. Or someone did.'

'True.'

'But why?'

'This is a waste of time,' Brugman said.

He closed the lid of the guitar case and looked ready to go.

Was it? Van der Berg wasn't sure. He didn't really know why Brugman wanted to talk in the first place. So he asked about Frans Lambert. What had happened to him.

'Frans was always on the edge. He liked to give you this tough-guy image. Karate and all that. But he couldn't stand the heat really. Jaap was always leaning on him. On all of us. More sessions. More tours. Frans hated being on the road.'

'So where is he?'

Brugman frowned.

'Why are you asking me? Aren't you supposed to know where people end up?'

'We're supposed to find out. Not quite the same thing. See . . . if no one talks to us . . . tells us what's going on . . . it all gets so much harder.'

Brugman scowled and said, 'Frans was into all that spiritual crap. Always heading off for meditation or something. Thailand. Bali and places. We did the talent contest that night. He had a plane booked. Then it's . . . bye, bye.'

'And you've never heard from him? In ten years? Some guy you grew up with? Made millions with once upon a time?'

Brugman looked at his watch. Not that he seemed a man pressed for time.

'No. Never heard from him. Don't you get it? After that family got killed, Rogier murdered . . . no one wanted to go near

The Cupids. No smoke without fire. That's what they all said. Maybe Frans saw it coming. If he did he was smarter than me.'

Van der Berg asked about money. Brugman turned shiftier and kept quiet.

'Come on, Gert. I still hear you on the radio. I don't know how the business works. There must be royalties. Where's his share? Who gets it?'

A pained shake of the head opposite.

'Where do you think? It's where all the money goes. To the manager. Jaap Blom. I talked to him maybe a year after Frans went missing. He reckoned he was gone for good. Not heard a thing. Probably dead in some shithole out there.'

'But the money must still come in . . .'

Brugman didn't look him in the face. Just told him to talk to Blom.

'Do I need to worry?'

Van der Berg sighed then asked, 'About what?'

'About those girls coming for me next?'

'Why would they do that?'

Brugman took out his phone and showed him the email and the pictures again.

'Is this meant to be a threat?' he asked. 'If it isn't . . . what the hell is it?'

'One thing you learn in this job,' Van der Berg said. 'It's when people are only telling you half of the story. If that.'

'I never touched any of them,' Brugman snapped. 'Not a hair on their heads.'

'Good.'

'Are you doing anything at all?'

'We're trying to find those girls. Do you really think they didn't murder Rogier Glas?'

Brugman closed his eyes and sighed.

'I mean,' Van der Berg went on, 'let's imagine it wasn't them. Yet still they confessed. They felt guilty. That's what happens with kids sometimes. When they're abused. They blame themselves. Not the bastard who messes with them. Not . . . the rest of us . . . for letting it happen in the first place.'

Brugman grabbed the guitar case and the amp and muttered, 'This is all beyond me.'

'Did anyone else have reason to hate Rogier? Reason enough to kill him?'

Brugman thought for a while then said, 'Not enough to kill him. No.'

'Who?'

A shrug. He wasn't happy saying this.

'You didn't mess with Jaap. He was the boss. He made us. He told us that day in and day out. You took what he offered and you didn't argue. Even when it meant we had to pretend we liked all that dance and rock shit he made us do. We were supposed to be these happy, smiling Volendam guys for the public. Legends who never got old. But honestly . . . it wasn't like that. God knows where most of the money went. And the pressure . . . it got ridiculous. Rogier kept nagging us to dump Jaap and find someone else. They were his songs. Jaap was making more money out of them than any of us. Rogier talked about going solo a few times too. We all had. Jaap hit the roof the moment he heard and put a stop to it. Said we didn't have the talent. Or the balls. He was right. Apart from Rogier. He was the golden goose. It wasn't just him who died that night. We all did.'

He stopped, remembering something.

'What is it?' Van der Berg wondered.

'I was really wasted that day. Been drinking since eleven or so. Truth is . . . most of the last ten years of The Cupids we'd broken up. Barely made a damned thing together. Jaap just wouldn't let us tell anyone. Things were really frosty between him and Rogier. Jaap had us under contract. None of us could get out of it. We had to do what he wanted. I knew there must have been some kind of blow-up when Frans slipped in the news he was headed for the airport. He always made himself scarce if there was an argument around.'

'Wait.' Van der Berg was trying to think this through. 'You didn't know Lambert was leaving until that very day?'

'Booked it that morning he said. Jaap wasn't pleased. We had some sessions the week after. We knew we'd have to use some local guy instead. Frans could be a real jerk when he wanted.'

He got up and Van der Berg saw how badly he moved. The limp. The shaky way he held the amp. He looked sick, not just decrepit.

'One question. Ever heard of a kid called Maria Koops?'

Brugman stopped and looked at him.

'Yeah.'

'Where?'

'She was that girl who killed herself in Marken a few years back. One of the fishermen picked her out of the lake. It was in the paper.'

'An orphan,' Van der Berg said.

'Has she got something to do with all this?'

'Maybe.'

Brugman looked interested.

'What are you going to do?'

'Not a lot we can do at the moment. It's all just . . . a mess.'

Brugman glared at him and said, 'Nice to see our tax money going to good use. Keeping us all safe at night.'

How many times had he heard that? Van der Berg couldn't count them.

'When do you play next?'

'Officially? Tonight in the Jordaan. Bar near Lindengracht.'

'Unofficially?'

Brugman lifted the amp.

'I may just try busking out here. Until the police come along and move me on. Do you want to listen?'

Van der Berg wrote his mobile number on a card and handed it over.

'Call me any time. There's something you know, Gert. Maybe you don't even realize it. If you'd like to share—'

But by then he was shambling out of the door.

Van der Berg paid for the coffee and checked his messages. Nothing happening anywhere. He hoped Vos and Bakker were having more luck. He still couldn't work out why Brugman had been so desperate to talk to someone. Would it have been different if Vos had turned up? The 'straight' one?

The phone rang.

Back in Marnixstraat Aisha Refai was doing her best to make the call unnoticed from a quiet corner of forensic. The ribbons of tape had returned from the lab. To her surprise there was something on them.

'I need to talk to you, Dirk. Right now.'

'Because?'

She glanced around then swore under her breath. Snyder was back from the clubhouse by the water. He had the beadiest eyes she'd ever seen and just then they were on her.

'Not on the phone. Just get in here.'

'Will do.'

She was trying to close down the window on her laptop when the man from Rotterdam got there. Too slow.

'Who sent this to the lab?' he asked. In his hands was a ribbon of VCR tape. 'I didn't know anything about it.'

'I was going to—'

He shoved her to one side and looked at the laptop. She didn't say a thing.

'Go home,' he ordered.

'What?'

'I said go home. I can't have people running around doing what the hell they like without my knowledge.'

'Snyder. You weren't here.'

'Don't give me that shit. You sent this stuff off last night and didn't even tell me.'

'*You weren't here.*'

'This is starting to offend me now. *You* are starting to offend me. Go home,' he ordered. 'I'll let you know if I want you back.'

Outside in the street, close to tears she called Van der Berg again and said they ought to meet for a coffee somewhere.

'I'm going to drown in coffee, Aisha.'

'I'll rescue you,' she said and told him the place to be, twenty minutes or so.

She sounded down and that was unusual.

Brugman had set up in the centre of the square, amp on the cobblestones, guitar out, ready to play. The local uniforms would move him on in fifteen minutes at the most.

Van der Berg wandered over and said good luck. He meant it.

The guitarist looked at him and said, 'That Koops kid?'

'Yes?'

'You said she was an orphan.'

'Or something. Single mother maybe.'

Brugman scratched his head.

'I don't like gossip. Especially with outsiders. But . . . that's not right. Not really.'

Van der Berg said he could handle gossip. Listened then asked for a name. When he heard it he closed his eyes and cursed his own stupidity.

Walking back towards the cafe and Aisha he called Vos.

'Where are you?'

Outside Ollie Haas's place on the edge of Volendam. Haas wasn't home.

'What did Brugman have to say?' Vos asked.

'That's a very good question,' Van der Berg replied. 'I'm still trying to work it out. But one thing. You remember I mentioned that cook . . . ?'

75

The sisters sat on the back seat all the way. People got on. People got off. No one looked at them much at all.

Invisible, Kim whispered as they pulled through Broek.

No we're not, Mia thought. Anything but.

The bus idled in Monnickendam for a while. They stared out of the windows at the bright summer day, the park they called the Green Heart, the verdant fields behind.

Waterland. Narrow dykes, broader streams. The grey lake ahead. Marken across the gentle summer waves, its long finger jabbing out towards Volendam.

They hadn't set foot in the place of their birth since the night their family and Rogier Glas were murdered. No one from the town had come to see them in custody or in Marken. Not even Uncle Stefan. But then he and their parents had never seen eye to eye.

Would anyone recognize them? Even as they were? She'd no idea and didn't want to know. They had to find somewhere to hide. Somewhere to think. And then . . .

The woman in front was reading the news on her tablet. It was easy to see over her shoulder. They were the lead item, alongside a picture of Vera the Englishwoman. Vera Sampson. They never knew her second name.

The headlines said it all.

Kim saw them too then leaned on her shoulder shivering. Pleading. For what? Answers. Release. Something they could cling to and hope it might bear the name of truth.

Then she whispered in Mia's ear, 'They're saying we killed

her. We didn't.' Her breath was too quick, her voice low and frightened. 'Did we?'

'No,' Mia whispered. 'We didn't. Kaatje was there. You brought her. Remember?'

The bus kept moving. Out into the countryside again, the last leg before the town by the water, with its harbour where a talent show once happened, three young girls singing their hearts out for all to see.

Kim's wild eyes roamed around. It was like this after the man died in his van. She went crazy then and Mia followed, just to keep her company.

In the narrow green channel by the road a family of ducks leapt squawking out of the water, surprised by the sudden sound of the bus.

'Quack!' Kim cried so loudly the other passengers turned and stared.

She giggled and put a hand over her mouth. Then kissed Mia quickly on the cheek and said sorry.

They weren't more than a kilometre from the town so Mia pressed the bell.

'Let's go,' she said. 'Kim.'

Her sister didn't move.

'We're not there.'

'We're where we're going. Remember? The chickens?'

She thought for a second.

'Chickens. Right. I remember.'

Mia wondered whether that was for real.

The bus came to a halt by a narrow dirt track. At the end was a ramshackle low farmhouse with wrecks of tractors and other machinery scattered around the yard.

They walked up the dusty lane. Mia rang the bell. No answer. Then she led Kim round the back. There was a barn there and a warm, fond sound that brought back so many pleasant memories.

Hens clucking round a grimy patch of enclosed grass and earth, a wooden house to keep them safe from foxes.

Kim laughed, crouched down and picked some fresh grass from the field to push through the wire.

Footsteps behind in the stifling day. Mia heard them first. They both turned.

'Well, girls,' Tonny Kok said. 'We saw you getting off the bus and walking down the drive. To what do we owe . . . ?'

He was bigger and much older than they remembered. The second man larger still.

'It's them, isn't it?' Willy asked his brother. 'Freya and Gus's kids.'

'Oh my,' Tonny muttered. 'Oh my.'

Mia stood up straight and said, very earnestly, 'We didn't do anything. Whatever they said. We never hurt anyone. Honest.'

'Honest,' Kim added.

The two men had their hands on their chins, watching them. They were brothers. Not twins. But maybe they had a bond too. They understood.

'You *are* different. But . . .' Tonny leaned down for a closer look. 'Maybe not underneath. Not when I think about it. All grown up now. As much as any of us ever gets.'

Mia took out all the money they had and held it in front of her, hands shaking.

'We can pay,' she said. 'Take it all. No use to us.'

'What do you want?' Tonny asked.

Mia couldn't think of a word to say.

It was Kim who spoke.

'Mum used to bring us here to feed the chickens.'

'You and your sister,' Willy said. 'Those were the days.'

'Jo.' Kim smiled. 'Little Jo.'

She started to sing. A line from a Cupids song. Mia took her hand and told her to be quiet.

'I bet you're hungry,' Tonny told them. 'I know. How about you two go out back and find some eggs from them there hens?'

Kim was through the gate in a flash. Mia could picture this so clearly. Lifting the birds and finding that magical thing beneath them, warm and shiny, smelling of feathers, and the birds didn't seem to mind them taking their eggs at all.

'Thank you,' she said.

'Nothing, girl,' Tonny told her. 'But best we get inside soon. So no one sees, eh?'

76

Vos insisted they visit the churchyard first. They parked in the narrow street of Kerkepad, a street back from the seafront. On one side a dense hedge next to the brown-brick church hid the graves. On the other a small iron bridge crossed the canal to an alley leading to the Gouwzee. They were past the harbour with its cafes and seafood shops and the hordes of day trippers hunting T-shirts and cheap gifts. Here Volendam was quiet and residential, small houses, most just about detached from one another, fronted by tiny gardens with neat flower beds competing for attention.

Still they could smell the ever-present water, a briny tang hanging over everything. There was the distant sound of too-loud pop music from a bar somewhere. Along the narrow canal a grey heron stood stiff on its stick-like legs, then jabbed its long spear beak into the weed and came out with a wriggling frog.

He checked his notebook. The Timmers had lived on the other side of town, in the cramped timber fishermen's cottages. So did Bea Arends.

'Let's take a look at the grave first.'

Bakker didn't move and he asked her why.

'I've never liked churchyards. Not since I buried my mum and dad.'

'We have to do this. We may have to come back and exhume that girl. I hope not. But . . .'

Still she didn't move. The events of the previous day hadn't left her, he guessed. No reason why they should. No more than a kilometre from here, in a hidden cabin now being probed by forensic, she'd looked death straight in the face.

'But if you really don't want—'

'Let's do it. I'm just being stupid,' she said, and led the way to the church.

The caretaker who'd talked to Van der Berg was in the nave, a small man in overalls, wielding a very old horsehair broom. He wasn't so friendly now the police had turned up in person.

Vos asked him about Maria Koops and whether he could check the records to see who'd paid for her grave.

'I told your man,' the caretaker replied, not even making a move for the office. 'It was an anonymous donation. We don't know. Why should we?'

'Who puts flowers on her grave?'

He grunted something under his breath then said, 'Lots of people come with flowers. You think I've got nothing better to do than follow them around the place?'

Volendam, Vos thought. The locals were never going to be easy with strangers. He asked for directions and said thanks. Then the two of them went outside. The headstone was near the hedge of shrubs close to where they'd parked. Recent, unstained by the years. The inscription in the cold grey stone seemed bolder than it appeared in Van der Berg's snapshot. The lyrics of the song especially.

> *Love is like a chain that binds me.*
> *Love is like a last goodbye.*

There was a small bouquet of yellow roses next to the grave, a white label around the stems. Bakker bent down to take a look then shook her head. It was just the price tag from a supermarket.

'We don't need to dig her up, do we?'

'If I have to I will.'

'To find out what? I read the report. She'd been in the water for two days. In the ground now for five years. Could there really be—?'

'If we don't look we won't know, will we?' he said, a touch peremptorily.

She went quiet.

'I'm sorry,' Vos added. 'I didn't mean to be abrupt. It's just that . . .' Laura Bakker had a way of bringing ideas and doubts and possibilities to the surface. It was a talent she possessed without knowing it. A useful one. 'The more we delve into this, the more you see people not looking. Just turning away. And if we don't look . . . who does?'

He gazed at the grave once more and then went back to the church, walked through the cool, quiet interior, didn't bother the caretaker. If the man knew something he wasn't saying.

It was ten minutes to Bea Arends' cottage. The place wasn't easy to find in the tangle of old streets behind the harbour. Eventually they located the address: a black wooden shack, tiny, with flowerpots on the front deck and white net curtains pulled back like curious eyebrows. The homes of both the Timmers family and their uncle Stefan couldn't have been more than a couple of minutes away on foot.

Bea Arends answered the door. She was about fifty, stocky with a ruddy face, greying brown hair, sad green eyes and the stance of someone used to years of manual work.

Vos showed his ID card and she scowled at it.

'Did Sherlock send you then? I wondered when he'd finally catch something with all that fishing.'

'Sherlock?'

'That big bloke of yours. The one who got biffed.'

A dog barked, loud but friendly. The German shepherd went straight for Bakker who bent down and stroked his handsome head.

'Funny that,' she said, tugging at his collar. 'I told the other one. Rex doesn't normally like strangers.'

She looked the two of them up and down.

'Best you come in, I suppose.'

77

Van der Berg bought two coffees, didn't even touch his, looked at Aisha and said, 'Let me guess. Stefan was busy churning out porn in that shack of his. Kiddie porn, probably. I reckon—'

'Possibly.' She seemed upset and for the moment he didn't want to know why. 'But it wasn't that.'

He opened his arms, grinned and pointed at the tablet in her bag.

'Something to show me?'

'Snyder kicked me out of the office.'

'Oh.' The young woman behind the counter put out some sandwiches. He wondered about a beer then decided against it. 'If you want to wait for Vos to come back . . .'

'I don't. Dammit!'

She banged her fist on the table. The coffee cups jumped.

He went and bought two sandwiches. Then listened.

The VCR tapes they found in Stefan Timmers' private studio had gone to a specialist lab that had managed to recreate the video from a few. Most of what they had recovered was unremarkable.

'The kind of stuff people took of their families,' she said. 'The seaside. Barbecues. Singing. A few things from the TV. Nothing sexual at all.'

'You mean the Timmers family? Gus. Freya. The triplets.'

'That's some of it,' she agreed. 'The lab said the material came from two different cameras. I'm guessing, but I'd tend to think one of them belonged to Gus. The other was Stefan's. All the other material Stefan had was later. Maybe it was a hobby of his. Going round just videoing stuff that happened there as far as I can see. Carnivals. Christmas parties. Harmless.'

The Timmers family were murdered. The videos they owned passed into the hands of the brother. He could see how that might happen.

'The camera he was using recently was different. Digital. It didn't use tape. He'd just plug it straight into the laptop. Not that we have that of course. It looks like he burned DVDs and kept a backup drive underneath the desk. We found the cables. No drive. All gone.'

Van der Berg tried to follow this. There was no doubt Stefan Timmers was a criminal. He had a pretty hefty record, and that was probably just scratching the surface.

'So he could have been making porn? We just didn't find it?'

'Correct.'

'In that shack Laura found? The Flamingo Club?'

She took a deep breath then smiled at him.

'I haven't been entrusted with any details about that place. Snyder's keeping it with his people.'

'I thought you liked him?'

'I thought so too. But I don't. As I said. He sent me home. For pursuing avenues he didn't know about.' Her dark finger pointed across the table. 'Your avenues.'

There was a long silence between them then she sipped at her coffee and gave him a curious look.

'I like my job. I worked damned hard to get it. I'm good. I could end up running that department, running it well too. Just a few years. A few quiet years.'

'Ah.'

He went to the counter and got himself a beer. Which was wrong but he could live with it.

'Ambition,' he said, sitting down again. 'The privilege of the young. An awkward thing, if I'm honest.'

'Awkward? We're supposed to aspire to something, aren't we?'

'We're supposed to aspire to lots of things. Some of them a bit contradictory. Let me tell you a story.'

It was short on detail and entirely free of names. A tale of when he was a young detective, planning to take the promotion exams. Dreaming of when he'd be a brigadier like the smart and well-paid men above him.

'Then one day someone told me to go and talk to one of the local hoods. Shake him down, but nicely. It was different back then. A few of the guys were . . . over-friendly with the wrong sort of people. The lines weren't so clearly drawn. The man didn't want shaking down. He was there to give me a present.'

She looked shocked.

'What happened?'

He laughed and said, 'I took it, of course.'

Aisha didn't utter a word.

'Then I went back to the office. Told my boss. Gave him the envelope. Asked what kind of report I should file.'

It was a long time ago. The brigadier was now dead. He'd seemed a decent enough man. Large family and all of them went to church on Sundays.

She waited. Finally she asked, 'Then what?'

'He took the money and said he'd deal with it. I told him I didn't follow. I saw the hood. I took the envelope. If anyone was going to start dealing with it . . . should have been me. But no. It wasn't. After that nothing. Nothing at all.'

She waited again.

'And?'

'And that was it. Some people kept talking to me. Vos would have but he wasn't around back then. Some of the others . . . not so much. After a while I realized I was standing at the bottom of the ladder looking up. And it was going to stay that way. Forever.'

'It's not like that now, is it?'

He thought about that.

'In the sense that we don't send out junior officers to pick up bribes for their bosses and see which way they fall . . . no. But sometimes . . .' This conversation was headed in a direction he dreaded. It was too depressing. 'The point is the world's different. When I was your age people looked up to us. They were innocent civilians. On our side. We were there to protect them. And their interests. Some of the guys who took those bribes were pretty good at that job if I'm honest. It wasn't black and white but it was close. Now . . .'

He took a long swig of the beer.

'Now the civilians aren't so innocent. They look at all the shit around them and think . . . if everyone else can get away with it . . . why can't I? Makes life more complicated. Back then it was money in a brown envelope. Now it could be a wink. A glance away. A file that just happens to get lost. Sorry . . .' She looked so guilty it hit him too. 'I don't mean to burst your bubble.'

'You didn't.'

'I just wanted you to know.'

'So what do I do? Go in there, face up to Snyder, ask for the stuff back? I can do it now—'

'No, no, no!' He laughed. 'He told you to go home, didn't he?'

'I can't—'

'Course you can. Go to the movies. Watch TV. Do some shopping. Forget about Marnixstraat for a while.' He smiled at her. 'Leave it to me.'

'To you?'

'Yes. Detective Van der Berg. Bottom of the ladder staring up and used to it. Nothing to lose.'

She was silent. Then she reached for his beer and took a sip. He didn't know what to say. She didn't drink.

'The trouble is,' Van der Berg added, 'you're thinking . . . but what if he buries this too? What if I can't trust him . . .'

'If I thought that I wouldn't have asked you here, would I?'

'So why the hesitation?'

Aisha reached into her bag and pulled out the tablet.

'Because Snyder's right to kick me out. I didn't just take that stuff to one side to get a look without telling him. Before he got there I managed to sneak a picture off it too.'

This was so unlike her. She was a cautious, ambitious young woman who almost always played by the rules.

'Why would you do that?'

She shot him a baleful glance, turned on the tablet and stared at the screen as if the answers to all the problems in the world might lie in a piece of plastic and glass. The young could be like that.

'This is a still from one of the VCR tapes. It's the day the family were killed. I know that because earlier I found some footage of the talent contest. There was a banner, a year. It looks continuous. It has to be then.'

Her finger stabbed at the touchscreen. An image came up, the colours bright like a vivid nightmare.

Along the Volendam harbour some of the gift shops had an extra trick. You could walk in and stand behind cardboard cutouts of traditional Waterland costumes – fishermen, women with pointed white hats and clogs, local yokels. You poked your head through the hole above the shoulders, smiled for the camera, and handed over some money.

Whoever was holding the video must have followed three men into one of the shops and shot some footage as they got their picture taken.

Van der Berg gazed at the screen and started to feel much as he had all those years ago when he fetched a brown envelope back to the station and never found out why.

'See the problem?' Aisha asked.

'Leave it with me.' He held up the tablet. 'Can I keep this?'

'If you like.'

'Go home. Do like I said. Find something to do.'

'I emailed myself a backup, Dirk. That thing's out of there whatever Snyder thinks. God knows what else . . .'

He reached over and took her arm.

'Go home, Aisha. Please. Don't call anyone. I'll talk to Pieter. We'll see this through.'

She got up then and left. He thought about another beer but realized it wouldn't be a great idea. Things were moving now in ways he couldn't begin to understand.

He tried to phone Vos but just got voicemail. Same with Bakker. Then, reluctantly, wishing he could draw himself away from the thing, he picked up the tablet and looked at it again.

Three cardboard figures in a tourist shop somewhere. Seemingly on the day the Timmers family and Rogier Glas were murdered.

The first figure was a podgy farmer with a beard and a pipe. A younger Jaap Blom poked his head through, smiling reluctantly as if he was too smart, too superior to be involved in such nonsense.

The middle one was a woman in a flowing black-and-white dress, dancing legs with clogs, a pointed hat. Ollie Haas's face was on her shoulders, grinning like the idiot he was.

The last was a fisherman with big galoshes, a striped shirt, a painted-on pipe and burly arms. He was holding a struggling fish that winked at the camera. The face was thinner, younger. But the moustache wasn't much different. Darker perhaps.

Frank de Groot in Volendam hours before death came to the town by the sea. He didn't look happy to be caught like this. But he was there, no mistake, all the same.

78

The pictures were everywhere in the tiny wooden fisherman's cottage. Pinned to the walls. On the small dining table, the sideboard. The Cupids back when the trio were young and handsome, feted everywhere. On stage, in record company offices holding up gold discs. Signing autographs. Larking around. Then later, the slide in the career mirrored in their ageing faces, the dreadful, needy stabs at fashion in their clothes.

Bakker wandered over and picked up a framed picture from the table. A young woman, short, tubby, embarrassed in an unflattering miniskirt, standing between Frans Lambert and Gert Brugman. They both had their arms round her. Rogier Glas stood behind holding up a sign: 'Our Biggest Fan!'

Bea Arends came over and smiled at it.

'I was too. In my own little world. But the boys had so many others. It was daft to say anyone was bigger than the rest. Back in the old days anyway. By the time it all fell apart there were just a few of us left, holding up a couple of candles in the dark.'

She took the picture from Bakker's fingers.

'What a mess I was back then. Lots of prettier girls than me around. Still. Nothing wrong with being born plain. No one's ever going to say you're losing your looks.'

The photo went back on the table.

'Had to put all this stuff in storage for a few years. Went away for a while. Wasn't going to lose it though. Too precious for that. Want some coffee?'

They said yes and took a seat on a small sofa while she bustled around in the kitchen. Laura Bakker couldn't stop smiling at the place. Vos quietly asked why.

'It's so cute,' she said.

'Cute?' the woman called from the kitchen. 'Don't think you can talk among yourselves. My hearing's sharp as a cat's.'

She came out with two china cups, biscuits in the saucers.

'I suppose it is cute. This is the last place I'm ever going to live. Had a few . . . turbulent years. That's all over now. I'm settled. Back in Volendam. Never going anywhere else again.'

It all came out then. How she'd grown up in the town, followed The Cupids from the time they were just a local band playing the bars. She'd started their first fan club, worked unpaid as its secretary while she did odd part-time jobs anywhere she could find. After a while the band became so big that Jaap Blom formed a management company around them. Professionals came in and took over the fan club. Everything grew bigger and bigger for a time and then, just as quickly, began to slide. No one wanted old pop stars, except old people and lots of them had better things to do.

'Were you here?' Bakker asked. 'The night it happened.'

'Ten years ago,' she said straight away. 'Summer. They'd put on a talent contest for the carnival. Those Timmers girls should have won it. They were lovely.'

'Why didn't they?'

A pause and then she said, very carefully, 'I wasn't a judge. Why ask me? To think of it . . . The Cupids at a seaside talent contest. How the mighty were fallen. They'd never have stooped to that in the old days.'

'And now,' Vos noted, 'you're a cook in Marken.'

'Not any more. They let us all go this morning. Eighteen months I've been working there. Good job. Won't find it easy to get another like it. Seems there's the whiff of scandal about the place.' She smiled. 'But then I imagine you know more about that than me.'

He asked the obvious question: what happened the night of the talent contest? The obvious answer came back: someone killed the Timmers family. The sisters, Kim and Mia, thought it was Rogier Glas and attacked him in his van three streets away.

'Poor lasses. God knows what must have been in their heads when they went into that house of theirs. Freya. Gus. Little Jo. All dead. It wasn't Rogier who did it. Couldn't have been. He was a lovely man. Only one of that lot who had a proper musical bone in his body if I'm honest.'

'Who then?'

'No idea. I'd had enough after that. Watching them all go downhill was bad enough. Seeing what happened after Rogier died . . . I upped sticks to Spain. Spent a good few years drinking myself stupid. The world here . . .' She glanced beyond the neatly parted net curtains. 'Everything fell apart that night. Couldn't take it any more. And then . . . then I came back.'

Bakker asked why.

'No friends. Not real ones. My mum and dad are gone but I know a few people here. Nice folk. Volendammers stick together. We have to. No else is going to look after us, are they?'

The dog came out of the kitchen still munching on some food and settled at the feet of Vos and Bakker.

'He does like you pair,' she said with a grin.

It was always a question of choosing the right moment. He wasn't sure when that was any more. Not out here, so far from the city, where life seemed to run to a different rhythm, to mores and rules he couldn't begin to understand.

Vos got up and retrieved another photo from the wall. A younger Bea with the band back when they looked fresh and smart and gleaming with fame. They were presenting her with a plaque. There was a cutting from the local paper by the side. The story had her real name: Bea Koops.

'No pictures of your daughter,' he said. 'Maria. Why's that?'

Her round, intelligent eyes started to fill with tears.

'Because I as good as killed her, Mr Policeman. That's why you're here. Isn't it?'

79

The sisters ate their eggs and ham. Then Tonny drove out to the shop and came back with yoghurt and ice cream, some pastries, fresh soap and towels. Willy had tidied up their mother's old room at the back of the farmhouse, lugging a vacuum cleaner in there for the first time in years, finding clean sheets for the bed, wiping the dust and cobwebs from the windows.

'We don't have guests much,' Tonny said, scratching his head.

'We've never had guests,' his brother added. 'Two old fools in galoshes and overalls. Who'd want to visit us? I ask you.'

Seated at the ancient kitchen table the sisters laughed at that. These two men were a part of their childhood. Figures in the hazy uncertain dream about the life that happened before. Quite what they represented Mia wasn't sure. All she knew was that her mother trusted the brothers. Enough at times to leave the three of them playing with the chickens at the farm when she was working for Mr Blom.

The one thing Mia couldn't put her finger on was the connection. Somehow they were always there, on the sidelines. Coming along to gigs. Clapping. Not quite a part of the family. Just two solitary, slightly shy men who hung around, laughing, joking, drinking beer.

There had to be more to it than that.

'What was it like in that place?' Tonny asked. 'Marken?'

Kim said it was okay and left it there. Mia stayed silent so they kept looking at her.

'It was where we were,' she said when she realized they needed to hear something. 'Where they sent us after it all happened.'

Willy shook his head and stared at the table.

'Terrible days. Our old mum died not long before. We were still reeling from that, weren't we?'

The other brother looked glum and angry.

'You never forget losing your mum. Like a part of you goes with her. Never forget it. Never.'

These two must have been thirty years older than her and Kim. Or more. There was still a bond between them she recognized, one not so far from the one that they possessed. Some of it was blood. Another part, a more subtle one, something shared, perhaps not fully recognized.

Willy looked straight at her and asked, 'Do you remember what happened that night? With you? And Little Jo and that?'

'Not really . . .'

Kim stared at the table then got up and walked out into the hall. The place was like a doll's house, full of tiny rooms. They didn't seem to mind where the sisters went.

What was there left to say?

We went home and walked into a nightmare.

We rushed out into the street and there he was.

It was our fault. The policeman said so. We had something, did something that started it all. And if it wasn't for us . . .

'No,' Mia said. 'We don't remember.'

'Had other people to remember it for us,' Kim added from the hall in a low and surly voice.

Willy didn't seem satisfied with that. He asked, 'Did some-one—?'

'Stop it.' Tonny put his big elbow on the table and raised a finger. 'Stop that now, Brother. The girls are our guests. We treat them that way. Don't get . . . pushy.'

Willy scowled then nodded.

'Sorry, lass. But don't it bother you? Not knowing? Would me—'

'I said stop it,' Tonny cut in.

She was owed a question then.

'How did you know us? Mum, Dad? All of us?'

Tonny laughed and looked friendly and agreeable when he did that.

'This is Volendam, sweetheart. Everyone knows everyone. We live in one another's pockets.'

'One another's beds sometimes too,' Willy grumbled.

'We used to go fishing with your dad now and then. He had a boat. We didn't.'

'Was that it?' she asked. 'Fishing.'

'Isn't fishing enough?'

'What are we going to do?' she wondered.

Tonny Kok looked straight at her in a way people hadn't in Marken. There they were always patients. Inmates. Guinea pigs for experimentation. Failures who might or might not be cured.

'What do you want to do?'

Kim started singing from another room. One of the old songs for three voices. Little Jo was in her head, Mia felt sure. If Kim kept on like this their dead sister would be back in her own imagination too before long.

'Be normal. Just that. Be like everyone else. Ordinary. Invisible.'

He reached over and patted her hand. It was a fond and sympathetic gesture but immediately she recoiled, shrinking from him.

'Sorry,' the big man said. 'I shouldn't have touched you, should I? We're just simple country brothers. Don't mean any harm.'

'Best you don't go wandering out of here,' Willy added. 'Not without us. The police are looking everywhere. We'll have a think. Talk to some friends. It'll be all right. In the end. Promise.'

Kim was singing more loudly. Mia wished she'd answered his question honestly. They couldn't be ordinary. That was always going to be denied them. Nor could they be invisible.

There was a clatter then, a deep boom, a loud metallic clash. Willy Kok's face creased with anger. She shrank further from the table, from them.

'Not that!' Willy yelled. 'Not that. Don't even—'

He was on his feet, dashing for the door and one of the rooms beyond. Too fast for his brother. Too fast for her even.

When she got there he was striding across the bare floor of a place at the back. A drum set, gold with glitter on it, stood in the corner. Kim was on a stool behind, messing around with a pair of brushes, swishing at the cymbals.

'Not a bloody toy,' Willy said and grabbed the sticks from her. 'Out of there now. Go to your room. The pair of you.'

Go to your room.

How often had they heard that? At home when they were small. In Marken when they said the wrong word, the forbidden one . . . *no.*

The farmhouse bedroom was long and narrow. Kim reckoned the brothers' old mum had died in the low bed in front of them.

Outside Waterland, dykes and ditches, animals seemingly too sleepy to move, stretched to the far horizon.

Mia wasn't really listening to her sister. There'd been a name painted on the front of the bass drum. The Cupids. She'd thought that only the good would remain in Volendam when they returned. It never occurred to her that the evil would hang around too.

Soon, exhausted from the dismal night before, she fell asleep and dreamed of the lake, a stage beside it, people playing music. Bad music, out of tune, so dissonant it hurt.

When she woke up the cheap digital clock by the side of the bed said she'd been out of it for almost three hours. The window was open. Kim wasn't there.

Mia looked out and saw how easy it would be climb onto the roof of the outbuilding below, then let yourself down to the ground.

Volendam was just over a kilometre across the fields. In the far distance a black shape moved towards the low houses, the church, the silvery, endless lake.

80

Bea Arends went and got herself a coffee then sat down and talked, freely, frankly for a good half-hour. The story didn't emerge quickly. But it came out in the end.

Maria was her daughter, just turned eight when the Timmers family were killed. A quiet, troubled child. There were problems at school, with the social services people. Bea was a single mother. Life was never easy.

Then, the night of the talent contest, everything fell to pieces.

'Couldn't do it any more. Any of it. Pretending I was a good mother. Making out I could cope.'

Bakker said, 'It wasn't anything to do with you, Bea. Was it?'

'They were kids! Gus and Freya were a family. A couple. If they couldn't manage how the hell could I? That girl deserved better. Better than anything I could give her. I'd been falling to pieces for ages anyway. When they got killed . . . and Rogier . . . I just went to pieces.' A grimace then. 'Halfway there already. Didn't take a lot. Took her to the social people and said they had to look after her. I couldn't. They didn't argue. One day later I was on a plane, crying my eyes out, swigging at vodka as if that was going to make it all right.'

She got up and went to the sideboard then came back with a slim photo album. A younger Bea, drawn and heavier, sitting on the Volendam waterfront with a quiet, pale child. Neither of them smiling. Just six photos, all taken on the same day.

'That's all I've got left. Burned the rest when I heard she was dead.'

They waited.

'Before you ask, Frans was her dad. A kind man. Generous.

Decent. He'd have married me if I'd let him but . . .' She gestured at the photos of The Cupids. 'How could that have worked? Surrounded by all those glamorous women. Throwing knickers at them night and day. And frumpy me standing there, stuck out like a sore thumb. Maria wasn't the only kid of theirs in Volendam. They were kings, weren't they? Kings who came up from the gutter. Kings do stuff like that. Toffs do it all the time. They're born to it. No one complains about them.'

Vos picked up a photo of Lambert. A tall man with a full head of dark hair, too Eighties for now.

'What made him run?'

She shrugged her shoulders and said, 'That was another thing that pushed me over. He came up and told me that morning. Off for good just a few hours later. I never saw it coming. I still got the money. And then . . .'

Her eyes grew glassy.

'Did he say why?' Bakker asked.

'There was trouble with Jaap. There was always trouble with Jaap. Money. Or the kind of music they were playing. I don't know. Jaap thought he was the band. He made them. They belonged to him.'

She traced the faces on the old photo with her fingers.

'Five years ago the payments stopped. I guess he must have heard Maria was dead and blamed me. He wasn't here. I should have been. Instead I was pissing away his money in Spain, out of it most of the time—'

'We think Frans Lambert changed his name,' Bakker cut in. 'He died in a boating accident in Bali. Around that time. It wasn't you . . .'

No answer.

'You don't seem too surprised,' he added.

The woman nodded.

'I wondered if he was gone if I'm honest. He came from here.

I always thought he'd want to be home some day. You know he's dead, do you? You're sure of that?'

Vos put the picture back on the table and said, 'As much as we're sure of anything. Why did you get a job at Marken?'

'Wanted to find out what happened. For myself. You don't think I believe what people tell you, do you?' She finished the coffee and sighed. 'There was always gossip about funny stuff going on there. I wanted to know for myself.'

'And?' Bakker asked.

She asked if they wanted more biscuits. They didn't.

'If there was I thought it must have stopped before I showed up. I talked to everyone in that place. Nurses. Irene Visser. Veerman. Just quietly. They all seemed genuinely sad. Ashamed they didn't pick up the way she was going. Maria was always a funny kid, even when I had her. Head up in the clouds. One night she got out and went for a swim. That was it.'

Vos and Bakker exchanged glances. It had to be broached.

'There was more to it than that,' he said. 'There's no easy way to say this. Someone had had sex with her. I'm sorry.'

A long silence filled the room punctured only by the bronchial breathing of the slumbering dog.

'Why didn't you do something about it?' she asked eventually.

'We weren't on the case. Brigadier Haas was—'

'Ollie Haas? That man was supposed to find out what happened to my girl? The one who said Mia and Kim killed Rogier? Who couldn't even find the bastard who murdered Freya and Jo and Gus?'

Vos nodded and didn't say a word.

'What are you going to do about it now, mister?'

'We'll look,' he promised. 'Once we've found the sisters. There are a lot of questions to be answered—'

'Always have been,' she cut in. 'But I don't see anybody asking them.'

'Bea,' Bakker said. 'All in good time . . .'

'Good time,' she muttered.

Vos asked about Simon Klerk. Her face fell.

'Creepy little man. Do you think it was him?'

'We don't know,' Vos replied. 'We may have to ask permission to exhume your daughter's body.'

There were tears then, and fury on her face.

'There's gossip round this place says Klerk was messing with our girls. Is that right?'

'What do you think, Bea?' Vos asked.

'Bloody police. You never tell us anything till it's too late. Well it was news to me. To everyone in Marken I think. But then he worked nights. Could have done whatever he liked there. We'd never know.' She raised the cup in a toast. 'Paid for it, didn't he? So maybe there is some justice in the end.'

He got up and walked around the room, thinking. There wasn't enough for a search warrant here let alone a trawl through her phone records.

'What about Vera Sampson?'

'That woman on the news? Do you really reckon Mia and Kim did that?' She scowled. 'I don't believe it. Any more than I think they killed Rogier that night. Two young kids. Not that you lot give a damn . . .'

'Did you know her?'

'How the hell would I? Stupid bloody question—'

'If people don't come to us,' Vos began. 'No one complained. No one said . . . this might have been wrong.'

She stood up and faced him.

'I guess it's what you'd call experience, mate. Little people round here. Don't count for much on your radar screen, do we?'

'Brigadier Haas got a confession out of those girls,' Bakker pointed out. 'They said they killed him.'

It was the right button.

'They were eleven years old! Ollie Haas could have got a confession out of Jesus! That evil bastard fitted up anyone he liked if they didn't do what he wanted. If—'

'So who was it?' Bakker asked. 'Who killed the family? Glas? Any ideas?'

She calmed down then, with some effort.

'No. I haven't. If I did I'd tell you. That brother of Gus's had some nasty friends. From Amsterdam. Not here. But Gus and Freya . . . those girls. They were just a family. And Rogier . . . he was a lovely man. All that stuff about him handing out sweeties to the kids. That's how he was. A real darling. It didn't mean anything bad. You'll never tell me otherwise.'

One last opening. Vos wasn't expecting much. He told her about Jaap Blom's revelation the previous day. The threat Freya Timmers had supposedly made to reveal someone connected with The Cupids as a child abuser.

She listened, blinking, getting ever more furious.

'Jaap told you that?'

'He did say he never believed the accusation. It was just her trying to pressure him into getting a contract.'

Bea Arends snorted.

'Freya had a contract with him already. For her and the three girls. Got it signed a week before they died. Maybe she was lying, but that's what she told me.'

She picked up one of the oldest photos. The Cupids in their prime. Glas was in the centre. A handsome, genial-looking man. Everyone's favourite uncle. There didn't seem anything sleazy about him at all.

'There was some trouble with her and Jaap now I think about it though. I'd assumed it was him trying it on with her.'

'Trying it on?' Vos asked.

'He couldn't keep his hands off anything in a skirt. Even went for me once. I told him where to get off.' A memory then. 'That was the only piece of gossip I heard when I went back to Marken.' She looked at them and laughed. 'There I was thinking I'd be helping out my dead daughter. And all I picked up was some tittle-tattle that told me what I knew already. He was a dirty old sod.'

They waited.

'You mean you don't know this either? Before I turned up there was some kind of board of friends of Marken. Jaap was on it. Used to come along for . . . charity work. Night times usually, from what I gather.' She smiled, not pleasantly. 'It was all organized by Irene Visser. They were special friends. Him and the psychiatrist. Friends with favours is what the young call it. Been going on for five years or so. I hope he kept it from Lotte. That wife of his is a Volendam girl. Got the temper to prove it.'

Five minutes later they were back in the car.

Bakker retrieved a packet of mints from her bag, offered him one and said, 'We're not supposed to go near him, are we?'

They were tiny mints. He took two.

'That was this morning.'

'He said he'd never been to Marken and he was there regularly. Having an affair with Irene Visser. That must have given him access to—'

'Jaap Blom lied,' Vos agreed. 'His wife must have known about some of it too.'

He got the address out of his notebook and tried to remember the difficult, cramped layout of Edam's pretty old town centre.

'We need to park near the bus station. Blom lives in a pedestrian street next to the canal.'

She was behind the wheel. And didn't move.

'I still don't understand why Bea Arends would go back to Marken after all that time. Her daughter's dead. Maybe it was an accident. Or suicide. What did she want to find? Closure?'

He grimaced.

'Please don't use that word in my presence. There's no such thing. It's a myth.'

'Why then?'

Good question, he thought.

81

Bea Arends watched them leave. Then she took out the cheap phone she'd bought the week before from a shop in the city and went out back. The cottage looked out onto a sluggish canal. The adjoining homes were owned by rich Amsterdammers who rented them to holidaymakers. Both were empty. The one piece of good fortune she'd had of late.

She banged on the door of the lean-to shed by the rear door and said he could come out. Then she went and sat on one of the three rusty garden chairs by the end of the garden overlooking the water.

'Did you hear all that?' she asked, staring at the messages from the past few days.

'Most.'

The hair was shorter, the moustache now a beard. She wasn't sure whether people would recognize him or not. Sooner or later he'd have to go public. Frans Lambert, the missing Cupid. Back in circulation. From the dead, or so the authorities thought.

'That police chap's as sharp as a razor,' she said. 'If he wanted he could clear up this mess like a shot.'

It had all seemed so simple to begin with. Get the girls out of the grip of the institutions when they were freed from Marken. Keep them hidden at Vera's. Taunt the police with some clues, a few apparent leads. Scare Veerman and the rest with some texts.

At some stage the silence had to break. They had to start reopening old files and realize something had gone badly wrong over the years, however hard the likes of Ollie Haas had tried to hide it.

Freya, Gus and Little Jo. Rogier Glas. Maria. God knows how many more along the way.

But they never imagined the wheels could come off so quickly and in such a violent and unpredictable fashion. She looked at the messages she'd sent Vera, anonymously, along with the cash. She'd used the same scheme leaving the notes, the money, the map for the sisters in Marken. Lambert suggested they say it was all from Little Jo. It had never occurred to her how cruel that trick had been.

Maybe that was why it all went wrong. They asked for it. They brought it on themselves. Worse, they brought it on Mia and Kim.

She glared at him and said, 'We screwed it up from the beginning. You ran. I ran. We left them all behind and now we think we can put it right. Is that for them or us?'

A big man. Strong when he wanted to be. But weak at heart. She appreciated that now.

'I'm sorry,' was all he said.

'Sorry? What use is that? You heard him. Someone had sex with her. With our own daughter.'

'I—'

'We screwed up, Frans! All those years ago. And here we are doing it all over again. Making it worse when we're supposed to be making it better. Ten times worse by the sound of it.' She looked at the messages on the phone and showed him them. 'Little Jo. For God's sake . . . how could we even think of that?'

'You wanted them out of there. You said it'd make them listen.'

That was true. It was her desperate idea.

She got up and threw the phone over the fence. It hit the green water and vanished beneath the algae and weed.

Then she turned on him, jabbing with a fat index finger.

'That sharp policeman isn't going to do a bloody thing. None of them are. It's down to us now. All of it. You got me?'

He took her arms, tried to hold her. She struggled away, hands flapping at him, puny, furious blows raining on his chest.

'Too late for that. Kings of Volendam my arse. You're just a bunch of weak and spineless cowards and we were too blind to see it. Just—'

'What do you want?' he yelled. 'What else?'

She raised a fist in his face.

'I want what I always wanted! Some bloody justice.'

He didn't say anything. She gripped his black shirt and pulled him to her.

'You vanished the moment you heard Maria was dead. Just cut me off—'

'While you were pissing it up in Spain. Don't throw it all at me, Bea. We're both guilty.'

'Why? Why'd you just run away twice over?'

He shrugged.

'Because I could. Because it was easier that way. No ties. No one to nag me. And besides.' He ran his finger down her cheek. 'What else could I do?'

'Why come back then?'

'I told you. I'm out of money. Nowhere else.' He glanced across the canal. 'Once we've fixed this mess I'll make my own way. Put things back together.'

'With her?' she demanded. 'Not me. Not ugly Bea.'

That accusation hurt him, and not for the first time.

'I can't fix everything,' he whispered. 'If we find some answers. The right ones.'

She pulled herself away.

'You mean the ones you want to hear? I should never have let you back here, Frans. Back in my life. What was I thinking?'

She didn't wait for an answer. Just went back into the house and found her real phone.

'Bea?'

He sounded hurt. That pained bleat was a cry for comfort.

'Too late,' she whispered and began to make some calls.

82

Van der Berg went back into the office, checked the logs, tried to call Vos, got voicemail. Found himself a coffee, went to the restrooms, swallowed some mouthwash. They got funny if they smelled beer on your breath and he wasn't in the mood to be sent home like Aisha Refai.

When he got back there was a message from De Groot demanding his presence.

One set of stairs. He took them slowly, peered through the window into the commissaris's office then knocked on the door. Snyder and Ollie Haas were inside. It looked as if they were having a meeting.

Haas let him in. He stood in the middle of the room and said nothing. They looked at him. Finally De Groot said, 'A report would be welcome.'

'It would, sir,' Van der Berg agreed. 'What would you like me to say?'

'That you're getting closer to bringing in the Timmers girls,' Haas said. 'I know those bitches of old. We don't want them out there. They've killed already. God knows who's next.'

Van der Berg took a deep breath then pulled his notebook out of his pocket, licked his fingers and slowly turned through the pages. They waited, getting cross.

'We have one lead,' he said finally. 'Vera Sampson. The Englishwoman who was killed. Her phone was used in Chinatown last night. All we have is a phone mast. It vanished first thing this morning. Either the battery ran out or they wised up and turned it off.'

He looked at Snyder and asked, 'Do you really think they killed her? The sisters?'

The forensic man squirmed in his seat and kept quiet.

'I'm asking out of curiosity,' Van der Berg added. 'It's just that from what we've learned so far it seems much more likely that the other kid, Kaatje Lammers, was responsible. Just one person. Not two. From the knife marks.'

'The fact one person wielded the knife doesn't mean it wasn't the sisters,' Haas observed. 'They work together. It was just one of them killed Rogier Glas.'

'I never knew that,' Van der Berg said. 'But then I couldn't find the report. Which one?'

De Groot muttered something inaudible.

'According to Marken, Kim's the more disturbed,' Snyder said. 'By far.'

Van der Berg screwed up his nose in puzzlement.

'Why would that be? Triplets? Brought up together? Through all that dreadful nightmare? Why would one be worse than the other? I mean—'

'This isn't the time,' De Groot barked. 'Maybe if you tracked them down we could find out.'

'True,' Van der Berg said, then put his notebook in his pocket. 'Anything else?'

'That's it?' De Groot looked desperate. 'I can't get through to Vos. He's out in Waterland somewhere. Is that really it?'

'Pretty much. I'll keep calling him. As soon as I know something, you'll hear.' He waved his notebook. 'All three of you. I promise.'

Five minutes later he was back at his desk wondering what the prospects were for a beery detective kicked out of the police in his mid-forties. Not as rosy as Ollie Haas's, he guessed.

The phone rang. He snatched at the handset. It was the dry cleaner's round the corner asking when he was going to pick up the suit that had been ready for ten days now.

'Soon,' he said. 'Very soon.'

83

The mansion where Jaap and Lotte Blom lived was a ten-minute drive from the modest timber cottages of Volendam, home to Bea Arends and once a family called Timmers. Only a strip of rich pasture separated the two communities but the contrast between the two could scarcely be more marked.

Edam was an ancient, genteel place. Tourists wandered through the town's pretty streets buying souvenirs. The shiny red-waxed cheese had made its name famous throughout the world. But the busy farmers' market from which they were sold had ceased to function almost a century before. Now it was nothing more than a holiday attraction, revived once a week during the summer months to bring in visitors.

Not that most of the locals needed the money. Selling trinkets to foreigners was a sideline at most, a minor economic ripple from the brash commercialism of its more raucous neighbour. Artists, musicians and business people fleeing the pressures of Amsterdam made up a large part of the modern population. The Bloms were, in many ways, typical of the new Edammer: wealthy, influential and barely connected to the bustling, more proletarian town just down the coast.

Vos and Bakker couldn't get near to the address so they had to park outside the centre and walk in along a sluggish canal. She kept checking the map on her phone. After a minute they could see the back of the Blom property across the water. There was a long garden and a large and ornate summer house, glass, wood and wrought iron set by the water surrounded by palms and pampas grass. Blom sat inside, hunched over a computer monitor, absorbed.

A white iron pedestrian bridge led across the canal. After that they found themselves in a narrow cobbled cul-de-sac with tall buildings on both sides.

These red-brick houses, with their careful cream mortar, looked plain from the street. But he'd been out here before and knew the façade was deceptive. Behind they could be huge, especially if they owned gardens stretching down to the green and dreamy waters of the canal. Blom's house had to be worth millions. All from the modest beginnings of the Palingsound and The Cupids in particular.

'Money,' Bakker said, getting the picture straight away. She pressed the doorbell. 'You can smell it here.'

His wife answered, cigarette in mouth, casual white shirt, loose jeans, bare feet. Not quite the politician's partner.

Before they could speak she asked, 'Is there news?'

'Of what?' Bakker wondered.

'Of those sisters you're supposed to be chasing. What else?'

Vos said they needed to speak to her husband.

'No news then?' she snapped. 'What do you people do for a living?'

Just a quick word with her husband, Vos repeated. Bakker was sighing very audibly, the way she did when people were obstructive.

'About what?'

'I need to confirm something,' Vos said. 'Won't take a minute.'

'Wait here,' she said then closed the door.

Bakker balled a fist and shook it at the shiny brass knocker: a lion, roaring.

'He's a politician. He's supposed to help people, isn't he?'

Vos was barely listening. He was wondering why Lotte Blom was so interested in the Timmers girls.

The door opened. Blom was there in a too-small green polo shirt and pink Bermuda shorts. He was sweating. There was the faintest hint of drink on his breath.

'Can we come in?' Bakker demanded.

'What is this?' He looked behind him, scared. 'Lotte's really pissed off with you two. I told her we wouldn't get pestered again.'

'We're not pestering,' Bakker snapped. 'We're investigating several homicides and the possible abuse of minors.'

Vos intervened.

'This really isn't a conversation for the doorstep. Please.'

He relented. They walked through the house. It seemed to go on forever. Rich wood floors, tapestries, paintings, antique furniture, everything polished and spotless.

Blom led them out into the garden. They stood by one of the palm trees. He lit up a small cigar and puffed on it nervously. They could see his wife watching them from the kitchen window, smoking too.

'There's a discrepancy,' Vos told him. 'I just want to get it clear in my own head.'

'What . . . discrepancy?'

He didn't mind where he blew the smoke. Laura Bakker did, waving it out of her face with an angry sweep.

'Where does the money go? From the band?'

Blom groaned.

'Do you have any idea how long it would take me to answer that question? It goes in multiple directions. Some into family trusts. Some abroad. Some to me. To my wife.'

'None to Gert Brugman, the only living band member?'

'I bought Gert out a few years ago. Very generously. He needed the money. I was doing him a favour.'

Bakker broke in, 'Were you having an affair with Irene Visser?'

Blom sucked on the cigar then threw it into the bushes. His eyes were on the kitchen window.

'You really have been fishing, haven't you? Is that a good use of your time? Does De Groot know?'

Vos said, 'It's a simple question. If—'

'My private life's no business of yours.'

Bakker was starting to get mad.

'You said you never went to Marken. But you were having an affair with Irene Visser. Going there for so-called charity visits. Getting the run of the place . . .'

He turned and glared at her. The politician had retreated and they saw a different man. Thuggish. Dominating.

'I don't have to take this kind of crap from you.'

'If you want me to repeat it,' Bakker told him, 'we can have your wife in on this conversation. Give you a witness.'

'Laura . . .' Vos began.

She waved away the smoke again and stepped back.

'Who told you this?' Blom repeated.

'That's irrelevant,' Vos replied. 'Is it true?'

He was watching his wife standing at the window again.

'I think you should leave. I need to talk to De Groot.'

Bakker was wandering down the garden, towards the canal and the fancy summer house. There was a big laptop on the desk, the lid down. Next to it sat stacks of DVDs and what looked like connected hard drives.

Vos said, 'You told us their mother was threatening you. That she said if you didn't give her a contract she'd go to the police and tell them someone connected with The Cupids had been abusing their daughters.'

He nodded.

'Freya just craved fame. It wasn't only about money. She needed . . . adulation. Never a good reason to do something. It was a complete fabrication. If there'd been anything in it she'd have given me a name, wouldn't she?'

'It's not true though, is it?' Vos butted in. 'You'd given them a contract already. It wasn't the band she was threatening to expose. It was you.'

Blom waited a moment then laughed.

'Is that meant to be a joke? Where do you get these fairy tales?'

'We've a statement from someone who was close to The Cupids at the time. They were heard talking about it. Your name was mentioned. If—'

'This was ten years ago!' Blom snarled. 'Dead and buried. Like Rogier and Freya and that brute of a husband of hers.'

'And their daughter,' Vos added. 'Little Jo. When we find her sisters we'll ask them.'

'Do that. In the meantime you can get the hell out of here. I told you the truth. I don't know who you spoke to in Volendam but half of those mean bastards hate me anyway. I got out of that dump. I made something of myself. Are you surprised they're jealous?'

A sound then and Vos knew what it was. Bakker had got to the summer house, opened the creaky door and was about to step inside.

She was still on the step when Blom got there and dragged her out with such force she stumbled down to the lawn.

'What the hell is this?' he roared. 'Who gave you the right to pry into my home?'

Vos helped Bakker to her feet. She wasn't looking him in the eye.

'What's in there?' she yelled, pointing at the laptop and the DVDs. 'What are you looking at? More kids? Someone else Irene Visser fixed for you?'

Lotte Blom marched down the steps into the garden, cocked her head to one side and said, 'Irene Visser? The woman from Marken? What—'

'If you go now – right now – I may overlook this,' her husband cut in. 'Just the once.' He pointed at the back door. 'On your way.'

His wife stared at them in silence.

It took a while to get Bakker out of the garden, then through the house into the street outside.

She stood there, hands on hips, breathless, furious.

'He's lying! For God's sake. He's lying through his teeth. We need a warrant—'

'A warrant? On the grounds he's got a computer?' Vos waved his car keys. 'We're going.'

'He lied to us about Irene Visser. About Freya's contract . . .'

Vos calmed her down and told her the truth: they only had the word of Bea Arends for that. In spite of what he'd said that didn't even amount to a statement.

'So this has been a complete waste of time! We've no idea where the Timmers sisters are. Not a clue who's telling the truth or not.'

He set off for the bridge over the canal, as mad with her as she seemed with the world.

'I need the toilet,' Bakker declared as they reached the steps. 'Where's the nearest?'

'How would I know? Do I look like a tour guide?'

She pointed back towards the centre of town.

'Over there. I'll see you at the car.'

Fine, Vos said. He called Marnixstraat as he crossed the canal and walked back to where they'd parked. That was an awkward conversation too. There was something Van der Berg wanted to say but wouldn't.

By the water opposite the gardens along Blom's road a couple of elderly men were seated on deckchairs, sipping at beers.

As he ambled by wondering when Bakker would turn up one of them pointed across the green water and said, 'Would you look at that? What is the world coming to?'

Vos muttered a quiet curse then turned to see.

She was a tall and fit young woman, if clumsy sometimes. Already she'd scaled the garden walls of the first two houses. Now she was stepping through the ornate, Chinese-style lilies and bonsai trees of the third.

'Laura!' he yelled across the canal. 'Get out of there.'

She waved at him then careered into what looked like an

expensive ceramic pot holding a tall bush full of red flowers. It crashed to the ground and shattered, sending soil and shrubbery everywhere. She jumped over it and walked on. One more wall to go and then she was back in Blom's place.

The summer house was empty. She stopped at the door, looked across at him. Shrugged and mouthed a single word, 'Sorry.'

Then she stepped inside and went for the laptop. The back door of the house was opening already. He heard Jaap Blom's furious shout rise over the canal.

84

Henk Veerman went home, packed hand baggage, looked under the bed and retrieved the two USB drives there. One stolen. The other carefully updated over the years. That second had been his quiet insurance. His get-out-of-jail card should it be needed.

He sat on the bed and thought of his wife, innocent of everything. There'd been a moment during that last illness when he'd thought perhaps she knew. The suicide of the Koops girl, Hendriks hanging himself not long after . . .

There were plenty of clues that all was not well inside the remote and private institution of Marken. Men outside Waterland had started to notice and worry. In spite of his promotion he'd felt far from safe.

But she'd never asked him outright. Instead she faded before his eyes while the guilt and shame grew inside him. What hurt almost as much as her painful, agonizing decline was the knowledge that a part of him still argued none of this was his business, his fault.

I only work days.

He'd wanted to scream when he told Jonker that. He'd said those words so often in the past.

I only work days so whatever you and your friends get up to when I've gone home doesn't touch me. I did nothing. Therefore I am innocent.

The truth was bleaker and more painful.

I did nothing so I'm as guilty as the rest.

Worse than them maybe. For acting out of deliberate, considered cowardice and self-interest instead of thoughtless, brazen pleasure. Perhaps that was what destroyed Hendriks, a decent, weak man, like himself, willing to turn a blind eye to those who thought themselves superior to the rest.

Acquiescence.

It was what kept them in their jobs. And the thing that destroyed them in the end.

Veerman checked his phone. He had the numbers he needed. Then he went to the downstairs computer and looked at flights out of Schiphol that evening. There was one to Istanbul. Outside the EU. A place where it would be easy to hide for a while, maybe sailing on a wooden gulet around Bodrum. That was one of the pipe dreams he and his wife had shared.

He bought a one-way ticket then hooked the USB drive into the back of the computer. There was so much material there, gigabytes and gigabytes of it. It was going to take an hour or more to upload.

Did he have that long?

Did he have a choice?

Veerman poured himself a tumbler of Scotch then sat and watched the progress bar crawl slowly left to right.

85

Bakker was inside the summer house, seated in front of the laptop. Jaap Blom stood over her, face red with fury. Lotte Blom was watching in silence, arms folded.

There was a video up on the screen. It was a beach somewhere, blue sea, blue sky, golden sand. Then a figure began to walk across it, headed for the waves. It was Blom's wife in a bikini.

'If you really think the police need to see my holiday videos,' Blom said, 'I'll burn some DVDs and you can take them with you.'

Bakker looked at the pile of disks next to the computer. Vos walked over and picked up a few. They all had exotic destinations on the label: Phuket, Barbados, the Seychelles.

'It's a hobby of mine,' Blom said, ambling over. He opened a drawer next to the desk. It was full of cameras, still and video. 'Taking pictures. Innocent pictures.'

'We need to take the computer,' Bakker told him. 'All your disks. All the . . . drives you have.'

'Laura . . .' Vos began.

'Why?' Blom walked over and closed the notebook lid. 'What possible business is this of yours?'

Bakker got up. She was struggling.

'If there's nothing to see you won't object. You said we could . . .'

He walked to the door and held it open.

'One chance, I said. You had one opportunity to get out of here and then it wouldn't go any further. You didn't take it.'

'Pieter.' She took Vos to one side, pleading in a quiet, worried voice. 'There has to be something. He lied to us.'

'Get out,' Blom ordered. 'This is illegal entry. I could have your backsides in court for this.'

'He . . .'

Vos put his arm round her and the two of them walked back into the street. They went over the bridge in silence, past the two old men who stared at them, puzzled, still sipping at their beers. Blom was on the other side of the canal in his summer house. Smoking another cigar. On the phone.

When they reached the car she looked at Vos and said, 'I made a bit of a mess of that, didn't I?'

'A bit,' he agreed.

Then his phone rang and he knew who it would be. Vos went away from her to take the call. De Groot wasn't even mad. Things had moved beyond that now.

'Put her on,' the commissaris ordered when he'd run through Blom's version of events and Vos hadn't argued with a single detail.

'Frank. Don't be hasty. There's more going on here than meets the eye. I do believe Jaap Blom's hiding something . . .'

'The sisters!' De Groot yelled down the line. 'Where are they? What are you doing to find them?'

'I'm trying to understand. Not making a great job of it I'll admit but—'

'Put her on now. I don't want to see her face inside this office until the disciplinary people ask for it.'

There was never any point in arguing with him when it was like this. So Vos went and handed her the phone then wandered off for a while, looking back along the canal. Modest houses on one side. Mansions on the other. Jaap Blom had crossed over, from Volendam to Edam, and probably made a good number of enemies along the way. He might be lying. So might Bea Arends. Or the pair of them. The only thing that was certain was that they couldn't both be telling the truth.

'Pieter?'

Her voice had a soft, hurt bleat to it, a tone he'd heard from time to time. He always hated the circumstances that caused it.

He wandered back to the car. She handed him the phone.

'De Groot says I'm suspended. He's calling in the disciplinary people. I'm going to get kicked out.'

'One step at a time. I'll talk to Frank tomorrow. When he's calmed down a bit—'

'He says I've pissed off one of the most important men around. Blom could make all our lives awkward. Someone has to take the blame.'

He took her arms.

'Tomorrow . . .'

'I've been a bloody idiot. Again.'

She swore, kicked the car hard with her heavy work shoes, then swore again, more vividly. The elderly pair along the track stared at them and shook their heads.

'Did that help?' Vos asked.

'Yes,' she said, climbing into the passenger seat. 'Why are you looking at me like that?'

He was and he hadn't realized it.

'Because you make me think. Good going for an idiot.'

'Thanks!'

'I mean . . .' He was struggling. 'I mean we're all idiots. That's what we do. Blunder about. In the dark mostly. Don't kill yourself for it. Sometimes we find something. Help someone. And then we're not idiots at all. For a while anyway.'

Laura Bakker looked deeply miserable.

'I make a good idiot, don't I? From what De Groot said—'

A different phone trill interrupted them. It puzzled her for a moment. Then she reached into her bag, retrieved her private mobile and looked at the number on screen.

'Why the hell is Dirk calling me on this number?' she wondered then answered, listened for a moment, looked at Vos and said, 'It's for you.'

86

When she let herself out of the farmhouse there was only one place for Kim Timmers to go. Back to the town by the lake, to wander along the waterfront trying not to stare at all the blank and aimless people there.

She couldn't remember being outside on her own like this. Even when there was family it rarely happened. There was always her mother, Little Jo, Mia by her side. Except when Freya asked her for a favour and for some reason Kim was always the first, the one who didn't object too much. The obedient one, for a while anyway. Which meant she wasn't alone for long either. Just with a stranger, or someone whose face she was supposed to forget.

She had a ten-euro note in her pocket and spent almost a quarter of it on an ice cream. It occurred to her she'd no idea what things cost. How any of this worked. And she wondered . . . would someone look at her white face and the chestnut hair and see what lay beneath?

Kim didn't intend to stare at any of the people round her but she couldn't stop herself. Some were familiar. Women working the stalls, selling fried fish and sweet waffles. They all looked older, more worn than she remembered. Still, they were the same people. They'd been here a decade before when a family called Timmers lived in a black-timbered cottage two streets behind this gaudy shoreline, dreaming of money and fame, all through nothing more than the sweet sounds three young girls and their mother could make when they wanted. When someone paid.

The harbour was too risky. She felt guilty for abandoning her sister after one more promise that only wound up broken. Mia was the good one, the calm one, the sister who saw sense. Kim couldn't help herself. She'd never been as awkward as Jo. When it all started she was the quiet one, the easy one, the one who did as she was told. Which was why they began with her at the outset and that knowledge nagged at her even now. On that black night some of her dead, troublesome sister had rubbed off. Perhaps over the long strange years in Marken that piece of Jo inside had grown.

For her anyway. Mia didn't really hear her light, bright voice high in her head. Mia just pretended, like the good and loving sister she was.

She lingered so long on that thought, the ice cream started to drip onto her black Goth clothes. Kim wiped off the stains and threw the cone into a bin. Why did she run? She wasn't sure. Maybe it was the sight of that drum kit in the farmhouse. Or just the fact that they'd been promised freedom for so long, and all they got when it happened was a cruel and new kind of captivity.

Where to go?

Back. To Mia in the end. There was nowhere else. Volendam wasn't the same. Without her family, without that warm bond around her, the place seemed alien. Strange. Hostile even.

She closed her eyes, trying to recall something different from the past. A memory surfaced. A cafe bar where her mother sang. Once they'd allowed the girls up onto the stage, though children weren't really supposed to be there.

The place had the oddest name: the Taveerne van de Zeven Duivels. The Inn of the Seven Devils. The sign outside had scared her to begin with. But the devils were funny really. And inside colourful dummies hung from the ceiling, with dreadlocks and stupid grins, brandishing pitchforks at the people below.

It was back towards the marina and the path to the bad place Simon Klerk knew about. The secret place he'd taken them until they said no. That was Mia's idea. Keep stringing him along. One day he'd grow so desperate they'd make the most of that.

One day.

This was freedom. Penniless and lost in the place they once called home. Eating soft ice cream that tasted of chemicals. Watching the lazy lake and Marken across the water. It felt as if that long spit of land that ran out from the institution was laughing at her.

Kim walked out of the town towards the marina. She remembered the bar as a grey, industrial-looking building down a cul-de-sac near the pleasure boat moorings. After ten minutes she saw it. Still there. Still with a sign at the start of the dead-end lane: a red devil leering, chasing a woman in a bikini who seemed to find it so very funny he was poking his pitchfork into her buttocks.

The only people around were a couple of dog walkers wandering by the water's edge. A good place to hide, she thought. Maybe that was what her mother had been doing all those years before.

She wandered in. Just three men at the bar. One about forty. Two younger ones. They stared as she put her change on the counter and asked what it could buy.

A Coke with rum appeared. The men came over. They weren't local. She could hear the city in the coarse, beery voices. One of them bought a glass of old jenever and put it on the counter in front of her.

Kim sipped at it, coughed on the strength of the drink, laughed as they laughed.

'You're a cute kid,' the old one said. 'What are you doing here?'

'Drinking,' she told them.

They laughed again and bought another round. She didn't touch the fresh glass that came. She was thinking of Mia. Her sister knew this place too. If she left the brothers' farmhouse she'd surely find her way here. They were different in some ways but shared the same thoughts. The self-same steps that brought Kim to this remote, grey building, with its small windows and stink of beer, its demons leering from the low ceiling, would surely lead Mia here too.

But when?

'Want to go for a ride?' the younger one asked, a look in his face she knew so well.

Kim told him she needed the toilet. On the way back she stopped by the empty kitchen. There was a cutlery stand by the door, napkins, knives, forks, spoons and plastic bottles full of ketchup and mustard. The place smelled of fried food. Burgers and chips, not much else.

She picked up a steak knife and tucked it down her jeans, pulling her shirt over it to hide the handle.

'Do you want a ride or not?' the kid demanded again when she got back and reached for the rum and Coke.

She looked outside. From her seat she could see the long, empty track back to the road into Volendam. Mia would find her. She always did. It was just a matter of time.

'In a while,' Kim said.

He went round the counter and put some music on the sound system. Loud, stupid rock. It didn't drown out the sound of Little Jo's voice in her head. Nothing would manage that. Ever.

87

Vos dropped Bakker at her flat in the city and told her to keep her head down for a while. Shoulders bent, still cursing herself, she shuffled through the door of her apartment block. She'd been like that when they first met, an awkward youngster from the provinces, someone who didn't fit in the hectic, sophisticated city. That part of her character would never retreat. It was selfish of him but he didn't want it to.

After that he went into the office unconcerned about the storm he knew would be waiting there. Van der Berg took him to one side and they had a brief, informative conversation in the place reserved for such discussions: the washroom. When Vos got back to his desk he found a padded envelope by the computer. Inside was Aisha Refai's tablet.

De Groot called not long after. The commissaris was waiting in his office with Snyder. The man from Rotterdam looked even more pissed off than he did.

'What a mess,' he grumbled when Vos walked in. 'You're damned lucky I'm not suspending you.'

'I didn't know she was going to try to get back into Blom's place. If the man had been a bit more forthcoming—'

'Jesus Christ, Pieter! A police officer breaking into private property? She was under your command.'

'She was. And yesterday when she wasn't she was a hero.' Vos turned to Snyder. 'Did you find anything in the boathouse?'

The forensic man frowned.

'Signs of sexual activity. The only semen we've come up with belonged to Simon Klerk.'

'A nurse?' Vos commented. 'With his own sex club by the water? There has to be more.'

'I can only report on what I find. Not what you wish was there.'

'Do you have any idea where the Timmers girls are?' De Groot demanded.

Vos was thinking about Bea Arends. She was the one who'd sent them to Blom's place. Told them about the affair with Visser – which he felt sure was accurate. Then contradicted Blom's claims about Freya's threats. He wasn't so sure about that. Bakker had asked an interesting question: why go back to Marken after her daughter had died there in an apparent suicide? It was an odd response. An unnatural one.

'Vos! I asked a question.'

'We drew a blank in Chinatown. That dump they stayed in was somewhere they found themselves. Someone set them up with the Englishwoman. That seems sure. Now . . . they must be out there on their own.'

Which had to be quite frightening, he thought. Two young women, institutionalized for almost half their lives, thrust into the modern world with no one to turn to.

'I've set someone looking at the buses and cabs to and from Waterland. It's going to take a while.'

'Relatives?' Snyder wondered.

'There aren't any. Not still alive. No friends. No . . .'

'Maybe they're not there at all,' De Groot cut in. 'They're just running.'

'Perhaps,' Vos agreed. 'Kaatje Lammers. We really need her back for interview about Vera Sampson. She's a much more likely suspect than the Timmers girls. All the evidence suggests—'

'Not much point until you find those two, is there?' De Groot snapped.

All the decisions were made already, Vos realized. He was there to hear them, not help frame them.

'You're right.' He tugged at his hair, thinking. 'Are you sure you want me on this case?'

'How many other officers do you think I have?'

'Thank you for the vote of confidence.'

'For God's—'

'I really need to brief the night people now. Can we continue this later? Come down to the boat, Frank. I'll get some pizza from round the corner. Sometimes I think better out of this place.' He smiled. 'And we can talk. Candidly.'

The invitation came out of the blue. De Groot understood there was something behind it.

'When?' he asked.

'Eight?'

'Eight,' the commissaris agreed.

Vos went back to the office and packed the envelope with the tablet into his shoulder bag. Then he found Rijnders, who'd just come on duty for the night. It was a simple enough request. Look into Bea Arends, also known as Bea Koops. Check the files to see if she'd ever been in trouble with the police.

'Did they sleep around a lot?' he added. 'The Cupids?'

Rijnders blinked and said, 'Is that a serious question?'

'Yes.'

'They were pop stars. Of course they slept around. I made a few calls last night to some people who hung about in their circles. Nothing came out of it. Except . . . they were real lads back then.'

Vos told him about Bea Arends and her child with Frans Lambert. Rijnders looked disappointed he hadn't managed to scoop up that piece of gossip the night before.

'Did any of the people you spoke to mention her?'

'Not one. Was she a looker?' Vos kept quiet. 'Because if she wasn't I doubt they'd remember. It's the lookers that stick in people's memory. The fat girl who ran the fan club . . . sorry.'

There was something so loose, so pointless about the way

these men lived that he couldn't picture what it was like. One other point from the Arends interview came to him.

'Jaap Blom's wife. Lotte. Have you got anything on her?'

He shuffled through his notes.

'Lotte. Lotte. Lotte . . . Yes. Here it is. Lotte Gerritsen.'

He went to the computer and pulled up some newspaper cuttings he'd assembled from the night before. Vos looked at the photos on the screen. Gert Brugman, young and full of life, clutching his bass in one hand, a glass of champagne in the other. Rogier Glas beaming at the camera, a girl on each arm. Young girls. No more than early teens. And Frans Lambert at the end, a lanky, shy-looking man with too much long black hair, not keen on being photographed at all. On his arm was a younger Lotte. She looked beautiful and happy and quite unlike the dry, sarcastic woman they'd met that afternoon.

Her face was close up to Lambert's. As if they were intimate. Behind he could just see a young Jaap Blom. He wore an interested, covetous look as he gazed on the band and the women with them.

'Wait,' Vos said. 'Lotte Blom was Frans Lambert's girlfriend?'

'Pop stars, remember?' Rijnders suggested. 'They look really nice together, don't they? Like a real couple.'

They did. He checked the date on the cutting. Six months before the bloody events in Volendam. Then another clipping. Lotte and Jaap Blom's wedding just a year later.

'Now *that*,' Rijnders said, 'is what I call getting hitched on the rebound.'

'Go back to what happened in Bali.'

'Looking . . . for what?' Rijnders wondered.

'Lies,' Vos said. 'Lots and lots of lies.'

'No, no, Pieter.' He was getting exasperated. 'There's nothing out in Bali. I talked to people at the embassy. They sent me all the press cuttings. Look . . .'

His fingers flashed across the keyboard. Some scans came up.

Stories from a local English-language paper. Behind were more, obscured by the number of documents on the screen.

'What about those?' Vos asked.

'Those are in Indonesian or something. I can't read it. If you want me to get a translator . . .'

Vos took the mouse and moved one of the clippings to the front. It looked like a court scene. Lawyers in black dress. Police officers. From what he could make out from the headline it was the inquest into the missing Bram Engels. Frans Lambert hiding under an alias.

'This one. How do you blow it up?'

Rijnders was quiet. He could see it too. There was a figure in the background.

'That's the woman who was with him on the boat,' he said. 'I recognize the name. Lia Bruin. She was . . .'

He made the picture bigger. It was obvious now. The same face, the same hair. Just older.

'Lotte,' Rijnders said. 'Lotte Blom. She gets around, doesn't she?' He reached for the phone. 'I'll fix an interview.'

Vos's hand got to his before he dialled.

'Leave it for now. I'll deal with everything in the morning.'

Rijnders looked uncomfortable.

'You're sure about that?'

'Very,' Vos said and left for the night.

88

Maybe they gave Kim two more rums and Coke. Or three. She wasn't counting. Sitting in the bar, beneath the leering devils, she was rolling back the years. To the time when they met their mother here after school, listened to her sing, joined in if the band let them.

Their young voices, tuneful mostly, occasionally scolded for missing a note, echoed in her head. She didn't hear the rock crap on the radio. Or the three men by her side, whispering among themselves. Sniggering. She knew what that meant, what it led to.

No one else came in. This concrete block on the edge of Volendam never got busy until nine at the earliest. Only once had their mother taken them back in the evening, to perform, nervously, for a prestige audience. The Cupids, their manager, a bunch of men – all men – she said were important people, from Amsterdam and beyond.

Was that the night just before it happened?

She wasn't sure. Everything from that time had a dreamlike fogginess to it and she was happy for it to stay that way.

Feeling bleary, stupid and a touch drunk, she sat on the bar stool, clinging to the sticky counter. The slowly circling fans above them stirred the hot summer air. The men were getting nervous.

Finally the youngest came and nudged her elbow.

'We're going for a ride. Maybe have a smoke. We've stuff they won't let you use around here.' He looked about her own age, thin with a straggly moustache and crooked teeth. The sweatshirt he'd just bought over the counter: a grinning devil jabbing his fork into a naked girl screaming with glee. 'Want to come?'

'Why?' she asked without thinking.

You never said an outright yes or no. They didn't like that. You were supposed to be persuaded. *Seduced.*

'We can have some fun.' He nudged her arm again. 'You'll love it. We'll run you home afterwards.' He looked disappointed she didn't leap at the offer. 'Where is home?'

'Round here,' she said. 'My dad's a big man. You wouldn't want to mess with him. He'd rip your head off and chuck the rest of you in a dyke.'

The kid looked worried by that.

'But it don't matter,' Kim added. 'He's dead. So he can't do anything now, can he?'

One of the older ones was listening. He was chewing gum and kept grabbing at his crotch.

'We're not from round here, girl. What you lot get up to doesn't bother us.'

'Oh,' she said softly.

He came closer, eyes running all over her.

'So are you coming or what? Might be a bit of money in it for you. If we think it's worth it.'

'Will you hurt me?' she asked in a girlish, faint voice, the kind they wanted to hear.

'Course not,' he said, like they all did.

''Kay.'

They waited until she moved then followed her outside. The car park was at the back, hidden from the road and the seafront. Anything could happen there. It was empty except for a dirty red Ford van with the name of a building company on the side and an address in Alkmaar, a town she'd heard of but couldn't place.

The third one had stayed silent. He was older than the rest. They seemed family. Not that they talked much.

Two of them walked ahead and opened the back doors of the van. Then the third ordered her to climb inside. There was a grubby mattress on the floor, some clothes next to it. Boxes of tools. They probably lived in the thing when they were moving round the country working.

She came to a halt.

It was the oldest one behind her. He shoved her in the back and said, 'Get the fuck in. Don't play the innocent now.'

That was enough. She jerked the knife out of her belt, let him see it, then swiped the air ahead of her, swearing just as much as he did, trying to stab him.

Too quick he took a couple of steps back and the others were on her. The young one twisted her wrist until the knife fell from her fingers. The other kicked her shin so hard she screeched with pain.

They held her arms behind her as she spat and yelled.

Not a face at a window in the bar. Not a single devil let alone seven.

The old one wiped the spittle from his face, glared at her and said, 'This will be fun.'

They'd dragged her, fighting, kicking, to the van doors when a huge black open-back truck rolled into the car park and came to a halt beside them, tyres shrieking, kicking up dry dust in the hot late-afternoon air.

The three of them were slow and didn't move. Kim saw her sister's concerned face through the windscreen and immediately felt a familiar, sickening stab of guilt start inside her head.

A big man got out of one side. Another came out of the other. Tonny Kok had a broken double-barrelled shotgun bent over his arm. Willy just kicked the gravel and looked at the three men in front of them.

'Sometimes strangers here make terrible mistakes,' he said in a casual, didn't-care-much kind of way. 'They think we're stupid. Or we're just not bothered. They think this is a town where anything goes. And maybe it does.'

Tonny took two orange cartridges out of his waistcoat, popped them into the barrels then locked the shotgun and lazily pointed it in their direction.

'But not for you,' Willy added. He held out his hand. 'Kim? We're going home now.'

She threw off their arms and walked away. Mia came out and hugged her. She was crying. That just made it worse.

The three builders from Alkmaar were still weighing this up. Maybe a fight was as good as the pleasure of dragging a screaming half-drunk girl down a country lane, then leaving her there like a damaged rag doll for someone else to find.

Tonny seemed to recognize this so he edged the shotgun just a shade to the left, loosed one barrel down the side the van. The pellets scraped the paint and blew the side mirror clean away. By the time the three men had recovered sufficient composure to look again he was breaking the gun quickly, popping in another cartridge, locking it then grinning at them, ready to start all over again.

'We're going,' the old one said and they climbed into the red Ford and drove down the narrow lane, back to the road.

The barman from the tavern was watching from the kitchen door by the bins. Back by the water a dog was barking and an old woman was looking their way.

'Just a friendly discussion, Koen,' Tonny called. 'No need for you to worry, is there?'

The two of them sat in the middle between the brothers, Mia still hugging her in silence. Tonny picked up some pizzas along the way. Then they drove back to the farmhouse. The day was fading. The green fields of Waterland were taking on the colour of a painting, timeless and perfect. Kim recalled dreaming of this moment in Marken, a memory from childhood, the inexplicable belief that somewhere among the grass and the dykes and the flat and endless horizon a perfect world might be waiting, anxious to be found.

They went into the dining room. Tonny Kok locked the front and back doors then put the keys in his baggy farmer's trouser pocket.

The pizzas were undercooked with rubbery cheese, cheap ham and slimy tomato.

'I've done my best to lock that window of yours, girls,' Tonny said. 'This isn't a prison though. Not like Marken. It's a house. Our home. We can't stop you running away if you want to. Wouldn't be right.'

'No,' Willy agreed. 'It wouldn't. Can't guarantee we can save you another time neither.'

'Where would we go?' Mia asked. 'We're home already.'

The two brothers thought about that. Willy smiled.

'You are. Both of you.'

'I'm sorry.' Kim was crying. 'I remembered that place. I always thought it was . . .' She sniffed and looked wretched. 'My head's not . . .'

Mia reached out, took her fingers and said, 'It's OK.' She looked at the brothers. 'Isn't it?'

'It's fine,' Tonny said and Willy nodded.

They ate in silence. After a while the girls went into the living room and watched TV.

Tonny and Willy Kok cleared the plates and washed them briskly, without much care. A bachelor routine. One they'd grown used to over the years.

'This can't go on, Brother,' Willy said. 'Now can it?'

'No,' Tonny agreed. 'Blood or no blood. It cannot.'

They found a couple of beers and sat staring in silence for a while.

Willy fetched two packets of crisps from the kitchen, threw one at Tonny, opened his and said, 'We told them we weren't going to get involved? Made that very clear.'

'Ja.'

Willy stared at him, waiting for more. When it didn't come he added, 'Well we are now, aren't we?'

'I reckon.' Tonny chinked his glass in a grim, reluctant toast.

89

Vos picked up Sam from the bar. The place was almost empty. Sofia was behind the counter. The American boyfriend was at a table reading the paper, a cup of coffee in front of him.

It didn't seem the hour for coffee. Or the time for conversation.

He walked Sam to the Italian slow-food place around the corner and ordered a couple of marinara pizzas to take away. One glass of red wine while he waited, staring at the wood oven as the two men threw pastry around and prodded at the logs. The waitress fussed over Sam as usual. Then it was back to the houseboat, the rickety rear deck table laid with the one plastic spread he owned. The only napkins he had bore Christmas trees, reindeer and dancing Santas. They probably went back to when he'd still had a partner and a daughter and a flat, brick walls, no ducks bobbing outside the bedroom at night. A kind of sanity. And that was an illusion too.

De Groot turned up just as he was opening a bottle of wine.

'Good timing,' Vos said and poured him a glass. The pizzas were perfect as always, thin, crispy, slightly burnt at the edges, with buffalo mozzarella and organic Tuscan tomatoes.

Then two men, one late thirties, the other a decade older, sat opposite one another on a shaky table at the back of the dilapidated houseboat on the Prinsengracht.

'I thought we'd be eating in the Drie Vaten,' De Groot said. 'We usually do.'

Vos looked up and down his stretch of canal. He felt he knew every turn of the waterway, all the bridges, the places the cobbles had failed in the pavement, the shops, the couple of dope cafes, a lot of the people too. It was a neighbourhood. A home.

'Things aren't usual, are they?'

The night was still warm. Mosquitoes were swimming in the haze coming off the water. Sam, dozing on the deck, snapped idly at them from time to time. The commissaris loosened his tie. His walrus moustache had too much colour. He must have been using some kind of dye. Vos didn't mind about getting older. Didn't think about it much at all. When he was trying to recover his life after his daughter's disappearance he'd made himself swear never to concern himself about matters he couldn't possibly affect. Age was one of them. Maybe he'd feel differently when he hit the half-century as De Groot had. But he doubted it.

'Look, Pieter. I know you don't like the fact I suspended her. I understand you've got a soft spot—'

'Don't say that,' Vos cut in. 'It's not true.'

'Really?'

'Really. Laura Bakker's not like us. Not jaundiced. Not experienced. Not worn down by all the crap we've dealt with. She sees things differently. She reminds me why I came into this job. I need her.'

De Groot picked up a piece of pizza, examined it in the soft evening light, removed a couple of capers, took a bite, then a swig of wine and said, 'Well. That's a shame, isn't it?'

'I want her back. I want Aisha Refai in the office tomorrow too.'

The pizza went back on the plate.

'Bakker's finished. She broke into the property of a prominent politician. Don't be stupid. Refai's Snyder's problem. Ask him.'

'Don't want to. I'd like Schuurman recalled from this course you sent him on. We need to be working with people we know.' He hesitated then said it anyway, 'People we can trust.'

De Groot really didn't like that.

'Anything else?'

Vos pulled the tablet out of his bag and put it on the table.

'No. Just that. Then I can find the Timmers girls. Close this case down. Don't ask why, Frank. I'm begging.'

'Not . . . possible.'

He turned on the tablet and pushed it across the table.

'You were in Volendam the day the Timmers family and Rogier Glas were murdered. You were with their manager, Jaap Blom. And Ollie Haas.'

De Groot picked up the thing and gazed at the picture.

'Where did you get this?'

'From a tape in Stefan Timmers' studio. Whoever broke in there and whacked Dirk Van der Berg around the head ripped it out of the cassette. I guess he thought we couldn't recover anything.' A thought and he had to say it. 'Where were you on Wednesday night? I tried to call. Nothing.'

That hurt.

'Are you seriously asking whether I assaulted one of my own officers?'

Vos shrugged and said, 'Just wondered where you were. As I said to Jaap Blom: you pay me to ask questions. Don't complain when I do.'

'I went for a walk in the Vondelpark. Felt like some fresh air. These cases get to us all.'

'On your own?'

'On my own.' He raised the tablet. 'The reason I was in Volendam back then was very simple. It was a charity event. We were offering some support. A few prizes. Showing the uniform. Trying to build some community spirit. Never easy in that place.' He turned the screen to show the picture of him behind the cut-out of the fisherman, holding the winking, struggling fish. 'If there was a nefarious reason do you really think I'd have allowed myself to be photographed like this?'

'You should have mentioned it.'

'Why? I was gone before that talent contest even started. Back here for dinner. I didn't know anything had happened until the next day.'

'So why did you delete the files?'

De Groot put down his glass and looked along the street. He seemed ready to leave.

'What?'

Vos pulled a printout from his pocket.

'These are the holiday schedules from five years ago. I know Ollie Haas has put his hand up and said he killed those records. But he was in the middle of a two-week break.'

'Maybe he came in the office and did it. You ask him.'

'And I'm sure he'll say that's what he did,' Vos replied. 'Why, Frank? Just between the two of us.'

A long silence then. The commissaris picked up his glass, drained it, reached down and was about to pat the dog when Sam growled without moving a single furry muscle. He always caught the mood.

'How long have we been friends?'

'Long time. As long as I remember.'

'In that case—'

'You want me to look the other way? Never mention it again?'

De Groot stayed quiet.

'Is that what friends do?' Vos wondered.

Some people walked past. De Groot waited till they were gone and said, 'You never mixed well, did you? Never went out much except with who you wanted. I'm one of the few people you really know and you don't even realize it. In most ways you're smarter than me. Than most of us. But here you are, living in this dump. On your own. Never going to get higher than brigadier. Lucky you've still got that. I've saved your backside so many times. I got you this job when everyone else had given up on you.'

Vos laughed.

'This job nearly destroyed me. And now you've brought me back to it. Why? So you can watch it destroy me again?'

'Because you deserve it!' Then, more quietly, 'It's easy where you are. Simple decisions. Right and wrong. Up and down.'

'This is easy?' Vos asked. 'I'd hate to see hard.'

De Groot seemed old and vulnerable at that moment.

'You don't know what it's like. People ask favours. Innocuous ones that don't really break the rules. Don't cost you anything. Don't keep you awake at night. And if you say no someone else says OK and the shit happens anyway. It's just that you get brought down with it.'

Vos poured some more wine. It was a good red. A primitivo from Puglia. Before De Groot and Laura Bakker persuaded him back into the police he might have downed the whole bottle in a mood like this. Then looked for something else afterwards and woken up the next morning, flat out on the cabin floor, head thick with hangover and regret, Sam licking his stubbly face.

'I just want to find those girls,' he said. 'Put all this to bed. I don't want to dig up the past.' He looked across the table. 'Truly. Just give me Bakker. Get Aisha in the building. Schuurman—'

'Schuurman's on a course! I told you!'

'Laura and Aisha then. I'll wrap up this up. Tomorrow. Those girls have to be in Waterland somewhere. But I can't work with people I don't know. My fault entirely. It's how I am. Too old to change.'

There'd always been a subtle divide between them. It was only natural. De Groot was a manager. Vos a lieutenant in the field. There were aspects to both their roles that were best not shared at times.

'Well,' the commissaris said, standing up, holding out his big hand. 'That's settled then. Keep Bakker in check. Don't go sticking your nose into the past any more than you need. Get those girls safe somewhere. When you've done that pull back Kaatje Lammers and ask her a few questions. Find out if they really did kill that Sampson woman. Then wrap it up. Let's try and get things back to normal. Deal with whatever's coming tomorrow instead of trying to dig up yesterday.'

'I couldn't agree more,' Vos said and shook his hand.

Sam got to his feet, wagged his tail, held up his head to be stroked. De Groot knew what was required and patted him gently.

'I spoke out of turn,' he said, not looking Vos in the eye. 'I'm sorry about that. Things haven't been easy for you either. I should remember that more.'

He wandered over the gangplank. The American was leaving the Drie Vaten. He seemed no happier than De Groot shuffling off down the canal.

Vos looked at the bottle. Then at the dog, wagging his tail.

'OK, boy,' he said. 'Let's go for a walk.'

90

Schiphol was busy as usual. Holiday travellers. Parents lugging children around the sprawling airport, trying to keep them amused. Henk Veerman found a quiet corner to wait, then went through to the gate when the flight was called.

Everything on time. It was important to leave this to the last moment. Five minutes before the flight was boarding he called Vos's number.

It took three rings then he heard the brigadier's gentle, interested voice. Behind it there were people talking and music. Then the low murmur of what had to be a boat somewhere. A canal in Amsterdam. Veerman could picture it and wondered if he'd ever see that sight again.

'Veerman here. How was your day, Vos?'

'Busy. Much like yours I imagine. I'm sorry I never got out to Marken to see you. We need to talk.'

He paused. The boat got louder. The music too. Veerman could see this all so clearly now. One of the tourist cruisers idling down the broad open waters in the Canal Ring somewhere.

'If you're willing to talk, that is,' Vos added. 'Most people aren't.'

'I'm sorry.' The flight desk people were getting ready, sifting through papers, looking at customers. Not long now. 'Everything was such a mess. Irene. Those Timmers girls. That bastard Klerk. It's as if . . .' They called the business-class passengers and anyone with children. 'It's as if all this shit was waiting for us in the wings. Just ready to burst. We should never have let them out. I knew it. I didn't have the guts to stop her.'

'Were you aware Irene Visser was having an affair with Jaap Blom?'

Veerman laughed.

'I never went near the private lives of my employees.'

'Did you go near anything? Blom was making evening visits. Supposedly social ones.'

'I'm sorry. Now's not the time.'

'Tomorrow then,' Vos promised. 'You will be brought in for interview. Whatever anyone else says.'

There were more announcements. Close now.

'What's your email address, Vos? I've something for you.'

Vos read out an official one in Marnixstraat.

'I mean your private email address. You really don't want this in the office.'

'I don't have a private email address. Just the work one.'

Veerman found this odd, but thinking about the man not entirely unexpected.

'You do have a computer? Your own? At home?'

'I've got a phone,' Vos objected. 'There are computers in the office. Why would I need one at home?'

'Christ . . .' A thought struck him. 'And this is a work number too?'

'It's my phone, Veerman. What is this?'

His seat was towards the front of the plane. They were boarding the back rows now.

'This is me about to open Pandora's box. Make things easy for you. I shouldn't even be calling on this number. I—'

'For God's sake say what you want to say. I've had a long day.'

'There's something I want to send you. I can do it as a link. A text to someone. A private number. Get that? Private.'

Along the Prinsengracht, close to the old courthouse, near the bar Van der Berg loved when he didn't want to be in the Drie Vaten, Vos pulled his notebook out of his pocket and read over Bakker's personal mobile.

'I'll send it there,' Veerman said down the line. 'You will need a computer to access it. I strongly suggest you do not do this anywhere near Marnixstraat.'

Sam was pulling on the lead. Someone at a table outside the bar was offering him a chunk of hot dog.

'Fine. I so much enjoy mysterious conversations late at night. Thank you.'

'Welcome,' the voice down the line said. 'That detective of yours. The big, inquisitive one. Van der Berg.'

'What about him?'

'Tell him I'm sorry I hit him. I hope he wasn't hurt.'

There was movement somewhere behind Veerman's voice. An announcement. A flight number. The name of a place.

'Irene and I . . . we thought we were doing the right thing. Someone had to look after those kids. We didn't want the place closed. Not after we thought we'd fixed it.'

'Stefan Timmers . . .'

'She said he had some information going back years. He'd been using it against a few of the people. Blom among them I think, which is probably how she heard. I . . . we just tried to make things right. They leaned on us. They said it'd never happen again.'

The sound changed. More announcements. Vos could picture him going down a gangway.

'We really need to talk,' Vos said.

'It's only when you stop and stand back you realize how much you hate yourself. Apologize to him for me. I hope that what I'm giving you makes amends. A bit anyway.'

The line went dead. Vos scribbled down some notes on what he'd heard. Then he called Laura Bakker. She sounded sleepy and down.

Before she could say much he broke in, 'You'll get a text any minute. From Henk Veerman.'

'A text?' There was a message beep. 'Oh. It's here already.'

'Good. I need you at the boat.'

'Now?'

'Now.'

After that he phoned Aisha Refai and Van der Berg. Then Vos walked the dog home, found the table at the back and picked at some chunks of cold pizza. Glass of wine in hand he made another call.

He was grateful she was the one who answered the phone.

'What the hell do you want, Vos?' Lotte Blom demanded. 'Haven't you caused enough trouble today?'

'Not really. I'd like to know why you went out to see your old boyfriend Frans Lambert in Bali five years ago. When he was calling himself Bram Engels and pretending to be dead. After that I'd like to know where he is now. Think before you answer.'

There was a long pause. Then the line went dead.

91

The girls were upstairs when Tonny Kok's phone went. Close to eleven. He was slumped in front of the TV with another beer, Willy snoring away in an armchair by the window.

Sometimes the council called late at night asking for some dyke clearances early the following morning. But that only happened when the weather had been extraordinary. This summer had been perfect. Dry, sunny, hot. The fields were full of rich grass, the water teeming with life, ducks feeding, fish and eels below. The kind of summer a man remembered from his childhood. A sultry sort of Eden.

He looked at the number and realized it wasn't the council.

'Lotte,' he said, taking the call in the kitchen so as not to disturb his brother. 'You have heard?'

'Heard what?'

'The girls are loose. They're here. One of them nearly got into trouble down that bar where Freya used to work.'

There was a deep sigh on the line then she said, 'They're with you?'

'*Ja*. Did I not say that?'

'Not exactly. Thank God.'

She told him about the call from Vos.

'That man is clever,' he said. 'A decent kind of fellow for an Amsterdammer. His girl, that one from Friesland who had the trouble with Sara Klerk . . . now she is a good one. A diamond—'

'We've waited,' she cut in. 'Long enough. They won't do a thing. We can't put it off any more. Gert and Bea, Frans . . . we're all agreed.' She waited then asked, 'Are you?'

Tonny Kok looked around the kitchen. They'd grown up

here. The farmhouse was more than home. It was their world. A sanctuary in the green fields of Waterland. A place of safety, of comfort. Somewhere to hide at times.

'*Ja.* I believe so.'

They'd had run-ins with the law aplenty. Drunken escapades. The odd fight. Never any dishonesty. That was plain wrong. They'd been brought up to hate lies and thieving. The Kok brothers' distaste for it was deep in their blood.

'Won't be no turning back from this one, Lotte,' he said. 'Will there?'

'No,' she said. 'There won't.'

There wasn't a lot to say after that. Just a lot to do.

92

The Drie Vaten had closed early for some reason. There were only security lights on. No music. No sign of life. It wasn't yet midnight. Vos rang the bell and banged on the door, Sam by his side, puzzled and yawning on his lead.

Finally Sofia Albers came downstairs. She was in a blue night-gown, fluffy slippers on her feet. Her eyes were red and bleary.

'This is bad. I'm sorry to wake you.'

'What do you want, Pieter? I don't feel so good. So I kicked everyone out early.'

The American friend, he thought. Something had happened.

'I need your help. You've got that wireless connection. Internet. I've Laura coming round. Aisha and Dirk. We need to work.'

'What? Don't you have that on the boat?'

'No. I've got a phone.'

'Why don't you go into the office?'

Sam took his chance and wandered past her legs until the lead stopped him.

'Can't. Don't ask.'

Sofia opened the door and he came in. She bent down and took the lead off Sam's collar. The terrier went over to the bar and found the dog bed behind the counter then curled up and fell instantly asleep.

The place smelled strongly of beer with a faint aroma of cigarettes behind. There were dirty glasses everywhere. This was so unlike her.

'Make yourself coffee. Pour yourself a drink. Don't care. I'm going upstairs. With any luck I'll sleep.'

He didn't know what to say.

'Is there . . . anything . . . ?'

'No.'

'The American. Er . . .'

Names usually eluded him unless they were important.

'Michael?'

'Him.'

'Gone.'

'Sorry.'

She laughed.

'I'm not. Or I am. One or the other. Or halfway in between.'

'If you want to talk—'

To his surprise she came close and pecked his cheek.

'Another time. You're so sweet. So fragile underneath it all. No one's ever going to want to touch you. They'll wonder if you'll break.'

That observation baffled him but all he said was, 'Right . . .'

Sofia walked back to the stairs, patted the dog once and got a growl in return from the slumbering animal.

'I just kept thinking about his wife and kids,' she said, turning on the first step. 'They're on the other side of the world. He was never going to tell them. They'd never know. It still nags you. I still felt guilty. Dirty. Ashamed. Why? If it was never going to harm anyone? Not a single soul? Why?'

He came over, found Sam's thin blanket and draped it over the dog.

'It's how we are I guess. Most people anyway.'

'I suppose.'

'I'm not that fragile by the way.'

Her hands went to her hips. The old Sofia Albers, a determined, individual woman, no one's fool.

'Is that so? Goodnight. Help yourself to anything you want. Don't make a noise.' She chuckled, a sound he liked. 'I wouldn't want the police on my back for staying open too late.'

Five minutes later there was a rap on the door. It was Laura

Bakker with Veerman's text on her phone. Within the next half-hour Aisha Refai had turned up followed shortly after by Van der Berg.

The detective looked round the empty bar and immediately started to clear up the dirty glasses, putting them in the machine behind the counter.

'I hate grubby places,' he said. 'Worked in a beer dive once upon a time. You'll be surprised to learn.'

Aisha was setting up her laptop and logging on to the wireless network.

'No drinking,' Vos ordered.

Van der Berg glared at him.

'Of course there's no drinking. Who wants what?'

Two coffees. One water. One orange juice.

Bakker passed her phone over to Aisha and asked, 'Why are we here?'

Vos told them as succinctly as he could. Then broke the news that both she and Aisha would be welcome back at work the following morning. He wasn't surprised that Bakker was suspicious about that.

'How did you get De Groot to change his mind?'

Van der Berg knew how to work the coffee machine. He came over with two cups and the soft drinks on a tray.

'See? I made a good waiter. Could always go back to it if I wanted.'

'I asked a question,' Bakker said.

'I'm very persuasive when I choose to be,' Vos told her.

Aisha was shaking her head. The link Veerman had sent to Bakker's phone was for a public folder on a cloud storage service. There were eighteen gigs of material there.

'Is that a lot?' Vos asked.

'Even I know that's a lot!' Van der Berg pointed out. 'What is it?'

Aisha was bent over the laptop, face close into the screen. Such a natural position for her it seemed.

'PDFs. Word files. Video. Pictures. There's stacks of it. We could be here all night. Is there another computer we could use?'

Van der Berg went behind the counter and found the laptop Sofia handed out to regulars. Aisha put it next to hers on the long table.

'Can you use both?' Vos asked.

'Sure.' She gave him a look. 'This is a public folder. Anyone with that link can see this stuff. No password needed.'

He pulled up a chair next to her and looked at the filenames. One seemed familiar. Van der Berg saw too. It followed the format for the Marnixstraat filing system. Aisha opened it and all four of them looked at the document names there.

'Where did you get this?' Van der Berg asked.

Vos told them.

'These are the case files, aren't they?' Bakker asked. 'The ones I was looking for. The ones that got deleted.'

The sisters had gone straight into Marken after they were detained. The medical staff there would have access to all the police reports about their case. De Groot might have managed to kill the copies within Marnixstraat. Whoever put him up to that never realized there were identical ones held in the institution, presumably by Irene Visser and her colleagues.

'What's the rest of this stuff?' Van der Berg asked.

'Big files,' Aisha said. 'Video. Lots of it. The connection here's just home broadband. This is going to take a while. Especially with two of us working down the same line.'

There was a folder called SimonK. Vos jabbed a finger at it. She opened the first video file there. A younger Kaatje Lammers' face came up on the screen. Perhaps thirteen or fourteen. Naked, grinning. Doped or drunk. The segment was shot from above, presumably by the man holding the camera. It wasn't hard to tell what she was doing.

'That,' Bakker said, pointing at the pink satin coverlet and the toy penguin to the girl's right, 'is the Flamingo Club.'

Aisha checked the file data. It had been recorded six years before. Then she brought up another video. Bakker looked away. It was another girl, this time with a man visible from the back only, face hidden, portly, middle-aged. The kid was red-faced and crying with fear and pain.

'We get the idea,' Van der Berg moaned. 'That's enough for me. I can't watch this stuff. Sorry.'

He was one of the most analytical officers Vos knew. Someone who could quickly skim through case files and form a picture of what lay behind them. Vos gave him the bar laptop and told him to check through Haas's original investigation.

Aisha shrugged and killed the videos.

'This is going to take days. Weeks.'

She found another folder. One of the files had the name of a local TV news programme. Aisha clicked on it.

The recording was shaky and old. A bright sunny day, summer on the Volendam waterfront. A news reporter's voiceover was talking about the charity talent contest supported by The Cupids. They were all there on three chairs set apart by the stage. Rogier Glas looking confident. Frans Lambert, a tall, powerful man with lots of hair who didn't smile much. Gert Brugman, red-faced, clutching a beer.

It was impossible not to watch. A tall, striking blonde woman led three young girls onto the stage. She was wearing a tight, short skirt. The kids were in scarlet shirts and skimpy hot pants. A few of the men were catcalling as they walked onto the platform.

Freya Timmers introduced herself and then the girls: Kim, Mia, Little Jo. Then said a brief thank you and waved at a stern-faced man in a fisherman's smock by the side of the stage. Her husband, Gus.

They watched in silence. A cruel and bloody fate was waiting for these people around the corner. And here they were, alive, engaged, seemingly happy, thinking a bright and starry future lay ahead.

'I can't take this either,' Van der Berg said and picked up the spare laptop then went to the adjoining table to start work.

Freya sashayed off the stage. The band got louder then the girls began to sing in perfect harmony, each voice clear, sweet and angelic. With the first few notes the crowd became quiet, listening to the song, lost in its curious, perfect loveliness.

The camera turned to the front row of the audience. Jaap Blom and Frank de Groot sat next to one another. There was no sign of their wives.

Laura Bakker sighed and put a finger against De Groot's head.

'Is that why we're not in Marnixstraat with all this stuff?'

It wasn't a question Vos wanted at that moment.

'Let's look at what we've got,' he said. 'Then take it from—'

Aisha's slim dark fingers were moving across the keyboard like crazy.

'What are you doing?'

'Moving all this stuff somewhere safe. A place of my own. Didn't you hear? It's a public folder. Anyone with that link can see it.'

Vos put his hand on hers.

'How about we move it somewhere safe. And leave it where it is as well. There's a word for that.'

'It's called copying,' Bakker said.

'Copying,' he agreed. 'That's what I'd like.'

93

Ollie Haas was alone in one of the tourist bars near the harbour. None of the locals spoke to him. They hadn't much since he left the police. No reason on his part. No desire on theirs. Tourists were different though. He could easily engage them in conversation. Spin them some local yarns. Get a free drink, not that he needed the money.

This wasn't going to last much longer anyway. He'd put the house on the market. The agents said it would sell too if only he could bring himself to lower the price a shade. Haas didn't like cutting corners. He wanted what he wanted. After that he'd take his savings and vanish from the Netherlands for a while. The Caribbean. Florida. Italy. Wherever he felt like. He was owed a break. There'd been too much in the way of awkward questions of late. He'd known the Timmers kids were going to come out of Marken around now. That was a matter of simple arithmetic. The place couldn't keep them much beyond the age of twenty-one.

It was by no means certain the past would rise up to greet them all when that happened. But it was a possibility. If he'd been smarter he'd have taken the opportunity to scoot out of Waterland months before. Now he couldn't wait. And perhaps wouldn't. If the agents couldn't clinch a quick deal he'd take what money he had and run anyway.

A small glass of beer and a jenever sat in front of him on the counter. An American couple from Oregon had allowed themselves to be engaged in conversation earlier. Then they gave him a look and said their taxi back to Amsterdam was waiting.

He'd watched them walk off to their hotel along the harbour road wondering if it was something he'd said. Or perhaps an awkward, needy air just hung around him these days. Either way this wasn't going to trouble anyone for long.

Haas didn't drink much but tonight could be an exception. He finished his beer and jenever and walked outside, then along the waterfront to the public car park where he'd left his Volvo. The place was deserted. All the Friday action happened elsewhere in Volendam, and would go on well into the morning.

By the car he stopped and fumbled for his keys.

'A man like you,' a bold, strong local voice said, heavy with sarcasm. 'Driving when you've got strong drink inside you. Brigadier Haas. What are you thinking?'

Sometimes the natives got heavy. They remembered him from when he was running the police here. Plenty of enemies. None with the guts to do much but wheedle and whine.

'I'm thinking you'd better piss off home, chum,' he said, still running through his pocket for the keys. 'Before your life takes a nasty turn for the worse.'

There were two of them, both in front of the car.

Haas looked up and they came out of the darkness into the light cast by a car park lamp.

'Tonny and Willy Kok,' he said. 'Shouldn't you two be tucked up in your cots by now? I know your old mum isn't around to read you bedtime stories—'

It was Tonny who was on him first. A big punch to the gut. Haas bent over, winded, scarcely able to believe it. No one had dared touch him in Volendam in years.

'It's other stories we want to hear, Mr Haas,' Willy hissed in his ear. 'We'll give you a night to think it over.'

Haas coughed, gasped for breath, wondered if he was going to retch.

'What the—?'

Tonny had him then, held him while his brother rifled his pockets for the car keys. A few more punches. He heard the boot fly open with a pop. Before he could shout or scream they'd belted him some more and thrown him inside.

Ollie Haas was just finding his voice when the world turned black and close, became nothing more than a cramped compartment that smelled of dust and diesel.

Then the engine started and they were moving God knows where.

Two kilometres away Jaap Blom was packing his small travel case. His wife watched him, smoking a cigarette, a look of distaste on her narrow, lined face.

'You're really going to drive all the way to The Hague? You've been drinking, Jaap. Is that wise?'

'Don't have to stay in this house. Not when I'm not wanted. Don't have to put up with you looking at me that way all the damned time.'

She laughed and asked, 'What way would that be?'

His shirt was open and sweaty under the armpits. He came up and poked a finger at her face.

'I've kept you. Paid for your life. Ten years. Ten miserable years. And what gratitude do I get?'

'I'm still here, aren't I? What more do you want?'

'Let it go, Lotte. Just let it go. All that shit's over and done with.'

She stubbed the cigarette into a vase by the door.

'If you say so.'

'We need to talk to lawyers,' he grunted. 'Can't keep on with this. Not any more.'

'Lawyers?' She put a finger to her cheek. 'That would be interesting. Whenever you like.'

He swore at her then she opened the door and he lurched out into the dark warm night.

The black Mercedes coupé was kept in a lockup on the far side of the canal. It was the nearest parking space he could find in this cramped, genteel corner of Edam.

He marched across the iron bridge still cursing. When he got to the garage a filthy Datsun pickup was parked across the entrance blocking his way. Someone was in the cab listening to music on the radio. Old music. The Cupids.

Blom swore, went to the door and yanked it open.

'Just move this piece of junk, will you? I've got places to go.'

No answer but the music did get turned down. A big man climbed out and stood by the driver's door. A beard he didn't recognize, almost hiding a face he did.

'Jaap,' Frans Lambert said. 'Been a long time.'

Across the water he could see the back of his house. Beyond the summer house and the palms the lights were still on in the kitchen.

'Get in, please. We need to go somewhere and talk.'

Blom laughed.

'Ten years since you ran away. And now you're back? Telling me what to do?'

He moved closer and said, 'Just get in, will you?'

Blom jerked out his arm and pushed him hard in the chest. Lambert stumbled against the Datsun, cursing. He was taller, stronger maybe. But Blom had always been the boss. He'd beaten him to a pulp when he was a mouthy kid, good at the drums, lousy at everything else. Things hadn't changed so much.

Lambert was coming back for more. A single, hard punch to the stomach stopped him, left him winded and gasping for breath.

'What the hell is this?' Blom yelled, getting mad, feeling aggrieved. 'Did you start all this crap? The police. Marken. For Christ's sake . . .'

'I didn't do anything,' Lambert moaned. 'None of us. Not me. Not Rogier. Not Gert. Just—'

Blom brought up his knee and caught the crouching figure hard in the gut. Lambert went down.

'You pathetic worm. Get the hell out of here. Crawl back to whatever shithole you came from.'

The figure in black lurched towards the pickup's cab.

'I don't want to see your face round here again,' Blom spat. 'Don't ever . . .'

He felt something cold then, hard against his neck. Heard a trigger cocked. A gun against his neck. Soft and certain breathing behind. There were two of them.

Lambert got to his feet. Courage found. By someone else.

He jerked back his arm. Big fist. Strong man. It was just that most of that strength went into stupid things like yoga and tai chi and other such crap.

'Think about this,' Blom mumbled. 'Just think . . .'

The punch was hard and cruel. He was half-conscious as they dragged him into the pickup. Gone completely when a second blow came to keep him quiet.

94

They didn't leave the Drie Vaten until three that Saturday morning. Even then Vos and his colleagues had only dealt with a fraction of the information Henk Veerman had left stored in a cloud folder for all the world to see . . . if they had the right address.

By that stage they were exhausted. Depressed. And full of anticipation. From the hours spent going through the files it was clear they could prove the basis of an extended investigation. Most of the information was old, pre-dating the death of Maria Koops, which appeared to mark a significant turning point in the Marken story. But a decade wasn't distant history. Vos felt sure there was enough promising material here to raise the prospect of conviction for anyone connected still alive. Photos. Names. Lists of visitors to the institution, politicians, people from the media and entertainment world, local councils, the police. The guilty liked to hide behind the innocent. It was inconceivable that every individual named in the records turned their visits into nights at the cabin called the Flamingo Club. But there was sufficient smoke to convince Vos he could make this case catch fire with some effort, a spot of luck and support from on high.

The key would be persuading the victims to talk and that was never easy. A good number would have been released already. From previous experience he knew how difficult it was to persuade the victims of historic sex crimes to reopen their wounds. For former inmates of an institution like Marken, frightened of another engagement with the legal system, it could be even harder. Others, like Kaatje Lammers, might be seen as unreliable witnesses, vindictive, inconsistent and proven liars. His best bet could be the Timmers sisters themselves.

It was obvious there'd been systematic abuse over an extended period. Perhaps even murder. The case to come might turn into one of the most protracted and difficult the department had faced in years. Marnixstraat would, for one thing, have to prise responsibility for the investigation from the ministry's own team now looking into Marken as if it were simply a case of institutional failure. Finding Kim and Mia Timmers and persuading them to talk had to be the first step.

In such situations a single false move early on could so easily scupper criminal charges months or years down the line. He needed legal advice, specialists, a detailed, reliable game plan to take the case forward. And all he possessed was a massive stack of leaked material, some of it the police's own, illicitly deleted to keep the incriminating information out of the hands of those who might use it.

Vos returned to his houseboat and watched Sam fall sleepily into his dog bed in the cabin aware he was terribly out of his depth. In the normal way of things he would have simply taken what he had to De Groot, asked for advisers to be assigned to the investigation, and followed their expert counsel to wherever the evidence led.

Now he felt stranded. Lost.

His head swimming with images of Waterland – endless green fields, dykes full of dark water where thick weed hid what lay below – he fell below the duvet. The next thing he knew his phone was ringing. Bright sunlight streamed through the houseboat's thin curtains. Ducks were quacking outside. Sam got up from his bed, yawned then ambled to the cabin door and started pawing at it.

Still in pyjamas Vos let him out, picking up the phone along the way.

'Pieter. Are you OK?'

It was De Groot and he sounded worried.

'Of course.' Sam had developed a habit of peeing off the side of the gangplank. Vos was torn over whether this was a good idea or one more offence to get him into trouble with the authorities, already cross with the ruinous state of the boat. 'Why wouldn't I be?'

'Last night—'

'Last night we had a candid talk. It's done with.'

Silence, then De Groot took a deep breath and said, 'I'm glad to hear it. Something's up.'

Vos listened to his rapid explanation. De Groot had phoned Haas first thing. There was no reply. When he sent a patrol car round to the house they found it empty.

'Why did you call him, Frank?'

'That doesn't matter now. His car's been outside a bar in town since last night. I can't raise Blom either. There's no answer from his place in Edam.'

Vos was wondering what to say about the stash of leaks from Veerman. Nothing seemed best.

'Perhaps they've gone on holiday together.'

'This isn't funny. If those two girls believe Haas and Blom were responsible for their family's murder they could be prime targets. I really don't want any more blood on our hands. Nor do you.'

Sam wandered down the gangplank and looked up at him, hunger written on his inquisitive face.

'Why would they think that?'

'Jesus! Will you stop being obtuse? The officer responsible for the case is missing. So's the man who was managing The Cupids at the time. I want them found. I want those girls back inside where they belong.'

'So you said. I need Aisha Refai. Snyder won't want her.'

'Done,' De Groot said.

'On it,' Vos told him and that was that.

Ten minutes later he took Sam over to the bar and picked up a coffee on the way to the office.

They were there already, three of them around the desk.

'So I gather we're looking for four people now?' Van der Berg said. 'Not two?'

'Sounds like it,' Vos agreed as he scanned through the morning reports. 'Dirk. Aisha. You two stay here. I've got some things I need you to check. Laura. Get us a car.'

95

They spent the night gagged, hands tied in a dusty shed that smelled of diesel and chemicals. At dawn a single cock crowed and then came the sound of chickens clucking busily. Animals were lowing somewhere, birds squawking. There was a distant buzz of traffic from time to time.

Haas kept mumbling through the rag around his mouth. He had scared eyes and struggled to piss in the corner once during the night. Jaap Blom checked his bonds, knew he couldn't shift them. Then crouched down by the corrugated iron wall to wait.

There'd been a few arguments with the Amsterdam gangs when The Cupids were starting to make money. Once one of the hood outfits had done this to him. Money sorted everything as usual. Another time he'd done the same to a rival band manager who'd had the temerity to think he could tempt the band from him.

Plenty of stupid people in the world. Plenty of cowards too. He had both with him in that tiny, rusty cell.

They waited. A long time he thought. Then in a sudden rush the door opened and three men came in, grabbed them, bundled them into a bigger space where straw flecks hovered in the hot light air, bound them to a couple of seats in the centre then went away.

It was a stage of a kind, Blom guessed. They wanted a performance.

If that was the case he'd give it to them.

When they came back it was Frans Lambert who removed their gags. Haas's first and he just shook and begged. All the idiotic pleading phrases. The man was too dumb to realize: they wanted something and wouldn't stop until they got it.

Lambert came and untied the gag round Blom's mouth. Jaap Blom looked up, grinned and said cheerfully, 'Frans! You never gave me the chance to say it last night. But you're looking good. Aged well.' A pause. 'All that time doing nothing out in nowhere I guess. Money gone now, has it?'

They were in a barn, the roof old and full of holes. Morning sunlight was working through the rusty gaps, casting shafts of yellow across the dusty interior. It was hard to work out how many people were there. They were just shapes in the shadows.

Lambert was still tall and muscular, still wore black jeans, black T-shirt. His hair was shorter, going grey in places and there was a new, heavy beard, bold and thick enough to fool people who didn't know him well.

He bent down in front of the two tethered men.

'Funny, Jaap. Any more jokes?'

Something swished through the air. It took a moment for Blom to realize what it was. A baseball bat in Lambert's strong hands.

'And you've taken up sport too. It's good that a man should look after himself—'

'Shut up!' Ollie Haas shrieked. 'For God's sake, Jaap—'

The man in black pulled both arms back then beat the club through the air so close to Ollie Haas's face he must have felt the sweep as it raced past. The old cop whimpered and fell silent.

'This cretin may be a sad bastard who lives on his own,' Blom said. 'I'm not. I've got a wife. An office in The Hague that's waiting for me.' He looked up at Lambert. 'Whatever nonsense this is, Frans, it's a waste of time. You'll go to jail. When they find out—'

Movement in the shadows, figures entering the light. One there that made his heart sink and his voice fall silent.

Lotte Blom came and stood next to the drummer then took

his arm. She had the look of victory on her. That hadn't been around for a while.

'No one knows you're missing, Jaap,' she said. 'I called your office and told them you'd gone away somewhere for a break. You could vanish off the face of the earth right now and no one would know. Or care. I wonder. How does that feel?'

A memory from the previous night. *Two of them.* The metal barrel cold against his neck, a figure behind. He'd been slow and stupid. There was a handgun he'd kept from the old days, for when the gangs came calling. Blom couldn't even remember where they hid it. His wife clearly did.

'Lotte,' he replied, quietly, seriously, with all the sincerity he could muster. 'Whatever we've been through . . . whatever you think I've done . . .'

She hung on Lambert's arm, gazing at him, amused.

'What I know you've done's bad enough,' she said. 'What I think . . .'

The man in black stepped forward. The long wooden bat slashed through the air again.

Lotte Blom laughed at the way they shrank back.

'Now's the time to find out, I guess,' she added.

'What in God's name do you want?' Haas screeched. 'Just say it.'

'Girls,' Lambert called.

Two shapes in black with hair the colour of burnished copper emerged from the shadows. Then Bea Arends. Gert Brugman, limping and looking sick. Finally the two yokel brothers Blom knew from his Volendam days. They had broken shotguns in their arms.

It was Kim who came up first. She looked wild-eyed, crazy. The other one held back.

'Hello, Mr Blom. Mr Haas,' the girl said. 'Remember me?'

96

He let Bakker drive for once and sat in the passenger seat making calls and reading messages on his phone. It was a calm summer day, pure blue sky the colour of a starling's egg, scarcely any traffic once they'd escaped the city.

Vos got through five emails and three texts before they'd reached the open fields of Waterland. Then he took a call from Aisha Refai. When it was over he stretched back in the car and announced he was still hungry.

'Isn't this urgent?' Bakker asked.

'It would be if we knew where we were going. Why do people need computers of their own? I mean really . . . what's wrong with a phone? We've got computers in the office.'

Bakker told him he was in an odd and antediluvian mood.

'What did Aisha have to say?' she added.

'We finally got something back on the call.'

That was it.

'The . . . call. Any call in particular?'

'The first one.'

'Still struggling, maestro.'

He sighed and scanned the green horizon. They were past Broek headed for Monnickendam. Soon they'd be in Volendam and she'd no idea where exactly they were headed.

'How did this start, Laura?'

She knew this game by now. Vos was challenging her to reconnect the pieces of a fragmented narrative. It was a bit like doing a jigsaw and she hated puzzles.

'With Mia and Kim Timmers getting let out of Marken. After which they went with Simon Klerk to that farmhouse for some reason. His reason I guess. Then they overpowered him and left him stark naked for his wife to discover.'

Things had been moving so quickly she hadn't had time to put all that together in her head. But it seemed to make sense.

'They can't have known she'd be mad enough to kill him. All the same that's what kicked it off.'

He frowned, looked at his watch then stared out of the window.

'Didn't it?'

'You took the phone call,' he said. 'Supposedly from Ollie Haas's old girlfriend.'

'Ah.' She remembered. 'Yes. That.'

'Who made it?'

'His old girlfriend? I don't know!'

'Aisha finally got something back from the switchboard. It came from Marken. The institution. A landline.'

'Visser?' she asked.

'Visser helped cover up whatever happened in that place. She was trying to hide things from us. No.'

Volendam was five kilometres away. He'd have to tell her where to go soon.

'Bea Arends then. Or Koops. From the kitchen.'

'That's my guess too. What Bea didn't tell us is that one of the places she worked ten years ago was the Waterland hospital in Purmerend. The Sampson woman was a staff nurse there, dividing her time with Marken. They must have known each other.'

The hazy picture was starting to turn clearer. Eighteen months before, Bea had come back and got a job in Marken under an assumed name. She found out nothing about her daughter's death. But when the Timmers sisters were set for release she arranged for them to hide out in Amsterdam.

Bakker tried to recall what the Arends woman had said the day before when Vos had asked why she'd never come to the police with their suspicions. The answer was simple: they had. To Ollie Haas. They'd been ignored.

'Someone's been dropping us breadcrumbs all along.'

'Quite,' Vos agreed. 'And if Kim and Mia stayed missing they reasoned we'd be forced to take another look at Marken and what put them there.'

'Maybe if Sara Klerk hadn't killed her husband . . .'

'No,' he said in a low, aggrieved voice. 'It wouldn't have worked anyway. All the files were gone. In Marnixstraat. In Visser's office too. If Veerman hadn't kept his own . . .'

'God. We really failed those people.'

'We did,' he agreed.

'So it's back to Bea's place?'

He shook his head.

'She's not there. I got a local car to check. Lotte Blom's not at home. Gert Brugman neither. And Frans Lambert's no more dead than you or me. It's just . . .' He closed his eyes and looked ready to go to sleep. 'We've been strung along from both sides and I was too idiotic to realize. I thought it was just one.'

Bakker stopped and waved at a smart red tractor waiting to cross the road and pull into a field by their side.

'You're so polite sometimes,' Vos noted.

'Country girl. Always give way to a farmer. Tractors are bigger than you for starters. So they've done a runner? Ollie Haas and Blom thought we might be on to them finally—'

He groaned and she knew she'd said the wrong thing.

'What—?'

'They've had ten years to run away. These people think they're untouchable. They know it. We've made them like that.'

Out of Marnixstraat, just the two of them ready to think out of the box, things were starting to make sense.

'Do you know what happens if people expect justice and you don't give it to them?' he asked.

'Mostly . . . nothing,' she said. 'Thank God. Otherwise we'd be knee deep in angry vigilantes.'

He roused himself in the seat and looked up. The town lay ahead, a collection of low roofs set against the placid silvery lake.

'Mostly. There's a white building coming up on the right. Before the roundabout. A bungalow cafe. Quaint place. White walls, black beams. Pancake house or something.'

'I see it.'

'Pull in there.'

'Why?'

'I'm hungry.'

'A pancake house won't be open at this time of day!'

'I said. It's a cafe too. People out here are . . . versatile. Independent. Strong-willed. I suppose you need lots of talents.'

'It won't be open.'

Vos held up his phone for her to see. There was a mobile page on the screen: *The Little Ducks Pancake House and Music Bar. We do breakfast too!*

'Thank you for keeping me in the picture as usual,' she said then pulled off the road and into the empty car park.

There was a sign along the way. A poster for a music night: 'Remembering The Cupids'.

Vos pointed it out.

'Now there's a coincidence, don't you think?'

Bakker growled.

'You can be really annoying sometimes, you know.'

97

In her black jeans and midnight T-shirt, sick of the cheap jewellery they'd bought, ashamed she'd got their beautiful hair dyed brown, Mia listened to her sister.

This was the old Kim. The forceful, demanding creature she'd become in Marken. Ranting and raving. Throwing out accusations. Never listening much to the answers.

Here, in the dry, hot dusty interior of the Kok brothers' barn, hens clucking happily outside and the faintest drone of traffic from the main road into Volendam, they might as well have been seated in front of Irene Visser. It was never about confession there either. Their presence demanded nothing less than an act of release, a purging of all the pent-up fury inside them. And then, in the exhausted aftermath, simple, blunt obedience.

Don't tell. Never tell. You'll only make things worse.

Kim kept screeching at the two bound men in front of her, Frans Lambert and the rest of the audience swallowing every word. Mia went to her side and whispered, 'Please, love. Not so—'

'Shut it!' the old Kim snapped. Then she bent her furious head into her sister's ear and half-sang, half-whispered a single musical line.

Love is gone and so am I.

That was enough. Mia closed her eyes and found herself in the last place she'd ever wanted to be, even in the beginning. A young girl dressed in blue hot pants, sparkly scarlet shirt, patent red leather shoes pinching her toes, yellow hair tied back in a bun, cheeks heavy with make-up, mascara stinging her eyes, lipstick thick and greasy on her mouth. Walking up the steps onto the Volendam stage.

Put on a show.

That was what her mother said. But to Kim. It was always the easy, obedient sister who came first.

Put on a show. Kim, give the gentlemen what they like. Your sisters can do their turn after. That's why we're here, girls. That's what'll let us leave this shithole forever. Just the four of us. The Timmers girls. Mother and her three daughters. Centre stage. No one'll ever forget us then. Will they?

But they did, Mia thought. So easily.

Kim was back to shrieking at the policeman who'd found them that night. Yelling about his lies. The people he'd hidden. What they'd got up to, year after year and no one cared.

Give the gentlemen everything they ask for. And then we walk away from the lot of them. That useless dad of yours too.

'It's why we're here,' Mia whispered.

Ollie Haas tried to say something. A plea. A denial. The man in black yelled at him.

The baseball bat went up.

The baseball bat came down.

The policeman screamed, his face a bloody mess.

Blom was bellowing too. All around her they watched and didn't move. It was like music. Another kind of performance, just as cruel as the ritual act the three of them had been forced to perform that distant balmy evening.

Mia took a deep breath and walked up to Lambert before he could strike the next blow.

'Don't do this, mister,' she said, putting a trembling hand on his arm, remembering what it was like to be a scared little girl on the Volendam waterfront all those years ago. Begging. Pleading. A small creature hoping against hope. 'Not for us. We're not . . .'

Worth it, she almost said.

Clawed fingers struck at her then, scratched her cheek,

pushed her out of the way. Hands to her face she waited, expecting the pain that was to come.

Because old Kim was here and in full flood. Fierce and uncontrollable, mad and wild.

'She's weak as a baby,' her sister yelled, reaching out for the bat. 'Let me. I'll beat the bastards for you.'

Lambert looked back at the rest of them. Gert Brugman sighed and stared at the dusty straw floor. Lotte Blom nodded. Willy Kok shook his head. His brother said, 'Any more of this and I'm walking out of here, Frans. I thought you lot wanted to put things right. Not do more wrong.'

No one spoke. Tonny shouldered his weapon and went for the door. Willy stayed all the same. Kim held out her shaking hand, trying to grab the bat. Lambert kept it from her, bent down in front of the bleeding Haas, the silent, sullen Blom.

'Who killed them?' he demanded, pushing the wooden stump hard into their faces in turn. 'The family. Rogier. Who killed them? That's what we want to know.'

98

An elderly couple, seventy at least, ran The Little Ducks Pancake House and Music Bar. They seemed surprised to get business before lunchtime, but grateful for it. The interior of the place was white walls with fake beams, neat wooden tables all carefully laid, paintings and photographs everywhere. At the end of the room stood a low wooden stage, a lone mike stand leaning at the back like a shiny drunken heron.

Vos ordered pancakes. Bakker stuck to coffee. When the man had gone to the kitchen she said, 'So this isn't just a random stop for a bite to eat?'

He checked his messages again. There were none. Then he got up and started walking round the walls, looking at the photos and the memorabilia. Bakker uttered a long, pained sigh and joined him. The place was like a shrine to The Cupids. Photos of them when they were young and starting out. Then in New York, playing the fool at the top of the Empire State Building. Picking up prizes. Posing with starlets.

The woman came out of the kitchen with coffee in two old-fashioned china cups with saucers bearing biscuits.

'You've seen our local heroes then,' she declared, bringing them their drinks. 'Those lovely boys came from Volendam. Back when they were doing the songs they wanted, you couldn't beat them. All that later stuff . . .' She winced. 'Well, we can forget that now, can't we? Poor lads. Time wasn't kind to them. Never is if you're in the music business I guess.'

She placed the cups on the nearest table and wiped her hands on her apron.

'Your girlfriend looks too young to remember but I reckon you do, mister.'

Bakker looked ready to explode.

'She's my niece,' Vos said quickly. 'Didn't something happen? Something bad?'

The friendliness vanished from her face in an instant.

'Lies. All them people from the city coming here telling their lies. Just because young Rogier liked to hand out sweeties to the kids. I ask you. Those lads never did anyone any harm. I'm not saying they were angels. You couldn't be in jobs like that. Everyone worshipping you. There was a time when they couldn't walk down the street without the ladies flocking round. Then, not long after, another time when it was just the fans like us, people who knew them, asking for autographs. Even though we had them already. Can't have been easy. They didn't do those terrible things some people said. Never would.'

She walked up to the photos and pointed out a more recent one. An older, frailer Gert Brugman performing solo on what looked like the cafe stage.

'They used to play here when they were teenagers and learning their tricks. Gert still comes back sometimes. Salt of the earth. Good Volendam folk. Here . . .'

She led them down the room. In the corner, mounted on a plaque halfway up the wall, sat a sunburst guitar. Next to it was a pair of drumsticks and what looked like thick long strands of wire.

'That was Rogier's first electric,' the woman told them. 'My husband paid off the hire purchase on that when the lad was broke. Frans Lambert's drumsticks. Some bass strings from Gert. We have a tribute band from time to time. Out here we still remember them for what they really were. Not all those nasty lies the press kept putting around.'

Bakker reached out and plucked the strings on the guitar. They were slack and barely made a sound.

'We'd buy more memorabilia if we could.'

'Not easy after all these years I imagine,' Bakker said.

'Not easy when the people who've got it won't sell,' she grumbled. 'I mean why hang on to stuff? Either have someone play it. Or let fans like us put it where people can see the things. I don't get it.'

Vos reached out and touched the drumsticks.

'He had a lovely golden set of drums,' the woman said. 'All glittery. We'd buy them if we could. But their relatives . . .'

Vos had got Van der Berg to go through that option. Rogier Glas's parents were dead. Lambert grew up with a single mother who'd moved to Florida. Brugman's father still lived somewhere nearby but the two weren't on speaking terms.

'What relatives?' he asked.

She threw up a dismissive hand.

'The kind you hope don't come around at Christmas. I don't even know they've got a right to own that stuff in the first place. I mean . . . why would Frans hop off and leave his drum kit with a pair of clowns who can't even get a girlfriend for themselves let alone play the things?'

Bakker said, 'Perhaps he thought he was coming back?'

The woman laughed.

'Left it a bit late, hasn't he? Only old folk like us going to pay to listen to him now. No one—'

Vos's phone beeped. He looked at the message and started to take out his wallet.

'What relatives?' Bakker asked again.

'I'm sorry,' Vos cut in. 'We have to go.'

He placed a twenty note in her hand. The kitchen doors opened. The man walked out bearing a plate.

'Go?' he asked. 'But I have cooked your pancakes. With my own hands. Here they are.' He thrust the food at them. 'Surely you've time for a bite.'

Vos nodded, picked up a piece in his fingers and was wolfing the thing down as they got to the car, spilling pieces everywhere.

He went to the driver's side, wiping his hands on his jeans as he reached out for Bakker's keys.

'I don't get it,' she said. 'Aren't we supposed to ask who the relatives are?'

'No need,' he said, getting behind the wheel. She climbed into the passenger seat. 'Aisha tracked it down finally.'

He brought the car to life and floored the pedal down the dusty track back to the road.

'Frans Lambert and the Kok brothers are cousins.'

'What?'

'Someone walking their dog in Volendam called in this morning. She saw two men threatening a couple of visitors with a firearm outside a bar last night. There was a pair of girls with them. Got a number for their truck. It's them.'

She gazed at him, open-mouthed.

'Tonny and Willy wouldn't hurt a fly.'

He cut in front of a bus as they reached the road and got hooted at for his pains.

'Would they?' she asked.

99

Another world was alive inside Kim Timmers' head. Here in the dusty barn where two men were getting beaten slowly, deliberately, chanting out the same pathetic refrain when they got the space to say the words.

It wasn't me. It wasn't me. It wasn't I swear . . .

Lies. Every word, every syllable they uttered through cracked and bleeding teeth.

Elsewhere. A lost place, bathed in the dreamy golden summer light of the town beside the lake.

One hot evening a short lifetime ago. Music and the smell of hot dogs and chips on the waterfront. People pushing and shoving. Laughing, too much drink inside them.

Their mother was there, bossing them around the way she always did. Their father, silent as usual, watching in his gruff, suspicious way.

We are a family of girls.

That was what their mother told them.

Men are just fools.

Dangerous fools though. Fools who knew what they wanted and hated when they didn't get it.

Uncomfortable in their tight clothes, the three of them lurked at the back of the stage.

'All things come to good children,' Freya said, listening to the cues, watching the hired band avidly as she waited for the moment to push them up onto the boards. 'And you three are so good. My golden angels.'

She kissed each in turn. Kim took the embrace happily. Mia

less so. Jo, Little Jo, always the one for an argument, tried to squirm out of her grip.

Freya Timmers held on to her tight, just to make the point: *You do as I say.*

'What's wrong, darling?' she asked in a hard voice as the band began to signal for the stage.

'Had enough,' Jo spat at her. '*Had enough.* We all have.'

She pinched Kim's bare arm hard.

'Haven't you?' Scared sister, timid sister, Kim kept quiet. 'It's always you she starts with. You've had enough. You said . . .'

'Didn't,' Kim whispered, too afraid to look her in the face. All the same a worm was slowly turning.

Mia looked up at her mother and said, 'Will we win, Mum? Will we win and then . . . then that's it?'

Freya stared at the three of them and there was none of her usual affection there.

'I could lie to you, darlings. But I won't. No one ever wins. Doesn't work like that. You've got to keep fighting. Never stop. You can have everything in the world or think you have. Love. Money. Fame.' She glanced at the three judges at their table. 'People at your beck and call telling you how wonderful you are. But if you don't keep fighting you lose the lot. And then you're ordinary. Common. Plain. Ugly.' She reached out and pinched Kim's cheek. 'We're not any of those things. So go and—'

'I'll tell him,' Jo cut in. 'If we don't win. If it doesn't stop. I'll tell him, Mum. I bloody will—'

A slap then. Quick and hard. Straight across the face. Jo glared at her, cheeks turning red from the blow, from her anger too. She was never scared. That was just her sisters.

'I'm taking you on that stage and you'll sing like I showed you,' Freya told her. 'And you watch your language, child—'

'I bloody will . . . I will . . .'

Freya's arm came back again. The music started. People were beginning to stare.

The angry, threatening scowl turned to a loving smile in an instant.

'You be sweet now, children,' she said, grabbing their hands. 'Do that and we'll all be fine.'

100

Down the dusty drive they sped, heading towards the ramshackle farmhouse. The graveyard of old tractors and machinery looked more than ever like the upturned toy box of a careless giant. Then they saw a car that wasn't there before. A shiny black Mercedes coupé standing out among the junk.

A man was leaning on the door of a rusty metal barn set in front of a field of endless green. There was a shotgun in his arms. Tonny Kok. Worriedly watching the unmarked police car race for his home.

Laura Bakker took her seat belt off before Vos had even found a space in the yard. She was opening the door as he came to a halt next to the corpse of an ancient John Deere.

Tonny hadn't moved, towards them or away. It was obvious what he was doing: guarding something.

'Call Control,' Vos ordered. 'Ask for backup.'

'No.' She was out of the car already. 'You call them.'

He wasn't pleased.

'This is no time for games . . .'

'True,' she said, leaning through the door. 'Listen to me, Pieter. I know these people. I grew up with their kind. You're . . . city. You're different. The enemy.'

'I'm your boss . . .'

'You're what they hate. You let them down. You hid all the things they wanted to see. Let me speak to Tonny first.' She nodded at the phone in his hands. 'You call Control. Get backup. Whatever you want. I'm going to talk to him.'

Then she closed the door and walked up to the man with the shotgun. He stood there, uncomfortable, shuffling on his big feet.

'Tonny.'

'Miss.'

'Laura. Laura Bakker. Remember?'

He nodded at the car.

'I remember. We don't want trouble. Best you and your friend get out of here. Lots of angry people around. Seeing you won't help.'

There was a cry of pain from behind the metal doors. Shouts and screams. Then silence.

'You'll find out all about it in the end.' He locked the shotgun with a quick, deliberate slam. 'Not now. This thing's started. Train's running. Can't stop it. Not even for you.'

'And if the train's going to the wrong place?' she asked.

Vos came up and stood next to her. The pair of them folded their arms and waited.

'You had all that time,' Tonny said. 'Years and years people round here have been waiting. But we don't count, do we? We're just small folk. Stupid farmers and fishermen. Nothing next to all those toffs in Amsterdam. The ones with the money. And your . . . your ear.'

Bakker glared at him then.

'The only voices I'm listening to right now come from two young girls in trouble. They need help and they're not getting it. Not from us. Not from people who think they're doing them a favour either.'

Another scream from inside. He raised the gun, the barrel half-pointed their way.

'I'm asking nicely, Laura,' he said.

'I heard. I'm just not listening. Best shoot me,' she said and pushed the grey barrel to one side.

There were more shouts inside the barn, more pained and frightened screams. From across the flat green meadows came the insect whine of far-off sirens.

101

'We didn't win,' Kim muttered in the dusty half-dark of the barn.

She could see it all so clearly as if then were now. And now nothing but a ridiculous never-ending nightmare.

They didn't even get second place. That hot night by the lake Freya Timmers sat listening to the judges, a stony stare on her face. All the trite remarks.

So much talent everywhere...

Such a hard decision...

It wasn't, Kim thought. It was an easy one. Give them what they wanted. What they'd suffered for. Earned. She even more than her sisters.

Instead a couple of long-haired, pretty teenagers from Amsterdam, strangers, foreigners, another boy-band in the making, walked off with first prize. Jaap Blom had told The Cupids to vote that way, or so her mother said. It didn't occur to her then that perhaps they'd paid too. Only later did that idea surface when the pair of them got a recording contract then vanished into obscurity.

Jo was so furious, spitting bile and curses everywhere. Their mother dragged her off home, Gus their father in prickly tow. Kim and Mia had to stay behind and pick up the poor consolation they'd won: third prize. A box of chocolates.

A box of chocolates.

'All that,' she whispered to herself, staring at the two men bruised and bleeding before her. 'For a box of bloody chocolates.'

They'd hung around the stage for a while. Then, when the beer was flowing and the men getting too friendly for their liking, they'd carefully detached themselves from the crowd, slid out from the show, walked along the waterfront away from everyone.

Mia was in tears. Kim was just mad.

Aware of their stupid clothes they went and sat by the car park near the museum. No one there. They opened the chocolates and tried a couple. Too sweet. Too cheap.

Like us, Kim thought. And nothing was ever going to change that.

After a while Mia stopped crying and said they ought to go home.

Kim threw the chocolates in a bin and said, 'I'll tell her I chucked this crap away too.'

That's brave, she thought as they trudged back to the cottage by the harbour. Next to the threat Little Jo had uttered, yelling curses right, left and centre. Shouting . . . *I'll tell.*

That's really brave.

When they got there the door was open. There were voices inside. Loud and violent. Mia hovered at the front step.

Kim had always been the timid one. Mia in the middle. Jo the angry sister, cursed with a caustic, too-free mouth.

That had changed though.

'Don't,' Mia said and tried to hold her back. 'There's some-thing—'

'No one's hurting me again,' Kim said. 'Or you. Or Little Jo. No one—'

Then she pushed her sister aside and walked straight in.

102

Inside the barn there were two men bound to chairs, heads down, bleeding, faces caught in shafts of sunlight from the broken roof. In front of them stood Lotte Blom and Bea Arends. A tall, athletic bearded figure who had to be Frans Lambert was cradling a baseball bat stained red, looking back at the door. Willy Kok lurked to one side, a shotgun broken in his arms. Gert Brugman was leaning against a wooden crate. Then a couple of slight, elusive shapes half in darkness.

Vos walked straight up and said the first words that came into his head.

'Amsterdam police. Put that thing down, Lambert. And the gun, Willy. I know why you're doing this. I know what brought you here—'

The tall man didn't move.

'Is that so, Sherlock?' Bea Arends rounded on him. 'Monday those two girls came out of Marken. We spirited them away and thought you'd finally notice something's wrong here. And what do you do? Nothing.'

'Nothing,' Lambert repeated.

Bakker stepped forward so they could see her clearly.

'Things don't happen overnight,' she said. 'There's an investigation under way. This time round—'

'Under way?' Lambert snarled, kicking at Haas's chair so hard it made him whimper. 'Like the one this fool did? You lot don't give a damn about us. All you want is to cover the backs of—'

'We've a lot of work right now,' Vos cut in. 'Lot of bodies. Simon Klerk. Irene Visser. Stefan Timmers—'

'Good riddance,' Bea Arends snapped. 'Filth, the lot of them.'

'Vera Sampson,' Bakker added. 'She was your friend, wasn't she?'

The woman hesitated at that, then nodded at the shapes in the corner.

'Don't try and lay Vera's death at the door of anyone here. Wasn't the girls who killed her. That crazy cow Kaatje Lammers was there, wasn't she? Cut your throat for five cents that one. And Veerman let her out. None of this would have happened if you lot were doing your job. If—'

'I agree,' Vos said and got nearer Blom and Haas. He'd seen worse. This was a beating. A nasty one. But nothing more. Yet.

The door opened. Tonny Kok stuck his head through and said there were people turning up. Police. Lots of them. Then he went back outside. Gun in arms again.

'All we want is the truth,' Lambert said. 'Bea and me lost a daughter. These girls their family. Then their freedom. There's blood spilled here. Ours. Got the right to know.'

Vos listened then asked, 'So why did you run?'

The drummer's arm stabbed out at Blom.

'Because you don't hang around and argue with the likes of him! Freya did. She knew he wasn't going to fix anything proper for those girls. And look what happened when she moaned about it. Like Hendriks, the man from Marken too. Dead and gone.'

Blom winked with one half-shut eye. Lambert pulled back the bat, ready to strike.

'You always made a lot of noise, Frans. Not much in the way of sense. Or action. First sign of trouble. On your way.'

'I had no part in your filthy games, you bastard! Why should Freya bring us all down because of you?'

'You really think I killed her?' Blom asked. He seemed ready to laugh.

Vos looked towards the girls in the corner.

'Mia,' he said. 'Kim.'

'They were kids,' Lambert barked. 'What do they know?'

All the files from Marken. Every last report written by Ollie Haas. They were more thorough than Vos could have expected but that was all part of the fog. The idea this was a cock-up, not a conspiracy. A clever tactic. A successful one. For a while.

'Let's ask them,' Vos said and called their names again.

103

There was no one in the hall of the black-timbered cottage. No one in the front room. Or seated at the familiar table in the kitchen where they sat and ate in silence after their father spoke a quiet grace.

The sounds came from above. Footsteps, shouts and screams. And then a terrible cry unlike anything they'd ever heard. A high-pitched shriek. It had to be Little Jo. And another scream.

At the foot of the stairs they stopped. Mia reached out for her sister's hand to drag her back. Kim shook herself free and took to the steps.

Blood on the walls. Blood on the cheap table where their mother kept what heirlooms they owned: old crockery, now smashed into sharp jagged pieces on the bare timber landing.

'Kim . . .'

They made their way to the big bedroom. The place her mother loved to take them when the house was empty, to sing, to hug, to dream.

Two bodies on the floor, spread-eagled like a pair of bloodied rag dolls. One tall. One small. Blonde hair both, bedraggled now and barely hiding faces the sisters knew would haunt them for all the long days and months and years to come.

The kitchen knife he'd used lay between their bodies. Kim picked it up and didn't know why.

Another sound then. A loud, commanding one.

His voice.

His presence.

They turned and saw Gus Timmers, shotgun in his arms. Weeping, angry, mouthing dreadful imprecations.

All aimed at them.

You dirty little bitches. How could you?

It was as if his hurt was greater than theirs. As if they'd somehow done all this to spite, to harm him. To spoil the precious illusion of family. And that was their fault, naturally. The guilt, the blame, all theirs.

The bloody knife trembled in Kim's sweating fingers as their sobbing father tried to aim the barrels their way.

'Run,' Mia said more loudly and snatched her sister's hand. '*Run!*'

Fearful, wailing, they turned and fled, away from the gore and the dead, away from the terror behind the black-timbered walls where they'd grown up always hoping for something better because Freya, their mother, said the golden days, a brilliant future, both were coming soon if only they could wait. Be good girls, like Kim was. Be willing, be polite and never cry.

Down the worn wooden planks of the landing, down the grimy carpet on the stairs, out through the hall, into the hot street.

Behind them the sound of an explosion so loud it seemed to tear a hole in their sunlit world.

That dull, dread noise spurred them on. Along the narrow cobbled lane, not knowing where to go. Until a van door opened blocking their path. And a familiar face came into view.

'Girls,' the big man said, all smiles. 'What is it? You look like you've seen a ghost.'

104

Mia and Kim didn't come when he called. So Vos told them about the case files anyway. How they'd been erased in Marnixstraat and resurrected with new information by Veerman as he fled the country.

'Henk Veerman?' Lotte Blom looked as angry as the rest of them. 'He was part of it. You believe him?'

'I do. He got an attack of conscience. We have the documents, videos, reports, interviews,' Vos repeated. He looked at Ollie Haas. 'The initial investigation. It was thorough. Which is why they had to hide it. They thought they'd destroyed pretty much everything after Maria Koops died. But Veerman had copies. Lots more from Marken too.'

He fed them some of what he'd uncovered the night before, leaving out the fact that it had happened in a bar by the Prinsengracht for fear of alerting anyone in Marnixstraat.

'Just pack this in, will you?' Laura Bakker cried. 'It's not needed. You'll only get yourselves into more trouble. And if you bugger about much further you're going to find these two—' She pointed at Blom and Haas. 'They start to get a load of sympathy they don't deserve.'

'The young lady speaks a lot of sense I think,' Willy declared. 'We should listen to her.'

Lotte Blom bent down over her husband, put a hand to his chin, forced him to look into her face.

'You told me this was finished, Jaap. For good. You said—'

'I told you the truth,' Blom spat at her through cracked and bleeding lips. A nod towards the shadows. 'Ask them.' The girls still didn't move. '*Ask them.*'

A moment of silence. Outside a sharp electronic noise broke the quiet. A bullhorn, a voice Vos recognized. De Groot calling for someone to come out. Then vague and pointless threats.

Mia Timmers stepped out of the dark. Copper hair. Black clothes. Pale, bloodless. Her sister joined her. They held hands.

'It hurts,' Kim said in the softest of whimpers. 'It hurts. It always hurts.'

105

A ghost. He was now. The famous man. The singer. The kind one all the kids loved because he penned those beautiful songs, patted them on the head and gave them sweets.

Love is like a chain that binds me.

They knew that so well. Had learned it along the way as their mother taught them how to deal with harmonies, to dance, to make men watch with greedy glinting eyes. And what to do when the important ones came asking, looking, checking. Wanting.

Rogier Glas leaned down from the open door of his van and grinned at them.

'What is it, sweethearts? What's up?'

They stood there, Kim hiding the bloody kitchen knife behind her back, nothing to say.

'I'm sorry about the contest,' he said with a shrug. 'You should have won it but Jaap had other ideas. Still . . .' The grin got bigger. 'There's another one next week. In the city. Big time. How about you come to that?' A pause then. 'I'm running the judging. Not Mr Blom. It'll be fun.'

The sisters stayed next to one another, too scared to move or speak.

He reached into the van and took out a bag of something. They'd seen things like this so many times before.

'Tell you what, girls. Have a sweetie.' He shook the bag and opened it. All the colours of the rainbow. A few more besides. 'Take as many as you want. Bit of candy. A few sweeties. Won't hurt, will it? Won't hurt a bit. I promise.'

That was all it took. Kim flew at him knife out, stabbing

manically, the bloodied blade flashing left to right. He fled into the van. She followed.

What happened next was a nightmare. Red and vivid.

When it was over they stayed there, waiting. Minds blankly fearful, wondering if any of this could be real.

106

Ollie Haas's face came up, angry and bitter.

'I told them all this! I told them!'

'And who'd trust lying scum like you?' Lotte Blom asked. A nod to her husband. 'Any more than we'd believe him.'

Bea Arends looked shell-shocked.

'Not Rogier. Never Rogier. He was a diamond. I don't believe it. He wouldn't touch—'

Jaap Blom threw back his bruised and bloody head and laughed.

'Of course he never touched them. He wasn't on Freya's list. Jesus . . .' There was something new in his face. Despair. Resignation. 'It's always the men, isn't it? Always . . .'

'Who was on her list?' Bakker asked.

'Anyone she wanted to get her talons into.' He glanced at Lambert. 'Frans knew what was going on. Why do you think he scuttled off like that?' Then a look at Brugman. 'Gert was too drunk to notice. Rogier too damned naive. Promoters. Record producers.' Then, more quietly, 'Managers. People who mattered.'

Lambert said in a quiet, shocked voice, 'Freya told me she was going to ruin us, Jaap. Wouldn't even say why. We never . . .'

Blom laughed in his face.

'You still hopped it, didn't you? And you never thought to ask? How it all happened? Three semi-pro bums from Volendam. Could barely play a note until I came along and schooled you. Got the work. The deals. Found people to clean up your act. You were dead in the water, the lot of you. Out of date. Old. Pathetic . . .' His voice died away. 'If I hadn't done something . . .'

'How many others?' Lotte Blom asked. 'Over the years.'

'You think I counted?' he bellowed. 'For God's sake . . . why? If—'

'Little Jo was going to tell Dad.' Mia's clear sad voice hushed them all. 'Tell him everything we'd done. What Mum . . . asked. To get us out of there.'

Ollie Haas shook his bloodied head.

'This pair killed Rogier Glas like I said all along.' More quietly then he added, 'Gus Timmers stabbed his wife and his daughter. After that he put the barrel of a shotgun in his mouth and pulled the trigger. It was as clear-cut a murder–suicide as you're likely to get. His prints on the gun. Her prints . . .' He nodded at Kim. 'On the knife we found in Glas's van. You wanted the truth. There. Happy now?'

Bakker leaned down and looked into his face.

'Then why did you hide it?'

He struggled against the ropes and glared at Jaap Blom.

'Because this one and his pals made me! I wasn't part of their mucky schemes. If it had been left to me I'd have thrown every last one of them in jail. Don't think . . .' His fierce stare was on Vos now. 'Don't think for one moment you'd have done differently either. They got friends. Big men. Try saying no to them.'

Haas tried his best to sit upright and look at them: Bea Arends, Lotte Blom, Brugman, Lambert and Willy Kok.

'That's the truth. If I'd put it down as a murder–suicide someone would have started poking around asking awkward questions. The social people were sniffing about already. All they needed was an excuse. As long as there was an inconclusive investigation they said we'd keep it away from Jaap and his mates. If we left the whole thing unresolved some day it would just fade away . . .'

Haas glanced at Mia and Kim, two hunched figures still to the side of everyone.

'I did as I was told. They didn't give me a choice. I put these two girls away like they deserved. Got a promise those bastards would pack in their mucky games. No more of this bloody—'

'But they didn't, did they?' Bea Arends interrupted. 'They murdered our kid. Killed Director Hendriks when he was going to rat on them. Five years ago. Not ten. *Five . . .*'

Haas nodded.

'I never knew about any of that. Not till . . .' He turned to the man next to him. 'You tell them, Jaap. It's your story. Not mine.'

107

The boat that ferried girls from Volendam to the Flamingo Club bobbed up and down on the night waves, lit up just enough for safety, not so much that it was obvious. It was three in the morning. Kees Hendriks was at the wheel. Jaap Blom sat in the back trying to interest the girl in a smoke.

She crouched on the hard deck crying. A small bundle of misery who seemed to hate herself more than she hated them.

Guilt was never far away at these moments. But the heat and the excitement that started with Freya Timmers' games in Volendam five years before . . . they stifled it. Usually.

'Don't want to do this,' the girl said finally. 'Don't want to go to that place any more. With you two. With Simon. With anyone.'

Without thinking Blom reached out and touched her bare arm. She recoiled instantly. The night was hot. The evening had been . . . difficult. He hadn't meant the gesture to be anything other than comforting. These were games. Kids played them. Lost kids, abandoned kids. What else did they have?

'OK. That's your choice.'

'My choice?' she asked and in the dim light from the wheelhouse he could see such hatred and anger in her young face it made him sick for a moment. 'My *choice*?'

'You'll get over it,' Blom said and told himself that was true. Then he went to the wheelhouse to find his cigarettes.

A few seconds later he heard the splash. No cry. Not a word. It seemed impossible her slight frame could make a noise so loud. Hendriks, a better boatman than he'd ever be, was yelling orders in an instant. Lobbing a life buoy into the dark water. Grabbing a boat hook and torches.

Hour upon hour they flailed like fools in the black night. Finding nothing at all.

108

'She jumped,' Blom said, eyes closed, voice close to a whisper. 'She jumped from the back of the boat. I couldn't stop her. I didn't even see.'

He gazed up at Lambert standing over him, the bat raised again.

'Don't look at me like that. I didn't put her in Marken. You did. Both of you. And now you're trying to fool yourself this is all about her.' A glance at the Timmers sisters. 'About them.' A grim, short laugh. 'Yeah. Right.'

He was blinking, trying to focus.

'And you didn't call anyone?' Bakker asked.

'What was the point? She was gone. It was dark. Three in the morning. Black. Endless. We kept looking till daybreak. It was . . .'

'You as good as murdered her,' Bea Arends broke in.

'Your kid should never have been in that place!' he bellowed. 'Where were you? Drinking yourself stupid in Spain. While her father . . .'

He squinted at Lambert.

'Where were you, Frans? How could you just leave her like that? And then when it all goes wrong you come back and think . . . Yeah. I'm the big man. I can put all our consciences straight. Just find someone to blame.'

Blom leaned forward on the old wicker chair.

'Let me tell you something. We paid. You never lose that voice in your head. Never. We told ourselves we'd stop then. Hendriks couldn't handle it. He went to pieces.' A shrug beneath the ropes. 'Then he killed himself. That's the truth. No one touched him. We weren't . . .' He was about to say something then checked himself.

426

'No more visits to Marken. No midnight rides across the *meer*. Irene Visser kind of guessed what happened but I managed to keep her sweet. Veerman too. They'd have lost everything if it had all come out. None of us knew that idiot Klerk was still playing those games. I'd have done something if—'

Lotte Blom marched across, drew back her arm and struck him hard across his bloodied face.

'You promised,' she yelled. 'You lying bastard . . .'

'Like you promised you'd stop seeing Frans. You don't know what it's like. With your little lives. Your puny dreams. Not me. I got offered things every day. Things you couldn't imagine. And you know who it came from? The likes of you. All staring at me now as if I'm the only villain here. Do you think I went to Freya asking for her girls? We got them on a plate. Lots else besides. All from you—'

Lotte Blom withdrew something from her jacket pocket and he fell silent. It was a small handgun, the barrel now pointed straight at her husband's temple.

'The weapon,' Vos said carefully, only to see the snub nose briefly point his way.

Blom looked up at her, eyes half closed, defiant still.

'Go ahead then, Lotte. If it makes you feel good. If it means you can go home and tell yourself none of this was anything to do with you and Frans and Freya at all. You're all the bloody innocents here. If it—'

Bakker had edged towards her, feet scuffing quietly through the straw on the barn floor. Before Vos could get there she launched herself at the woman's outstretched arm. The weapon went up. One bullet fired into the metal roof, rattling round like a pebble in the tin. Then the handgun slipped from Lotte Blom's fingers and tumbled to the ground.

Vos was there by then. The two of them dragged her to the floor, Bakker reaching round for the cuffs, Vos bringing the woman's wrists round ready to be tethered.

'Can't even manage that, can you?' Blom yelled, lurching to his feet still tethered to the chair, cursing, trying to reach her.

De Groot's armed entry team, on tenterhooks already, reacted to the gunshot straight away. On cue they burst through the barn doors yelling, weapons aimed, combat gear in place.

Terrified chickens flapped their wings beyond the tin walls. Straw motes flew in tiny whirlwinds in the hot dense air.

'It's fine,' Vos started to say, getting to his feet. 'No need—'

A single shot. Jaap Blom's head jerked up with the impact of the bullet and his hefty body fell backwards with the chair. Then four more until the gun rattled empty to the desperate trigger.

Bea Arends stood above him, the discarded handgun now in her shaking fingers, a look of shock and surprise, satisfaction mixed with shame, on her taut, white face.

One groan, one last breath from the bloody mess on the grimy floor, head back, mouth open.

'There,' she said, slinging the weapon at the bloodied body before her. Masked men were drawing all around them, rifles up, yelling all the time. 'That's justice now. Done.'

'On the floor all of you. Hands on head,' the lead officer bellowed.

Bakker was turning to tell him to shut up. Vos got to her, made her do it.

Down in the hard straw they lay, just as they were told, faces turned to one another. Jaap Blom was no more than a footstep away.

Dead eyes open. Gone.

109

Outside lay chaos. Ambulances, weapons officers armed to the teeth slowly standing down after the tense anticlimax in the barn. The first of what would doubtless be a succession of TV crews was trying to push past the 'don't cross' tape some uniform officers were placing at the entrance to the Kok brothers' yard. A couple of medics had Ollie Haas on a stretcher and were ferrying him into an ambulance. Jaap Blom was beyond help. That was obvious from the outset. A corpse getting cold in the old barn, surrounded by medics and forensic officers assembling the tools of their trade.

Bea Arends was the first to be taken away, cuffed inside a custody van all to herself. Laura Bakker was helping shepherd the others to the edge of the cluttered yard to await a larger vehicle, Tonny and Willy Koks whining all the way.

There was a conversation coming and Vos dreaded it. Finally Frank de Groot walked over.

'Well this was a mess, I must say. Could you really not stop that woman? What the hell did she think she was doing?'

Vos looked at him and thought it best to keep quiet.

'Am I speaking out of turn?' De Groot wondered.

He told him then. About Veerman's flight to Istanbul and the documentation he'd left behind. The lost reports. The images and the visitor lists to Marken. The kind of names mentioned there.

'Ah,' De Groot said when Vos was finished. Nothing more.

'Busy times ahead, Frank.'

'I believe we covered the general principles of this last night,' the commissaris said eventually.

Vos shrugged.

'Sometimes you just can't keep a lid on things. Doesn't matter how hard you try.'

De Groot thought for a moment.

'Blom's name appears on those documents you got from Veerman? Frequently?'

'From what I've seen,' Vos agreed.

'Well there's your solution.' He made a cutting gesture with his right hand. 'There has to be a limit somewhere. We go so far, no further. No fallout . . .'

'I want Haas,' Vos broke in. 'I want Kaatje Lammers in an interview room answering for that Englishwoman's murder. Anyone else on that list I can nail.'

De Groot looked at the confusion around them. It wasn't getting much better. Too many people. No one seemingly in charge.

'Shouldn't you be running this show?'

'Now?' Vos demanded. It was almost a shout. Some of the nearby officers were starting to notice. 'When you've been trying to rein me in ever since those kids went missing.'

'Those kids murdered a man.'

'Do you know why?'

'No. Do you?'

'Because we failed them. God knows how many more too.'

'Wait . . .'

'No.' Vos shook his head. 'I'm not waiting any more. Haas is in an interview room as soon as he's well enough. I'm opposing bail. We need counselling for those girls. I want a team—'

The commissaris held out a hand and said something about taking things steadily.

'Too late, Frank. This *show* is going to run and run.'

'Really.' His voice stayed calm and quiet. 'Think about this before you go any further. There were no miscarriages of justice here. No one was convicted of something they didn't do. No fit-ups. No one got away with anything that happened that night.'

Vos almost shrieked.

'Not that night. Just the rest of the time because of who they were. Kim and Mia Timmers and their sister were kids. Little girls—'

'Little girls getting pimped by the mother, a Volendam tart.'

'And that makes it OK?'

De Groot came closer, jabbed a finger in Vos's face.

'Are you suggesting I was part of this? Just because I had my picture taken down there? I told you. I was there on duty. I knew nothing about what went on. Five years later I went along with removing those files on the strict understanding . . . that was all over. Done with. In the past. Never going to happen again. Besides, there was no guarantee we could have got anyone in court. No witnesses. A good lawyer would have wiped the floor with us—'

'Don't tell me these things, Frank. I shouldn't hear them.'

De Groot was back to being commissaris again. Wily and in charge.

'You're out of your league. You can pursue this as far as you wish so long as it travels no higher than I allow. I'll make sure Ollie Haas goes along with that. Blom's dead. Dump what you can on him. But there are limits and if you cross them I will know.' A pause then, 'You can't put everyone in jail. If you try they'll come for you. Trust me. I've been there.'

The second custody van still hadn't turned up so Frans Lambert and the Kok brothers were being bundled into the back of a patrol car, cuffed, the uniform officers pushing down their heads the way they usually did. Laura Bakker was arguing with the men, demanding gentler treatment. Willy Kok had started crying openly, gazing round the wrecks of the farmyard as if he'd never see them again.

'We are fine on this?' De Groot asked again. 'I'm talking from experience here. You can only tilt at so many windmills, Pieter. Go too far and they start to tilt at you.'

It took a while but finally Vos said, 'We're fine, Frank. Just get out of here.'

The commissaris squeezed his arm.

'I know. It's unpleasant. That's life.'

'Please go.'

De Groot didn't move.

'When this is under wraps we should have a chat. I'll see what I can do for you. Quietly. Bakker too. Van der Berg . . . I don't know. If only he could stay off the beer. There are pay grades I can play with maybe. Leave it to me . . .'

He stopped. The atmosphere had changed.

'Is that how it happens?' Vos wondered. 'Shred some files. Look the other way. When it's all over we'll hand you a pay rise and a promotion and everything will be fine?'

'You really have no idea how things work. That's why you're where you are.'

'I'm just one of the little people too, Frank. Happy that way.'

'This conversation's going nowhere . . .' De Groot sighed and looked at his watch. 'Get this Arends woman in an interview room and charged. The Timmers girls somewhere they won't escape this time. Fill me in on where we are tomorrow. Big dinner tonight. Sandra's coming home with her new husband. The honeymoon had to be delayed because of his work or something. The young these days . . .'

The car with Lambert and the Kok brothers was leaving. Tonny and Willy were both in tears now. The ambulance had gone ahead. Three uniform officers were dealing with Lotte Haas and Gert Brugman.

He couldn't see Kim and Mia Timmers anywhere.

'Did you hear me?' De Groot demanded.

'I did. This is what you have to do. Go back to the office and suspend yourself. If you don't I'll start the process for you.' He smiled and wished he hadn't. 'Enjoy your dinner. I want a formal interview in Marnixstraat in the morning. Don't make me come and arrest you. Choose the room you like best. You ought to bring a lawyer.'

De Groot raised his hand and prodded Vos hard in the chest.

'You sanctimonious shit. All the times I've saved your skin. Do you really think you're up to this? I can bury anything I want if you make me. Stuck-up brigadiers included.'

Vos held up his phone.

'No you can't. Every piece of information Veerman sent me – every report, every list of names, all the photos and videos – is sitting in a folder out there on the web. I can make that public with a single message. Give it to all the media. Let them have a field day.'

He'd got Bakker to forward him the text with the file location. Vos brought it up.

'If you haven't suspended yourself by the time I get back I'm putting this out there. Every last piece of it. Every—'

'This is crazy,' De Groot snapped. 'All the things we've worked for. All the years—'

'They don't mean a thing, Frank. One last time . . . get out of here. If you don't I'll arrest you right now.'

He walked away and found Laura Bakker talking to the police-women dealing with Brugman and Bea Arends.

Vos interrupted and took her to one side.

'Kim and Mia Timmers. They've gone ahead already? We need to get some specialist people to look at them . . .'

'Um . . .' She looked round the farmyard. 'Sorry. It was a real mess getting out of that place. De Groot's toy soldiers didn't help, poking their guns at everyone. I haven't dealt with them. Dirk?'

Van der Berg was on the far side of the yard talking to the medics. Vos and Bakker walked over and asked. He hadn't seen the girls either.

'They did come out of the barn, didn't they?' Vos demanded, getting worried.

The three of them went back to the rusty iron building. The

big sliding doors were wide open. The place was empty. At the rear was a tiny exit leading out onto open meadow behind.

Through it they could just make out two small shapes scuttling across the pastures, fast-moving black dots past a couple of low hedges already.

'Oh God,' Bakker murmured.

110

Out in the fields, the green fields, places they knew from when they were small. From picnics and walks, countless pleasant, winding rambles. Freya and the three of them, meandering across the meadows, listening to the larks that would lead them from their precious nests limping, pretending they had a broken wing only to rise into the blue sky trilling a song so ornate and beautiful they had to stop and wonder.

Then walk on. Always walk on. Life was a journey, their mother said. You either went forward or went back. There was no in between.

The town with all its dark memories lay behind them. They couldn't leave that for good though. Something black and evil lived there, lived inside them too. However much they tried to push the beast down into the confused tangle of dreams and memories and delusions they thought of as the past.

What they'd always hoped was false proved true. They knew it really. Just as they understood there never would be a glittering golden prize for their harmonies and their precisely pretty movements on the stage.

They were scum from the fishermen's cottages and only men like The Cupids rose from that grim poverty to escape to a world that was bright and warm and new.

Hand in hand they went, black shapes, copper hair, pale faces, stumbling over the rich summer pasture. Somewhere ahead in the hidden dykes, beneath the low bridges the cows used to cross from field to field, they heard ducks squabbling, webbed feet splashing through water.

Pylons crossed the distant horizon, stiff like giant iron herons seeking prey. Somewhere a duck would be leading her chicks to safety, the task she was born to, the way the world wanted. Birds and animals were everywhere, watching them, judging them. By a rise of rushes a lone sparrowhawk perched on the edge of an old metal water trough gazing across with its beady yellow eye. Overhead a perfect V-formation of geese flew against a line of puffy white clouds.

Then came grunts and the stamp of heavy feet. A herd of Friesians, black and white, bright doe eyes, long lashes, mouths that dripped water and slime as they followed the sisters' lumbering progress with a look of offended bovine outrage as if to say *This place is ours, not yours.*

But this was Waterland, their home too. The land that made them. The only place they belonged.

Behind, at some distance, they could hear a man's voice pleading. The officer from the barn, the one with the sad face and long unkempt hair, half-angry, half-lost.

'Mia! Kim! Please . . .' he begged.

They didn't listen after that last word, barked through the tinny metallic medium of a loudhailer. All the men said please. It never meant a thing and the memory of that fact only made them scuttle more rapidly across the meadows, breaking into a jog when they heard the steady chop of a helicopter rotor cutting through the sky.

Jogging. Then sprinting.

A triplet of steps marked in their heads.

One, two, three . . . one, two, three.

Even the young cannot run forever. Out of breath, panting, they came to a halt by a larger bridge, crumbly red brick with a gentle hump back. Cowpats on the stones along with straw and dried mud. Beneath it the channel was wider than most. Bulrushes grew in a dense forest at the edges. Mayflies and dragonflies, shiny blue and red and green, darted through buzzing swarms of smaller insects hovering over the thick duckweed that covered the sluggish water below.

There was a narrow dirt path that led to a dry mud ledge by the low bank. They scrambled down and sat there in the shadow of the brick arch above them. The stone structure muffled the racket of the helicopter, the frantic cries of the policeman with his loudhailer, behind him the yapping of eager dogs.

Next to each other on the hard ground, hands around their aching knees, they watched a coot scavenge through the green weed, stare at them, then skitter across the water, busy wings beating up the surface until it fell cackling into the rushes in the daylight beyond the path.

'It was me,' Kim said and looked at her sister, eyes wide with shock and shame and wonder. Not crying. Not quite. 'It was me all along.'

'It was us,' Mia told her. 'You. Me. Little Jo . . .'

Love is like a chain that binds me.

The words, the notes flew out of Kim's mouth with such ease it seemed as if they'd always lived there.

Begging company. The holy perfection. The magic number. Three.

Love is like a last goodbye.

Mia sang that solo and wondered . . . did they hear? Did she?

Love is all I have to keep you.

Two of them together, still waiting on a third.

Love is gone. And so am I.

All in melodious harmony. The low notes, the middle and a soprano faint yet as real as could be.

The coot came back, swimming quickly, curious to see them.

And here we sit, Mia whispered. Like ugly trolls trapped beneath a bridge.

The helicopter was nearer. So were the dogs and the policeman's importunate cries.

She moved her sister's copper hair to one side and tenderly kissed Kim's cheek.

'They'll send you one place,' Kim said. 'Me another. Me the mad one. The bad one. So weak I started it. Me—'

'No.' Her hand pulled Kim's face closer. 'You didn't start anything. It was there all along.'

And it always will be, she thought.

The bird with the gleaming black feathers and white beak leaned its head to one side and peered at them. Then squawked and paddled on its way.

A dog barked, so close now the violent sound of it made Kim jump and shudder against her sister.

Mia looked at the depthless stream, one more ever-circulating artery of Waterland leading through meadow and pasture down to the endless lake.

'I won't let them,' she whispered.

The voices were getting nearer all the time. One louder yet more fragile than the rest. The man from the barn again, the one with the sad eyes and the downcast kindly face.

'Mia! Kim!' he cried. 'Don't worry. It's fine.'

'Not fine,' she whispered. 'Never fine.'

The sound of feet crashing through meadow. Above the bank by the field the long grass started to stir.

They saw just a glimpse of him, desperate as he looked around, not noticing two small shapes crouched together hiding beneath the brick hump.

'Girls!'

Girls.

He sounded broken, lost. He was wrong even if he didn't know it.

'We never were girls,' Mia murmured. 'Not really.'

On the sluggish surface something moved. Wild white roses, dislodged by the sullen summer breeze, floated gently downstream towards the *meer*. Yellow lilies, curved and beautiful, followed like a scattered wild bouquet for a country funeral.

One step forward. A moment and their eyes met.

Then hand in hand, slowly, hearts in consummate harmony, under the water, the sweet green water, gracefully, joyously they slipped.

extracts reading groups
competitions books new
discounts extracts
competitions
books new
events books
extracts
new reading groups
interviews
events extracts
discounts
new books events
events new
discounts extracts discounts
www.panmacmillan.com
extracts events reading groups
competitions books extracts new